Sebastian's Way

The Paladin

BOOK II of A Tale of the Time of Charlemagne

George Steger

For my grandchildren, with hope that they might always know and cope wisely with the difference between duty and conscience.

Table of Contents

Persons of the Story

Abul-Abbas	Indian elephant, gift from Harun al-Rashid to Charlemagne
Adela	Sebastian's wife; daughter of Duke Gonduin
Adelaide	Count Leudegar's daughter; a free spirited wanderer
Alcuin of York	English-born scholar, educational reformer, advisor to Charlemagne
Askold	Danish shipbuilder for Charlemagne in Dorestad, Frisia
Archambald	Soldier at Fernshanz, Sebastian's companion
Arno	Count and Mayor of Charlemagne's Palace at Worms
Attalus	Sebastian's first son by Adela
Audulf	Charlemagne's seneschal and army general
Bardulf	A free peasant; personal servant of Sebastian
Barbero	Venetian ship captain
Bernard	Frankish veteran soldier; member of Sebastian's company
Bodoc	Monk of Brittany
Charlemagne	Karl der Grosse, High King, later Emperor of the Franks
Drogo	Peasant serf; companion of Bardulf
Elias II	Patriarch of Jerusalem
Eric of Friuli	Duke of Friuli, Italy and Margrave of the Pannonian March
Fastrada	Charlemagne's wife and queen

1

Father Pippin	Chaplain at Fernshanz; Adela's confessor and friend
Fra Fardulf	Benedictine monk; spy for Charlemagne; later abbot of St. Denis
George	Syncellus of Jerusalem; later Patriarch
Gonduin	Duke of Andernach and the Lower Rhine; general in Charlemagne's army. Adela's father
Harun al-Rashid	Caliph of Baghdad and Ruler of the Islamic Empire
Heimdal	Blind hermit, soothsayer, and longtime friend and advisor to Sebastian
Herlindis	Mother Superior of Adela's order of Benedictine nuns
Ibrahim	Emir of Ifriqiya; ruler of the northwest coast of Africa
Irene	Empress (later Emperor) of the Byzantine Empire
Isaac	Radhanite Jewish trader; merchant to kings and caliphs
Ivor the Bold	Danish pirate; leader of a band of Viking raiders
John the Eparch	Eparch of Constantinople; imperial Enforcer for Irene
Karl	Sebastian's second son by Adela
Konrad	Former Count of Adalgray turned Renegade, Sebastian's mortal enemy
Lantfrid	Charlemagne's official emissary to the Caliph of Baghdad
Leo	Nobleman of Constantinople; agent for the Byzantine Emperor
Magdala	Holy woman of Jerusalem; mystic healer
Milo	Sebastian's son by the peasant girl Gersvind
Pepin the Hunchback	Charlemagne's illegitimate first son by Himultrude

2

Pepin of Italy	King of Italy; Charlemagne's son by Hildegard
Rahul	Mahout; driver of Abul-Abbas
Sebastian	Count of Fernshanz and Adalgray; Paladin for the King
Sigismund	Second official emissary of the King to the Baghdad court
Simon	Radhanite Jewish trader; Sebastian's friend
Tasillo	Duke of Bavaria
The Tudun	Governor of the Ring City of the Avars
Turpin of Mayence	Frankish count and troop captain in Charlemagne's army
Wonomir the Slav	Croat Ally of Charlemagne against the Avars

Europe c.782

Prologue

Konrad

The King's Court at Attigny on the River Aisne Western Francia

Winter 785

"He's alive!"

Sebastian was stunned. He stood at the open door of his quarters, momentarily paralyzed by the appalling news. He had just come from a long war council with Charlemagne. When at last he returned to his quarters, he was delighted to see his friend Simon, the Radhanite merchant, whose storied travels to the East had always captivated Sebastian's imagination. But the anxious look on Simon's face told him that the news this time would not be good.

"I truly hate to tell you this, my good friend, but there's no avoiding it. Konrad is alive," Simon repeated.

"What?" Sebastian exploded in horror. He grabbed the hapless trader by the shoulders and shook him violently. "Are you sure?" he demanded. "Did you see him yourself? Do you even know him well enough to recognize him?"

"Calm down, Sebastian. Let me tell you what I saw. It *was* Konrad. No doubt about it. I recognized him at once."

The news could not have been more devastating for Sebastian. His worst enemy, whom everyone thought long dead, had suddenly been resurrected. It was not just that Konrad was a dreaded foe who had sworn to kill him. Far worse. Before everyone thought he had been killed by the Saxons, he was married to Sebastian's beloved wife, Adela—by the king's mandate. The news meant that in the eyes of the Church, she would still be Konrad's legitimate wife.

5

"I met him personally once before," Simon explained, "at the king's court when it was in Worms. He's hard to miss. I was trading in Hedeby. It's a growing town in Denmark, and it prospers mostly because it's a nest of Viking pirates who bring their loot back to the town. Konrad was strutting down the main street with the scurviest bunch of cold-blooded killers I've ever seen, as if they were all great victors and he had always been part of the Viking band. The gossip was all over town about him boasting openly of how easy it had been to overpower the three guards assigned by the Saxon war chief Widukind to execute him. Apparently, he managed to kill all three. He cut the head off one of them, burned it beyond recognition in the campfire, and sent it to Charlemagne, along with his own sword and a personal amulet. Charlemagne never suspected it was not Konrad's head. Once safe in Denmark, Konrad often told the story in elaborate detail while drinking with his Viking friends and laughing about how he had fooled everyone, even the gullible king.

"But it was not only I who saw him," Simon continued. "Everyone in Denmark knows who he is now. He's famous up there. He's been on several raids with Ivor the Bold, one of the leading pirates in that part of Denmark. He even thinks of himself as a Viking now. It's some old Nordic word that means more than just pirating at sea. Now they also occasionally raid on land, and against the very towns of Frisia and Britain. It's just beginning, but it's a growing business; more and more of the Danes have decided to go 'a-Viking,' as they say, for plunder and fame and fortune. And Konrad is in the thick of it. They say he's already rich from it."

"But how?" Sebastian wondered. "The only ships he knows are river boats on the Rhine."

"Well, he certainly doesn't know how to navigate a Viking ship. The Danes do all the sailing," Simon said. "But he's a ferocious fighter, and whenever they attack a ship at sea or venture a quick raid on some island or exposed port, he's a terror. And he's recognized as a fearless leader of men as well. He commands half of Ivor's raiders."

Sebastian collapsed onto a bench and buried his head in his hands. His stomach had turned sour, and he felt ill. Not again, he thought. It had taken them so long to be together, and now Konrad had come back from the dead to rip up their lives again.

"This is the worst news you could have brought me, Simon. Do you have any idea how bad this will be for me? I wish you'd never come."

"That's precisely why I did come, thank you very much. Do you think I would travel all the way back here just to visit? I could have gone on to Constantinople and Baghdad, as I planned. But you would have heard soon enough that Konrad is still alive. Too many people know about him now, and you will not be able to keep the news from Adela. I just wanted to be sure that you didn't hear it from a stranger and that you had some time to prepare for what you're going to say to her."

Sebastian took a deep breath and regained possession of himself. This was not the way he usually dealt with bad news. But this was Adela. She was no meek and submissive Frankish wife. She thought for herself, and he remembered vividly how hard it had been to pry her away from her Church even after they thought Konrad was dead.

"Well, thank you for that at least. I'm sorry. You're a true friend, Simon, and you are right. If he's alive, it won't be long before everyone knows it—as if that bloody savage could remain invisible! But nothing is going to make it easy to tell Adela. You don't know her. There's no telling what she might think or do. I dread her response."

"Wait a moment. It can't be that bad. Konrad is a long way from here. And if he should try to come back to Francia, the king would have his head. He's no longer *Count* Konrad of Adalgray, nor a leader in Charlemagne's army. He has no power in Francia now, and he's a traitor. He's an escapee from the king's justice. Besides, from what you've told me over the years, he's a completely wicked man who treated Adela very badly. He could not possibly have any hold on her now."

7

"Of course not. That's not the problem. She hates him. What I'm afraid of is what the *Church* will decide about it and how Adela will react after they do. I've got a very bad feeling about this."

He took another deep breath, walked to the window, and said in a calm, low voice, "But if it does make a difference to her, I will go to Denmark and kill him."

Chapter 1

Adela's Choice

Adela was with the two younger children at her father's villa at Andernach on the Rhine. Using three horses, Sebastian raced there nonstop, night and day, in order to bring her the bad news before she might hear it from someone else. As he pushed the horses relentlessly, he kept himself awake by conjuring up each of their three boys, one by one, seeing them in his mind's eye, examining every minute feature, gesture, and trait that made them different, trying to see beyond their limited present existence into who and what kind of men they might eventually become. He fretted they would be reflections of himself, at least to some extent, but he hoped for better.

First there was Milo, the illegitimate son he had sired in an impulsive, youthful liaison with a comely village girl. Though Milo was not her son, Sebastian marveled that Adela came so quickly to love the pensive, withdrawn child with his bright yellow Saxon hair and angelic appearance. She had immediately taken him under her wing and treated him as if he had always been her own. They had soon discovered that he was uncommonly bright, keen to learn, and singularly inclined to an almost mystical spirituality. Milo was a constant source of delight and surprise to them both. Since Sebastian was often away with the army or the king, Adela became the boy's primary influence. Within a year, she had taught him to read, and he was already well on his way to becoming the scholar he would be for the rest of his life.

Much different were their other two boys, Attalus and Karl, now four and three years old, respectively. Both had Adela's handsome features and thick hair, though Attalus's was a deep glossy black color to match the dark eyes he inherited from his father and Aquitanian grandfather. Not so the sturdy Karl, who was as ruddy and fair as any Frank and had the astonishing violet eyes of his mother. Even at three years, he showed the muscular definition of a tiny wrestler. Both boys had quick minds and hands—and wonderful endurance. They could play all day at high speed and then collapse into sleep at night like stones. They were as lively and noisy as Milo was serious and quiet, and they filled whatever space they occupied with laughter and noise.

As much as he forced himself to think of his sons in minute detail, he spent far more time over the rough trail reflecting on his wife, whom he loved to distraction, more than anything else in the world.

Sebastian's relationship with Adela had been near perfect in his remembrances. After Konrad's assumed death, when they were finally free to marry, their delight with each other had only been heightened by the fact that Sebastian spent much of his time away on the king's business. True to his word, Charlemagne had made Sebastian one of his *missi dominici*, royal messengers who spoke with the voice of the sovereign and had the power to adjudicate in the king's name. It was a daunting responsibility, and it kept him away for weeks at a time.

But his absences only served to inspire Sebastian to make elaborate plans for whatever precious time they did have together. During long hours on the road, he dreamed up special days to spend with Adela upon his return. They organized long rides to beautiful places and picnics where they wound up lying naked in the sun by some brook or sparkling pool of water. They made love as if it were the first time, saving it until the moment was perfect and they could no longer wait, exploring each other as if they might discover each other's souls in the minute examination of their bodies. When they finally made love, Sebastian deliberately held back so he could drink in the sight of her. She never needed the enhancement of clothes; she was far more beautiful without them, and every movement proclaimed her lustrous sensuality.

Afterward, they would talk for hours, revealing every detail of their thoughts and actions while apart, until each felt they had filled the interim of separation with the exact knowledge of what had occurred in each other's separate experiences. They felt charged and vitalized in each other's presence, and after these reunions, they came away from each other feeling intoxicated.

From the first day of their marriage, Sebastian had the feeling that he had been far too lucky. Adela was not only physically beautiful, but she was truly compassionate and amazing in her ability to sense the needs of others. She reached out to everyone, and everyone thought her purely "good," though she would have cringed to hear herself so described.

After so many years of celibacy and solitude, he reveled in their mutual happiness, but in the back of his mind there lurked a guilty sense that he was unworthy of such a charmed life. Now, as he rode toward her with the bad news, he felt that old foreboding rise out of his knotted belly and into his throat, forewarning that his luck was about to change.

Nevertheless, Sebastian clung to his love for Adela and the boys and knew that, no matter how things changed or how bad life might become, the memories of those early years with his family would forever be the way he judged true happiness.

***

As always, she welcomed him into her bed even in the middle of the night, and he made love to her as if there would never be another time. But he did not sleep. Instead, he waited till she stirred in the morning light.

Adela awakened slowly, rubbing her eyes and giving herself a long, luxurious stretch. At last, her eyes focused on him, and he was heartened as the lovely smile she gave him transitioned into an impish grin as she remembered the pleasure of the night before. She held out her arms to him, but he sat on the edge of the bed and held up a hand in caution.

"My darling love, my sweet girl, do you still love me?" he said, not knowing where to begin and fearing her reaction in his knotted stomach.

"Well," she said playfully, "you might have been a bit more passionate, I suppose—and if you could have lasted just a bit longer, I might have really enjoyed myself." She laughed at the long face he made.

"Oh, for pity's sake, my love, last night was truly wonderful, and of course I love you—more than anything. Now come back down here with me, you randy brute."

"No, Adela, I have to tell you something." He searched his brain for the right words. In the five years they had been married, Sebastian had learned he could not manipulate his self-confident wife. She was too intelligent and far too perceptive. He decided he would just have to come out with it.

"Two days ago, Simon came to me at Attigny and told me he saw Konrad in Denmark. He was running with a pack of Danish pirates in a place called Hedeby. He's alive and apparently as well as may be.

"No!" she said, bolting upright in the bed. "That can't be true. The king. . . the Church. . . they let us marry. Even the king said he was dead. He saw the charred head, and there was Konrad's sword and amulet."

"I don't know, Adela. I don't know what to say. Obviously, there was a misidentification. In any case, it won't matter."

"What do you mean it won't matter? Of course it matters. Is Simon sure it's him? Has he ever seen Konrad before?" Her face had turned white, and her eyes were already welling up in fear and anger. "How can this be, Sebastian? How can something as terrible as this happen? Tell me. Tell me everything."

When he had finished recounting what Simon had reported, she sat motionless for a long time, head down, hands clasped at her knees. Finally, she raised her eyes, already streaming with tears. "I knew it," she murmured angrily. "Somehow I sensed it. We were too happy. It was all too easy—our marriage, the children, the promotion to Charlemagne's court. I knew it wouldn't last. Konrad is my cross, damn his miserable soul. He will always be so. It's the burden God has given me in this life."

"Rubbish, Adela," Sebastian reasoned, trying to speak in a calm, matter-of-fact tone. "You aren't predestined to suffer. How can you think that? The news is not even relevant to us. Your marriage to Konrad was never real in the first place. The king forced you to do it because he needed Konrad to captain his new fortress inside the Saxon territory, and you were what Konrad wanted in return. Besides that, we were able to marry because everyone had a clear understanding that Konrad had been executed. The king as well as the Church acknowledged it. You cannot think he still has any claim on you."

She stood up and walked over to the window. Turning, she looked him in the eyes and said softly, almost inaudibly, but with a voice full of conviction, "You asked me a moment ago if I still loved you. How can you doubt that? We've already sacrificed more in a few years than most people do in a lifetime. We almost died and made shocking choices just to have each other at last. We've had beautiful children together. You know I love you and will love you to my last breath and with all my heart."

Sebastian waited for the "but," trying to control the grinding in his stomach. He had never met a more complex person in his life than his own wife, and he knew in his guts, in spite of all his careful logic and reasoning, that she would not be able to take such news lightly.

"I know what you want me to say, my love. You want to go on as if we had never heard this news. I want it, too."

Here it comes, Sebastian thought, those absurd Church notions. Her next words came out in a whisper. "But there are other things to consider, other people, my conscience, my vows. . ." He waited, knowing it was no use to argue at this point. Adela never made decisions easily.

"Give me some time, my heart. Let me go away for a bit, just a day or two. I must think. You can have some time with the boys, take them on an outing, set your things in order. I'll return soon, my sweet husband, my only love. I promise."

He kissed her and went quietly from the room to go look in on the boys. By the time he had roused them and got them dressed and ready to have breakfast, she was gone. She had dressed simply, taken a cloak, and had her horse brought to her by a household serf. Without another word to anyone, she had ridden away.

***

It took her two days to decide. Later he learned she had gone to see her old friend and counselor Father Pippin, who had always been a guiding light for both of them. Then early on the third morning, she returned, gaunt from lack of sleep and nourishment. They walked together across the fields and into the shadows of a nearby copse. She clung tightly to his arm as she began.

"Sebastian, do you not believe that the Church is God's agent here on earth? Do you not agree that there must be someone, some authority, some guiding agent who can interpret what God wants here on earth? Who is it if not the Church? Certainly not the king. He would do whatever he likes if it were not for his bishops telling him constantly that he must not do thus and so or God will be angry. They have a hard enough time controlling him as it is."

As she struggled to explain the depth of her feelings, he could already feel a swelling pang of regret. She went on, tearful eyes and quaking voice imploring him to understand, "The bishops have declared that marriage must be considered a sacred bond. They want to make it a sacrament, not to be broken simply because those involved wish it to be. As it is now, any man can simply put his wife away somewhere, in a nunnery or by sending her back to her father, as Charlemagne did with that poor Lombard princess he married. And God help those women who have nowhere to go. At least for their sakes, we must support this decision of the Church."

"But what if the Church is wrong, Adela? Surely, this cannot be right—to allow you to remain married to that devil. He's not even a man. He's an unthinking beast, and he certainly cannot be considered a husband, especially not yours. All he did was abuse you and cause your son's death.

Who but a vainglorious fool would try to teach a three-year-old child how to be a soldier by taking him up on the wall during a Saxon attack? What has he ever done for you but cause you grief? What possible good has there ever been out of this so-called 'marriage' your Church forced you to make?"

"Someone must represent my faith; someone must tell me what is right in the eyes of God. It is only selfish if I allow myself to think that *I* know what God wants—or that *you* do.

She stood up, straightening her back and looking him directly in the eye. Sebastian recognized that old strength of will he knew so well. She had made up her mind. "My love," she went on, taking a deep breath, "I can't dismiss the facts. I cannot. You must believe me when I tell you how agonizing this is for me. I want to be with you with all my heart and soul. Love is the one eternal thing we have between us."

At that point, Sebastian knew she wanted to be engulfed in his arms, as if she could recover their former peace and end her doubt. But he hesitated, and she doggedly went on. "After my little son Hugo died, in my grief I went to the convent, and there I came to know God as never before. And then you came when we heard Konrad was dead, and I believed that God wanted me to be happy with you and have a family.

"Now I realize that it is not my will that matters. I must do what God asks of me. And the Church, as God's agent and voice here on earth, has told me what to do. Don't you see? My faith is my 'pearl of great price.' I must be willing to sacrifice everything for it—no matter how it hurts or how unjust it may seem. That is my decision, my heart, my precious love. I must cling to it or it will drive me mad. Please understand me. I beg you not to hate me for it."

***

He left the next day after multiple attempts to change Adela's mind. In the end, however, she could only cry his name and beg him to understand. He became angry at last and refused to accept her decision. But rather than curse and raise his voice to her, he finally dropped his head and hands, stood for a long moment in silence, and then walked resolutely out of the room.

When he left, her distress tore at Sebastian's heart, and it was all he could do then to wrench his gaze from her pleading eyes and spur the horses into a canter toward the waiting barge at the landing. He had wanted with all his heart to turn around and gallop back to her. But he knew he could not have changed her mind, nor could he have stayed under the conditions she had imposed upon them both. She would tell him again, pitifully and full of shame and guilt, that she could no longer live with him as man and wife, that they must refrain from further physical contact, that he must accept that henceforth she must live as a celibate laywoman, if not a nun. Not because she wanted it so—far from it; he was sure of her love for him. But that love battled with her unshakeable conviction that she must obey the higher call to which she had been summoned. He had always felt his own faith was strong, but he realized now that in the past few days that faith had been profoundly shaken. As he revisited yet again that unhappy scene, his stomach lurched and his heart burned, and he felt he would sooner die than continue to live in this wretched state.

That feeling lay behind his decision to go to Denmark, come what may. He would go there and find Konrad, and this time he would see to it that he ceased to be a problem once and for all.

Chapter 2

Becoming the Paladin

At the Maifeld in Worms, Spring 786

As he did almost every year of his long reign, the king called for the *Maifeld* gathering, the call-up of the army in early spring to plan and organize for a new campaign. The king went to Worms for the gathering and announced that this year there would be two campaigns. He would send part of the army to Brittany while he led another part into Italy.

Sebastian waited nervously in the anteroom of the king's quarters of the palace at Worms, devoutly wishing he could find some way to be excused from the coming campaign. But it was impossible to be indifferent around the king, and Sebastian felt the old excitement mounting in spite of his misgivings about the king's intentions. At last, Charlemagne burst in from the latest war council and swept Sebastian with him into his quarters. "Come in, come in, old lad. Good to see you! By all the saints, it's been far too long!"

It had indeed been a while since Sebastian last saw the king, and he watched him admiringly as he threw off his cloak and sword belt and bellowed at a waiting serf to bring in some ale. At forty-four years, Charlemagne was at the top of his form; he was as fit as a young man from years of campaigning and hunting, and he looked like one. He disdained a beard, preferring long, drooping mustaches and a shaven face, which gave him a distinctly rakish air. He had a voracious appetite for food as well as everything else he enjoyed. His court was alive wherever he went, full of interesting people and spirited discussion.

As the king gave him an exuberant embrace and slapped him roundly on the shoulders, Sebastian realized once again that King Karl also loved mightily—his children, his

17

dogs and horses, his trusted advisors, the women in his life—both wives and concubines, his warriors and his entire army, which would do anything he asked without question and to the death. Charlemagne loved learning and luxury, listening to stories, singing, laughing, and swimming.

But he was a singularly focused monarch. At this point in his life, he was still very ambitious, ruthless in the pursuit of his goals, supremely confident and fearless. He was the most important man in the realm, and he knew it. It filled him with satisfaction.

"Listen," the king said, throwing himself down on a padded bench near the fireplace, "we must be about some serious business, you and I. We've no time to lose. Where's that damned ale?" he sang out.

Sebastian's heart sank as he sensed that his plans for Denmark were about to be suspended.

"Sit down, sit down, Sebastian," the king barked. "It's a tonic to see you, truly. There's never enough time to share with those one really likes. I spend most of my days suffering fools, it seems. Well, I suppose you know why you're here, do you not? I hinted at it the other night at the war council."

"I believe so, my king. You want me to go to Brittany in advance of the army."

"Don't look so glum about it, lad. I know it's a very big ask, but it'll be a splendid adventure! Just the sort of thing you fancy, innt?

And I can think of no one else who can get me what I need there as well as you. Here, have some of this brown ale. Excellent stuff! It's from Denmark," the king said as the pot was set before them.

Sebastian flinched at the sound of that fateful name. But he gamely held up his cup with subdued thanks. "And what exactly is it you wish me to do, sire?"

"Right, then, straight to business. That's more like it. It's what I always liked about you. No nonsense. Here's the problem: we're having trouble with those bloody Bretons again. They won't pay their taxes. They owe me tribute every year, by thunder, not just when they feel like paying it. We've got to go there and give the buggers a good seeing to." The king took a long draught of ale and belched absentmindedly.

He leaned forward and looked his champion squarely in the eye to emphasize the importance of his message. Sebastian could already feel the precious time slipping away. "The thing is, I must go to Italy this year with part of the army, and there's a great deal of preparation to be done before we march. You know, don't you, that we've locked up that scheming devil, King Desiderius, and now I own Lombardy? I just haven't made it official yet. I need to go there and do what is proper, as they say—let 'em know to whom they truly need to bend the knee. And I've got some things to say to the pope as well, and to that scoundrel Duke Arighis in Benevento down in the south. He's getting entirely too clever with the Greeks again. I want them the devil out of Italy. In short, there's much to do down there, and I can't go to Brittany.

"It's a bit of a dilemma, though. Count Audulf will be in charge of the Brittany expedition, but I'm not sure Audulf knows what to do. He's my seneschal, and he's a damned fine general, no doubt. But Brittany is no easy place, not even to visit. It's rough country—all up and down and full of bloody bogs and thick forests, and you can't find a blasted thing there. Even my poor Roland, whom we lost down there in that godforsaken mountain pass in Iberia, used to complain bitterly about how hard it was to find one's way in that ruddy country. He was my captain of the Breton March, you know. And a damned good one he was, too. I miss him, even now." The king looked away and cleared his throat.

"Here's the thing," he continued, "I want you to do a bit of snooping about in Brittany. Go there and scout out the country for Audulf. If you can poke about and point the way for him and perhaps warn him of what he may be up against, it might make the difference between a successful campaign and bugger all. Audulf needs to be able to bash in there boldly and bring them all to heel. He just needs to know where to go and how to choose the way so he doesn't waste time. A campaign can be ruinous if there's too much mucking about finding the road and such. And he needs to know where the strong points are and where to put some pressure. Can you do that for me, Sebastian?"

Sebastian shifted uneasily and cleared his throat. "I trust I can, my liege, if you wish it."

"There's a good lad!" the king said, rubbing his hands together briskly. "I knew you'd be up for it. Will you need any troops?"

Sebastian was momentarily struck dumb. It was a shock to realize that the king was actually offering him command of part of the army. But he knew that would cause serious delay, and there was a good chance any show of force would only serve to stir the Bretons up like hornets and set them to fevered preparation behind their walls. After a long moment, he replied, "None, sire. I need only a few good men, and I will choose them, by your leave. I think it would be better to go into Brittany with as little stir as possible. We might even slip in unnoticed if we're careful."

"Right, then, that's the word. Be very careful. I don't want to lose you. And brief Audulf thoroughly before you leave. Make sure you have a good dispatch rider and he knows where you are at all times so he can bring up the army quickly if you run into trouble."

"Aye, my lord king."

"Right, then. Is there anything else you need?"

"Well, as a matter of fact, my king, there is something I would ask of you."

"Ask away, Sebastian. There's little I wouldn't give you."

"I need a bit of time, my liege," Sebastian said quietly, looking at the floor and knowing he was about to lie to his king. "After this business in Brittany is done, I would like," he struggled for the right words, "to spend some time away—for my family's sake, that is." He sat up straight and spoke with more confidence. "And then I need to be about some private business for a while. I've been so much on the road lately as one of your *missi dominici* that I've neglected some important parts of my life. After we're done in Brittany, will you excuse me from your service until I can attend to these matters? It will be only for a little while, I hope. I will be back as soon as I have settled my affairs."

"Hmm," the king mused, eyes narrowing, pulling on his mustaches. "I'm not sure what to make of that. I hate to lose you for any time at all. You've been doing superb work as one of the *missi*. You truly are my voice in the provinces, and you're doing exactly the kind of job I had in mind when we started the business. When you come back from a tour of one of the provinces, I believe I know it and what its problems are as well as any who live there, which is excellent!

"But you've been hard done by lately with the travel and all, and I wouldn't even blame you if you said no to the Brittany venture. After all, what's that lovely wife of yours doing while you're out there trooping about? I know you've got to have some time to give her a proper romp now and then, eh?"

He paused to consider. "So here's my decision: I can't think of anyone who deserves a good rest more than you. But I do need you on this one. When it's over in Brittany, it's off with you. I won't poke into your private affairs any further, but promise me you'll come back to the court just as soon as you rest up a bit and tend to your business, whatever it is."

"I assure you, sire," Sebastian said with huge relief, "just as soon as I have done what I need to do, I will come back to you. I love being an agent of the court. It's what I've always wanted, but there's a pressing affair to attend to, one I can't ignore. Thank you for letting me sort it out and for not holding me to account for what it is. I'm truly grateful. I assure you, my king, it's a most important business for me. Otherwise, I wouldn't ask it of you."

"Right, right, Sebastian. I understand. Don't like it, but I understand. Go and do what you must. I trust you'll do as you say, but I wish you'd let me help you if it's all that bloody important. But I won't insist. You've always had good sense, and you seem to know what you're doing. So until you ask, I'll stay out of your private life. But remember, your first duty is to me. And I expect to have you back as soon as possible. Understand?"

"Absolutely, sire."

***

Upon leaving the king's quarters, Sebastian wondered how he could be so miserable while Charlemagne was in such high spirits. The king, too, had lost a wife. His beautiful Hildegard had died after the birth of their ninth child in twelve years. She had been only twenty-five when she died. His mother, Bertrada, always his staunchest ally, also died only a few months later. Sebastian learned of both tragedies while on the road doing the king's business. The word was that the king had grieved deeply and prayed unceasingly for a month after each of their deaths. Everyone knew how much he loved them both. But a state of mourning and sadness was alien to Charlemagne's nature, and it had lasted only a short while. Now the king was back to his usual exuberant self, surging with energy and enterprise.

On the other side of the door, Sebastian discovered the reason the king was so full of life and optimism. Her name was Fastrada.

Sebastian recognized the king's new wife at once by her reputation. Even in the morning, she was exquisitely dressed, and her character burst out immediately, as bold as her clothing—bright, beautiful, and pretentious.

She was Charlemagne's fourth wife, and, like all the others, she was very young. The king not only loved beautiful women in general, he preferred them young, knowing that their chief function as queen would be to give him heirs, as many as possible.

Sebastian found it hard not to stare, for Fastrada was indeed striking—a classic, gracefully slim face with high cheekbones and elegantly arching eyebrows, a wide, bowlike mouth, lustrous chestnut hair, and, unlike so many sturdy Frankish women, a long, willowy body. Sebastian was taken aback to find this lovely, regal woman alone and apparently waiting for him in the anteroom.

"Ah, there you are, finally! You're Sebastian, are you not? My husband's darling, right? You're his invincible, charmed warrior," she said as she brazenly looked him up and down. "He brags about you all the time and says you can do anything he asks of you and that you cannot be killed. Is that true? Are you supernatural, perhaps?"

"Not at all, my queen," Sebastian hastened to say, not knowing how he was supposed to react to this bold woman with her provocative eyes and sensuous manner. "I am lord of two very small pieces of your husband's vast kingdom, both on the rough border of Saxon territory. The king has graciously called me to service now with his court. He is most kind to mention me, but it's his custom to boast of all his warriors."

"And modest, too! I'm impressed. Come, walk with me in the garden," she said, taking him firmly by the arm and whisking him out of the building. "No matter what you may say, you fit his description of you." She stopped and walked boldly around him, keeping a delicate finger on one of his shoulders and running the finger across the back of his neck to the other shoulder, observing every part of his body as she moved.

He felt as if she was trying to draw out of him through her fingers and eyes his total worth as a man and a potential ally. Stopping directly in front of him, she leaned in closely and locked her eyes on his. For an odd second or two, he felt like she might either kiss him on the mouth or bite him. "Listen, Lord Sebastian," the queen said in a low voice, suddenly becoming serious, "I will tell you frankly why I am interested in you. There is much that I would do to help the king in all of the great things he wishes to accomplish. But I am in need of friends, men of proven quality, warriors who would be special to me—as well as to the king—who would help me accomplish my goal of being the king's right hand. If you would be one of them, you would find me a very grateful patron." She grasped his hands and squeezed them hard.

God and all the saints! Sebastian thought, stepping back. He knew at once he was being lured down a very queer

23

road, and he could feel the hairs on the back of his neck rising. He took a deep breath, squared his shoulders, and withdrew his hands, wrenching his eyes away from her gaze. Finding his voice, he replied formally, "I am honored, Your Grace, and I would be most happy to assist you in any way—as long as it does not interfere with my service to the king. I fear, however, he keeps me quite busy."

Her eyes narrowed as she studied him, but she gave it a second effort, once more stepping close and locking her eyes on his. She placed one graceful hand on his forearm. "I would not want you to be any other way, good Sebastian. I merely suggest that we can be friends, you and I. You can be my champion as well and entertain me with your stories when you return from your adventures for the king. You're one of his *missi dominici*, his personal messenger, his 'trusted eyes and ears.' They say you know as much as anyone about how the kingdom is managed, how it works, and that the king is forever seeking your counsel. I too wish to be of great service to my lord the king, but as yet I know so little of such things, and the king is often too busy to keep me informed. Won't you help me learn? Won't you be my little bird—nay, my brave falcon, who sees everything and shares his wisdom with me? I would be forever indebted to you, and we would become great friends."

Sebastian was so astonished at this speech and the way Fastrada was moving her hand up and down his arm as she spoke that he almost jumped back from her.

"I. . . uh. . . I'm sorry, Your Grace," he stuttered, clearing his throat. "I just have never been so close to a queen before. I feel. . . uh. . . it is not my station." He took another step back and gazed distantly over her left shoulder.

Fastrada smiled thinly and looked away, lifting her head as if discovering a new scent in the air. "Well, Master Sebastian," she pronounced precisely, moving toward the door, "do give what I have said some serious thought. Have a care that you don't lose a very fruitful opportunity—to be my friend, that is. We shall see. The next time we meet, I hope you will find me—my offer—more enticing. Good day to you, sir." She glided from the garden without another glance at him.

Charlemagne barged into the courtyard a bare few seconds later, trailed by an entourage of war captains and priests. He found Sebastian mouth open and in a mild state of shock. "Sebastian! Still here? Why are you looking so addled?" Then the king burst out laughing.

"Oh, I see, you've met my young bride. We passed her in the hallway." Grasping Sebastian by the arm, he declared jovially, "Stunning, isn't she? I swear, she amazes me more every day, the minx. She's into everything. Always wanting to know this and that and telling me what I should do, like she was one of my high counselors or one of my generals. My God, what does she think she knows about war and running the country?" He laughed as he thought of it and then turned serious. "It's a bit of a pain in the backside, actually." He sniffed and furrowed his brow thoughtfully for a moment but then returned to his jovial mood. "But she's such a saucy, beautiful creature! I have a hard time denying her anything. Anyway, hope she didn't scare you, did she?"

"Oh no, my lord king, I. . . I'm just not used to talking to queens."

"Think no more about it, dear boy. It's just who she is. She means no harm. You'll get used to her."

I sincerely hope not, Sebastian thought, stepping back with a low bow as the king swept past toward the stables, escorted by a noisy convoy of advisors.

***

The next day, Sebastian made haste to gather a small corps of his closest companions for the Brittany expedition. He already had Archambald, a mate from his childhood at Fernshanz and his shadow ever since he became one of Charlemagne's *missi,* and the two peasants, Bardulf and Drogo, who had attached themselves to him like tar as his personal servants. He sent immediately for both Liudolf, the best friend of his youth and his right hand in a fight, and

Bernard, his mother's longtime guardian, now the senior sergeant at Fernshanz fortress, and, happily, a native of Brittany, having been born of a Breton mother and a Frankish father and raised speaking the strange Celtic language of the region.

When all were assembled, he gestured for the company to be seated around a crude table in the upper room of a nearby tavern. "Friends," he announced without preamble, "we're going to Brittany on the king's business. King Karl has decided to go against the Bretons and force them to pay the tribute they owe him as vassals, which they haven't done for two years now. He wants us to find out everything we can about them before the army comes in. So that's what we're going to do."

"But, Sebastian, how are we going to get into that wild country without everybody knowing we're spies for King Karl?" broke in Archambald, already alarmed at the prospect. "As soon as they find out we're Franks, they'll probably roast and eat us. I've heard that's what they like to do. I've heard those people are very queer, not at all like us."

"They are Christians, Archambald, just like you, and they don't eat people, though they do cling to a few of the traditions of the old Celtic gods. But there's more than a little touch of paganism in our own people, and the Bretons are no worse."

At that point the door opened, and a blind man carefully felt his way in. "Greetings and salutations, gentlemen," the old man said in a low, spectral voice as he eased himself into the room.

"Heimdal! How in blazes did you get wind of this? Archambald. . ." Sebastian said, his voice rising.

"Wait now, before you say anything, Sebastian, "Heimdal raised a hand against the protest he knew would be coming, "I am wounded and surprised that you did not invite me. After all, I am the lifelong confidant of your father and of yourself, for that matter. Did we not make a dangerous pilgrimage together to the shrine of Saint Martin in Tours when you lost your Lady Adela the first time? Did I not save your life several times on that hazardous journey? Has not my wisdom always been useful to your house and to you? I should have thought you would have invited me first."

He hastened to continue, "I already know all about your little jaunt into Brittany; I even know what you have to do. I also know that you have some sort of half-baked plan and that you're going to need me to straighten it out."

"Well, you are right, Heimdal, I should have consulted you first. I haven't forgotten the service you've given to me and my family. And I'll never forget it was you who saved me when I almost died on that pilgrimage. Actually, I was going to consult you. . . before we went," Sebastian finished lamely.

"But that journey was a long time ago, and I'm afraid the days of your tramping about on grand adventures are long past, old friend. How bloody old are you anyway?"

"Age, my not-so-young man, is not important. It is attitude and strength of spirit that count. I have both—more than most—and I am still spry enough to ride a mule."

"Mules? What's this?"

"Tell me, my son, have you even got a plan yet?"

"We were just about to put our heads together about it when you barged in. I have a general notion of how to go about it."

"Right, then. Let's hear it, and we'll see if it has any legs. If it does, then I will allow that you don't need me."

"Well, the plan is relatively simple," Sebastian said. "We'll ride into Brittany under cover of darkness, camp out in the woods close by, and walk into the towns we encounter in the morning, wearing simple clothes and assuming the role of minor merchants. We'll ask where the biggest markets are and what governing officials we might need to see to gain permission to seek future trade arrangements. As we go, we're bound to discover the seats of power and the status of the local garrisons. If there's a standing army somewhere, we'll find it."

"In other words, my boy, you don't know dog's bollocks about the way forward."

"Come now, Heimdal, we've just started. We'll collect a load of information before we go and have a better idea. And

Bernard here was born and brought up in his youth in Brittany. He can be our mouthpiece. None need know anything more about us other than that we are merchants."

"Oh, I see, merchants without wares asking a lot of questions, and all of you, excepting Bardulf and Drogo, looking exactly like soldiers, not merchants. And even if you could avoid suspicion and go about your plan, it would take you a year without better intelligence than you have at this point."

"All right, then, Heimdal, persuade me. You obviously have already given it considerable thought. What's in that fertile brain of yours? But mind, I haven't said you could go— even if you do have a better plan."

"Very well, I do have a plan, and it is based on a lifetime of listening—to travelers, soldiers, merchants, pilgrims—anyone who has been somewhere else and done something of note there. For instance, I know that the routes into Brittany need not be a cause for much worry. Our ancient friends, the old Romans, managed to conquer Brittany long ago, and with the help of legions of Gallic slaves, they built three still very serviceable Roman roads into that country. These roads lead to all of the major towns and military strong points: Rennes, Nantes, Vannes, and etcetera.

"Better still, they lead past all seven of the major holy places in Brittany. These famous places were founded by seven founding Celtic holy men who actually accomplished the amazing feat of bringing Christianity over from Britain a few hundred years or so ago. Those so-called holy men are highly revered in Brittany. The monasteries they founded contain well-known relics and are the objectives of countless pilgrims who visit them each year. In fact, their Christianity and those holy places just might be the key to our success."

Oh, right," Archambald scoffed. "We'll just ride in and tell 'em we're visiting churches."

"Not exactly, my good man. But you do need to practice your Latin—because we'll be going in as monks."

Chapter 3

Brittany

Spring and Summer 786

Like all of Heimdal's adventures, this one was of highly dubious nature. Sebastian's head still swam with the risks of the plan being exposed at any point for the audacious lie that it was. As they patiently endured the mule-paced approach to the border of the old Breton March, land now vehemently opposed to the return of Frankish control, Sebastian reviewed Heimdal's flamboyant exposition of his bizarre scheme.

"We must have a good reason to be coming into Brittany," Heimdal had gestured dramatically as if about to conjure magic, "one beyond mere pilgrim visits, else we will never get to meet with the men we must see, the men who control the levers of power in both Church and State. We will start with the monasteries, the holy places that are the goals of legions of pilgrims every year. But we must have a spectacular attraction, something no ambitious abbot or lord can resist." He paused to heighten the suspense.

"And what might that be, oh great weaver of outlandish plots?" Sebastian prompted.

"We must have something the abbots want. And what do they want most of all, you ask?" A longer pregnant pause followed. "They want *relics*!" he boomed with a great gesture of his arms to the sky. "They want bones and teeth and hair and skulls—anything that pilgrims might swoon over as they think of the blessed indulgences to be had just by gazing on the sacred parts of some long-dead and exalted holy man. To gain access to important places and people, we have only to have such items to offer."

"Oh, right, all we have to do is steal a few holy bones from some of our own shrines and trade them away for information," scoffed Archambald.

"Again, not exactly, my good simpleton. We shall simply gather the bones of poor men from any common graveyard and *pretend* they are the bones of saints. Who knows, perhaps the unfortunates from whom we gather such relics really were saints in their lifetimes? Brothers, many a good man has died without fanfare or fuss about him. Yet is he not a saint in God's eyes nonetheless?"

Sebastian shuddered and shook his head in amazement. "I can't do that, Heimdal. I can't lie like that. I could never look anyone in the eye and tell such a story—without laughing out loud at the absurdity of it."

"You will not have to, my boy. Like the pilgrimage you and I took to Tours when you became so ill, I shall do all the talking—through Bernard of course, who is fluent in the Breton tongue. You and the others will be simple Frankish monks from the small and little-known monastery of Alta Ripa at the foot of the Spanish mountains far to the south. No one will have even heard of it, but if they have, I shall know all about it, for that is where I prayed and begged and learned all there is to know about the Mass and the monkish life. Trust me, lad, all you and the others will have to do is nod sagely and look humbly at the floor."

"But what about the pilgrims who might worship before such bones? Isn't it a grievous sacrilege to ask *them* to believe such a lie?"

"Not at all, my good man. Look at it logically. Is it more important that a pilgrim knows for a certainty that the bones are genuine or simply to *believe* them to be so? If he worships genuinely, with praise in his heart for the holiness of God and for holiness in men in general, does he not get the same benefit?"

"Oh, for God's sake, Heimdal, it will never work," Sebastian proclaimed in exasperation.

"There is a very good chance that it *will* work, Sebastian. The people of Brittany, I have heard, are extremely pious as well as highly superstitious. All we have to do is produce the bones along with a plausible story of their origin. There are hundreds of saints, some real and some not so real. I wager that half the great churches in Francia contain highly dubious holy bones, gotten here and there by enterprising priests or abbots. I am an excellent storyteller, as you well know. I can spin a tale that will make every bone a coveted treasure wherever we choose to go."

***

No one bothered to interfere with the small company of black-robed monks riding inconspicuously into Brittany on the backs of mules. Sebastian chafed at the slow pace. Each long day put off the reckoning he felt compelled to make in Denmark, but at least the complexity of the task before them took his mind off the constant urge to find Konrad and kill him.

He forbade weapons and any trappings of luxury. He even insisted that each man be tonsured like the Benedictine monks of most of the abbeys in Francia. Only Liudolf, who took on the duties of dispatch rider, escaped the role of humble monk.

Sebastian was still shaking his head as they rode into Nantes with two pack mules bearing the bones of long-dead peasant serfs obtained from a common graveyard near the town of Cologne. Against Sebastian's better judgment, Heimdal convinced him to let Liudolf, the only one of the band not wearing monk's cloth, hire a more-than-willing gravedigger for a piece of silver to load the pack mules full of bones and skulls from the oldest part of the town's paupers' graveyard.

Nantes was one of the region's most important cities and a seat of government. More than half the population of the city was Frankish, but the count in control of the district was a Breton and famous as a vociferous opponent to the King of the Franks. No one raised an eyebrow, however, upon the arrival of yet another troop of pilgrim monks seeking to visit the holy sites of the famed *Tro Breizh* pilgrim road.

They sought the well-known monastery of Nantes and found it across from the town on Monks' Island in the middle of the Loire River. It was already an ancient abbey, having been founded three centuries earlier by Celtic holy men from Britain.

Rapping persistently on the massive wooden door of the abbey, they were finally rewarded by the appearance of a diminutive, red-cheeked monk of a cheerful but decidedly odd demeanor and wild red hair to match the apparent scramble inside his head. "Yer too late for sext and the midday meal, and it's too early for supper and vespers," he announced in the Frankish tongue with a lopsided grin and a high-pitched, singsong voice. "But I can bring ye a bit of bread if it please ye. No wine or beer, though—oh no, no, not in the afternoon! That would never do, no sir, no siree!"

Eventually, the little man led them into a waiting hall with benches against the wall and went off to bring them a tray of bread and water, as he promised. The bread was stale, but their host presented it as if it were true manna from heaven. Ain't it a blessin', then?" he said, giggling like a child.

His name was Brother Bodoc, one of the monks but not yet a priest and, from the looks of him, unlikely ever to be one. Sebastian had trouble following his disconnected chatter and inane asides, but he seemed fit enough for the easy role of greeter and servant to pilgrims, being outgoing, friendly, and welcoming.

As they got to know him, however, this funny little middle-aged fellow, with his unruly hair flaring upward like flames, his bulging blue eyes, and his perennially smiling fool's face, could scarcely hide another, quite sly and self-serving side to his character. He looked longingly at the skin of wine Sebastian pulled from his pack to share with the group.

"Would you like a little taste, then, of our own vintage, Brother?" Sebastian offered. "It's certainly not as good as what you make here, I'm sure, but perhaps it will please." He offered Bodoc the first cup. The monk's eyes lit up, and he eagerly took the cup with both hands, murmuring thanks. Before the others even had a cup in their hands, Bodoc held out his own for a refill and began to try to impress his guests.

"I know yer plannin' to go on the *Tro Breizh* pilgrim road on the morrow. I can tell ye it's a long, hard journey. Why, it must be a thousand leagues! I myself have walked that very same road—thrice, don't ye know! I know where every holy place and abbey is where a poor pilgrim can stay the night and find a bit of bread to eat."

Bodoc downed several cups of the sweet wine before the abbot sent word that the band was welcome to stay the night. They were allowed to wash and share a loaf of bread, and when it was evening, Bodoc unsteadily led them with much tittering and elaborate, if irrelevant, commentary to the large barracks-like pilgrims' room with its row upon row of simple straw mattresses lined up along the walls. As they prepared to settle for the night, he left them with a single candle and tottered off, wishing them oddly, "Sweet dreams in the arms of the Lamb of Dod! Dod is dood!" Giggling, he stumbled his way out of the cavernous public quarters.

"Well, who woulda thought that a few drams of wine would turn that old lad into a stuttering three-year-old?" Bardulf said, snickering at the discovery of such a glaring weakness in the little monk. "No wonder he's just a door minder."

"Don't be so hard on him, Bardulf," Sebastian said. "He's not a bad little fellow, and such a weakness might prove very useful to us in the long run. His brains might be a bit scattered, but he knows all the roads and probably all the churches and abbeys where we could stay a night and get the kind of information we need on local leaders and the strength of their militias. We might tempt him to go with us."

"Well, how did ye know, m'lord? Ye gave him a drink right off, like ye already knew he was a tippler."

"Simple, Bardulf, just look at him—shiny, red face and nose, unable to be still even for a moment. He's a loose bolt, no denying, but he might just be the key to our getting where we want to go."

"Why not, dear boy?" Heimdal added. "He might also add to our cover to boot. After all, there's no greater distraction in any assembly than that of a jester."

***

The abbot was only too happy to release Bodoc to accompany the Franks on a tour of the holy places along the *Tro Briezh*. He did so, he said, as a sign of the brotherhood of fellow monks, but it was clear from his beaming face that he was only too glad to get rid of the vexatious little brother, at least for a while. He even gave Heimdal an introductory letter to the duke of the province in Nantes.

For his part, Brother Bodoc could not hide his glee at the prospect of a new adventure on the road and a cup or two of wine or beer every evening with Heimdal and the others. They could not get him to settle down as they prepared to leave the next morning; he talked unceasingly and was as nervous and jumpy as a flea. But finally the mules were ready, and the band rode off at midmorning, with Bodoc bringing up the rear, singing to himself and chortling joyfully upon the back of an ass not much bigger than himself.

Their first destination lay right across the river at the palace of the governor of the region, Duke Bordred, born a Frank but an outspoken opponent of Charlemagne and the irksome annual tribute. Heimdal gained an audience by virtue of the abbot's letter, which included a note hinting at the possibility of mysterious potential benefits to be had from the band of monks from Alta Ripa.

The duke's curiosity was aroused, and he admitted the group as soon as they arrived. Completely undisturbed by the prospect of an interview with a powerful lord, Heimdal entered the council chamber on the arm of Sebastian and breezed up to the duke's dais at the upper end of the great room as if he, and not the duke, were the most important person in the room. He bowed low and, without a word, unrolled a soft leather cloth on the floor, revealing a glistening pile of bones and a gleaming skull.

"Esteemed Duke Bordred, grand protector of the faith and all the people of this great province, we humble monks come to you bearing a precious gift. You see before you none other than the bones of Saint Sebastian himself, the first Christian martyr." Heimdal paused dramatically to allow all to take in this surprising phenomenon.

"We bring these holy relics to you, great lord, to save them from what we fear will soon be war in Francia."

"War?" exclaimed the duke. "What war? I have heard nothing about that."

"Oh yes, my lord. It seems King Karl is preparing the army for a new campaign against rebels in Aquitania. We feel the holy bones of this splendid saint are no longer safe in our humble, undefended monastery, which lies in southern Aquitania. We ask only that you preserve them and reverence them and display them to the multitudes of pilgrims who will no doubt flock to see and pray before them for the good of their immortal souls. Who knows? There may even be miracles here, in your beautiful cathedral, as there were at our poor monastery."

"Wh-what?" stammered the duke, unable to take in the magnitude of the blind man's proposal. A hooded priest standing behind the duke suddenly stepped forward to whisper in his ear.

"See here," the duke said irascibly, "we understand the bones of that particular saint lie in Rome, where they have been for centuries."

"Your Grace, pardon me, but you have only the partial truth of the bones. It is true that the good saint was murdered in Rome, but that is not the whole story, Excellency. More than four hundred years ago, the saint's bones were gifted by the pope to the Merovingian king, Dagobert, in return for his protection and as a sign of good will. They were eventually brought to our isolated monastery to safeguard them from a rebellion in Paris."

The duke conferred once again with the shadowy priest behind him. "What proof have you to support this fantastic story?" the duke said, his voice still icy with skepticism.

Heimdal promptly drew out of his pouch a hoary parchment wrapped in crimson silk cloth. Unfolding it, he held it before the duke. "I believe you can see for yourself, honorable Duke, the Latin words in Merovingian script and the signatures of both King Dagobert and Blessed Hilduin, the abbot of Saint Denys during the time of Dagobert. You can see there clearly the papal seal as well."

Heimdal quickly stooped and groped for the skull. Picking it up, he held it before the duke. "You can see for yourself the crack in the skull where the poor saint was finally clubbed to death. And if you examine the bones, you will see the marks of the arrows that pelted his body."

Of course, the letter was sheer fantasy, invented in entirety in the imaginative mind of Heimdal, who mixed the facts and dates with wild abandon in order to enhance the story. He had in his saddlebags identically produced scrolls "authenticating" every bone in the mules' packs as those of well-known saints. And like a great gambler, he betrayed by no word or gesture his righteous attitude of conviction. Meanwhile, Sebastian and the other "monks" kept their eyes firmly on the floor and their folded hands upon their hearts. All the while, Sebastian felt his hair was standing on end.

Eventually, however, Duke Bordred was thoroughly convinced by Heimdal's compelling arguments, particularly when the blind man waxed eloquent about the number of pilgrims who were sure to journey to Nantes and crowd into its famous cathedral to see the glorious relics of the sainted martyr—and while doing so would be sure to visit the inns, taverns, and markets of Nantes, bringing silver by the barrel full.

The duke was even disposed to give Heimdal letters of introduction to one other Breton duke and a number of other chieftains of the clans of Brittany. In doing so, he warned them away from several other clan leaders, saying these were unruly lords with whom he did not agree and could not recommend, nearly spitting their names as he said so. He even gave Heimdal a few small pieces of silver to stand him and his monkish band in good stead on the road ahead.

***

The surpassing success with Duke Bordred made the rest of their mission in Brittany comparatively easy. Brother Bodoc had no difficulty pointing the way, which he did with unbridled enthusiasm and a raft of stories that he related madly and as fast as he could speak.

Letters from the duke eased their way into the inner chambers of war chiefs and abbots alike. Heimdal waxed more convincing at every audience and generously bestowed the "relics" to all they met, asking only to be allowed to observe the way the famous monasteries used their precious holy objects.

In the process, they learned firsthand about Brittany's current problems with clan divisions and lack of communication and saw for themselves the less-than-formidable state of their defenses. Sebastian carefully noted both strengths and weaknesses and every other day stayed behind to rendezvous after dark with Liudolf at a prominent church on the road behind them. Liudolf then raced back on a fast horse to Count Audulf to advise him what roads to take and what defenses he might expect to face.

At one of these meetings late in their mission, Sebastian hurried to the steps of the cathedral in the port city of Vannes in southern Brittany. Sebastian arrived soon after dark and spotted what appeared to be a beggar with his back against the church door. It was Liudolf—with some disconcerting news.

"You've got to get out of here," he exclaimed without preamble, after they had hurriedly scanned the open square in front of the church. "The word is out against you and your fake monks. The abbot in Nantes wasn't so sure about the bones you gave him, and he sent messengers all the way to Paris to verify your story about the bones of Saint Sebastian.

By the way, why on earth couldn't you have chosen another saint? Using your own name for that colossal hoax makes my flesh crawl."

"It was Heimdal's idea, not mine. But it doesn't matter now. How can you help us get out of here?"

"Well, you're lucky; Count Audulf says he has enough information now, and he's already launched the invasion. He says for you to pull out at once, and he sent a contingent this way with horses and clothes for you if you can get your men out of here."

"Can't be done tonight. It would raise too much suspicion."

"First thing in the morning, then. Don't delay. I'll meet you on the east road outside of town. The sooner we're out of here, the better. Damn Heimdal. I knew he was going to get us into big trouble."

Sebastian did not share the harrowing news with the others for fear of their possible overreaction. But he did not sleep that night and got them up well before dawn the next morning. They were dressed, fed, saddled, and ready to go before the sun came up, including the jubilant Brother Bodoc, who said he "might enjoy a little holiday" before making his way back to the monastery.

A few miles out of Vannes, they encountered Liudolf with a troop of Frankish cavalry and gladly exchanged mules and monkish garb for horses and weapons. They stayed off the major roads and made their way back to the main body of the army without incident, the only unfortunate consequence being a very bad reputation in Brittany for Frankish clergy of any sort.

***

Sebastian returned with most of the army before the end of summer. The campaign had proven so uncomplicated and quick that Charlemagne had not even had time to finish his preparations for Italy. Audulf triumphantly presented the captive leaders of the Bretons at the assembly of the army in

Worms. The king was delighted with the results of the campaign and couldn't wait to sit Sebastian down to hear the full account.

"Stone the crows, lad, you've done it again!" the king proclaimed loudly as he poured Sebastian a large cup of new wine. "How on earth did you manage it? Tell me everything. They say you went all over the country in the guise of a band of monks!"

Sebastian spun out the story at length and concluded, "It's all true, my liege. We posed as monks on pilgrimage and rode in on mules—no war horses, no weapons—and carried our baggage of 'relics' on pack mules. No one even bothered to question us seriously—until nearly the end, that is. By then, Audulf had all the information he needed. We got out by the hair of our chins and joined the army back at Nantes."

"By Saint Martin and all the martyrs! What a pair of iron bollocks you've got! I've never been anywhere without at least a sword and a good horse under me my whole life long. What of routes? Everyone has said that Brittany is particularly difficult to move an army through."

"Not really, my lord king. The Romans did it when they conquered Brittany long ago. And they left very good Roman roads into the country. Soon enough, we discovered where to find the great lords of Brittany and where they had the bulk of their fighting men."

"Splendid!" the king exclaimed. "Audulf brags that he succeeded in taking one fortress after another against weak resistance. What do you make of that?"

"That was the key, sire. What we learned from the lords we saw and other pilgrims early on was that there were bitter territorial squabbles going on among the three tribal kingdoms Brittany is divided into. No fortress we attacked was reinforced from another. In the end, we moved so swiftly the Bretons never had a chance to organize a viable resistance. They wound up reluctantly agreeing to pay our annual tribute and reaffirm your authority. I believe the seneschal left some garrison troops and brought back hostages."

"He did, and he made a good show of the whole thing. But you, my amazing young champion, opened the door for him. If Audulf had gone in there without all that scouting you did, he would have gotten lost in that Breton wilderness and likely would have been buggered by those savages well and proper, like poor Roland down in the Spanish mountains. We would be licking our wounds now instead of celebrating a successful campaign. And it hardly cost me a bloody thing! Once again I find myself indebted to you. How can I reward you?"

"Sire, you allowed that I might have time away from court to spend with my family and to tend to some urgent personal business."

"I did indeed. And I'm as good as my word. Too bad, though, you won't be available for our next adventure. I'm off to Italy as soon as I can raise the rest of the troops. I've got plenty to settle there, and I need to sit our own man down on the Lombard throne. Can't have old Desiderius plotting against me in Pavia or threatening the pope again in Rome. Sorry you can't be with me on this one, Sebastian. You've not see Rome, have you?"

"No, my lord king."

"Well, you will someday, God willing. It's an impressive old pile of stones, even as run-down as it is. They have some first-rate churches still—many of 'em quite beautiful. And Hadrian does put on a good show at High Mass. His Latin is a bit plummy, but it's a good job, nonetheless."

The king took hold of Sebastian's shoulders and looked him in the eye. "Take care of yourself, lad. Can't afford to lose you. In fact, I'm thinking of making you one of my paladins, my special champions. What you did in Brittany is exactly the kind of thing I need my paladins to do. I admit I set you a test there, but you came through, dog's bollocks! There'll be more of that, I can assure you."

Sebastian froze for a moment. He felt a pang of guilt that the confrontation with Konrad might very well make irrelevant all of Charlemagne's plans for him. Even if he

40

survived, he dreaded to think of what being a paladin might mean for his future. At length, he only said quietly, "I'm unworthy, my lord king."

"Nonsense, old lad. Get on with you now, and good luck. Come back soon."

The Saxon March

Chapter 4

Hedeby

Denmark, Autumn 786

On the long ride into Denmark, two thoughts kept competing in Sebastian's head. The first was the rage and hatred he felt toward Konrad for ruining his life. It seemed that everything that had ever gone wrong in Sebastian's life—the murder of his father, the loss of Adela, the lonely life he was compelled to lead now—was all Konrad's fault. Adela was right; Konrad was a curse upon them both. He was like a malignant canker in the flesh; the only thing to do was cut it out.

The other thing was what the king had said to him after the Brittany expedition. His thoughts kept returning to that last audience. The king wanted him to be one of his paladins! Fancy that! It was an enormous honor. There were only a few of them, all great men. Roland had been one of them. But there was a heavy price to pay. Most of them never lived to grow old, and they certainly didn't have any life except to be at the king's beck and call at every moment. There would be precious little time for home life and family. The recent escapade into Brittany was only a taste of what it would be like to be a paladin.

But what does it matter? he thought bitterly. I've already lost my family—unless I can settle with Konrad once and for all.

It was precisely because Adela was the answer to every prayer Sebastian had ever uttered that he now found himself, as in a bad dream, on a reckless road to Denmark, even though his journey held out as little hope for success as his chances of becoming king. But without her, he did not care what might happen to him. His only regret was that he risked the lives of

43

his companions, and the nearer they drew to Hedeby, the guiltier he felt about the risk they, too, were taking.

He racked his brain for a way to keep them out of harm's way once they reached their destination. But he could not go back; Adela was for him the fountain of his life and its significance as well. Thus he had resolved to die if necessary in an attempt to have back what they once had held so perfectly.

His comrades had tried everything to deter Sebastian from his intent. Liudolf had even threatened to go the king, but the king was deep into organizing the army for the campaign into Italy, and Sebastian had already received Charlemagne's blessing to attend to personal business.

Sebastian would not be deterred. The more they argued, the more stolid and silent he became as he prepared for the journey. Despite their doubts and reservations, on the morning of his departure they were waiting for him, packed, armed, and mounted as well as he: Liudolf and Archambald, the friends of his youth, closer to him than anyone besides his family; Bardulf and Drogo, who had become as devoted to him as the family hounds; Bernard, who continued to regard Sebastian's safety as a family responsibility; and even Heimdal, whose blindness, infirmities, and age did not deter him from assuming the role he had always played as personal advisor and conscience for Sebastian and his father, Attalus, before him.

The trip was long and uneventful despite the fact that much of the way led through Saxon territory. But the Saxons had been beaten too many times and were, for the moment, at peace with Charlemagne. Sebastian spoke little during the entire journey. It was as if he had put his life behind him and no longer cared what might occur. No attempt by Archambald to be jolly and none of Bardulf's ribald folktales could stir him or even win a smile. He was impervious to all but the road ahead of them.

Liudolf, who never spoke more than two sentences a day if he could help it, made several attempts to talk sense to Sebastian. Always the practical one, he had become

Sebastian's constant companion since they moved to the king's court, perennially at his right hand, guarding and guiding as much as anyone could with Sebastian. They had been together since their boyhood at the frontier fortress of Fernshanz. Born a peasant in a soldier's family, everything good that had ever happened in Liudolf's life had come through Sebastian. Now that they had ascended to the king's court, Liudolf rarely left his friend's side. When he traveled, Liudolf went with him; when he fought, Liudolf was at his right arm. Tall and strong, lean and wary, he trusted few and befriended even fewer. He rarely questioned Sebastian or even offered his advice, but he was watchdog, caretaker, and confidant and as good a friend as Sebastian could have had.

On this journey, however, Liudolf uncharacteristically offered his grave reservations about the venture.

"This is hare-brained, Sebastian," he said in a low voice, riding up closer so the others would not hear. "You're going to get us all killed, yourself as well. You can't go riding into a town full of pirates and expect to call one out and do justice to him in front of God and everybody. Besides, this is not just any pirate, this is Konrad. You beat him once because he was drunk. What makes you think you can beat him when he's sober? He's a terror, and you know it. And maybe he won't even give you a chance to fight him alone. He's more likely to set his pack of mangy dogs on you and watch them eat your liver if you challenge him up there."

"I told you not to come, Liudolf," was Sebastian's terse reply. "I have no choice."

"You damned well do, by all the saints! Your choice is to live or to die. If you go into that town looking for Konrad without an army, you're going to die. I know something terrible has happened between you and Adela, but do you think she'd want you to do this? I'll wager you've not even told her what you're up to. I don't want to ride back to Andernach with your dead body over a horse's back and tell her you died doing a damn foolish thing."

"See here, Liudolf," Sebastian hissed back, growing angrier by the second in his frustration, "this is something I

45

have to do because if I don't, I will lose Adela, and I will never be happy again without her. I don't expect you to understand. And the best thing you could do for me now is go back—and take these other fools with you." He spurred ahead to signal an end to the argument.

***

Once in Denmark, they wasted several days in misdirection but finally stumbled on a well-traveled road leading to a busy Danish town. As they sat their horses on a low rise above the town, Sebastian was surprised to find such a large and thriving place. Since the Saracens controlled most of what used to be called the Roman Sea, trade had almost dried up north of the Alps, and many cities and towns in Francia and even in Italy had lost their vitality. Populations shrank drastically, and manufacturing all but ceased. Major cities like Rome had been reduced mainly to administrative centers for the Church. Consequently, power and wealth in the realm came to reside almost exclusively in the land and what it could produce. But this, surprisingly, appeared to be a major trading center. As was his habit in new situations, Sebastian decided to consult his old advisor.

"Heimdal," he called. "Come up and tell me what you think." The blind man had the reputation of being able to "see" better than an ordinary man with two good eyes. He was the most intelligent man Sebastian had ever met. On the long and dangerous pilgrimage they had made to the shrine of Saint Martin in Tours, Heimdal's wisdom and vast knowledge of the world of the Franks had saved them from disaster more than once. Before that, Heimdal had been the traveling companion of Sebastian's father, Attalus.

As usual, Heimdal merely listened as Sebastian described the town. "I see a middling town, crowded with small houses. It lies behind a rough semicircular wall. At the bottom end of the town, there's an estuary of a large river flowing eastward as far as I can see. There are three bulky cargo boats moored to large poles driven into the mud a short distance from the shore. And there's a stream channeled right through the town so they can easily bring goods by skiff from the large boats into the town's center. There's a big marketplace there with considerable activity. To the west, there's a busy road with many carts and people. I believe this must be Hedeby."

"I'm sure it is, my boy," Heimdal affirmed. "What you see is a long fjord leading to the Mare Balticum, and the road to the west must lead to the Northern Sea. Hedeby is a fairly new town, I've heard, and it seems it is now at the apex of what trade there is here in the north.

"More ominously," Heimdal went on, dipping into the vast warehouse of his mind where he dumped every bit of information from every conversation he ever had, "it is also ideally suited as a base for Danish pirates. They pose as traders here in the town and then ride a short distance to the Northern Sea, where they transfer into lean, fast-sailing warships and prey on trading vessels sailing between the rich towns of Frisia and England. Once a prize or two is taken, I'm sure they return to Hedeby and sell their captured treasures for staggering sums. No wonder Konrad is here."

"Well, it certainly is busy and crowded with people. But it doesn't look very comfortable or healthy. The houses are so close together their roofs nearly meet over narrow wooden streets. Most of them have tiny fenced-in yards with a few chickens and a pig or two. And they've got their outhouses far too close to their wells. I certainly wouldn't care to live there.

"It also must rain a great deal," Sebastian continued. "There's mud everywhere. That's why they have to build their streets out of timber. Not much farming either, hardly any barns. Appears they bring in all their food or fish for it."

"One thing you may count on, my friend, this is going to be a very important town. That enormous earth-and-timber barrier you described to me a few leagues back means that the Danish chieftains may have already set their course. They intend to take advantage of towns like Hedeby to pursue a very aggressive policy, most of it having to do with piracy—or worse. I have heard they call that wall the Danewirk and that it extends all the way across this narrow part of Denmark in order to protect the whole peninsula—from Charlemagne and his army, in case all this plundering they're beginning to do draws a Frankish invasion. That huge wall is not occupied now, but you can be certain it will be if this Viking business results in a war. Hedeby is only the beginning."

Heimdal paused a moment to let his words sink in. "Lad, this is information the king needs. We should go back at once and tell him."

Sebastian snorted. "No, Heimdal, that hound won't hunt. You can't argue duty to dissuade me from my purpose here. If you think Hedeby is so important to the king, *you* can go back, or all of you." And he turned his horse into the nearby woods to begin his preparations.

***

"M'Lord Sebastian," Bardulf began nervously, "let me and Drogo go in first. It's a big town, mainly, but not so big as nobody's going to notice ye, with all yer swords and spears and lovely big horses. We will just be poor buggers lookin' for work or somethin' to eat. And we'll nose around, up and down, till we finds a place where Konrad is likely to want to drink. Because he laps his ale like a hound, and he's always at it. We'll set ourselves down in front of the place and pretend like we be peddlers or some such. Sooner or later, if he's in the town, we'll see him. I know him right enough. Who don't that's ever seen him? And he's not likely to hide, I reckon. Just give us a night and a couple of days, and we'll bring ye back such news as ye can make a plan with. Let us do that for ye at least, m'lord. It ain't like me and Drogo be in any danger. Nobody'll bother with folk as innocent lookin' as we be."

"Right, Bardulf,"Archambald remarked scornfully, "you're about as innocent as a weasel in the pigeon cote."

"No, wait," Liudolf interjected with unusual interest, "Bardulf is right. If we all go in together, we'll make a stir, and if Konrad is there, he'll know it and have us at a disadvantage. Let them go in, Sebastian; it won't hurt to wait a day or two, and we can watch the roads in the meantime."

Bardulf and Drogo spent the rest of the day disguising themselves for entering the town. They got rid of any items that smacked of life above the poverty level. They scoured the nearby woods for berries, nuts, and roots to stash in the small rough bags they tied to their belts. They muddied their boots to make them look old and worn. And in lieu of weapons, they took only a crude knife good only for eating and a pair of stout walking sticks. In the morning, they trudged toward the town, looking like needy, down-at-the-heels peasants with no other prospects beyond a quest for the next meal.

Falling in with a family of peasants pushing a small cart full of vegetables for sale at the town's marketplace, they passed easily through the main gate. Just beyond it, they came upon two brightly painted stones set upright on a small mound. Strange rows of runic inscriptions decorated both stones.

They blended easily with the busy crowd going to and fro in the large central marketplace. A few Wilzi slaves, captured in some raid to the east, were standing shirtless in the crisp air, on display for prospective buyers. A blacksmith plied his clangorous trade in the open between two houses.

And women as well as men were purposefully going in and out of a larger wooden lodging at the edge of the marketplace. Smoke pouring from the fire hole in the middle of its thatched roof indicated that cooking was continuous. It was immediately apparent to Bardulf that this primitive inn was a multipurpose public house, where one might buy food, strong drink, information, or a woman, and where one would eventually see anyone of consequence in the town or any visitors to it.

They quickly found a dry place at the edge of the village green, and spreading out a dirty piece of linen on the ground, they displayed their meager wares of roots and nuts.

Two days went by with no sign of Konrad or any of the warrior crew of Ivor the Bold. On the first night, Bardulf went back to the wooded area where Sebastian and the others made camp and collected from them a few small spare knives, random items of tin and soapstone, woolen cloths, and a bag of salt. The next morning, he and Drogo began the vigil again, watching the life of the town from the village green and becoming familiar with its folk.

Bardulf was in his element as a peddler. He exuded a congenial, non-threatening air. He knew better than to try to pressure a potential customer to barter with him. Instead, he began by complaining of the weather, his aches and pains, or the difficulties of constantly traveling a dangerous road. And then he would wax into elaborate stories of fictional adventures or exotic places he and Drogo had seen. He was best as a teller of farcical tales so ridiculous and surprising that he would end up astounding his audience or driving them into fits of laughter—after which, he would invariably make a good trade.

On the morning of the third day, surrounded by a growing covey of peasants eager to hear another of his stories, Bardulf was in the midst of a fanciful boast of his familiarity with none other than the great Charlemagne.

"Why, us have been to the very court of Karl the Great, King of all the Franks. He likes to buy from me and Drogo from time to time. Ye see, we have access to a delicacy the king just cannot resist. We catches it, and we cooks it—with turnips! Just so, and it becomes the most delicious, mouth-waterin' supper that ye can find to eat outside of the palace of the pope. What is it, ye say, that the king cannot do without? I'll tell ye, if ye don't tell nobody else, for I wouldn't want to spread the word that the great king has got a weakness. But ye know, he does have such a tooth for it, and he'll pay a good price for a good one. What is it, ye say? Well, I'll tell ye, it's a porkypine," he said after a significant pause for effect.

"The king loves it," Bardulf went on quickly to ward off their disbelief. "I have seen him eat a whole porkypine at one sittin' while we stood by countin' the silver he give us for it. And ye know, while he was eatin' it, a great delegation of Saxons come to surrender to him. Everybody knows the king has been fightin' them Saxons for a score of years or more. And he has beat them over and over, year after year. And after they gets beat, they always promise to give up their bloody ways and become good Christian folk like the Franks themselves. But no sooner than they do this, they goes back to their worshipin' tree, the giant ash tree of Odin hisself, and they unswears themselves.

"Well, it does make the great king a bit put out with 'em. But on this here occasion, he don't let on. He just accepts their apologies and keeps on eatin' his porkypine and turnips. They says to him: 'Is it all right if we goes now, and are we forgiven?' The king says, without missin' a bite, 'Yes, ye may go, and I forgive ye, but before ye go, ye must be measured.'

"'Measured,' they says, 'how is that, great king?'

"'Just go on out into the courtyard,' says the king, continuin' to eat, 'and they will show ye. Ye must be measured.'

"And so all them Saxons filed on out into the courtyard, which was now surrounded by soldiers. And there in the middle, a tall Frankish soldier is standin' up on a platform holdin' a sharp, double-edged Frankish battle sword with its point stuck into the platform. He says, 'Come on up here, ye Saxons, and be measured. Ye must be measured by the sword. And if ye be taller than the sword. . . ye must be shortened by a head."

As the villagers howled with laughter and Bardulf protested loudly in feigned indignation and swore it was all true, Konrad rode up on a spent Danish pony and barged into the public house.

Chapter 5

The Dirty Shame

"So I told 'em I had a hankerin' for porkypine meself, and I slipped outta the marketplace while they was all a-gawkin' at Konrad ridin' up. It was him all right. I got a good look at him. And everbody knew him too. They know what a bastard he be. Everybody's feared of him."

"Was he alone?" Sebastian demanded. "How many men does he have?"

"Well, he was alone when he rode up, but the tavern was already full of his men. They musta come in durin' the night. They be about thirty of 'em in there. I left Drogo there to watch 'em."

"That's it, Sebastian," Liudolf asserted. "There's no way we're going to take on Konrad and thirty of his warriors. We'd be better off to ride out the way he came and wait for him to go back there. We can lay an ambush for him if he's alone or with just a few men."

Sebastian was up, pacing the floor nervously. He even buckled on his sword belt, preparing to barge right down to the town and call Konrad out into the street.

"We don't know if he'll ever go back that way, Liudolf. What if he decides to go east to the Balticum? We'd lose him."

"What if we just invite him out here, Sebastian?" Archambald chimed in. "We could say we have a message from his wife. Er. . . in a way, we do."

"Nonsense, Archambald. He'd come with his whole band, and then all of you would be at risk."

"Well, you can't go in there alone, Sebastian. Don't think of it—unless you want to die. You don't, do you?" Heimdal added uneasily.

"No," was the terse reply, but Sebastian was beginning to feel certain that going in alone was the only way to avoid risking the lives of his comrades. The devil with it! he said to himself in disgust. He would probably die, but he had to go. It wasn't worth living if Konrad was still alive and standing between Adela and himself. At least Sebastian could spare his friends.

"Look," he said, mustering a weak smile. "We're all tired. Let's get a good night's sleep and approach the problem with fresh minds in the morning."

"There's a good man," Heimdal said with relief. "Excellent advice. A bit of bread and wine and then to bed. Everyone thinks better with a full stomach and some rest."

Sebastian waited only an hour after everyone else was soundly asleep and then slipped out of the camp on foot, carrying only the weapons he expected to use. As he anticipated, the town gate was barred, and a sentry challenged him as he came up.

Sebastian had long since decided what he was going to do when this moment came. Without an army at his back, he really had only a single choice: to challenge Konrad once again to single combat and hope that the arrogant man's pride as a famous fighter would make him accept. Obviously, Konrad would not be alone.

There was at best only the slimmest chance that, come morning, Sebastian would walk out of the town alive. But he had given up hope of recovering Adela any other way and was prepared for that fate. He was not really afraid; he had been in such circumstances several times before a battle. He knew that a warrior must give himself totally to the fight if he hoped to be clear-headed enough to stay alive. One simply had to be ready to die and be reconciled to it, not looking or caring for anything beyond the battle in order to concentrate methodically, one step at a time, on the foe before him. After the long, hollow journey to Hedeby with nothing to do but think, he was relieved now at the prospect of action, abandoning at once all doubts and calculations

Not surprisingly, the guard at the gate refused Sebastian's request to be admitted to go to the town's inn for a night's rest.

"Halt, you! Vas be you? Say vat you vant here by *uns*? I *Wachtmeister,* me, *und* I no *kenn* you," the guard said in a loud voice, clearly mistrustful of the hooded figure standing before the gate, who, though cloaked, could not conceal that he was armed at least with spear and sword.

"Speak," the guard repeated, "or I make alarum. You mebbe spy for Franks, *ja*? You look like spy, by Gott*s*!

Sebastian discarded his hope of getting into the town unrecognized and finally declared, "I am a Frank, but I mean you no harm. I am Sebastian, a count at the court of the great King Karl. I am here on business with a certain Konrad, who is supposed to be here with the men of a Danish trader called Ivor the Bold."

"*Donder! Das ist eine Antwort!* I tink you must be vat you say. Only such high man say so like dat. *Aber entschuldigung, Hoheit,* I must not say you come in widout my chief say so. You must here staying. I send to Dirty Shame, *und* they come, bring in you."

"The Dirty Shame? What in the world is that?"

"*Das ist unser Weinstube, mein herr, unser* tavern. Ve call it so to make honor for old Bolli, who vas first innkeeper. Bolli vas friendly fella, good *Gastgeber. Sehr gastfreundlich. Aber eine Nacht*, many sailors come, *sehr vild und verrueckt, ja*? They drink und fight *mit einander*, und *unser* Bolli vas in between. They kill him dead. Too bad. Ve all love old Bolli. So ve say it is dirty shame. So now *das ist Namen unser* tavern—Dirty Shame, *ja*?"

"Sergeant," Sebastian declared formally, "I would be obliged to you if you would send to the tavern and tell whoever is in charge there that I am at the gate and request to come in to the inn and meet with Konrad. If he is there, I would be obliged if he would be informed of my presence."

***

Sebastian watched Konrad come down the crude stairs of the inn, buckling on his sword belt. He had obviously been roused from some whore's bed in the loft above by the astounding news that a count from the court of Charlemagne awaited him below. From long association with Konrad when they were youths at Adalgray, Sebastian knew him to be a man who thrived on hatred; he hated and scorned almost everyone he met, even the whores with whom he had almost daily intercourse. This universal hate was what drove him to be such a terror in battle. It propelled his furious, unthinking onslaughts and gave him additional strength. Men said that merely his face, contorted with savage rage and the lust to kill, caused horror in the hearts of his opponents and gave Konrad a tremendous advantage. He had such a fiery temperament that he was always on the tipping point of releasing that fury. It was clear to Sebastian that the older his dreaded cousin got, the more murderous his moods became.

Konrad paused now in mid-descent as his eyes identified the hooded face of the man he hated more than any other on earth—the only man who had ever bested him in personal combat. He screamed in recognition. "YOU! You bastard! You whore's son. You filthy piece of *scheisse*. You . . ." He leaped down the stairs, pulling at his sword.

Sebastian, too, reacted to the meeting of their eyes and quickly drew his own sword, actually smiling with the realization that perhaps he would be able to have the single combat he sought after all.

However, just as Konrad propelled himself toward Sebastian, several of the Vikings stepped out to bar his way. The men quickly relieved Sebastian of his sword and spear as a grotesque figure emerged from the midst of them.

Sebastian stepped back cautiously and considered the abrupt change in the situation. Uh-oh, he thought as he took in the sudden appearance of the bizarre leader of the Viking band. So this was the infamous Ivor the Bold that he had heard so much about. This was the thug he was going to have to go through to get to Konrad. His mind raced to grasp an idea of how to deal with him.

It was not Ivor's physical bulk that startled Sebastian as he tried to size up the newcomer—the Viking leader was merely of middling build, though heavily muscled. It was the implicit threat in his tight death's-head face and the way he held his tattooed body, naked to the waist, like a coiled snake, always ready, watching everything through ice-blue slit eyes, unpredictable, mean, and dangerous. The sides of his head were shaven, and a long rope of heavy dark hair trailed down his back. Three small black lines of runic symbols were tattooed across each cheek. He elaborated his startling face with a perpetual thin and incongruous smile.

It was clear to Sebastian the man had a formidable aura, for Konrad stopped in mid-stride when Ivor held up his hand. "Halt now, Konrad, you great hulk of Frankish wild boar; it will not do for you to bang into a fight here in our nice tavern—especially without introductions. I mean, is that a fine way to treat guests? No, no, no! Such mysterious person as we have here must be important fella. They say he comes from court of Karl der Grosse himself. Well, we cannot be so impolite to such a noble visitor, *ja*? Let us wait a bit and not blow up like summer squall before we know what is what."

"I'll tell you what's what," yelled Konrad at the top of his voice, straining against the men who held him. "This man is my mortal enemy, the man I hate more than any other on this earth, the man I'd give a fortune to kill, as I have said many times before. This is Sebastian, the bastard, the man who's been sleeping with my wife, who has usurped my lands and patrimony, the man who poisoned my name with the King of the Franks. And now here he is, just as if God himself sent him to me. If I prayed at all, which I don't, he would be the answer to my prayers. And I can kill him now once and for all, in the midst of many witnesses, so he will stay dead, well and truly."

"Well now," Ivor replied in a silky tone of misdirection, "that is quite big evil you say against this poor hooded fella. But maybe we just see first what he looks like and hear what he will say. After all, you did say your piece, *ja*?"

Konrad roared again and struggled in the arms of the husky bruisers who restrained him, furious that he could not immediately satisfy his lust for Sebastian's blood.

Good! Good, you cursed devil! Sebastian thought. Get mad! Get furious. You'll insist on fighting me now. And you'll make a mistake, you bumptious fool!

Ivor went on as if Konrad's rage were only the senseless squalling of a child. "Let us see now," he said, spinning out his web, "who are you, stranger? Tell us your story before you die, if indeed you must. Let it never be said that Ivor the Bold is not fair-handed. Besides, it has been a most dull evening, and we could enjoy a good tale, told well, and perhaps a bit of sport at the end, *ja*? Kindly unmask yourself and tell us who it is you must be."

Sebastian decided quickly that the only way to deal with Ivor was to tell him the truth boldly and without showing doubt or fear. He must at least win Ivor's respect. He calmly pulled aside the cowl of his cloak. His voice, low and even, betraying no evidence of fear or panic, was magnetic. He spoke quietly, never taking his eyes off the face of Konrad.

"I am Sebastian, lord of the fortresses of Adalgray and Fernshanz, a royal count of the court of Karl der Grosse, King of all the Franks. But I am here on my own business, not that of the king, to seek justice on the body of that creature there." And he nodded his head toward the nearly apoplectic Konrad.

"Uffda!" breathed Ivor, increasingly warming to the unfolding scene. "This tale is more interesting each moment. But tell us, pray you, why it is you are so worried to have justice on the body of our man Konrad? He is my second in command. You must know that we love him like brother, *ja*? You are taking terrible risk to jump so quickly into what some would say is your most bad dream. Here is a man who hates you and would kill you in one quick moment if we would let him. And here are us, Danish. . . uh, adventurers, who do not know you from nobody and for sure do not much like your King of Franks, who you say you serve. What evil could drive you to risk such stormy waters? You must know this Dirty Shame tavern where we are is like to be the last place you will

ever see. Too bad, you look like you might be somebody a man could like. It is truly dirty shame what is likely to happen to you tonight, *ja?*"

"I don't care what happens to me tonight. I have made my peace, and I'm ready to die, if I must. But that devil there must die first. At least I'll have the satisfaction of ridding the world of his villainous presence in it and sending him to hell."

"Oh! Izzat so? Well, we will see about all that. But you must have dire reason for such awful opinion of our good friend Konrad here. My, my, my! You say he is so bad, I wonder if I should like him myself anymore. What has he done, if you don't mind me asking? I would wager it is about a woman, *ja?*" he whispered as an aside to the men lounging against the wall and grinning in anticipation.

Sebastian took a deep breath, waited a few seconds, and began, "He poisoned my father and, I suspect, caused the death of his own father. He stole the woman I love by bribing the king into letting him marry her. Then he treated her like a whore, beat her, killed her little child through his insane actions, and nearly killed her as well. He led a foolish charge against an entrenched Saxon cohort. It was a trap, and the Frankish cavalry were cut to pieces by Widukind, the most famous of all the Saxon princes. When the king sent for him and demanded explanation, this coward refused to go to him and tried to start a conspiracy against the crown. I was sent to arrest him, and we fought. I bested him and could have killed him. But I spared his miserable life, God forgive me. I should have killed him then before he did more harm. He escaped the king's justice, and now I am here to finish the job."

"*Uffda!* That is bold talk for one who is not so big and strong as this Konrad here—with nobody here to back him up and in a place that is not his own, among folk who might be not so friendly to him or to what he wants to do. However, I will say this for you: you do have some big pair of bollocks, as they say.

"One more thing," Ivor continued, "why should we let you do what you come here to do? Even was you to kill our old Konrad here, which I have some big doubts you can do, what good would come of this for us? We don't like your king. But we like our friend here; he is good man in fight. I might be sorry to lose him from our little band."

"I will pay you to let me kill him," Sebastian blurted out. "I have access to a great deal of gold, and I will give it to you."

"Oh? Where is this precious gold, pray?"

"Well, I did not bring it, but I swear by my oath to the king and by all that is holy that I will make this worth your while."

"Hmm. Why have I got this feeling that what you say is true? But even so, my honest-looking stranger, we do not trust your king, and we are not so holy as your own self, maybe. It is a good offer, 'tis true, but it sounds much like a risk. Say we let you fight, and by some miracle you kill him; then you go home, and what we got is only your word that you will send us some treasure. You must forgive me, but I have some small doubts. I want to say, even if I trust you, and you go back on your word, what does that make me in front of my men?" He turned to the gaggle of rough-cut thugs lining the sides of the room. "Should I do this thing, my good soldiers? Should I trust this man?"

They responded as one with a resounding, "Noooo!"

"Well, well, well, now you see it, my Lord Sebastian, they don't see no profits in all this for us. And, unfortunate for you, we are in the business of making profits."

"I will give you profit," burst out Konrad, no longer able to restrain himself. "Let me fight him, Ivor, and I will give you my share of the profit from the next three ships we take."

"Whuh!" Ivor breathed out with a mercenary grin. "I am beginning to truly love this tale." He paused a moment to consider his options. "Look here, Konrad, I don't like to mention, but we all know you be a demon as brawler, but this fella here, he say he beat you once. If it is true, what will happen to us if he beats you again? We would have nothing, no profits at all save some little satisfaction of killing the man who kills you. And that might not be so much fun neither, *ja*?"

"Bollocks! I was drunk at the time. He took me by surprise. Besides, he had over two hundred men at his back."

"Did they butt in on fight?"

"No, damn it, they were just there, but I kept expecting them to horn in.

"Ah, but they did not, and he beat you, *ja*?"

"I'm telling you, I was drunk. And I was sick. Hell and damnation! You've seen me fight. Is there any man you've ever seen who could beat me?"

"That is true. I have seen you fight many times. And you do well—for a Frank—better than most. In fact, you might just be fiercest Frank I ever see." Ivor paused to consider, shrugged his shoulders, and smiled roguishly. "Still, I have not seen *him* fight, *ja*? When I bet, I like sure thing."

"Listen, Ivor, you know me. You know what I can do. Give this bastard to me, and you can have my share of the next three ships we take. And if by some trick he should win, you can have everything I've got here now—all the treasure we've taken over the last year. It's yours. How can you lose?"

"Well now, that is truly generous offer, friend Konrad." He spun around, arms open to his men. "What say you, my brave warriors, do you want see a good knock-about this night?"

The response was a deafening roar of assent.

The jubilant reaction of the men to the fight triggered an immediate response from both Sebastian and Konrad. Both lunged forward against the guards restraining them. But Ivor stepped quickly between them and held up his hands.

"No, no, no, my impatient friends. Do you think I wish to have blood all over my lovely inn where I eat my supper? Not to mention what you might do to the fine furnishings of this place. No, it would be, as they say here, one dirty shame. We must move out onto market square, where you can have room to kill each other properly. And let us bring some torches outside. You, Konrad, will do nothing until I give

60

word. Is clear?" he said menacingly toward Konrad, still heaving against his hulking captors.

Once in the yard, Ivor's men formed a square. Sebastian stepped into it along with a glaring, furious Konrad. Oddly, he felt exhilarated. This was what he had asked for. So be it. At this point, there was nothing to lose, and an eerie calm began to take over his consciousness, almost detaching him from the raucous preparations and noise of the onlookers. Out of the corner of his eye, he spied Drogo, perched innocuously at the edge of the green on some empty wine barrels with a stricken look on his face.

Ivor stepped officiously into the square, facing the two combatants. "Now, my fine friends, since you are so eager to cut each other's throats, we have decided to let you—for our sport and gratification, and for the profits, *ja,* which we will enjoy no matter who wins this lovely fight. But let us be fair from beginning. How can we make all fair, eh? What weapons do you wish to use, Lord Sebastian?"

"If you will be good enough to return my spear and sword. . ."

"Will you not use shield? I see that you did not bring one."

"No, this is enough—for him," was his calm reply. Konrad uttered a growl and a curse. Sebastian smiled.

"Well, then," Ivor said in surprise, "that is settled, but I must marvel at your confidence." He gestured toward a warrior, who returned the weapons at once. Sebastian shifted the spear into his left hand and grasped his sword with the right. "And you, Master Konrad, with what weapons will you fight?"

"I will have my shield and this sword." With that, he drew once again the enormous sword from its scabbard and brandished it above his head.

Ivor held up his hand. "We are agreed, then, my quarrelsome friends, that you will fight until one of you is no longer able, dead or alive. When I drop my hand, you may begin." He waited overlong in order to raise the level of excitement among his men and then swiftly dropped his hand and stepped adroitly aside.

Konrad lunged forward bullishly in his typical explosive manner, roaring at the top of his voice and vilifying Sebastian with each breath. Sebastian skipped away easily, circling to his left and then quickly back to the right, all the time thrusting out with sharp jabs of his spear at Konrad's head or legs and causing the burly fighter to protect himself constantly with his shield.

The fight soon revealed how much faster and more flexible Sebastian was than his lumbering opponent. No matter how many times Konrad rushed forward, he found no target for the huge sword he brandished. Sebastian became a blur in the torchlight, moving like a wasp, darting in and out, waiting to sting, spear held low in his left hand, sword in his right hand at high guard.

Finally, the moment came. Konrad rushed forward, and Sebastian let him get close. He lingered just a short breath longer than before, and Konrad swung his sword down forcefully from a high guard. As he did so, he let his shield fall too far to the left, away from his body. That was the moment Sebastian needed. He sidestepped neatly to his left and drove the spear into Konrad's side. The chain mail kept the spear from going in too deeply, but Konrad was hurt. He staggered back, glancing down with disbelief at the blood seeping out of the wound. The hesitation almost cost him his life as Sebastian thrust the spear again, this time at Konrad's head, connecting briefly with his helmet and skimming across Konrad's brow. Blood streamed down the big man's face and into his eyes, but his reflexes saved him. He raised his shield just in time to block Sebastian's sword sweeping down from the right.

After the close call, Konrad moved more cautiously, pausing often to wipe the blood out of his eyes with the thumb of his sword hand. But his style of fighting still depended primarily on furious attacks. He continued to plod doggedly after his enemy, swinging away with his huge sword but jumping back skittishly to avoid Sebastian's deft riposte with the spear. At last, he resorted to an untypical move; he lunged forward with another wide swing from the side. When Sebastian leaped back, Konrad suddenly turned his back to him and spun around again with a vicious backhand to the head, but the sword slipped in his bloody hand, and the blow fell too weakly against Sebastian's helmet.

Sebastian ducked quickly under Konrad's arm and used the burly man's momentum to step past and slash at his knee with the sword. The blow caught Konrad just above the back of his right knee, causing his leg to buckle. But he braced himself against the ground with the shield, regained his balance, and managed just in time to strike the onrushing Sebastian powerfully with his uplifted shield. The blow caught Sebastian on the shoulder and sent him reeling into the dirt. Konrad rushed forward, slashing down, but Sebastian rolled away quickly and was up again, jabbing at his foe with the spear and holding the sword behind his ear in readiness. Clearly, Konrad's crippled leg and injured side were becoming a growing disadvantage, and his face began to show a mounting doubt.

Both men were tiring visibly. Konrad was breathing hard but still pressing forward doggedly. He attempted another heavy downward blow, followed by a sweeping upward stroke toward Sebastian's retreating head. Sebastian ducked again and passed to the right under Konrad's extended arm. He then swung his foot hard against Konrad's injured knee. The big man fell at once, flat on his face. As he rolled frantically onto his back, Sebastian hovered over him and smashed his shield away, stepping at the same time upon his sword. He threw away his own sword and grasped the spear with both hands to drive it straight down into Konrad's neck.

In the blink of an eye, between Konrad falling and rolling over on his back, Ivor signaled two of his men. From behind, the first one drove his spear into Sebastian's back. The other swung his sword hard against Sebastian's exposed left thigh. God! Sebastian thought as he went down. I should have known better than to trust that snake for a fair fight.

Konrad, seeing his opponent momentarily immobilized, rolled over on him, and drawing his small sword, drove it with all his might through the chain mail into Sebastian's shoulder. He then drew it out and prepared to finish off his stricken foe.

But before he brought the blade down into Sebastian's neck, he hesitated. A glint came into his eye as he observed how completely at his mercy his enemy was. Sebastian was bleeding from multiple deep wounds. His breathing came in short gasps, and he struggled to focus. *So this is how it ends,* he thought. *I almost succeeded. . . Adela!*

Konrad stayed his hand, pulled back, and then bent low to whisper into Sebastian's ear, "That's for you, you stinking wife stealer. I can kill you now, finally. Good! But maybe I will just watch you die, slowly and painfully. Also very good!" He drew back, open-mouthed and drooling, to gloat over his victim.

Ivor came up to inspect the outcome. "Well, you have done it, my large, fierce friend—with a little help from friends," he added with a suppressed snicker. "I suppose you will kill him now, *ja*? But wait one moment. I thought you hated him! Don't you want him to suffer some more? If I had such hate, I would make such a man pay. It would take much more to satisfy my anger than just to kill him quickly and end his pain."

"Right!" Konrad agreed readily. "I do want him to suffer more, much more. Maybe I'll just let him lie here in his pain until he bleeds to death."

"Hmm! That may take some time, I think. He is healthy fella. I have idea. You say you hate him and want him to suffer more. Just look at what you have done to him. His leg is cut through to the bone. And I think we may have punctured a lung. You may be right; he may bleed to death first. But even if he does not, he will never walk again. He will be a cripple, no good for nothing.

"It will be morning in some few hours. Why you not just let him live, if he can? He must have some friends here somewhere close by. We will let them take him home to Francia? Everyone will see his disgrace. His wife—uh, your wife—will know that you beat him. The word will return to King Karl, and you will have back his respect, eh?"

"No," Sebastian moaned. "Just kill me, you fat donkey pizzle. Get it over with."

"Yes," Konrad hissed, smiling in delight as he thought over Ivor's suggestion. "I want them to know. I want her to know! You will be no good as a fighter ever again. I think it's better if you do live, bastard! You can crawl back to Francia and let my wife see you like this. I would cut your balls off if I thought it wouldn't kill you. But now I just want her to see you and know who is the better man. I want her to see how weak you are, how pitiful a man you will be now. Tell her," he shouted into Sebastian's semi-conscious ear. "Tell her, 'Lord' Sebastian, who beat you. Tell her it was Konrad, her true husband. Tell her that someday, when she doesn't expect it, I will come back. I will come for her someday. Tell her!"

Oh, God, no! This cannot be happening! Fighting to stay conscious, Sebastian denounced his fate. God, why was I born? What sin have I committed just to come to this? Why must Konrad prevail? Why do you let this foul, evil man continue to live? Mercifully, his pain and despair finally faded into black.

Chapter 6

Bleak Road

The Vikings staunched Sebastian's wounds with some dirty rags to keep him from bleeding to death, draped his broken body over the back of a pony, and dumped him unceremoniously in the dirt of the road beyond the gate. They guessed correctly that someone, whoever had traveled with him, would gather him up and try to save him.

At the end of the fight, Drogo slipped over the wall and ran furiously, as fast as his short legs would take him, back to the camp in the grove. Liudolf and Archambald galloped at once to the gate, and in less than two breaths spirited Sebastian away in a makeshift stretcher secured between their saddles. By midnight, the small company was furiously trying to patch Sebastian up enough so that they could, with all haste, put as much distance as possible between themselves and Hedeby.

***

To fill the darkness in his life, Heimdal had made it a lifelong habit to study sickness, disease, and healing. In his early years, his wanderings had taken him to the monastery of Alta Ripa in southern Aquitania, where he learned medicine among the monks there. Though he could not see, he understood the body and made it a point wherever he was to attend any disaster or illness and learn from it. He had saved Sebastian once before on their long pilgrimage to Tours, when he had been stricken by a severe illness and all had shunned the fallen young man for fear of the plague. From many similar experiences, Heimdal had learned never to set out on an expedition without a fat bag of healing potions, herbs, and roots. He needed almost all of them to cope with the wreckage they put before him.

Sebastian had suffered three major wounds. The spear to his back had been stopped in the main by his chain mail, but the force of the blow was enough to break one of his ribs. The sword stroke to his thigh had bitten deeply into the flesh and stubbornly continued to bleed. Even had he been able to stand, he could not have walked. He was not only disabled but completely immobilized. The worst was Konrad's thrust into Sebastian's upper chest. By the time they got him back to camp, he was struggling to breathe.

As soon as they brought Sebastian's fractured body into the camp, Heimdal began to bark orders. Somewhat taken aback by the tirade, Bardulf growled, "Wait a bleedin' minute, old man, what makes you think you can do somethin', blind as ye be?"

"Listen, you ignoramus, I have been studying human illness since before you were born. Now go and boil me some water. We've got to wash him. *Macht schnell*, idiot!"

While Bardulf stoked up the fire, Heimdal explained more calmly, "If you knew anything at all about sickness or wounds, you would know that one learns more by listening—listening to how the man breathes and what he says in his pain. You might be surprised to know I can learn much by just feeling the wounds. Even how the body smells tells me something. Right now it tells me we've got to close these wounds at once."

Heimdal felt the body until he was sure exactly where the wounds were and how badly hurt Sebastian was. He then began to force Sebastian to swallow a thick, sweet brandy, brought along for exactly such a circumstance. He poured and coaxed patiently until he could see Sebastian was beginning to lose consciousness. Then, already sweating copiously, he growled at the others, "Hold him tight now, you lot. Don't let him move while I do this."

Heimdal took a knife from the embers of the campfire and, with the red-hot blade, cauterized each of the wounds while the others held their heaving leader to the ground. They placed a cloth between Sebastian's teeth, fearing that even his weak screams might bring prowling Danes into the woods.

The next step was to cover the wounds completely with animal fat and clean dressings to shut out air and staunch the bleeding. Heimdal knew that Sebastian's chances depended on whether or not they could manage to close the chest wound enough to allow the lung to reinflate.

The whole process took less than an hour. When it was done, Liudolf knelt beside Heimdal and whispered tentatively, "What happens if we move him now?"

"He will probably die," was his terse reply. "Why do you mention it?"

"Because I just came in from watching the road. A group of armed men left the fort just now and rode off down the road in a hurry. Someone may have changed his mind about what to do with Sebastian. We're too close. Once it's daylight, I'm afraid they'll find us—if they really want to. I think we have to get away from here."

Heimdal objected heatedly, but Liudolf convinced the others that Sebastian—and everyone else—would likely die anyway if they were found. So they fashioned a primitive stretcher of wood and blankets and suspended it with ropes and braces between the gentle mares that Bardulf and Drogo had ridden. Sebastian lay in the middle between the two palfreys while the two peasants took turns leading the horses and forcing them to walk in tandem. They left the grove in the middle of the night, heading west toward the sea for fear the southern route to Francia would be patrolled by Ivor's men. They walked lest a riding pace would start the bleeding again. With Liudolf scouting ahead on horseback to choose the way and avoid potential danger, they stumbled down dark paths and uneven terrain, stopping often to coax Sebastian to drink water and broth. The pace was agonizingly slow. At daybreak, they found a wood and went as deeply into the brush as they could manage. Sebastian was still alive.

Traveling only at night, it took them nearly two weeks to reach the sea. Meanwhile, Sebastian remained for the most part delirious or unconscious, mercifully lost in his dreams.

***

One of his most consistent dreams was of a wheat field, golden in the warm sun of late afternoon on a midsummer day. It was a long field, running north to south, but not very wide at any point, bordered by magnificent old oak trees, perhaps more than two hundred years old. They lined the field on three sides with great green walls of leaves and sturdy branches.

Where Sebastian lay in the middle of the field, it rose into a small knoll, from which he could see all around himself, field and forest. He lay back and disappeared into the wheat. From his nest among the stalks, the sky appeared an endless deep blue. Every now and then, a goshawk drifted effortlessly over his small window of sky, and swallows occasionally swooped low over his head. A lark sang in the distance, and a raven called out raucously.

He got up and walked toward the open end of the field. There, the forest yielded on one side to a small enclave where a simple peasant hut sat surrounded by a wattle fence. Inside the fence was a garden, a cornucopia of vegetables, herbs, and flowers of all kinds.

The house was the home of a widow, an old woman who had lived without her husband for half her life. Sebastian unfastened the gate and went in. The woman was bent over her flowers, weeding and pruning, unconcerned that someone had entered the garden. Sebastian knelt beside her and began to mimic her work. When they had finished, she turned her face to him and gave him a toothless smile. She motioned to the flowers and herbs, urging him to pick as many as he liked. Then she gave him a cup of cool water to drink. They sat silently together on a small stump, enjoying the sun on their faces. The old woman was timelessness itself. In her presence, there was no conflict, no striving, only beauty and serenity. He had never felt such peace. When Sebastian got up to go, they had become friends.

Sebastian had chosen some bright yellow flowers with wide petals, long stems, and dark centers. He went back into the field, sat down once more, and began to weave the flowers into garlands, which he draped around his neck. He took the sharp-smelling bunches of herbs he had picked and stuffed them into his belt and the pocket of his tunic—mint, sage, basil, and fragrant rosemary—so that he could enjoy their scent as he walked.

As he rose and began walking again in the field, a figure appeared, coming through the wheat over the small knoll. It was Adela. She wore a blue dress the color of the sky and a white silk shawl against the summer sun. She carried a baby.

It was their baby, a lovely little girl who had died on the first day of her life. But now the child lay peacefully, perfectly alive and beautiful, in her mother's arms. Adela came to Sebastian and held him in her gaze. Absolutely astounded to see her again and not knowing what else to do, Sebastian gave her one of the wreaths of flowers from around his neck. She reached into the pocket of her dress and handed him a gift as well. It was her wedding ring on a silver chain. He put it around his neck. She said, "I have found it very hard not to love you, but I must not, and I must go away again soon, my dear, this time forever." All he could say in reply was, "I'm sorry, I'm so sorry."

They walked back then through the field to the end closed in by the forest. In one corner, a spring-fed pond sparkled, blue in the late afternoon sun. They kept walking together, hand in hand, out into the pond up to their waists. The water was cool and relaxing on this warm day. But it was more than just refreshing. It was magical. For out of his soul, the pond drew a memory, a barb of pain and regret. The pond took it, and the pain and regret dissipated into the water.

They left the pond and walked to an old fire pit nearby. Sebastian kindled a flame and built up a good blaze, where they warmed themselves dry. They sat and talked about old joys and good memories shared together. An owl hooted now and then in the distance.

Then she said, "It is time. I must go." They stood and held each other for a long moment. She backed away and said in parting, "Please try and understand. Forgive me. I love you still, without reservation, forever."

He said simply, "Thank you, thank you with all my heart. But you will never be gone from me, never."

***

Whenever they went to ground to hide during daylight hours, Liudolf was the caregiver. He became Sebastian's nurse while Heimdal rested. To keep himself awake and soothe his friend, Liudolf spoke of their days growing up together at Fernshanz.

"Listen, my old comrade," he whispered into Sebastian's ear, watching every movement and reaction of his stricken friend, "do you remember that time we went pig hunting by ourselves into that big wildwood near the Rhine? All the old hunters said that's where the biggest boars could be found. I would never have told you then, but I'll admit it freely now: I nearly soiled my britches when we jumped that one old grandfather boar. You remember him? My Lord, he looked as big as a horse, and his tusks looked as long as swords. And we were barely fourteen years old or so. Thank God it started to rain. It poured down on us so thick I couldn't even see. And the thunder and lightning was like the end of the world. We had to hobble the horses, they were so skittish, and tie 'em tight to a tree, hoping the lightning wouldn't strike it. Then you and me skirred into a hollow log and waited out the storm. I swear it rained all night, and in the morning we came out to find ourselves on an island in the middle of an ocean filled with the tops of trees. That old Rhine just left her banks and flooded everything halfway to Fernshanz. The horses were gone, of course, and it was a week before we found our way home. I've never seen old Attalus so mad. I know he was glad to see us, but once he got over seeing us again, I thought he was going to kill us. Remember how many days we had to be in the stables cleaning out all that *scheisse*? It made me want to give up riding horseback."

During that desperate time, Liudolf must have reviewed every adventure the two ever had together, every learning experience and trial. For a man who hardly spoke twenty words from one day to the next, he waxed articulate out of fear for his friend's life. He unburdened himself lest Sebastian should die without knowing how much Liudolf admired and loved him.

"You know, Sebastian, I would have never amounted to anything if not for you. I would have been just a peasant farmer all my life or at best just a part-time soldier at Fernshanz, like my father. I never would have learned anything or been anywhere outside our little settlement. Now I know how to fight, and I can even a read a little, thanks to you. I don't know what I would have done with my life without you taking me in—just like a brother. That's it! Why, you *are* my brother, the only one I've got.

"And so you mustn't die now. We have much more to do together, you and me. Why, we might see the world. We might even astound the king again with something we come up with. What do you say, old mate? Don't you die on me now. We have just begun, you and me. The wondrous things we'll see, the marvelous deeds we'll do. Don't you die, you hear? I am your brother, and I command you not to die. There's still too much of life to live, and I want to live it. But it all depends on you. So don't you die. . . don't you. . ." He drifted to sleep with his head on Sebastian's good shoulder.

***

Riding east from Hedeby, they finally reached the coast, fearing as each day ended that Sebastian would not live to the morrow. Finally, Liudolf came upon a ramshackle hut on a solitary, windswept beach, watched it for a while from a distance, and then raced back to the struggling group with the news.

"At last," Heimdal said impatiently, "but is it someplace we can stay? We've got to go to ground somewhere and soon if we want our man here to survive."

"It's the only place around here. There's an old hermit named Jacob that lives there. Nobody else. And he looks as crazy as a loon. It's only a shack, but at least we can get Sebastian out of this bloody wind and keep him warm. There's also a little ramshackle barn where we can bring in the horses. The rest of us might have to rough it a bit outside. But I don't think there's another soul alive for seven leagues in any direction."

Once Liudolf had described the old man to him, Heimdal knew the type at once: Jacob was just a superstitious old hermit who had abandoned a hidebound society where he didn't fit in, preferring the seabirds and the waves lapping endlessly on the deserted beach to the company of people. "It's likely he's more than a bit crazy, Liudolf, from living alone all the time. He probably sees only one or two people in a year. So of course Jacob's going to be sore afraid of all you heavily armed men and great horses invading his house and little barn."

After a single night, Jacob stopped sleeping in the house and made a bed for himself in an abandoned pigsty next to the barn.

"What kind of ol' fart is that, Heimdal?" Bardulf demanded. "I can't figure him out. Even Bernard has a hard time makin' him out. He says he be a Christian, and he's got a little wooden cross on a string round his neck, but Bernard seen him playin' with some little charms in a pocket bag strapped to his waist, and then he snuck up close and heard him prayin' to the Earth Mother and to Father Heaven. And then he sits down on the sand and takes out a knife and puts the point on a sore place on his belly and starts chantin' these crazy words and bowin' low."

"Why, Bardulf, I'm surprised you don't recognize him. Old Jacob—for that is his name, and it is a Christian name at that—is just a typical peasant of these wild parts. He probably was baptized as a Christian by some wandering monk long ago. But he's long forgotten everything but the name. Now he prays to little household gods and the gods of wind and sea to protect him and let him catch fish. These are the gods of the old earth religions. It's nothing unusual. Half the peasants of Francia have still got quite a bit of that still in them.

"As for the ritual with the knife, it's simple—he considers pain and sickness the work of a devilish worm inside his bones. And his cure is to place a knife on the sore place and say a charm to call out the little worm, 'From marrow to bone, from bone to flesh, from flesh to skin, and out of skin into this knife.' It's a common practice among the peasant folk both here and in our country. And it serves as their doctor as well as their priest."

But for Jacob's guests, the simple, changeless days by the empty beach turned into a month as Sebastian was racked with fever and so weak from loss of blood it was dangerous to put him back on a horse. He simply languished in the primitive straw pile that served as a bed and listened to the sea wind howling against the thin wattle and daub of the peasant's hut.

Heimdal spent much of his time sitting beside Sebastian's bed, bathing his forehead or making him drink as much as possible. Often his delusional patient would speak to him of imagined conversations on disconnected themes, most having to do with Adela and the boys or the king and his need to get back to him, or of Konrad. . . always of Konrad. "He kills everything I love, Heimdal! He killed my father, and now he wants to kill my boys next and. . . and Adela. He even wants to kill the king!" Sebastian lifted himself up with great effort and gripped Heimdal's hand. "We must stop him, Heimdal! He's the dark angel of death, don't you see? That's why I went to Denmark in the first place. We will never be safe until we kill him. We must kill him!"

***

For three days after they arrived at Jacob's hut, Sebastian tossed and turned, shivered with fever, and alternately sweated profusely. Finally, he regained a fitful consciousness, the dream still fresh in his mind. But it fell into pieces the moment he remembered that Konrad, the devil's

74

beast, was still alive while he had become an invalid who might never recover, never find the happiness he longed for with Adela, never again be the man he once was.

When he had recovered enough to think more clearly, he pondered the dream and its meaning over and over. There had been no little girl born to them, though they had often said to each other a girl child would complete their happiness together. It came to him eventually that the girl baby stood for what their separation had cost them. But Adela had not returned the ring he gave her as she did in the dream. This thought gave him some hope. He puzzled endlessly over the meaning of the pond and how it could have drawn away his pain and regret, but it remained a mystery. Alternating between pain and despair over his circumstances, he wished with all his heart that such a pond might exist somewhere and that someday he might find it.

***

Gradually, as Sebastian began to remain awake for a few hours of the day, Heimdal bade Bardulf and Drogo carry him on the makeshift stretcher to the beach if it was sunny and leave him to lie back in the warmth and light. Their patient had lost so much weight they were reluctant to resume the journey for fear his limbs would break.

The two peasants were instructed to keep watch over Sebastian. "Lookee there, Bardulf. There he comes again," Drogo said, pointing at old Jacob. "He spends all his days walkin' up and down in front of his hut, diggin' for shellfish and chasin' them little crabs. But look at what he does when he gets to where Lord Sebastian is; he won't come near him, he just wades way out into the water, singin' them weird chants of his and crossin' hisself like a monk. And then he shakes that old medicine bag he's got in his belt. And lookee there, ain't that a wonder? Lord Sebastian is smilin'!"

Gradually, slowly, Sebastian began to recover.

***

From the day they arrived at Jacob's hut on the beach, Liudolf began a daily regimen of patrolling. He rode out every morning, watching the trails to the east for Ivor's men and searching for anything, a town or village, a movement or activity in the neighborhood that might threaten them. He explored the coast systematically, looking for a means of sea transport by which they might get Sebastian back into Francia more easily and as soon as possible.

In the third week, he found what he was looking for, a small port in a tiny, obscure village, surrounded by salt marshes. The score or so of souls who eked out a living in that windswept place were Frisians and not particularly friendly toward their Danish overlords. One of them directed Liudolf to Hartvig, the village headman.

"Listen to me, fellow, my friends and I are in need of a ship. Do they ever put in here?"

"They do indeed, sir, as well as Danish boats that puts in here sometimes. They wants our fish and barley, and they pays a good price for such amber as we can find and sealskins, even soapstone. I have a good bit I'm holdin' onto now for the next ship."

"Excellent, my good Hartvig. You see this in my hand?" Liudolf held up a small silver coin, knowing that it was more than the poor man could earn in a year. "This is yours and more if you will send word to me when the next ship comes in and keep your mouth shut about it. Can you do that?"

Hartvig started back as if he had been struck in the head. "Of course, of course, sir. I can do this, for surely. And I am the best man here to help you. I say nothing to nobody. You can trust me, for surely. Never to fear, never to fear."

Liudolf stepped in close and grasped the man by the front of his cloak. "All right, you can tell the villagers I was just a lost traveler seeking to find his way home. But listen to me, if you want to get rich, you will do exactly as I tell you. If you betray me and tell one soul about what I have said to you, I will know it, and I will cut off your testicles and stuff them in your mouth. And then I will sit you down on a pointed stick and see how long it takes you to die. Do you understand me?"

The poor man bobbed up and down, trembling in assent, mumbling over and over, "Yes, Lord, yes, yes, yes, yes, I understand so good, so good!" They arranged to meet every third day by a spot on the river a league away from the village and any potential informers.

On Liudolf's third meeting with Hartvig, he learned that a boat had sailed into the port and was taking on cargo. "Go to the captain of the boat at once, get him alone, and offer him three of these four pieces of silver. Keep one for yourself, and there will be more later if all goes well. Tell the captain there is much more for him if he will delay his departure for two days until I can return. He will be transporting six men and six horses to a place in Frisia, which I will reveal to him when we come on board. Make sure you tell him we will make it well worth his while. Tell him he will profit far more for transporting us than for betraying us. And tell him there must be room for the horses. Do you understand?"

"Yes, yes, m'lord," the peasant affirmed eagerly. "I can do it. I will do it. You will not regret trusting me."

"Well, be sure that I can, man. Tell no one of this besides the captain. You and he must be absolutely silent. If something goes wrong when we come, you will be the first to die."

Liudolf's fears were put to rest when they arrived two days later with Sebastian trussed up again on the makeshift stretcher between the horses. Hartvig met them at the meeting place and took them straight to the boat. A show of silver was all the captain needed, and the boat pulled away from the port as soon as the horses were blindfolded and brought on board. They left Hartvig waving happily from the shore, with a hand in his pocket on more silver than he had ever seen in his life and a broad smile on his face.

The sea journey was brief and happily uneventful. Liudolf instructed the captain to sail west to the mouth of the Ems River and then south, down the river, as far as the boat would go. They would then be deep into friendly territory and safe from the Danes. Charlemagne was overlord of all Frisia.

The boat proved too big and unwieldy to go far up the Ems, a river full of sandbars and debris. But Archambald used his talents of persuasion and soon rented a small cart and driver to take them south along the Ems to the Rhine. There they embarked again on a barge pulled slowly up-current by horses.

As they set out on the big familiar river, Liudolf made the mistake of telling Sebastian of their plans. "Listen, Brother, this flatboat will take us all the way to Andernach, and you will soon see your beloved Adela. What do you think of that? And perhaps she might join us, and, if you're up to it, we could even continue all the way up the river to the king's court at Worms."

Sebastian, still plagued off and on by a persistent fever, reacted immediately, raising himself up in the makeshift bed. "No!" he shouted, flailing about violently. "No, I cannot see her. I will not! Don't you see? I have been beaten. He beat me. The beast is still alive. Don't you see? She is still his wife. Oh God, I failed. I cannot face her. I cannot face the king. I told him a lie. I am no paladin—far from it. I'm a disgrace. I won't go. I'd rather die," he moaned.

He became so agitated that he threatened to throw himself out of the boat. Heimdal stepped in calmly and took Sebastian's hand, whispering to him reassuringly, "It's all right, dear boy, I have a better plan. How would you like to go home? To Fernshanz, I mean, where you grew up and where you are still lord of the manor. You and I can hire a small boat at the mouth of the Lippe. The others can follow on the road with the horses. Wouldn't you like to see the old place again? It will be peaceful and beautiful as always, and you can rest easy there, lad. Won't that be fine?" Sebastian calmed down slowly and soon fell into a deep sleep.

Heimdal, however, had other plans which he shared with Liudolf but did not tell Sebastian. Before they parted on the Lippe, he instructed Bardulf and Drogo, "Go upriver to

Andernach, find Adela, and tell her Sebastian is hurt and sick and she must come at once to Fernshanz."

Chapter 7

Light and Shadows

Fernshanz, Winter 786

Adela was not long in coming. She bombarded poor Bardulf with pleas and threats until he told her what had happened in Denmark. Over and over, she blamed herself as she feverishly packed for the trip. It was exactly what she feared he would do. But she had hoped the king would keep him close. She had lived in fear since Sebastian's departure, and now she was racked with guilt. *If only I had waited,* she wailed to herself. If only she had given him time to understand how she felt. She had to go to him. He would die unless she flew to him at once. She had to let him know how much she loved him. If only she didn't feel that God wanted her too.

She assembled half a troop of her father's men, crossed the Rhine with men and horses on barges, and rode night and day through snow and wind to Fernshanz. As she feared, she found Sebastian sick and still delirious from the trip, running a high fever and coughing up a thick greenish fluid, his body alternating between chills and heavy sweating.

Consulting with Heimdal, hands trembling, Adela immediately began pouring fluids into Sebastian. "I'm here now, my love, it's Adela," she murmured. "I will take care of you now. I will love you and hold you. I will make you well again. You'll see." She never left his side the whole day, humming to him softly and bathing his forehead and chest whenever the fever shook him. In the evening, she slipped naked into his bed to keep him warm against the chills with her own body. Heimdal's herbs and her constant tenderness finally began to calm Sebastian so that he could rest and sleep more deeply. Adela was constantly with him until he began to recover, and then she only left him for an hour or two of sleep or exercise.

***

"Adela. Is it you?" Sebastian mumbled as he came out of his long sleep to see her bending over him, wiping his brow. She bent nearer and took his face between her hands, holding her breath. She could not stop her tears as she realized that the fever was gone. His mind was finally clear and his color better. She recognized at once the radiant smile she had known so well when there had been only love between them. She returned it with joy as she gathered him into her arms.

"It is, my treasure," she whispered. "And you are going to be well now. I'm here."

"Where are we?"

"We are in Fernshanz, my love—you're home. This is the place you love most. So now you're going to let Fernshanz, and me, make you well again."

"Have you come back to me? Will you stay?"

Adela hesitated. "I'm here now, my own heart, and I will be with you as long as you need me."

"I will always need you," he said. Her stomach lurched, and the tears continued to flow—with relief, with love, but also with a brooding sense of transience.

***

The process of Sebastian's healing took several months. They passed into deep winter, and still Adela stayed at his side. Sebastian could tell he was making daily progress with Adela's support, and by the Advent season he had begun to walk again, slowly and tentatively. He was happy. He smiled all the time now and greeted his comrades with joy and appreciation. Adela was a constant presence.

Adela sent for the boys, and they arrived in time for the celebration of Christmas, along with Father Pippen, who, as her chaplain, had moved with Adela from Fernshanz and now traveled with her wherever she went. Sebastian was overjoyed to see his sons and the diminutive priest. It was like the early golden days of their marriage when they had all lived together at Fernshanz.

Accompanied by an entourage of attendants and servants, the younger boys rolled in like a small avalanche and engulfed their father, who endured the pain of their exuberant embraces rather than forego the outburst of their love. Milo had to be brought from the king's palace at Aachen, where he had begun to study. Sebastian was fascinated by the growth of character and maturity he saw in his oldest son. At twelve years, Milo was decidedly different from the younger boys, far more restrained, quiet, reflective, but highly perceptive.

He embraced his father briefly but with some embarrassment, and Sebastian realized that the boy now considered himself almost a man. Later, however, when the two were alone, Sebastian was gratified to see that some of the affection Milo had always felt for him began to show through his newly acquired reserve.

"Sit, my good son, sit! It's so good to see you again. I can't believe you're so tall already. Why, that's even a bit of a mustache there, isn't it? And good Lord, how your voice is changing! You sound like a man—already!"

"Thank you, Father," Milo said quietly, dropping his eyes to the floor.

"Well, tell me, then. How is it there with that Englishman? Are you learning anything?"

"Of course, Father," Milo said, looking up enthusiastically. "Alcuin of York is the greatest scholar and theologian outside of Rome. The king himself considers him the most intelligent and perceptive man he has ever met. I heard him say so. They say King Karl practically kidnapped Alcuin and spirited him away to Aachen. Even I can tell he is the wisest of all the wise men the king has been bringing into his court. It's wonderful to be in such a school, Father. I'm very grateful you have let me study there."

"Thank the king, son. It was he who recognized your potential. He did the same thing for me when I first came to his court. He has a knack for recognizing talent in men. It's one of the things that makes him great. And thank your mother, too. It was she who used all her wiles to persuade the king to get you into Alcuin's school, young as you are.

"Alcuin has vision and ideas. That's what the king likes," Sebastian continued. "I like his ideas too; they're similar to mine in many ways."

"What ideas, Father? What is it you both want?"

"Well, for one thing, I think we both would like to convince the king that his rule and his people could be so much better off if only he would see things in a broader way and not try to hammer everyone into submission if they don't agree with him. Haven't you realized we go to war almost every single year?"

"Yes, and I'm exceedingly sorry for that. Because you, Father, are one of his hammers, are you not? And look what it has done to you."

"I'm sworn to the king, Milo. And I believe in him. He is a truly great man. He and Alcuin are changing the face of Francia, and they're doing it through law and learning. There's a school attached to every cathedral in the land now, and they are meant eventually to educate laymen, not just churchmen. Alcuin is making that happen on the king's orders.

"More than that, to the king's credit, he's changing the harsh laws he wrote to control the Saxons and other conquered tribes, and he's finally trying to find a way to have peace through negotiation and alliances. You know of Widukind, don't you? He was the fiercest of the Saxon chieftains, and he warred against us for more than twenty years. The king offered him better land, inside of Francia, for his Westphalians and places for his men in our own army. And it worked—for a while. Those that remained in Saxony still rise up now and then. It's in their blood, God help them. But at least Widukind never fought again."

They continued to talk by the fireside late into that night and on many nights after that. Sebastian encouraged Milo to tell him everything, and the boy poured out his enthusiasm to Sebastian in those long late night sessions. Sebastian was relieved to learn that Milo considered his father p>2</p>

different from the swaggering warriors he saw at Charlemagne's court.

Adela noticed the change in Milo's reserved demeanor at once and enthusiastically expressed her pleasure and pride. "My love, what have you been doing with our boy staying up so late by the fire?" she demanded. "Have you fed him some marvelous elixir? He seems so animated and glad to be here. It's not typical. He's usually so contemplative and sober-sided."

"Yes, he's changing. I see it, too. He's finding out who I am, and he's not too unhappy with it, thank God. He's also finding out who he is and what he wants out of life. It's splendid to watch. We have many similar values, I'm happy to say. I feel certain now he's going to flourish at the court. Almost every man he meets there is lettered, articulate, and marvelously free of the fetters of custom. It suits him perfectly—and me."

***

Winter turned into an early spring. As the spring waxed, so did Sebastian. Every day he gained more strength. He began to hope that things might once again return to the way they were. The joy of having his family around him and watching his sons grow and flourish paled in comparison, however, to Sebastian's pleasure at having Adela return to him fully and intimately. She was always with him, and her presence alone was more healing than any herbs, ointments, or potions. Whenever she left him for exercise or fresh air, he waited anxiously for her return. When she re-entered the room, it seemed to blaze with new light, and the air was charged with the genuineness of her smile, her graceful movements, and the smell of her, which was often like the forest she rode in every morning—fresh, pungent, and sweet.

As he recovered his strength, they drew physically closer. She touched him often and kissed his eyes and forehead. Once in a while, she would bend and kiss him on the lips, briefly, almost as if by accident, moving away quickly and almost shyly. When she did this, Sebastian felt the same thrill he had known when he had first kissed her on the hill above the Rhine at Andernach. He reached out to her as well, tracing the curve of her neck as she bent to him, the arch of her back, and the fullness of her hips and thighs. She never resisted or drew back.

With time on his hands, Sebastian studied his beloved as never before. Childbirth had made her softer, though she still held her back so straight and firm that her breasts retained their youthful thrust and her figure its elegant shape. She was, for him, the summary of a woman, beautiful in body and spirit, compassionate, tender, challenging, alluring, and endlessly interesting.

They spent many hours with the boys, as they used to do, embarking when the weather turned warmer on limited local expeditions and small adventures and enjoying dinners that were like parties, with all their favorite food and much laughter.

He particularly loved the evenings after the boys were asleep and the servants dismissed. After his talks with Milo, they sat long hours into the night before the fireplace, talking of this and that but often falling into a comfortable silence in which they remained totally present to one another. In those quiet moments, they knew each other as never before and arrived at a magical place of mutual understanding. Adela was the fountainhead and purpose of Sebastian's life, and he was explosively and achingly happy.

Every day, as he grew stronger, they became increasingly intimate, touching and kissing each other at every appropriate moment. Finally, on one late evening in early spring, they lay together by the hearth. Sebastian thought Adela had never been more beautiful, her auburn hair glowing copper, red, and gold in the firelight. Together, they remembered their old way of making love, their eyes never leaving the other's face. Finally, inevitably, having waited so long, they poured their love into each other urgently and completely. Sebastian felt he had been lifted out of the human world and into Elysium.

In the morning, Adela was gone.

***

"No!" Sebastian cried out, shouting into the courtyard, "Liudolf, Archambald! Get the horses!"

Adela had left in the dark at a very early hour of the morning. She had taken her bags on a packhorse, and the men from her Andernach household had ridden away with her. Sebastian was beside himself with fury and fear.

As he pulled on his chainmail, Father Pippin knocked and waited, stepping back in alarm as Sebastian flung open the door to his quarters.

"What!" Sebastian shouted in the poor priest's face. "You didn't go with her, you traitor? I'll wager you were the one who told her it would be all right to leave me for the convent. That's where she's headed, isn't it? False priest!"

"Sebastian, my friend," Pippin began in a conciliatory tone, full of sympathy, "I have been greatly privileged to share in your happiness for the last few years. It has been perhaps the best time in my life to be part of this wonderful family and to share your joy and success."

"Bah!" Sebastian grumbled.

Father Pippen reached out both hands as if to hold back the tide of Sebastian's anger. "Your life has already been so exemplary and of such great value to your wife and children, to the king, and, indeed, to the Frankish people. And I've been most gratified to witness the love between you and Adela and the sacrifices you have had to make in order for that love to flourish as it has. I've never seen two people more bound to one another by love. It's been wonderful to see."

"What are you playing at, Father?" Sebastian scoffed. "Where's Adela? Tell me where's she's gone, what road she took."

The diminutive priest kept trying courageously to reason with Sebastian. "Adela has been a great light for you. She has helped you become the great man God has meant you to be. You have been deeply blessed to have her—and she you."

"Has been, have been? What are you babbling about, Father Pippin? Are you saying Adela is leaving me for good? Out with it! Is that it? Stop mucking about. Tell me plainly."

"Count Sebastian, please," the priest said, hurrying his speech as if to hold back the torrent of emotion he knew would come. "Try to understand what I must tell you. Very early this morning, when Adela went away, she came to me and told me to beg you to understand and let her go. She said she loves you more than life itself, more than anything at all—except God." He paused as a look of fear and horror flooded Sebastian's face. "But it is God who calls her now—away from you."

Normally a shy and timid man, Father Pippin suddenly launched himself at Sebastian, grasping his face between his hands in order to look into his panicked eyes. "You must listen, Sebastian. She has promised herself to God. She feels she has been called and that she owes God her life. She thinks that Konrad's coming back from the dead is God's way of telling her she must give you up and return to the convent."

He continued rapidly as Sebastian jammed his feet into his boots and buckled on his sword belt. "Please believe me. I tried to reason with her that God is just as much here with you and the boys as he is in the convent. But she has always harbored a doubt, a fear that she is somehow stealing happiness when God wishes her to devote her life to his service. The news about Konrad made up her mind. Only your illness held her back. Now she feels she must go."

"I will get her back," Sebastian erupted, wrenching himself away from the priest. He felt fear, then confusion, then rising anger when he thought of her deception over the past months. How could she have let him think that she had returned to him wholeheartedly and for good? "Liudolf!" he shouted, grabbing for his helmet.

"Please, Sebastian. She will not come back, even if you find her. Listen, she told me to say to you that out of the darkness will come an even greater light for you. It did for her, and now it will for you."

"Bloody rubbish! Get out of my way, priest." Sebastian stormed out of the room.

***

Adela knew Sebastian would try to stop her and bring her back, so she had planned her escape well in advance. Instead of taking the main road back to the Rhine, she and her Andernach cohort took less traveled trails to the south, boarded a waiting barge at the Rhine near Cologne, then traveled overland again to Bischoffsheim. Sebastian followed, riding furiously with Liudolf and Archambald. But he guessed wrongly that Adela would go first to her old home at Andernach and so remained always a step behind her.

When they finally did catch up with her, Adela was already ensconced in her convent and had gone into retreat. Mother Herlindis responded to Sebastian's pounding on the convent gate.

"She won't see you, Count Sebastian. When she got here, she put on her convent habit and retired to a retreat cell. She is on bread and water and has requested that her silence not be interrupted for two weeks."

"I will wait, by the rood. I will not go home until I see her. This is insane. I know she loves me. I can make her see reason. She will reconsider this foolishness. I know it!"

"I'm afraid she will not, my lord—at least not at this time. She said you would react this way, and she told me to tell you that if you persisted, she would shave her hair, strip herself, and ride naked down the streets of the nearest town. And she warned that if you succeeded in dragging her back with you to Fernshanz, you would have to make her a prisoner, for she would not stay."

Sebastian shook his head, desperately trying to think of some way he could reach Adela and convince her not to abandon him, not to give up the good life together they had finally gained after so many sacrifices.

"What can I do, Mother? You know her. You know how much she loves me. She has told you everything. I can't believe she's making such a cruel choice."

"I do know, Sebastian. My heart cries out for you—and for her, because this will be no easy road for her either. She will miss you terribly and mourn for you every day. But you must understand—the only answer is that she has come to feel that God has called her, and as painful as it is, it is the higher calling."

Sebastian groaned. "Can't you do anything?"

Mother Herlindis hesitated and then said quietly, "If it's any comfort, Sebastian, I think she has made a mistake. But I can no more go against the Church than she. I will say only this—go home, go and do your duty to the king. One day I believe your fortune will change. And because I believe that, I will advise Adela to postpone taking her final vows indefinitely. She can serve God just as well without them until we know for certain. Meanwhile, go and serve your king. Lose yourself in whatever he gives you to do. You will be doing good work, and perhaps it will give you peace."

Sebastian stood in the rain in front of the convent for two more days until Archambald and Liudolf came and wrapped his shivering body in a blanket and coaxed him back to the inn. The next day, they got him on the back of his beloved horse, Joyeuse, for the wretched trip home.

Chapter 8

The King's Will

Sebastian was drunk when Simon arrived with word from the king's messenger. He had been in such condition for three days and lay stinking and puking in a back room of the inn where Simon preferred to stay when in the town of Worms. He could see through bloodshot eyes that his friend was profoundly shocked, and he held up one hand to try and ward off the scolding he knew he was about to receive.

But it was to no avail; Simon lit into him. "*Feh! Du Klots! Du smutziges Schwein!* What on earth have you been doing? *Ach, du lieber*! How you stink!" Simon flung the fetid blankets off the bed and onto the floor and dragged Sebastian to an open window. Propping him up in the window, Simon emptied an entire wooden bucket of cold water over his head. "Don't blame me, Sebastian. I've got orders from the king himself. And if you don't bring yourself right, and quickly, my son, you might lose your head. The king's man said *sofort*, and in case you've forgotten your High German, that means *right now*. Here, drink this." He forced Sebastian's mouth open and poured in a ghastly green concoction that almost immediately made him lunge for the window and retch convulsively.

Sebastian dreaded the meeting with the king. It had been several months since Adela had left him, and he finally had to admit that this time she was probably gone for good. Ever since, he had been on a ruinous tear, drinking and carousing until he lost consciousness. It had only made things worse. Now he must see the king and give an accounting.

He dressed glumly and painfully, remembering for the thousandth time that wretched scene on the morning when she had left and the whole disaster in Denmark that had led to the miserable state he was in now.

***

Two hours later a wilted, morose, and totally dispirited Sebastian appeared in the doorway of the royal quarters. "Strewth!" the king breathed, looking the bedraggled young count up and down. "I've never seen you like this. You look like you've been mangled by a pack of wolves. What do you mean coming into my presence smelling like that? *Ach*, you're disgusting, Sebastian. Stand over there by the window."

After several uncomfortable moments of silence, during which the king stroked his long mustaches and observed the sad mess that Sebastian had become, Charlemagne spoke. This time there was no lighthearted teasing. "Look here at me, Sebastian. And stand up straight, damn you. You're one of my war captains. I can't have you falling apart on me like this. I need you. We have much to do. And you swore an oath to me. Remember?"

"Yes, my lord king," was his miserable reply.

"Well, then, it's high time you did me some service, by thunder. You've been away from court too long. I could have used you in Italy."

"I'm sorry, my lord king," Sebastian mumbled, feeling like a man with his head on the block waiting for the axe to fall.

"Good lord, is that all you can manage to say? What's happened to you?"

"I've been ill, my liege."

"Nonsense! Don't you try to muck about with me. I know what you've been up to. Everyone knows it. You bloody well went up to Denmark to deal with that scoundrel Konrad and failed, didn't you? For God's sake, Sebastian, what were you thinking? It would take an army to dig Konrad out of those stinking Danish bogs. And then I'd have to fight their king as well. I bloody well won't do it, not even for you, as much as we both hate that bastard. Leave him be. He'll have his soon enough, fool that he is."

For another moment, the king observed his crestfallen favorite, swaying unsteadily by the window, and softened a bit. "Why did you feel you had to go up there anyway, now of all times?"

"Sire, my wife has left me. Adela is gone."

"But why? You two were completely mad for one another."

"When she learned Konrad was still alive, she couldn't escape the conviction that she must still be married to him, at least in the eyes of the Church. She felt it was a sign from God that she must return to the convent and devote the rest of her life to God's service."

"Jesus, Mary, and Joseph! That bloody rogue!" The king smashed one hand into the other. "He's supposed to be dead. Why was I not told about this? If he's alive, whose blasted head did they send me? Christ and all the saints, why am I the last to know such things? And what in heaven's name is that wife of yours thinking? She needn't have left you, Sebastian. Konrad no longer matters here. He might as well be dead."

"Sire, she left in the middle of the night. I had no chance to reason with her. I even chased after her, all the way to the convent in Bischoffsheim, but she wouldn't even see me."

"Damn it, Sebastian, what a mess," commiserated the king. "Sit, man, before you fall." Charlemagne also sat silently for a long, pregnant time, twirling his mustaches and watching Sebastian's downcast face, weighing what he should do with the stricken young man.

Sebastian glanced out of the side of his eye at the gloomy face of the king. He's going to write me off, he thought.

Finally, the king broke the long silence. "Listen, old boy, I believe in you in spite of all that's happened. I'm giving you another chance, do you hear?"

Sebastian began to breathe again. He looked up hopefully into the king's face.

"I may regret it if you can't pull yourself out of this bloody funk you're in, but you've given me some excellent service in the past, far beyond the conventional, and you think more uniquely than any of my other warriors.

"My God, we've had such differences in the past, but you've been right most of the time. In fact, I hardly know how to keep you reined in; you tend to *cause* real change rather than react to it wherever you go. That's good. It's what I'm looking for, in spite of myself. Men who tell me 'yes' without question and will do anything I ask are valuable to me, but one who will stand up to me when he believes he's right is invaluable, even if I have to knock him down occasionally—which I will do if you don't put yourself back together, you hear me?"

"Thank you, my lord king. You're too kind."

"Rubbish. I just see clearly is all. Now there's something I want to propose to you. I have a special corps of men—just a few, only eleven of them right now. They serve me exclusively. Roland was one of them—the paladins. I've talked to you about them before, haven't I?"

"You've spoken of them many times, my king."

"They are the finest men I've got—absolutely fearless. Totally trustworthy. And not afraid to die. They'll do anything I ask of them. I want you to agree to become one of them. You'd be the twelfth man. Like the rest of them, you'd take on the role of being my eyes and ears throughout the kingdom and abroad, wherever my interests and the welfare of the Franks are at risk."

Sebastian drew in his breath and said in a barely audible voice, "I cannot, my lord king; I don't feel I'm able—not worthy to be mentioned in the same group as Roland and the others. I couldn't do it, sire."

"Of course you're able. I wouldn't ask you if I didn't think so," the king said huffily. "Don't try my patience, Sebastian. I shall be the judge of that, not you."

"But, sire, that's not all. I have. . . there are some troubles. . . problems at home. . ."

"Listen, Sebastian, I know you've suffered a terrible loss. And I bleed for you, believe me. If I could make it right, I would. There's very little that I wouldn't do for you. But what's happened to you with Adela is beyond even my power. I cannot order her to come out of the convent and be your wife again. And even if I could, the Church would not support me. Devil take it, Sebastian, you must give her up."

Sebastian dropped his head farther toward the floor, and the king reached out to grasp his shoulder. "I felt the same way when Hildegard died. Lord, she was lovely. And she bore me so many superb sons and beautiful daughters. But she died. And there was nothing I could do about it.

"It will be all right, my good old fellow. In fact, you're doing exactly what I did when Hildegard died. I moped about for a month or two—thought I would die without her. But finally I came out of it and decided life is too short, and it's a grand sight better when there's a woman in it.

"You've still got your whole life ahead of you. And the world is full of women. You could have almost anyone you wanted. I fixed my own grief by marrying Fastrada. I say, Sebastian, find a luscious lady like that, and she will raise your passions, for certain. You'll soon have no time to think of another."

"I don't want another, my king."

"Be that as it may, you're still a young man, more or less. You can't go long without a woman. But whether you have one or not is not important. What you need now is something serious and important to do—something that will take up all your time and effort and get your mind off those other problems. From now on, I want you to be totally committed to me, and I have some very hard work that needs doing. Will you do it?"

Sebastian closed his eyes, took a deep breath, and then, like a man stepping off a precipice, unable to see below, he looked into the king's eyes. "I will, sire," he said firmly, straightening his shoulders, "if you wish it."

"Good! That's that, then. But are you fit? Will you be able to fight again as you did before? Does everything still work?"

"I believe so, my lord, for the most part."

"By all the saints, you don't look it. Blast! It's a bad time for you to be in this condition. I've decided to march an army down to Bavaria and take control of the whole mess down there. I've got to do something about that bastard Duke Tassilo!

"And the pope told me Tassilo thinks he owes me no allegiance. It's time he's learnt a lesson. By God, I won't have him whining about Bavarian autonomy and then cozying up to the Avars behind my back. I'd wager it's him who's been goading that bunch of Asian jackals to raid into my territory in northern Italy. My father and grandfather wouldn't put up with Bavarian nonsense, and neither will I. They need to know, and no mistake, who is overlord of the Bavarians. I'm afraid we'll have to bloody that fool's nose this time.

"I was going to send you down there to ferret out what we're up against before I bring the army. Well, there's nothing for it. You're in no state to go. For now, I want you to do nothing but stay in the palace here and sort yourself out, do you hear? Eat. Ride. Swim. Get to the exercise yard and hone your skills again."

"Yes, my liege."

"See my constable and enlist him to help you get stronger. I want you fit at least by the end of this year, do you understand?"

"Yes, my king."

"Right, then. And remember, Sebastian, you swore an oath to me. Your highest allegiance, your single most important duty is to your king. Are you ready to serve me without reservation—in whatever I need and as long as I shall need you?"

"I am, my lord king."

"Embrace me, then, lad. It gives me joy to have you at my side again. We shall do great things together, you and I, and all will be well."

95

Book II Sebastian's Way

Chapter 9

A Paladin, Well and True

Worms, Winter 787

The King's Court at Ingelheim, Spring 788

Midwinter snow lined the practice yard at the king's palace at Worms, and Sebastian stood in the middle of it, sweating like a horse after a long gallop. Warner, the king's constable and horse master, had just put him through yet another grueling session with the heavy wooden practice swords, pitting one young warrior after another against Sebastian, each of them hoping to best one of the king's finest swordsmen. Sebastian had stood his ground, patiently studying each challenger's style and approach to the match and then finessing each one until a blow or counterblow clearly represented his defeat.

Sebastian drove himself each day until he was exhausted. Ever since the king left for Bavaria, he had faced three sessions a day under Warner's relentless regimen, and he was sick to death of the endless routine of violence. He stood head down and eyes closed in the empty courtyard, leaning heavily on the clumsy practice sword.

"Well, you are stronger, are you not?" announced a deep voice out of the gathering gloom of the early evening. "Everyone says so. They say there's no one around who can beat you."

"Hullo, Heimdal," he replied wearily.

"What's this? Do I detect some resentment from the king's champion? I would have thought you could not get enough of this rough play. Can it be you've finally tired of playing at war?"

"Get away, old man. I'm not in the mood for your philosophies."

"Oh, come along, my fine lad. It's been a while since we've had a good chat, and it seems you could use one now. Come, wash up a bit, and let's retire to the tavern down the road. I hear they have some very good late wine, a bit sweet, but delicious nonetheless."

Sebastian did not often step outside the grounds of the king's palace. He had not even had a cup of ale since the king departed for Italy. But in the mind-numbing sameness of rebuilding his strength and skills each day, and in the absence of most of his friends, his spirits had fallen to a new low. So in spite of his surly response to Heimdal, he jumped at the chance for a little conversation with the old sage.

The tavern was stuffy and filled with the smell of stale bread and burnt fish, but it was warm and mercifully empty of other guests. They settled at a low table by the fire and were served a thick porridge of oats and vegetables with a few chunks of tough goat meat and a cup of sweet white wine.

"Well, out with it, Sebastian. You sound worse than before. I thought you were on the road to recovery."

"Where is this God we're supposed to believe in, Heimdal?" Sebastian began, all at once pouring out his discontent. "Why is my life so difficult and full of such strife and loss? Surely, I've paid my debts enough to deserve a little happiness and peace."

"No one guarantees you a life of happiness, Sebastian. The best thing you can do is find a way to conduct your life so that you find tranquility and a sense of moral worth."

"How in blazes does one find that, Heimdal?"

"You know from your experience, my friend, that human conditions do not naturally reflect order and calm. And without order, there can be no peace, no calm, no sense of virtue in the world. It becomes a place of animals, where 'eat or be eaten' is the only rule. I believe that reason alone offers some kind of order and value in life. It is what one must pursue above all else."

"Not God, Heimdal? What of our Christian beliefs?"

"I do believe there is some kind of God, Sebastian. Reason tells me there must be something or someone who began everything. But the concepts of divinity and creation are so far above our puny minds that we cannot possibly know them. How can we know the mind of God, let alone what or who that God really is?

"Therefore, we must cling to reason—because we can at least understand *it*, and we know that only reason can provide some kind of order in this chaotic world in which we live. If we follow reason, we will see that justice and duty are the loftiest virtues—because they will lead to order. And if we pursue these virtues, we can at least have peace of mind."

"But what of those Christian virtues we are taught? What of mercy, forgiveness, faith, and love?"

"We cannot know, my boy, but personally I tend to believe that such virtues can lead one away from reason. Is it reasonable, for example, to forgive an implacable enemy? Should one have mercy on the Saxons after they have betrayed our trust so many times? And, my good man, I hesitate to say it since you have obviously encountered love in all its intensity, but I have found, over my long lifetime, that love is fickle. It does not last, sometimes not even for very long, certainly not for a whole lifetime. Reason, on the other hand, tells us to raise duty above love, for duty creates necessary order while love distracts, confuses, and disappoints—and often creates absolute chaos, not order. Look at your own great love for Adela. Has it created order---or chaos?"

"Never mind that, Heimdal, damn you. Talk of something else."

This was not the first of such conversations with Heimdal, but in his present disillusioned state, this one stuck profoundly in Sebastian's brain. He could see how love had been the cause of his great joy and how much the loss of it had made him bitter and his life empty and meaningless. He knew too well the chaos of the world, and eventually he resolved that, henceforth, if he were to feel any worth at all, he must concentrate on duty alone. He would become the king's paladin, well and truly.

***

While Sebastian was recovering, the king, never one to rest when there was unfinished business, was in Bavaria disciplining the unfortunate Count Tassilo to the point of actually annexing Bavaria to the Frankish crown.

His successes there put him in almost giddy spirits upon his return to Francia. He spent the winter in Ingelheim, near Mayence, calling a general assembly there in the spring to put Duke Tassilo on trial and discuss the acquisition of Bavaria with his magnates. He sent for Sebastian almost as soon as he returned.

"Come in, Sebastian. Good man!" the king exuded, hurriedly dressing himself for a ride. "Sit while I ready myself. I've a new stallion, and I want to have a go at him before supper. Well, I do say," he said, looking Sebastian over with interest, "it's true what they told me; you're in fine fettle—and more than that, you look a proper pushing lad once again. I can see why Arno told me you can't be beaten in the practice yard lately. Good show!"

"Thank you, my lord king," Sebastian responded indifferently to the mayor of the palace's praise.

"Tonight I'm celebrating! Not only did we have a rattling good campaign in Bavaria—couldn't have gone off better—but Fastrada has given me another child, a girl. I'm delighted with her—with both of them. We're having a banquet, and I want you there."

"If you wish it, my liege."

"I do indeed. The only thing better would be if you had been along in Bavaria to share our good fortune. But let me tell you quickly what's next for you—there won't be time tonight. I want you to go back up north—not to Denmark, mind! You're to stay completely away from that bloody Konrad. You understand?"

"Yes, my lord king."

"I want you to go to Frisia. I've been getting more unsettling reports about those bloody Vikings again. They're not just a nuisance now, they're beginning to be a real thorn in my side. They've been raiding all over Frisia, right up into the towns. We've got to stop 'em. You once told me the best way to do it would be to build our own boats so we could find them quicker and fight them on their own level. Well, I want you to go up there and find a way to build me some ships such as the Vikings have. We could never catch them in the old buckets we've been using for trade.

"You're one of my paladins now, you know. You're supposed to be capable of anything," he added almost offhandedly. "Do you think you could do that?"

"I do, my king," Sebastian replied, feeling a spark of enthusiasm for the first time. "I know something about that region. Attalus and I were often in those ports when the Saxons were trying to stir up the Frisians against us. I might be able to find someone there who knows the secrets of the Viking boats."

"Good on you, then. That's what you'll do. Unfortunately, I must go back down to Bavaria with another army in a few weeks. That villain Tassilo has gone back on his word already and refuses to be my vassal. He's acting a proper fool. I'm afraid I shall have to remove him from the duchy completely and put him in a monastery. I should have his bloody head lopped off, but he's my cousin. Wouldn't do."

As Sebastian and the king were leaving, Charlemagne saw Fastrada in the garden and pushed Sebastian toward her. "Go pay your respects to my lady queen. She's been asking about you. And she'll need a young and handsome lad like you to talk to tonight. She won't say a word to most of my 'old boy' retinue here." With that, he bounded away toward the stables, leaving Sebastian with a disconcerting prospect.

He paused to put himself on guard as he approached the queen. He already knew how bold and unpredictable she was. Their last meeting, just before the king sent him to Brittany, had almost shocked him senseless. He could still feel her fingers tracing the muscles of his arms and back, her dark eyes probing into his brain. He had felt virtually seduced.

For a minute or so, he watched her from a distance out of the corner of his eye, taking in her luxurious dress—purple silk, clinging to her body like a glove, definitely not a conventional choice for morning. With purple and silver ribbons in her hair, a riot of silver jewelry, and a boldly open bodice, she looked as if she were going to a celebratory festival instead of a morning stroll. She's fancy, no mistake, he thought. Too rich for my blood. But the king was over the moon about her. He vowed to pay no mind to the allure and just keep his distance. But he kept on walking toward her.

She was talking animatedly to two obviously captivated young warriors. They bowed and moved off quickly when they saw Sebastian approaching. Fastrada turned in surprise. "Ah, Lord Sebastian," she cooed softly, embracing him briefly but very warmly. "I am so happy to have found you at last."

Sebastian was rapidly routed from his resolve by this unexpected display of familiarity. Most Frankish women would never do such a thing, especially with a man they hardly knew. But Fastrada was decidedly an exception. She was the queen, and she exulted in her beauty and the feel of her power. Sebastian felt all that in her ardent, magnetic embrace. He could not help but be more than a little stirred by it.

At this point in their marriage, Charlemagne was besotted with Fastrada, with her elegant beauty, exceptional intelligence, and palpable carnality. It occurred to Sebastian that she was like original sin, impossible to ignore or avoid. The queen did as she pleased, more or less. And it took Sebastian only a few moments to see she was not content just to be Charlemagne's queen, his woman of the moment. She wanted much more. She didn't want to replace the king, she just wanted to control him and anyone else who had power and influence.

"Congratulations, my queen," Sebastian began, bowing low before Fastrada. "The king told me of your new child. He's very pleased."

"Ah," she murmured, reaching across to take his hand in hers. "Is that all you can say? The baby is old news. I had her months ago. The king is just now getting around to celebrating her birth. I would have thought you might say you were glad to see *me*."

"Of course I am, Your Grace." He cleared his throat and ventured lamely, "You are looking very well and healthy."

"Heavens! You certainly know how to charm a lady. Never mind. Take my arm. Let us get to know one another better." She walked him into the part of the garden where there were thicker shrubs. "You seem to be avoiding me, my handsome hero," she said, holding his arm tightly up against her bosom. "Why is that? I so want to be your friend."

"What?" Sebastian croaked, stunned at her familiarity. "Your friend, Your Grace? That is impossible; you are the queen. It would not be seemly."

Fastrada laughed derisively. "My good Lord Sebastian! Seemly? What kind of word is that? Don't be so stuffy and formal. Do you not think that queens are like all other women? They have feelings and emotions—needs, just like men or any other woman."

Despite his smug confidence that he was aware of Fastrada's game, Sebastian flushed red with embarrassment. The queen was speaking to him with highly inappropriate familiarity and holding him far too closely to her side as she led him rapidly into a nest of high flowering bushes, her hip firmly thrust against his own. Whenever she spoke, she leaned into him, pressing her bosom into his arm. "Look here, Sebastian," she insisted, stopping and fixing him with the unwavering eyes of a cat on the hunt. "I want you to be my good friend. I admire you ever so much, and I always listen eagerly for news of you. You are the most interesting man in my husband's court. I follow your doings everywhere. I even know some of your secrets." She paused a moment to let this pregnant phrase sink in.

"I know, for example, that you are a man of great passion and determination, that you love unreservedly and you would do anything for the one you love, even to the point of heedlessly intruding into the den of a notorious bandit to fight him in the midst of his bloodthirsty friends. What passion! What consuming desire drove you to do such a reckless thing?

They almost killed you. And yet you live. Perhaps it's true what the people say about you—that you cannot be killed. And you appear now even stronger, more vital than before. I marvel at you, my intrepid Achilles! Can you blame anyone for wanting to be closer to you?"

"You do me far too much honor, Your Grace, and I am truly sorry you know about that unfortunate business in Denmark. I was a fool, not a hero there."

"Of course you weren't a fool—only passionate and dogged in your devotion. Would that the king would love *me* with such ardor."

"He does, I assure you, Your Grace. He dotes upon you."

"Yes, at the present moment he does. But would he go to such extremes as you have done for love of me?" She let the question hang in the air as Sebastian struggled in stunned confusion.

Finally, she continued, "My dear Sebastian, I want you to be my confidant. I want you to be close to me—very close. Did you know that it was I who recommended to the king that he choose you to be his paladin? Yes, it's true. I told him he could find no greater devotion or loyalty in a man and that he could have no greater champion." She drew in a breath, pulling him closer. "So you see, you are *my* paladin as well as the king's. You will be the new Roland, and I will be the muse for all your future adventures."

By this time, Sebastian's head was pounding, and he looked desperately around for a way out of the sensuous bonds Fastrada was coiling around him. He had never met such a seductively attractive woman, one who wielded her charms with such terrifying confidence, as if she wanted to devour him in order to own him. He was at once horrified and charmed, like a rabbit before a snake, and he could think of nothing to say.

She continued, snuggling boldly up to his chest. "I have dreamed of you, my paladin. I see you one day as a great general, a leader of all King's Karl's armies, and myself as the source of your power and the inspiration for your deeds." She tugged him off the path and behind a spreading bush. "Here, kiss me, my champion, and seal the pact between us."

"No!" Sebastian blurted, tripping and almost falling over his own feet in his haste to escape Fastrada's grasp. He retreated two more steps, took a deep breath, and bowed low. Recovering some control over his emotions, he said evenly, not daring to meet her eyes, "My dear lady queen, you think far too much of me, but you are mistaken. I am nothing like what you assume. I am in many ways the least of the servants of the king, your husband. But one thing you said about me is true: I am perhaps his most loyal subject, and I cannot imagine remaining so and assuming at the same time the intimacy which you offer. I revere you as the king's wife and his most beautiful queen. And I will serve you as I serve him—if it be his will. Please forgive me if I disappoint you. But I seek no fame, no special place among the Frankish host. I only live to serve the king, and that is enough for me."

With that, he bowed low one more time, turned, and hurried from the garden. Later that afternoon, he sent a message to the court excusing himself from the banquet that evening due to 'pressing family concerns.'

Chapter 10

The Shell Begins to Harden

Frisia, Autumn788

The King's Villa at Aachen, Winter 789

"There he is! See him? Ye can't miss that skull head of his and them black markin's on his ugly face."

It was unmistakably Ivor the Bold, walking down the one long road of the Frisian town of Dorestad with a half dozen of his roughneck thugs. They came up from the harbor in the lower town, strolling in the middle of the road as if they owned it, calling out insults to anyone passing by and laughing uproariously at the frightened reactions of the townsfolk, who gave them a wide berth and hastily disappeared indoors.

Bardulf, keeping watch outside a small dockyard, had seen their ship row into the harbor while Sebastian was working with a local shipbuilder. He ran immediately to bring the news as soon as Ivor and the small crew set off into the town.

"It's him, ain't it, Lord Sebastian? And some of the same scurvy lot of cutthroats he had in Hedeby."

"It is, Bardulf. It's Ivor. Go and tell the others. I'm going to see where he goes."

"No, sir, I won't. Ye'll be seen, and they'll know ye. Let me follow. I'll find out where they goes and come back to the house and tell ye."

"You're right. He mustn't know I'm here. Stay with him. I'll send Drogo to find you, and you can come back to the house and tell me what you've seen. Leave Drogo to keep watch. I'll wait with Liudolf and Archambald until you come."

Sebastian was nearing the end of negotiations with Askold, a Danish shipwright who had come to Dorestad to build a boat for a Frisian wine merchant. They had noticed it in the harbor area and straightaway recognized the Viking design. They bought the wine merchant off with Frankish silver, and now Askold worked for the realm.

Returning to the dockyard, Sebastian retrieved Askold from the building site and walked with him toward the newly arrived Danish boat. "Listen, my friend, when we first met did you not tell me that you left Denmark because of Ivor the Bold?"

"I did, yer honor. He was like to kill me if I'd stayed. He found out I'd been sleeping with a woman he fancied, and it made him murderous mad. He grabbed a knife and came looking for me. I just barely managed to slip over the walls and get away through the woods. I can't tell ye what hardship I had to endure to get here to Frisia. I didn't have no money or anything. It's only my shipbuilding skills what saved me."

"Well, look at that boat right there. What do you make of it?"

"Why, it's one of ours. I mean, it's a Danish boat—not a war boat, but a cargo one. We used 'em to transfer the takings we got on raids with the longboats. Hold on! I've seen that one before. Cor! I believe I might've helped build it!

"See!" he went on excitedly. "It's longer and wider and deeper than a warship. It's for carrying cargo, and it'll have a smaller crew than a war boat. It's a thorough Danish job, though, don't ye know.

"I hate to tell you this, Askold, but your old friend Ivor the Bold just stepped off that boat. He's in the upper town right now with a bunch of his bully boys."

The little man started and looked around himself in panic. "Oh God! I must get out of here. If he sees me, he'll kill me. I know it. He might even be looking for me. I must go now! I must get my tools." The little man set off at a run toward his workplace. Sebastian caught him and slowed him to a walk.

"Calm down, Askold. If you start running out of town right now, someone will see you, and Ivor might find out. We will keep out of sight until nightfall. But listen to me. You know that I am King Karl's agent. The king wants a warship, several warships, and he is not a man to disappoint, you understand? He is not intimidated by a two-penny pirate. Neither am I. I have issues of my own with Ivor the Bold, and I can find a way to remove him as a problem for you. I will do whatever I must to make that happen. We need you for the king's business."

"Begging yer pardon, yer honor, but the king ain't here, and Ivor is! You don't know that man, Lord Sebastian. He might be Ivor over in Hedeby, but here in Frisia they calls him Black Hrotberck. I don't know why, but he's black all right—down to his liver and his gizzard. Why, I've seen him cut open a man's chest and let his lungs hang out just to see how long he would keep breathing. The local lord who is supposed to keep the peace in this open trading place don't even dare to bring his men to town when Ivor is here. I best be going now, I tell ye."

"Wait, Askold. I have a plan. If it works, I'll be able to get rid of Ivor for you. If it doesn't, you can leave. I have a personal score to settle with that scum."

"I'm telling ye, Ivor be a hard man to bash down; he's always surrounded by that bunch of slobbering killers. It don't appear you've got enough men for the job."

Sebastian tightened his grip on the little man's neck. "Listen to me, Askold. I can't let you go. You're too important to my king. But I won't put you in any danger either. Just wait with my men until dark. If I can't settle this thing tonight, we'll get you out of town on a fast horse before morning. Agreed?"

Sebastian covered Askold in a hooded cloak and spirited him through the alleyways to his own quarters in the upper town, where they waited for Bardulf to return and keep watch over the thoroughly shaken shipwright.

***

108

After making some trading arrangements for the morrow, Ivor and his men found a tavern and settled into it by nightfall. Sounds of celebration and debauchery spilled out of every window. Sebastian lurked in the shadows across the road.

Eventually, Ivor came out to relieve himself against the side of the building. Taking advantage of a rare moment when no one else was on the road, Sebastian crossed quickly and drew his dagger just as Ivor turned around, pulling up his trousers. Sebastian had the knife at his throat. "One loud word and you die, you scum-sucking snake. Is Konrad with you? I warn you, tell me the truth. You're this close to going to hell. I'll know if you're lying."

Even in the dim light, Sebastian could see Ivor's cynical smile. "So you are alive, king's man. I wondered if you would survive. But I see you are tougher than we thought. Let me remind you that it was I who saved you. Konrad wanted to kill you, chop-chop, right there. I convinced him he might like it better if you lived so you would be a pathetic, crippled witness to his prowess. Of course, we did not think you would ever be whole again."

"Where is Konrad? Is he here?"

"Unfortunately, no, my fine friend. He came not with us this time. It seems he is having a health problem just now. You know he will have a hump with just about anything, even the ugliest slag. And one of the pigs he rutted with apparently has given him a dirty louse or two. He is most uncomfortable just now. But he will survive. I have seen it before. He killed the unfortunate girl who gave it to him, I'm afraid."

"I don't doubt it. What are you doing here, Ivor?"

"I have some small business here. I like this town. It has some good girls and plenty of good wine. And we make a bit of profits now and then. No one bothers us here—until you."

"I don't like you, Ivor. And I have business here too. I want you gone from here tomorrow. Or you will answer to me. Is that clear?

"Well, since you have big knife to my throat, I suppose I must agree. But you must know that I am Ivor the Bold. I have a certain reputations, shall we say. I cannot run from every man who say he don't like me."

"You won't give me your word, then, that you will go?"

"Oh, I will give you my word to save my life this time. But I am prideful man. I cannot promise that I will stay gone once I leave."

Sebastian wrestled with his conscience. He could kill this dangerous man now and be done with it. Without a leader, his men might leave Dorestad rather than face an unknown threat. But he hesitated, unwilling to kill a man in cold blood.

"Listen to me, you ugly wharf rat. I intend to send Frankish soldiers here. If you come back, we will destroy you. Promise me you will not come here again, and I will let you live."

At that moment, a commotion occurred at the tavern door, and two Danish sailors lurched out drunkenly into the road. Ivor cried out to them and heaved himself at Sebastian in an attempt to break away. Without another thought, Sebastian drove his dagger into the pirate's throat.

The sailors gathered their wits and lurched across the road to investigate Ivor's cry. When they reached the shadows, Sebastian skewered one with his dagger, drew his sword, and cut down the other one as he turned to run. He left all three bodies lying where they were and slipped away into the darkness.

***

"Listen, men," Sebastian counseled when he got back to his comrades, "the Vikings will soon discover the bodies of Ivor and those others I killed. They probably won't do anything tonight, drunk as most of them are likely to be. But they'll find out soon enough that there are Franks in town, and they'll torture someone until they find out just where we are. They'll come for us, don't doubt it. But they won't know how many of us there are, and they might not expect us to be ready for them. So we'll give them a little surprise. Prepare yourselves, set a strong watch, and be ready for the morning."

Fairly early the next morning, the Vikings made a reconnaissance in force.

"Steady now," Sebastian warned as a troop of heavily armed Danes came up the lane to the Franks' small inn. "Let them come. Don't show yourselves until the signal."

When the Vikings came closer he gave the word, and his men stepped to the open windows and loosed a shower of arrows into their midst. Several of Ivor's men went down. The others hesitated and began backing away behind their shields.

"Now, men, now!" Sebastian shouted, and all twenty of the handpicked men he had brought with him, including Liudolf and Bernard, raced out of the door.

The fight was vicious but short. The Vikings had sent too few men, and all were cut down in the melee that followed. Sebastian had their bodies piled into two carts and driven back down to the waterfront, where they were dumped adjacent to the tethered Viking ship. Thereafter, the Franks waited and watched, picking off with arrows or attacking any Vikings venturing beyond the lower end of town. The next day, the remains of Ivor's band gathered their dead into the ship and set sail with the tide.

***

Amid much ado and excitement, the king made his way to Aachen during the winter of Sebastian's encounter with the Vikings at Dorestad. He was engrossed in the building of a new palace on the site of his old villa and had great plans for it. He was already in an exuberant mood and more so when the word came that Sebastian had been successful in finding a way to build a Frankish navy and was just now arriving at court. Charlemagne sent for him immediately.

"I'm amazed you found that shipbuilder in such a short time! But what in blazes is all this talk about the bloody

Vikings you ran into up there? They say you fought a pitched battle. Your message was far too short," he said, pulling Sebastian down onto a bench beside him at the fireplace.

"Sire, I think we can build that navy you've been wanting. We've got a real Danish shipbuilder on our side now, and we made a lethal statement to some of the Vikings who've been threatening our ports in Frisia.

"What do you mean threatening? Surely they weren't trying to take over in Dorestad?"

"Well, in a way, sire, they were. They've been coming to Frisia as traders, but they're so bold and aggressive that they intimidate the local leaders and just take over whatever town they're in." Sebastian hesitated, not wanting to give the king too much information about what happened in Dorestad. He decided he'd better fill in at least some of the blanks.

"Uh. . . there was this fellow, Ivor the Bold. I believe you've heard of him, my liege. He was an infamous pirate, but he came into Dorestad masquerading as a trader. He was definitely scouting for a big raid because he brought too many men, and all of them were warriors, heavily armed. He ran into us the day he got there, and there was a bit of a brawl."

"Aha, so you did have some trouble?"

Sebastian kept trying to play down the fight and his part in it regarding Ivor. "A small thing, sire. . . an incident, really."

The king was not going to be put off. "What sort of incident, Sebastian. What are you hiding?"

"It was nothing, my king. We had to deal with Ivor the Bold and his gang is all."

"Oh, is that all?" the king said derisively. "And?"

"I don't believe he will be a problem now, sire."

"Sebastian. . ." the king's voice began to rise. "I do remember that name. He was the fellow with Konrad in Hedeby, wasn't he? I thought I told you to stay away from Konrad and his scurvy chums."

"Sire, Konrad was not there. But I'm sure Ivor would have murdered our shipbuilder if he had discovered him. He's not a problem anymore, however; he was. . . uh. . . a casualty of the fight. But there will be other Vikings. On your authority, I ordered a detachment of soldiers from your garrison in Nijmegen to be sent to Dorestad. They will keep our man, Askold, and his workmen safe."

Sebastian braced himself for the king's reaction. But the king merely replied, "Well, I suppose you've done what I would have done. And you were certainly right to send for help from Nijmegen. I'll reinforce your decision. The stakes are high. We must look ahead and build those ships."

Sebastian relaxed a bit and changed the subject. "Let me tell you about those ships, sire. You will be amazed. They're very different from what we've been using all this time. Our boats can hardly get out beyond the sight of land, and they're clumsy and not very seaworthy.

"We saw Ivor's ship in the harbor when he came in. It was a true Viking boat all right, but a trading vessel, wider and deeper than a warship. It had room for a crew of fifteen or twenty men and could carry livestock as well as cargo. What Askold has begun to build for us is a real longboat—a warship. The genius of it is the way it's constructed, with thin, curved and overlapping planks, which they hew to fit perfectly, using only an axe. And then they nail the planks together and attach them to the keel of the ship running from stem to stern. Crossbeams are laid from side to side to support the rowing benches and any necessary decking. It's considerably lighter than a cargo ship, and it will have a very shallow draft and marvelous maneuverability. It'll be able to run up shallow rivers as well as survive on the open sea."

"Wonderful! Well done, you! I am pleased indeed. We've had a splendid stroke of luck! But when will we have some of those ships?"

"Well, sire, it's not as easy as all that. The shipbuilding business is complicated, especially if one is building the way the Danes do. It takes a great deal of time. First our man needs to train more workers. Then each vessel needs to be thoroughly tested by long voyages on the open sea as well as up rivers. That takes gifted seamen, those who can navigate on the high seas when you cannot see the land. Such men are hard to find. But the hardest part of all will be training sailors who must also be soldiers, like the Vikings. We will not have a navy overnight."

"No, I suppose not. But it can't wait forever; the Danes get stronger every year. I have no doubt that one day we shall have to fight them. And well we should—they're a load of bloody pagans as well as pirates. Do you want to oversee the project?"

"No, my king, I'd prefer to move on. The job right now is mostly about boards and nails and finding men to work with them. Later, when we're training sailors and fighters to man the boats, I may be interested again. But it probably should be one of the western Franks who lives in those coastal regions and knows them well."

"Right, then," the king said enthusiastically, rubbing his hands together, "it's a splendid beginning, old lad!" He paused to observe Sebastian and stroke his mustaches. "But now you need to rest, Sebastian. You must look in on your son Milo, of course. He's here in my villa. Making marvelous progress, that young man! All say so, even Alcuin. If he keeps it up, he'll be as smart as our prize Englishman before we know it.

"By the way," the king continued, "it wouldn't hurt you to spend some time with Alcuin yourself. He's a splendid scholar. You love Latin anyway. And he's a damned fine gentleman to boot, not even a priest, by the saints. Why, he even thinks like you do, bless him—always trying to get me to ease up on the sodding Saxons. He's even drafted a new capitulary for them. Blast! It eliminates most of the serious punishment I've meted out to them over the years for backsliding on their oaths to me. I devised most of the old Saxon laws myself to frighten the bloody savages and keep them from rebelling every flaming spring. Didn't work, though, damn their eyes."

"I will certainly see him while I'm here, sire, as well as Milo. I much appreciate Alcuin already, and it will be a great pleasure. Later I want to go down to Andernach and see how my little boys are faring under Duke Gonduin's tender care."

114

"Bosh, you needn't worry about those boys of yours. From what I know of them, they're not likely to be frightened by the likes of that old toothless lion. I imagine they're already running that villa of his right now, and he loves it. After all, he is their grandfather."

"I'm only concerned that they have people around them who care for them and comfort them. It can't be easy to grow up without their mother. And God knows I've not done much of a job of being a father to them."

"Nonsense, old boy. They're as fortunate as most of the sons of warrior fathers. You see them when you can, and you provide a good example for them. They know who you are. God's blood, everyone does. They can't help but be proud of you. Besides, there's a whole troop of teachers and servants around them all the time. And as for playmates, I reckon there are youngsters aplenty at Andernach running about getting training in Gonduin's 'school for young soldiers.' He's as good as you will find at bringing up youngsters to be warriors. He's done it for a legion of 'em. No, they'll be fine. Not to worry.

"Listen, there's another thing. . .I must go on campaign again soon—into Wilzi country, our first fight against the bloody Slavs to the east of the Saxons. The Wilzi hate us, and they've been harassing our allies. So I've got to go and show 'em some Frankish muscle, eh? Scare 'em back into their wretched bogs, the pagan buggers."

The king paused to consider for a moment. "I could use you with me this time to scout out what we're up against. Ah, but you'd best go down and see your boys. I've got plans enough for you later—the damned Avars in Pannonia, the blasted Umayyad Moors in Spain. There's plenty to choose from.

"Ever been to Spain, lad?"

"No, my lord king."

"Of course you haven't. Well, high time you saw some of it. Lovely country—warm, beautiful rivers and rolling hills, and full of good food like you've never tasted before. And women! Sensuous, beguiling. Nothing like 'em. I'll wager

115

you'd come back with a tale or two about it all. Meanwhile, I may soon need someone to go down there and do a bit of spying on those Umayyad Saracens who are threatening our allies in Barcelona. The men on our side are Moors, too, God forgive them, but they are Abbasid Mussulmen, connected to the caliph in Baghdad, not to that bloody butcher in Cordoba. And we've got to stand by them, or we'll lose our toehold there in Al Andalus. I may want you to go down there and see what needs doing about all that."

"Aye, my liege. Whenever you like. Whatever you like." Sebastian was just glad to be out of the king's disfavor and he didn't care what came next as long as it filled up his time and helped him to forget. All he needed was a sense of doing things right again.

"Right, then. But for now, go see your boys. Give them a jolly hug from the king, will you? I miss 'em."

"Aye, sire." Sebastian backed out of the room.

On the other side of the door, he turned to find Fastrada waiting for him once again, like a black widow on a web.

"Count Sebastian," she began in a silken voice loaded with feigned hurt feelings, "you have not come to see me as I asked. I am most disappointed. You will not be my champion, then?"

"No, my lady queen, I must decline. The king has made me one of his paladins, thanks to your, ah, thoughtful help. But the honor means that I must be committed to the king alone now. We are forbidden to have any other loyalties. I humbly beg your pardon, Your Grace."

"Nonsense, Sebastian. No one need know. I certainly would say nothing." She stepped forward quickly and grasped the neck of his tunic, bringing her face within inches of his own. "Why, if you did not wish to be seen coming to me publicly," she whispered, "you might visit my quarters in the late evening, after the torches have been put out. We can have a cup or two of good wine, and I will tell you my plans to serve the king as you tell me yours. Together, we will find a way to serve him much better and to the advantage of all."

Sebastian was dumbstruck, and for a moment he hesitated, not knowing what to say. Her eyes bored into him as if she could simply invade his mind and compel him to love her. He could feel her breath on his face, and one of her knees touched his own. She smelled of lavender and the sharp scent of cloves. He knew the veins in his temples were beginning to stand out.

If he rejected her offer with indignation or distaste, she would be sure to take offense. But doing what she asked was unthinkable. He took a deep breath and thought for a moment, staring into the black pools of her eyes. Finally, he cleared his throat, backed gently away from the queen, bowed low, and said calmly, "I am truly sorry, Your Grace, but I could never put you at such a risk. It would be most inappropriate of me and far too dangerous for yourself. I could never forgive myself if somehow we were discovered and someone got the wrong impression. You might be made to suffer the consequences, even though we would be meeting merely to talk on behalf of the king. Ahem."

He hesitated only a moment more, cleared his throat again, and began to back away, bowing low.

"Wait, Sebastian." She rushed to him again and clutched both his hands tightly. "I will come to you tonight, my hero. It will be safer. No one would question the queen if I'm roaming about the villa. I must confess, dear Sebastian, I am so strongly drawn to you. I cannot help myself. Will you be sweet to me? I adore you, I do."

Sebastian held up both hands to ward off the queen's approach. "My queen, please do not. I beg you. It is most unwise. And I'm afraid you have the wrong impression of me. I'm a simple soldier; I have little to offer besides my service to the king. And that is all I wish to pursue."

"Ah, but that is what I love—a great hero but a modest man. Very rare. I will come, Sebastian. Wait for me. Don't be afraid. I shall be able to handle any problem if it arises. You only need to be my good friend and bow to my wishes. You will see how good I can be to you."

Before he could recover, she had turned and left the anteroom. Sebastian was already in a sweat. He turned and almost ran to find Heimdal.

***

That night, as she had promised, the queen came to his quarters about an hour or so after the torches had been put out. She was accompanied by one of the women of her entourage, who stood at the door as she let herself into Sebastian's quarters. Fastrada was dressed seductively in a flowing silk nightdress and a robe over her shoulders. She had let her long hair down, and she carried a small candle and a leather flagon of wine. Immediately, the room was filled with her perfume. Smiling sweetly, she turned from the door.

The queen was totally unprepared for what she saw. The room was well lit by many candles, and Sebastian stood fully dressed in the middle of the anteroom, waiting. He did not return her smile.

Archbishop Regwald and Count Edelrath stepped out from the bedchamber into the anteroom. Without a word, both bowed low and formally to the queen. Her mouth fell open as she realized what was happening. She hesitated only a moment and then shrieked and fled, slamming the door as she went out. Unfortunately for the distressed queen, the train of her gown caught in the door. Rather than open the door again to further ignominy, she jerked furiously at the gown with all her weight and finally managed to tear it free, leaving a piece of delicate purple silk hanging conspicuously inside the room.

"My God, Edelrath, did you see her face?" the archbishop boomed after the queen had fled, almost doubling over in laughter. "I thought she was going to be sick right there in front of us. And then her gown got stuck in the door. Look at it there. What a testament! We have something here that might truly keep that audacious woman in check should the need ever arise."

A perennially serious and dignified man, Count Edelrath's eyes were wide with indignation. But he could not suppress a smile at Regwald's unabashed glee. Sebastian kept clearing his throat, his expression alternating between abject horror and the almost uncontrollable urge to laugh.

"Well," Edelrath said reflectively, "she has certainly brought this on herself. We suspected she would be a different sort of queen than our dear Hildegard, but who would have thought she would be this bold?"

Heimdal emerged from the bedroom and joined in the general critique of the evening's excitement. It was he who had thought of the solution to Sebastian's quandary. He had grasped at once how precarious the situation was. The queen would try to ruin Sebastian if he disdained her and was not in his quarters when she came. But he would be even worse off if he allowed her entry. The only way out was to catch the queen in her own web by providing witnesses to her latent infidelity. Regwald and Edelrath were highly placed in Charlemagne's hierarchy of advisors. Indeed, Regwald was his archchaplain now and Edelrath one of his most important generals. Both men were beyond reproach in the king's eyes. And they were both old friends of Sebastian's, having known him since he was a boy and sponsored his growth as a warrior. They regarded him as a count with much responsibility, a leader and fighter of high renown. As much as the king doted on Fastrada, there was no way he would be likely to take her word against men he had fought with and depended upon for most of his life.

When the excitement died down a bit, the three conspired with Heimdal on what to do next.

"I think, Your Excellencies," the blind man began, stroking his short beard, "that we must be charitable to Her Grace. After all, she is young and ambitious. The good king will find out soon enough that she has this, ah. . . tendency, shall we say, for adventure. Besides, we really don't want to drag poor Sebastian into an ugly confrontation. I suggest we say nothing unless we must—unless, of course, the queen tries to seduce our dear boy once again or she tries to ruin him."

"Excellent, Heimdal, I entirely agree," the archbishop said, rubbing his hands. "It was a delicious episode, and I hope

119

it will go a long way toward foiling the queen's machinations. Good Lord, what does she want to do, get rid of the king and run the kingdom herself? Heaven help us! No, she knows that we know. That's enough to curb her enthusiasm a bit. And the less said about Sebastian, the better."

"I am agreed about that course of action, Regwald," Count Edelrath said, stepping back into his dignified persona. "But I don't believe the queen strives to replace our good King Karl; I think she wishes to conquer him mentally and emotionally—and anyone else, like our poor Sebastian, who is handsome, powerful, or famous. I have never seen a more ambitious or reckless woman.

"You are right, Heimdal, we should force no scene or embarrass the queen further. Perhaps it will be enough of a lesson for her. But she will bear much watching nonetheless. We cannot let her do some other silly thing that might cause the king harm, good intentions or not."

Sebastian said nothing except to bid them all goodnight, but he sat for hours in the darkness pondering his close call and its possible future consequences. He found, to his surprise, that he could not condemn the queen. God knows, he thought, I wanted her. She was attractive enough—no, much more than that—she was damned near irresistible, mesmerizing. Now I know how Ulysses must have felt tied to that mast while the Sirens sang. Who knows what I might have done if she hadn't been the queen? He got up with a shudder and sent word to Liudolf to prepare to leave for Andernach on the morrow as soon as he had seen his son and Alcuin.

Chapter 11

Aix-La-Chapelle

The King's Villa at Aachen, Spring 789

Sebastian was uneasy about the prospect of visiting his sons. He loved them dearly, to be sure, but seeing them outside the context of family and in the absence of their mother, who had been the heart of the family, tainted his joy of them. Nevertheless, as soon as the sun was up, he sent a message to Milo's dormitory to arrange a meeting in the newest part of the palace.

It was the first time Sebastian had seen the king's new villa at Aachen, a resurrected country estate many of the western Franks were already calling Aix-la-Chapelle in honor of the grand basilica to be built there. Judging from the vast resources being poured into the project and the size it was taking on, Sebastian knew this was not just another palace in the chain of administrative residences Charlemagne used to control his sprawling kingdom. This one might actually be the permanent capital the king often promised to build.

Passing through the new wall that enclosed the palace, he came to the garrison building in the center of the new construction. On one side was an enormous edifice still in the early stages of construction. On another were the beginnings of a circular complex of heavy polished stones. The two parts were connected by a long, covered gallery, divided in the middle by the garrison building, which was the only structure yet completed. Accustomed to the Frankish practice of building with wood, Sebastian marveled that all the buildings were to be constructed of stone. As he waited for Milo, a steady stream of carts loaded with stone and brick trundled through the gate on the old Roman road that still served as the main artery.

Milo walked into the anteroom where Sebastian waited. The boy was dressed simply in a cleric's dark cassock. He walked slowly and serenely, in complete control of himself, as if he were strolling in a garden.

He was tall for fourteen, Sebastian thought with satisfaction as Milo made his way across the crowded room. And handsome, too. He had a shock of yellow hair, proof enough that he was part Saxon. The innocent, beautiful face of Gersvind, the village girl who had been Milo's mother and Sebastian's mistress for a short summer, came back to him with a shock. Milo looked just like her. He had her innocence, her grace of body and expression.

But he had his father's dark eyes, as lively as starshine on a dark night. From the look of him alone, Sebastian was sure Milo would become a brilliant scholar. He would have bet a good horse on it.

"Well, you are a surprise," Sebastian ventured, giving his son an embrace. "I see from your clothes you intend to be a monk, yes?"

"No, father, I do not wish to live in a monastery."

"I see. Well, that's a relief. I wouldn't want to live in one either. Tell me, then," he said, leading the boy out into the interior courtyard, "where is it that you would wish to live? And what work would you like to do?"

"I wish to be a scholar, my lord father, like Master Alcuin."

"Of course, you do. Excellent. You certainly have my blessing, and I will help you in any way I can."

"But that's not all, Father," the youth hastened to say.

"What else, then? Go on."

"I want to stay here for a while—until I have learned all Master Alcuin can teach me. And then I want to see what you see. I want to see the world—or at least as much as I can. So far, all I know is Fernshanz, Andernach, and here. I want to see how other people live and think. I want to know, Father. I want to know everything."

"Ah, is that all?" Sebastian smiled at his son's directness and the breadth of his thought. "I'm not surprised.

122

It's quite a fine ambition, and it's exactly what I wanted to do at your age. You do realize such a lofty goal will only take you a lifetime? But tell me, what is it you wish to discover about people?"

"I want to know why there are so many differences between people, why there is so much war. I want to meet some Saxons and find out how a pagan thinks and why they are so murderously angry at us. I want to meet a black man or an Arab. What would such a man think? Would it be different from the way we think? I want to go to Rome and meet the pope. I would like to ask him why he cannot bring Christ's peace to the world."

"Whoa, my good son! You've got some exceedingly grand notions. It will take you years just to find a poor answer to only the first of your questions. And you must understand very clearly that the world beyond what you know is a dangerous place. You can't just walk out into it as if strolling into the next village. You need to be prepared."

"Take me with you, then, Father. You have been many places already. I would go with you wherever you go."

Just then, another monkish figure entered the courtyard. "There you are, my good friend! How glad I am to see you," the man exclaimed, rushing forward to embrace Sebastian.

"Well met, Master Alcuin. I was afraid you would have no time to see me since I'm here only till the morrow."

"Sebastian, please don't call me Master. You and I are equals. Call me Flacco, why don't you? That's what the king likes to call me. He is David, and I am his Horace, or Flacco, as he likes to call me as a nickname."

"Thank you, uh, Flacco. It's certainly a good time to be here. Let me tell you straightaway how intrigued I am about what is happening here in Aachen. They say it will become the new Rome and that the king may wish to make it his capital. I was hoping you would have the time to give me a quick walkabout since you have had much to do with it. They say it was you who found the architect."

"You have heard correctly. The king can talk of nothing else lately, and he has indeed enlisted the services of Odo of Metz, an architect—nay, a magician—who has the most wondrous ideas and has amazed everyone with what he wants to do. His drawings and the preliminary work clearly show that this will be a palace to rival those in Rome and even Ravenna, which has some of the most beautiful buildings in the world.

"Come. Let us go at once to the chapel area. It is truly going to be magnificent, certainly the most beautiful creation since the halcyon days of Rome. You come, too, Milo. I don't want to take you away from your father for a single minute. You must be part of your father's education on the new Aix-la- Chapelle, as it is being called in the western Frankish tongue."

As they walked, Alcuin renewed his welcome. "And why would I not have time for you, my friend? Of all King Karl's officers, I find you by far the most compatible. Why, I would go so far as to say that we are kindred spirits."

Walking along the new gallery, Alcuin gestured grandly at the mountain of stones at the south end of the complex. "This is to be the chapel. Imagine what it will look like, how glorious it will be! It will have eight massive marble pillars, brought from Ravenna and Rome itself, at the behest of the pope, and marble walls inside a central octagonal core. It will have a cupola of bronze, topped—a bit comically, I think—with a large golden apple as well as a cross. The king will have a marble throne on the second floor, approached by a staircase of marble. From the throne, he will be able to see three altars across the central space. The walls and cupola will be decorated with brilliant mosaics depicting the evangelists and an angelic host. The doors will be of massive bronze, and there will be two rows of windows in the arched Roman style, so the chapel will be filled with glorious light.

"The connection between temporal and heavenly power through the king will be unmistakable. Aix-la-Chapelle will represent the New Jerusalem, and the king will be seen for what he is—the equal of any of the ancient Roman

124

emperors. He will truly be 'a Holy Roman Emperor.' And he must have a palace worthy of such a great ruler."

Alcuin gave them the grand tour. After the chapel, he explained the plans for the enormous council hall at the other end of the gallery, which would be able to contain the hundreds of Frankish leaders who came every spring for the annual assembly. It would be two stories of solid stone and would house the king and all his retinue, including his library and treasure room. It would be the place where the king received embassies and where all official ceremonies would be held. The walls would be covered with frescoes, tapestries, and murals depicting the great deeds of the king and the Frankish people.

"I'm exhausted just to think of it," Sebastian commented. "It's too much to consider all at once. It will be magnificent indeed. I hope the king has enough treasure to cover the enormous costs."

"Well, that is the problem, isn't it? At this point, I am inclined to believe he has not nearly enough to pay for all his ideas. But he is not deterred. He truly believes God will show him the way."

When they had finished the tour, Alcuin took Sebastian aside. "Listen, Sebastian, I want to tell you how glad I am to have you as a friend and ally. You and I think almost exactly alike. And we must stay together before the king. Ever since I have been here, I've been trying to persuade our gentle Karl to stop using the sword to try and make Christians out of the pagan Saxons. Good Lord, does he really think they will believe that Christ is their savior if he forces them to choose between baptism and execution? And then I discover that you have already had the courage to suggest the same thing to him years ago. I understand you had to face his considerable wrath because of it."

"Well, that's true, I'm afraid. Unfortunately, most of my poor efforts were like chaff in a strong wind. But, yes, I did approach him once or twice in that vein. I hope that your ventures have borne more fruit."

"I wish it were so. That is why I need your support. The king listens to his newest paladin, does he not? He does show small signs every now and then of changing his mind, but he has still to repeal the capitulary that imposes the death penalty for Saxons who go back to paganism after being baptized as Christians."

"I don't believe in summary executions either. But I must tell you, I've been through some rather bad times with the Saxons for over twenty years, and I've had some time to think. The Saxons still fight us after all these years and all our efforts to win them over, and our enemies on all sides assail us because we're too strong for their comfort and we presume to lead them against their will. And yet if we left them alone, they would continue to worship their loathsome pagan gods and keep on tearing each other apart. Frankly, I find it hard to care anymore about trying to convert them. Perhaps the king is right when he imposes order by any means available. I've come to think, reluctantly, that order is the only thing that will bring even a semblance of peace to this dog-eat-dog world we live in."

"I'm surprised, Sebastian, and deeply disappointed to hear you say that. You didn't always think in such ways. What has happened? It is strange for one who was brought up so carefully by Christian folk."

"Listen, my friend Flacco, we do have much in common. And I am truly grateful to know someone as wise as yourself. But you live in a different world than I. Yours is a world of books and ideas. As attractive and full of hope as they are, they don't seem to change much of anything in the way men behave. My world is one of violence and hatred, but we Franks are the force that matters; we use our power to create change so that there can be at least some progress toward a saner and less brutal world. And we forgive the evil that men do at our peril."

***

Sebastian walked with Milo back to the building outside the walls that served for Alcuin's famous seminars. He watched the young men as they showed up for class, the early ones engrossed in earnest talk as they strolled into the building, the late ones running up with looks of panic, their cassocks flying out behind them. Sebastian realized with satisfaction that not all of them were young men studying for the Church. Many, he knew, were from the families of the nobility, warrior families. It seemed an encouraging sign of change.

"That's right, Father," Milo said. "Master Alcuin boasts that these young men and boys have been collected from the far reaches of the realm and beyond, and they represent the finest young minds to be found outside of Baghdad or Constantinople. The king expects nothing less than to make Aix-la-Chapelle a grand capital of the Franks and establish it as the new axis of learning in the West."

Sebastian lingered a few more minutes to say good-bye to his son. Parting with Milo was strange. On the one hand, he felt keenly drawn to the boy, recognizing in him his own thirst for knowledge and wisdom. But he also felt separated from Milo, who was clearly under the influence of Alcuin. As young as he was, Milo did not agree with his father about the fickle nature of mankind or the need to achieve a kind of "Roman Peace" through unrelenting force and retribution. It was clear that Milo, too, felt the separation. Sebastian was sure that when they lived together as a family, Milo had loved him without reservation. But now, without Adela, who made the family whole, Milo had become distant, keeping his thoughts to himself.

"Good-bye, my son," Sebastian whispered into Milo's ear as he gave him a long embrace. "I'm glad to know you are in a good place, with good friends and teachers, and that you have prospects here you could find nowhere else in the kingdom. Learn well. Be a scholar. Fill your head to bursting with what Alcuin can teach you. Look for the answers to the deepest questions. Do not give up if you don't find them at once. I shall be proud of you whatever you do."

He paused and held Milo at arm's length to savor one last time the look and spirit of his son. "One day," he said quietly, "when you have become a man and you feel you've learned as much as you can here, send for me. I will return, and you will go with me to 'see the world,' as you put it. I'm not sure how much of a world that would be, and I warn you that it might cause you to change your mind and come to agree with me about how to make the world a better place. Nevertheless, one day you will share a road with me, and it will open your eyes. You will then see if that road confirms or denies what you have come to believe here. I promise you, I will come."

***

By midmorning, the horses were saddled, and Sebastian's small group awaited him in the stables. He had returned to his quarters for his armor and a small pack. On the way to the stable area, he found his way blocked by a large blond man with bulging muscles and a scowl on his bearded face.

"You! Count Sebastian! That's who you be, right?"

"I am Sebastian, yes. Do I know you?"

"Yes, you bastard. I am Turpin of Mayence. I have my own cavalry squadron in the king's army. You stole my captive after that big battle near Braunsberg near the Weser several years ago. She was Widukind's bastard daughter. I could have had a fortune in ransom for a Saxon prince's daughter, bastard or not—except for you. And then you let her go, you fool!"

"You would have raped her and left her bloody before you handed her over," Sebastian replied hotly. "Besides, I paid you half a herd of horses for her."

"Humpf! Saxon horses. Not worth a damn. I've not forgot."

"Neither have I. Do you still hold a grievance against me?"

"Yes, I do, you false comrade. No one steals another man's war prize. But it's not only I who has a grievance. You have offended the queen."

"Oh, really? And how do you know I have done that, sir? Are you a friend of the queen?"

"I am her champion as well as her good friend, I'm proud to say. She is a great lady. I take her cause, whatever it might be."

"And Fastrada has told you I have offended her."

"You will address that lady as the queen, you churl! Lowborn men like you may not take liberties with the queen's name. And, no, she has not named an offense in so many words; she is a charitable lady after all. But she has suggested that there has been an insult."

"I see. Well, please convey my sincere apologies to your *good friend* the queen," Sebastian said caustically. "Now I must go." He paused, narrowing his eyes at Turpin. "Unless you plan to call for satisfaction for my 'suggested' offense or for the loss of that little girl who was your prize—whom you never got to enjoy as you might have liked."

"You bloody hound!" Turpin's face turned red, and he grasped the hilt of his sword and took a step toward Sebastian. "I do indeed demand satisfaction," he shouted. "And *now*, in fact. Defend yourself." With that, Turpin tugged at his sword.

Sebastian was quicker. He did not even bother to draw his own sword but closed with the bigger man at once, wrapping his left arm around Turpin's neck and clasping it tightly with his right. Then he swung his hip hard into Turpin's midsection, lifting him briefly, and finished by twisting his body and throwing him violently to the ground. Taking advantage of the shock, Sebastian clambered quickly on top and immediately smashed his elbow into Turpin's jaw, following with a backhand that broke the big man's nose. Before his stunned foe could gather his wits to fight back, Sebastian hammered him with a vicious head butt and then grabbed Turpin by the hair and began to beat his head against the hard ground until Liudolf ran shouting into the courtyard and quickly pulled Sebastian free of his victim.

"My God, Sebastian! What are you doing? You'll kill him. Who is this?"

"No one," Sebastian growled. "A dog, perhaps. Nothing more."

"Well, leave him be, then, if he's nobody. You've hurt him enough. Good God, look at the blood on his face. I hope he's going to live. Meanwhile, let's get out of here before you're called to account. We don't need the delay." Pulling Sebastian roughly, Liudolf led him to the waiting horses, and they were away, leaving incredulous stable hands open-mouthed and still trying to comprehend the sudden violent scene and its bloody result.

***

Sebastian's small troop stopped at Andernach to see the younger boys, Karl and Attalus. Duke Gonduin was at home for a change.

"I have a letter for you, Sebastian," he said gravely. "From Adela. I presume you can read the Latin, can't you? "

"I can, Your Eminence, though not without some effort and certainly not as well as your daughter can write it."

"Before you read it, my son, please know how sad I am for you. I know how hard her absence has been for you and how much you have always loved her. I don't understand her, as close to my heart as she has always been. To choose the convent over you and the boys is a mad choice, so unlike the practical, rational Adela I've always known and admired. It's past understanding."

"I know, my lord. I can't grasp it either. But at least I know she still loves me. It's just that now she seems to love something else far more. But I can't believe her God would ask her to choose between us."

"*Her* God, Sebastian? Have you ceased to believe?"

"I don't know, my lord. I don't understand, and so I suppose I have come to doubt. I am angry—and bitter. Perhaps one day it will pass. May I read the letter now, sir?"

Gonduin handed the letter over without another word and quietly left the room. As he unrolled the parchment, Sebastian recognized at once Adela's beautiful hand and her careful choice of words in composing the lengthy message.

My Dearest Sebastian,

I must ask you once more to grant me a great boon. I was wrong to leave you and the boys in such haste. But I feared if I did not run as I did, I could never have had the courage to follow the command I feel I have heard so clearly from God himself. I do not understand this call, and I have little idea what it is God wants me to do. But there is no doubt in my mind that I must heed his message. It is the clearest thing in my brain, and I hear it every day I live.

But the mother in me yearns to see my little ones. I was wrong to leave them. They need me, and they are too young to be without their mother. I beg you with all my heart to bring them to me. I promise I will send them back when they are old enough to train and learn the way I know they must go. There will be no problem with convent rules. My father gives so much money to this place that no one will dare to object. In fact, I think most of the sisters will be delighted.

I do not worry about Milo, though I long to see him. He will make his way and one day become a great man.

The wife in me longs for you. I must fast and pray and deny myself constantly for want of you. You must know that we are truly one. We will always be so in spirit. God bless you and keep you safe. Please, please do not despair. Know that I love you without end.

Adela

Contrary to Adela's hopes, the letter filled Sebastian with a sense of impotence. She had closed the door to his hope of reunion. He felt helpless in a competition with God. But he loved her, so there was nothing left to do but bring the boys to her. At least it was the one gift he could still give her.

***

At Bischoffsheim, he paused on a hill above the convent and let Heimdal and Archambald take the boys to her. He watched as they ran delightedly to their mother. He could almost feel her joy as she hugged them to her. After the first riotous moment, she looked up anxiously in search of him, and he met her gaze for one brief moment before turning Joyeuse and disappearing behind the hill.

Chapter 12

The Ring of the Avars

The King's Court at Worms, Spring 790

"Ah, Sebastian, good man," the king said warmly as his newest paladin strode into Charlemagne's private quarters, where the king was having a vigorous rubdown by a heavily muscled giant. "I hope you're thankful you weren't with the army on this last bloody escapade! I'm completely done in. Did you know we rode across the whole of Saxony this time, all the way across the bleeding Elbe River? Never been there before, have you?"

"No, sire. I'm sorry I missed it. Was it a good fight?"

"It was. We fought the Wilzi Slavs this time. First time I ever warred against Slavs, but they were attacking some of the Saxons who came over to our side. I had to show 'em we could protect them. Turns out we beat those mangy wild men hollow. Wasn't all that difficult; they can't really fight. Lots of yelling, no order at all. Bloody hard to get there, though. Country's nothing but bogs and woods. I had to build two wobbly floating bridges over some wide rivers to get in. It was a dog's breakfast."

The king paused to study Sebastian for a moment. "Good," he said emphatically. "You look fit. Did you see your boys? Any hope for Adela?"

"I saw them, sire. All's well with them. Growing up fine. Left Milo in Aachen with Alcuin, took the younger boys to Bischoffsheim to be with their mother for a while. But I wasn't able to see Adela."

"Ah, I am sorry, old lad. Well, time will tell. At least the boys are thriving."

"They are, sire."

"I have something that might perk you up, Sebastian. It's a completely new adventure. I want you to go down to Lombardy and help Duke Eric of Friuli find out what the bloody Avars are up to and whether I need to worry about them."

The king's voice became edgy. "Those damned Asian savages used to raid against the Greeks. God knows how much treasure and tribute they carried off as 'gifts' from Constantinople. But lately they've been pushed westward by some other Asian rotters, the Bulgars, and now they're on our doorstep, raiding into Bavaria and Friuli. The army's exhausted. I'm not going to fight this year—there'll be no Maifeld this spring. But I need to know if those bloody Avars are going to be a threat to me. And I want you to go down there and work with Eric to find out. You know, don't you, that Duke Eric protects my eastern flank against the Avars?"

"I do, sire."

"He's the brother of my poor dead Hildegard, and I don't know a better man. I would trust him with my life. Just ask Alcuin; they're good friends. Alcuin will tell you that Duke Eric of Friuli is, first and foremost, a shining example of a morally upright Christian man, who also happens to be a great military leader. You must get to know him. He might even help you get through this brown funk you're going through right now."

Sebastian looked away and cleared his throat but decided not to protest the king's good, but unwelcome, intentions. "I've heard much of him already, my king. He is one of the paladins, is he not?"

"He is indeed. Perhaps the best now that Roland is gone."

"Sire, he's a duke and a very famous and capable man. I'm not sure how much I could help him."

"Nonsense! You'll get on famously. Eric is almost the same age as you. And he doesn't give a fig about rank or position. He'll become your comrade immediately. Besides, you've shown a real talent for ferreting out what's going on in dangerous places, and at this point, I know bugger all about the bloody Avars.

"However," the king paused forebodingly, "I won't send you if you think you're not up to the task. I've been worried about you lately. You've had a change since you lost Adela. Your attitude is different. Oh, you've done some excellent work for me, I won't deny. That nifty scouting you did there in Brittany—and the excellent beginning with the ships up in Frisia and all. But I've also had some disturbing reports about you. There are some who gossip that you're a man who drinks to excess. Good Lord, I've seen that for myself. And they say you have a fiery temper and act before you think. You even have a reputation as a brawler. Don't think I don't know about that business with Turpin when you left Aachen. My God, you almost killed him. I said nothing because I think Fastrada was mixed up in all that, God save her."

"The queen, my lord?" Sebastian mumbled uneasily.

"Right. She's incorrigible sometimes—always meddling in my business. I hear the damnedest things about her from time to time—which, if half of them were true, I'd have to chop off her head.

"I never liked Turpin either. But that doesn't excuse you for nearly beating the life out of him."

"I'm sorry, my lord king."

"I don't like this willfulness on your part, Sebastian. It's almost as if you don't care what you do or what happens to you. It's unhealthy. That's why I want you to go down to Friuli and get to know Eric. He's a fine man; you will like him at once. And if you listen to him and imitate him, he can teach you much."

Sebastian took the reproof restlessly and with some resentment. But he responded dutifully. "Yes, my lord king. I'll leave tomorrow for Lombardy. Do you have a specific plan in mind?"

"Well, it's early. I'm not sure if I need to worry yet. But there have been increasingly ominous reports that the Avars are encroaching more and more onto our side of the

Enns River border, and Eric has sent me reports of raids on villages in the easternmost parts of Friuli. They're acting up, no question. Do you know anything about the Avars?"

"Very little, sire, except that our people call them the Huns, the same sort of people that ravaged the Roman Empire a long time ago. They are supposed to be fierce warriors, excellent horsemen, with ten-foot lances and the skill to cause havoc with bow and arrow from horseback at full gallop. They're supposed to be very ugly, and they wear their hair in two long pigtails down their backs."

"That's right—a bloody bunch of wild savages. Well, whatever they look like and are, I want you and Eric to find out. It probably means you will have to go into their heartland—into Pannonia itself. But you've done that sort of thing before. So has Eric. I want to know just what kind of threat these wild nomads are to me and how soon I must deal with them, if at all. It will be treacherous, I'll warrant. But Eric's a clever man and a bold one when the time is right. You must learn from him—about war as well as about the conduct I expect from a paladin. Go now, with my blessing. I'm putting my faith in you. Be worthy of it."

***

From their first meeting, Sebastian could see that Eric of Friuli was a highly composed kind of man, supremely confident without being arrogant, even serene, as if he always knew things would turn out all right no matter what occurred. It was clear at the outset that he was devoted to the king and to his duties as a paladin. Sebastian was immediately drawn to him.

"Welcome to Friuli, Count Sebastian. I am honored and very pleased to know you. Your reputation precedes you." Eric smiled broadly as he welcomed Sebastian's small band of king's men to his modest villa on the outskirts of the old Roman town of Aquileia. It lay at the head of the Adriatic, a day's ride eastward from the city of Venice, and was more a frontier fortress than a villa, with high walls and a strong keep.

"I apologize for my rather rough accommodations," the young duke said as they gave over the horses and walked toward the barracks area. "I could have put you up in the town. But we'll be staging from here, and the town would just distract us. It used to be a great city in Roman times, a commercial center. We still have a lively trade in amber and metal. And I've a thriving Jewish settlement that does really fine glasswork. Perhaps I'll have a chance to show you when we're done with our business in Pannonia."

"Quite all right, Your Grace. We didn't come for a holiday, not that I wouldn't enjoy seeing your capital."

"Oh, please call me Eric. We'll get on much better if you do."

"Right, then—Eric. Can you tell me what you have in mind for our little venture? King Karl only told me to come down here and find out what the Avars are up to."

"Of course. I'm sure you noticed our beautiful mountains to the north and east of us. They're called the Dolomites, and we must go through them to get into Pannonia. If you've never been there before, you should know the mountain passes lead eventually into a vast plain, a basin actually, into which drains all these huge Alpine rivers. One of them is your beloved *Donau*—the Danube—which begins in the heart of Francia.

"The Avars use these mountain passes to raid into our land as well as into Bavaria. And we use them to retaliate, though we never go too deeply into Pannonia. The Avars have very good cavalry, and we don't really want to fight them on their own ground. But we may be able to do a little spying on them, and these mountains might help us get in without being noticed."

"I understand, but what do we expect to see once we get into this Avar basin?"

"Well, it will be what we make of it. We're to see how well they're defended and how far out and in what strength they patrol from their capital—the Hringum, the so-called Ring of the Avars. It's a fabled treasure city that is rumored to store the plunder of generations within a massive circular fortress with no less than ten thick earthen walls.

"We won't get near the Hringum, of course; it would take an army. I see this as a scouting expedition in force—fifty or sixty good men from the heavy cavalry, well-mounted. No supply carts, just packhorses. We'll send out patrols , move at night, and watch by day, fighting only if we have to. When we come out of the mountains, we'll make our way up to the Enns River border and follow it along to the Danube and then down the big river as far as the Raab. We know the Avars have forts along those rivers. If we can get that far, we'll have a fair idea of what strength the Avars have west of where the big river turns to the south. The Hringum is on the other side, the eastern side of the Danube. It's too dangerous to try and cross that river. So… what do you think?"

"Is it open country once we get out of the mountains?"

"Very. Grass everywhere. Trees only along the waterways. Best horse-raising country in the world."

"Well, I don't see how we could find out what we need to know any other way. We certainly can't go in disguised, as I once did in Brittany—as a monk, would you believe? Can't do that here, though. I don't suppose we'll recognize the language of anyone we meet."

"That, at least, won't be a problem. I brought interpreters for any language we might encounter. You might be surprised to know the Avars are a fairly diverse lot. They've conquered and absorbed so many people over time that they often don't look very Asian. I mean, there are bearded Slavs, swarthy Bulgars and Turks, and even members of old German tribes mixed in among them. But we'll talk more about all that later. Right now a bit of supper and early to bed, right?"

Eric's quarters were in the barracks with his soldiers, and he had a small suite on the second floor of the large building. He invited Sebastian to eat with his officers since the duke preferred "a simpler supper." But Sebastian chose to eat with him, and they shared a meal of bread, cheese, and cold fish with a handful of grapes and an apple as dessert. In the morning, Sebastian joined the duke for Mass before dawn and then spent two hours in the training yard with him before breakfast, where they practiced with every weapon they would take on the journey. On the fourth day, they were ready to go.

Chapter 13

Pannonia

Summer and Autumn, 790

It took a week to make their way through the mountains. Eric brought forty of his best men to add to Sebastian's fifteen, including his closest comrades. The trip was harder than normal because they traveled at night and on less frequented trails. But eventually they emerged from the narrow mountain valley out into the Pannonian Plain.

Sebastian's men had seen the Alps, but they were awed by the beauty of the Dolomites. At the same time, everyone was uneasy. Bardulf expressed their misgivings: "This ain't our country, m'lord. What are we doin' here? I feel like them mountains is closin' in on me. Makes me queasy-like. It's an odd place, right enough."

"Not to worry," Sebastian replied calmly. "We'll be out of this valley soon, and you'll be at home in the flatter country we're coming to." But Sebastian felt the same uneasiness, not just from the high altitude but from the feeling that they were not getting through the long valley unnoticed.

When they camped in the daytime, Eric and Sebastian plotted the next march and discussed their concerns. "Well, I haven't seen anything," Eric admitted, "but if I were the Avars, I'd have scouts in here, too. Let's face it; we're a paltry number to be entering such a wild field as Pannonia. This is the land of some of the best horse soldiers in the world, and they've been terrorizing the Greeks for a century. We'll just have to try to keep our heads down and see what we can see."

For two weeks, the mission went according to plan. They hid during the day in thick woods along the river routes and sent scouts out during dawn and early evening, two or three at a time, to observe traffic on the roads or set up watch over whatever forts or encampments they encountered along the river. Once in a while, the scouts encountered one or two riders, sighted from a distance, but the riders disappeared as soon as the scouts moved toward them. While the scouts were out, Eric insisted that the horses and men remain in battle readiness throughout the day, even though no activity was reported.

At the end of the second week, they encountered Kaumberg, the big Avar fort on the Danube, and spent several days observing it from a distance. "I'm confounded, Sebastian," Eric said after sending the scouts out one morning, "that we've seen so little movement. Just messengers now and then. Even Kaumburg looks more like an outpost than a major fortification. So far, Pannonia seems tame indeed. Not what one would expect from the great Avar nation. I thought we'd have had at least a skirmish by now."

"I don't like it either. There's something going on we don't know about. This has been far too easy.

"Uh-oh. I may have spoken too soon. Do you see them?"

"What? Where?"

"The scouts—they're coming back, and they're not sparing the horses. Oh yes. Now I can see why. It's an Avar cavalry troop, and there's a lot of them."

They watched as column after column of heavily armed Avar horsemen emerged over a rise, coming at a gallop behind the retreating scouts. Suddenly, the long line peeled off into three columns, the flanking columns clearly moving to surround the watching Franks.

"Ha, so much for going unnoticed!" the duke said with a groan. "Better get the troop into battle formation. Or do you think we should make a run for it?"

"A little late for that, my lord. They're already flanking us. Looks like we're in for a fight." He turned and signaled Liudolf to rouse the troops into battle formation.

"Steady . . . wait!" Eric said, stepping out into the open. "They're stopping. What's that? By the saints, they're sending a delegation. See that flag? It's the banner of the khagan of the Avar kingdom. They want to talk to us. Imagine that!"

As three riders emerged from the center column and made their way riding slowly up the low rise, Eric made a curious digression from the approaching danger. "You're married, Sebastian, are you not? And you have children?"

"What? Why, yes. Yes, I am married, and I have three children. Why in the world would you ask that now—at this particular moment?"

"Hmm. Pity." He paused a long moment. "I just think that we could die very soon. Look at them. We're outnumbered ten to one. Chances are we won't prevail if they attack. It's possible you might never see that wife and family again. Are you afraid?"

"Well, this is comforting talk," Sebastian countered, somewhat bewildered by such an incongruous conversation. "Yes, I'm afraid. Aren't you?"

"No, not really. I've been in this place many times already. I've fought in at least two score of pitched battles. There was always a good chance I might die. I was never afraid. I suppose that's one reason why I never married or had children. If I had, I would be afraid I'd never see them again—as you are. You see, I don't believe that a lifetime soldier should be married, especially not a paladin. It seems to me that would be a terrible distraction. I'm devoted to one thing only—my sovereign. I believe in what he is doing. He's uniting the Christian world and annihilating the dragon of paganism. He's raising his people from their poverty and misery. He's shining a great light for the world to see. If I die in his service, I could do no better.

"Besides that, I am close to my God. So close I don't really want to be here—on this earth—for very long. I would rather go to God than live a long life in this imperfect place."

"Great heavens!" Sebastian blurted, staring agog at the calm face of the duke. "Do you expect me to comment on such a statement—now?"

"Oh no, of course not; I just thought it was a good moment for sharing. Besides, you don't have the time. Here's the delegation. Perhaps later—if we should survive against these odds."

Somewhat shaken by the strange conversation, Sebastian tried to prepare himself mentally as the three emissaries advanced slowly, but he stored Eric's words in the back of his mind as something that could very well profoundly change him should he live through the present critical moment.

None of the three emissaries fit the common Frankish notion that the Avars were a swarthy, slant-eyed lot of Asian barbarians. They looked more like a rough mixture of all the nomadic tribes that had ranged back and forth for centuries from the vast Russian plains to the Carpathian Mountains—Scythians, Goths, Tartars, Slavs.

The obvious leader of the delegation was a short, heavily bearded fat man who looked more like a Serb than an Asian except that he had drooping mustaches separated from his beard, and his hair was worn in the signature long double braids trailing halfway down his back. Like most Avars, he was bandy-legged from years spent on horseback and short-armed. He was completely unarmored. Instead, he wore a long white tunic with a large gold buckle on a broad belt. Several gold chains adorned his neck along with a silver medallion proclaiming his office. "Welcome, my friends," he shouted cheerily as he rode up casually to greet the Frankish leaders. Sebastian thought uneasily that his broad smile seemed more a mask than a genuine sign of welcome.

"Welcome, my friends. I am the tudun of western Pannonia, the governor of this province," he said in passable Latin. But then he switched hopefully to his own tongue. Eric quickly motioned to one of his interpreters. The tudun beamed in relief and continued his welcome. "On behalf of the glorious khagan—the sovereign of all the Avars—I wish to welcome you, our Frankish guests, most warmly and assure you of our love and good intentions."

"Thank you, my lord tudun," Eric responded through the interpreter. "But I'm afraid the position of your troops does not exactly speak of your love and good intentions."

"Them?" the tudun responded with a dismissive wave of his hand. "They are merely your honor guard. I wish to invite you and your men to my capital. Actually, it is the capital of the entire Avar kingdom. Unfortunately, the khagan is not in residence at the moment. He is away in the east tending to urgent matters. But I am in charge of this part of Pannonia. And I have good reason to invite you. May I get down?"

A strange parley then took place as Eric and Sebastian led the tudun and his aides to a small fire where they shared water and a small bottle of Frankish *schnapps*. Squatting down in the middle of the wide windswept plain, surrounded by a hodgepodge of wild nomad soldiers, and exchanging pleasantries with a gaudy, obsequious fat man with his persistent catlike smile, Sebastian had never been in such a strange setting, and he thought that he must somehow have come to the end of the world or, possibly, to the end of his own existence in it.

The tudun wasted no time. Speaking in a slightly conspiratorial tone, he revealed his concerns, all the while incongruously smiling away. "You see, my friends, there is dissension among the Avars about whether we should be friends with the Frankish king or consider him an enemy. I am a strong advocate of the former opinion." He vigorously poked his finger in the air for emphasis.

"We do not wish a war with the Franks. We cannot have one! We already have too many enemies. I should like to see peace between our peoples and a flourishing trade arrangement. We have much to offer. Would you agree, Duke Eric?"

"How is it you know my name, good tudun? We have never met, have we?"

"Ah, my good duke, you underestimate us. We have long known who you are and we also knew about your presence since you emerged from the mountain passes. We have seen the banner of Friuli and the standard of the King of the Franks, carried by the men of your friend there. Count

Sebastian, is it not? We have heard much of you, sir. You are well known—even here."

The tudun laughed good-naturedly at the astonished looks on their faces but continued. "Have you ever seen the Ring City, my friends? It is a wonder of the world. I should like nothing better than to show it to you. I would like you to be the guests of our fabled Hringum. Few Westerners have ever seen it. It would only be for a few days, and then you could return to your king and tell him we wish him no harm— that I personally wish to be friends with him. I want you to tell him that I am ready to be his ally. I would go so far as to say I am even interested in his religion. I find it fascinating. You may tell him so," the tudun concluded, emitting a silly giggle.

They exchanged pleasantries for a few more minutes, and then Eric responded to the invitation. "My lord tudun, you do us much honor. But I'm sure you realize this could be considered a hazardous step on our part. After all, we don't know you at all, and we have reason to think the Avar nation is not that friendly toward our king. There have been attacks into Bavaria and Friuli, my own duchy. I hesitate to put my head into the lion's mouth, as they say."

"Oh, my good duke," the tudun hastened to say, rubbing his hands together, "things have changed a great deal here lately. If you only knew the trials we currently face. I am trying to save my people. It is that important. I want to show them that the King of Franks does not want war with us—that he has actually sent a peace delegation to us—yourselves. In this way, I may convince my people not to make a dangerous mistake by attracting the wrath of a powerful king when we already have enough troubles."

"And what are those troubles, sir, may I ask?" Sebastian asked, trying to resist the feeling of rising doubt in the pit of his stomach.

The tudun paused and looked around him as if fearing that he might be overheard. For the first time, he abandoned the irritating smile and spoke in grim tones. "I will tell you, my lord, but only because I know both you and Duke Eric as honorable men, and right now I need you. You could be the key to my. . . uh, our survival.

"For one thing," he continued with urgency, "we have had a pestilence amongst our livestock, especially our horses. Imagine that! The Avars without enough horses! And we are hard-pressed at the moment on our eastern front by the Bulgars and the Greeks. There are many such concerns, and instead of unifying us, these misfortunes have caused a serious rift. I beg you, please come with us. You will not regret it. Together, we can prevent a war."

"Excuse me, my lord tudun," Sebastian insisted again. "But how do we know you are being honorable with us? You could lure us into your den and simply destroy us in front of your people. What is to prevent that?"

"Lord Sebastian, you see these two young men beside me? These are my sons. I am willing to leave them here with your soldiers. We will withdraw, all of us. You and the good duke will come with us. If you do notreturn within two weeks, I will lose my only sons."

They agreed to suspend the parley for an hour to consider the proposal. The tudun retired. His sons remained.

When the tudun had departed, Sebastian and Eric looked at each other uneasily. "This is a fine pass," the duke said. "He either wants to lure us into his heartland and torture and kill us for his people's amusement, or he really is afraid of something and wishes to add the strength of the Franks to his own purposes. That last bit about the religion makes him sound a bit desperate. Something's going on here, and we only have a hint. What do you think, Sebastian?"

"Well, I have serious misgivings, but I think we must do it. If we don't, chances are he'll attack us. If he does, considering the numbers, I'm afraid we'll be past praying for."

"I agree. But we won't take everybody. If we leave most of the men here, they can watch the roads, and if we don't come back, they might at least have a fighting chance to run for it. Do you think those are really his sons?"

"Hmm, they look very like him, and they certainly treat him with great respect."

"Right, then, we'll go. And, touch wood, we'll get back again. If it works out, we certainly will have the information the king sent us to get. If not, he'll have to choose two new paladins."

***

They took only Sebastian's men from Fernshanz, some fifteen riders, including Liudolf and Archambald, leaving Duke Eric's men to watch over the hostages. The duke was resolute in his parting instructions: "Make haste for home the moment the two weeks are up! Make sure you secure the hostages in case we should somehow make it back. Keep your guard up at all times. If you're attacked, fight your way out as best you can and head for home. Spread the alarm."

After a few days on the road and a shaky crossing of the Danube on small barges, they reached the Ring City. The tudun halted the column at a distance to allow the Franks to absorb their first look at the fabled city.

Sebastian marveled at the panorama before them, continuing to feel he'd never been in such an exotic place. "It's much more than a town and a fortress," he whispered to Eric. "Can you make out what all that is? There must be thousands of people down there. And look at those walls!"

"I know a bit about it; it's the legendary Avar stronghold. No one I know has ever seen it, but it's rumored to be a place of untold treasure. All those tents outside the walls mean it's a large military encampment. It's also said to be the spiritual heart of the *Huni* as well as their center of power."

"Do you really think we can trust the tudun?"

"I don't know, friend. It's a giant gamble at best, the stakes of which are our lives. But I think we've got a good chance of getting out of here without losing them. The tudun knew exactly when we passed into Pannonia from Friuli. He could have attacked us at any time. It's almost as if he'd been waiting for some representation from the Franks."

"But why did *he* reach out to us? Why not someone from the khagan? It's *his* city."

"If it's true the khagan is not in the city right now, it would mean the tudun's in charge and has a lot of power. We'll find out soon."

As they rode through the first gates of the fortress, the welcome of the soldiers and citizens lining the streets was anything but warm. Scowls and muted harsh comments, accompanied by emphatic spitting at the hooves of the Frankish horses, revealed the genuine feelings of many of those witnessing the reception. Sebastian cautioned the men to keep their eyes straight ahead and their backs straight, but each of his men rode with his hand on his sword.

The tudun's escort led them through huge gates and past the ten spectacular earthen walls until they reached a spacious center square surrounded by huge conical warehouses interspersed with stately palace dwellings made of earthen brick, like small manor houses. Sebastian and Eric were conducted to one of these near the central meeting lodge, and the men were led to a large stable and dormitory nearby, where they were invited to settle themselves and their horses for the night. Before they were led off to meet with the tudun, Sebastian addressed his men briefly: "Hear me, Fernshanz men! Keep your heads now. Tend to your business and don't be provoked. Be vigilant. Set a guard for all hours. With any luck, we we'll be out of here tomorrow or the next day."

The tudun, however, did not seem to be in a hurry. He showed Eric and Sebastian to their elaborate quarters, leaving them to clean up and refresh themselves. Several young women remained in attendance, bringing cool drinks and fruit and gesturing eagerly for them to get into the baths already prepared for them. Such pleasures were clouded, however, by the presence of guards at every door as well as outside the building.

In the late afternoon, the tudun returned and escorted them on a tour of the inner city. "Ah, my friends," he said, taking them both by the elbows, "I wish to show you off to my people as my honored guests and, as such, under my personal protection."

They strolled through the huge square, the tudun pointing out buildings and explaining their functions. Suddenly, he stopped before one of the huge conical warehouses. "I say, I wonder if you would like to see the inside of an Avar treasure house," he said with his gleeful smile.

"Well, of course, my lord tudun," Eric said nonchalantly. "I've heard so many stories of fabulous Avar wealth; I'd like to see for myself if they are really true."

"Ah," the tudun said, rubbing his hands. "Then you really must see it. Let us proceed."

The walls of the huge building were built of several thicknesses of crude dried bricks, with no windows at all, only a large hole in the ceiling that cast an eerie light on the central chamber of the building. To get to that point, they were escorted by a squad of guards carrying torches. Sebastian covered his nose and mouth against the fetid, heavy air.

From the center of the building, corridors led off in all directions. Along each hallway, doors led into inner chambers. A tomb-like quiet hung over the whole place. When they reached the central chamber, the tudun explained the treasure house in hushed tones.

"Down each one of these corridors, there are rooms stacked to the ceiling with treasure." He chuckled as they entered a room. "You see, we Avars are like ravens; we like bright and shiny objects and tend to hoard them away in our nest. I'm afraid we really don't know what to do with all this."

The guards raised their torches high and revealed glimmering solid-gold walls and wooden buckets and trunks of silver plate and jewels. Both Eric and Sebastian caught their breath, unprepared for what they saw.

"Is that wall really gold?" Eric exclaimed.

"Oh yes, my good duke, but it's not really a wall. Rather, those are gold ingots stacked one upon another, several thicknesses deep—up to the ceiling. And this is only one room in one building—only a small part of what we have. I confess, most of it came from your fellow Christians in Constantinople. They have been giving it to us annually for years. You see, they would rather give us gold and jewels than fight us."

The tudun led them through several such rooms until the sameness of each room's gleaming aureate began to lose its fascination. The tudun seemed to realize the tour had saturated their minds. He apologized with a laugh. "There are many, many such rooms, my friends. I know it is hard to comprehend. But now we must go back and seek a good drink after all this.

"I don't know why we keep so much," he expounded, shaking his head. "We hardly spend it. But then, there you are, we are barbarians, as they say."

***

In the evening, the tudun sent for them and received them in the banquet hall of the lodge, where the headmen and war captains of the several hordes of troops at the fortress had already gathered. All lounged on rugs and pillows scattered on the floor and around low tables. No one stood to meet the guests.

The two Franks reclined at one of the larger tables in the center of the hall with several of the tudun's closest advisors and the interpreter. The hall seethed with a low and threatening murmur. There were no welcoming smiles from the dour captains, who stared openly, as if their strange guests were inhabitants from another planet.

Their taut attention was broken by the appearance of slaves bringing sizzling trays of goat and horse meat and cornucopian baskets of bread and fruit. Jugs of strong drink were passed around freely, quickly changing the mood of many. A dancing troop suddenly appeared, and young male and female performers dressed in turbans and silk pantaloons began to spin and whirl, swaying gracefully between the tables, accompanied by the seductive sounds of muted drums, lyre, and flute. The tension in the hall began to dissipate.

As it did, the tudun became more loquacious, sharing more and more of the story behind his overture to the Franks.

At one point, he leaned toward them and offered a toast through the interpreter: "Welcome, once more, honored guests. You come at a most propitious time. It seems the world is becoming smaller, and our two peoples are suddenly neighbors. I have invited you to our palace in the hope that we will become very good neighbors, nay, even friends—friends who will come to love and help each other. Here's to that budding friendship and to that mutual assistance." He raised his cup.

Eric bowed and tasted the coarse drink they had been offered. "My thanks, honorable tudun. I, too, have hopes our two nations may live in peace and treat each other benevolently. We are grateful for your hospitality and this opportunity to know you. What, if I may ask, is the specific nature of the help you mentioned you might need from us?"

Sebastian watched this polite interchange in a state of charged anticipation and not a little suspicion. At the other tables, the eyes of all were upon the tudun as he lifted his cup. When Eric returned the cordiality, some relaxed and some others looked angrily from one to the other. It was obvious they were in the middle of a divided house.

"I know you, Duke Eric. I have heard much about you. They say you are a tireless defender of your lands and that you are held in high esteem by King Karl, are you not? And this fine gentleman, your friend Sebastian, is also a war hero and high in the trust of the king. I have a great favor to ask of you both, and I hope you will do me the honor of trusting me as well, believing that I have only our mutual interests at heart."

The tudun leaned so close that only Eric, Sebastian, and the interpreter could hear. "I will be frank with you, my friends, we Avars are a contentious lot, and sometimes our petty family squabbles can make us roaring beasts. I'm afraid we find ourselves now in the path of a storm among us. I regret to tell you all is not well within our great nation. We have fallen onto very dangerous times. There is dissonance among our leaders. Our great khagan finds himself challenged by his kinsman and chosen successor, the jugur, who no longer believes the khagan is fit to rule. Even now they have journeyed to an ancient council grounds where they are meeting to confront each other. I fear the outcome may not be pleasant. We may be in for some vicious family infighting."

He paused a moment to look around nervously, his smile gone. "I risk my life by approaching you like this. But there is little time, and you must leave as soon as possible, perhaps as early as tomorrow morning. There are several factions within the camp, and some of them despise the Franks and any Christians. I am not one of those, I hasten to assure you. In fact, as I mentioned to you, I am strongly attracted to your Christian faith and would like to know more about it. Beyond that, I'm a peaceable man, and I would like to avoid a conflict, if it is indeed coming."

Sebastian had seen this before in negotiations with the Saxons and realized that here was a man who was desperately trying to survive by playing both ends against the middle.

"Here is my proposal," the tudun continued, "and I apologize that I have no time to put it more delicately or with more subtlety. You know that I am governor of this province of Pannonia. I command a substantial part of the Avar army. If I could ally myself with my strong Frankish neighbors so that I could count on the support of their armed might, if need be. . ." He paused to let his next words sink in. "I would be willing to convert myself to the Christian faith and become the firm friend and ally of the great Karl, King of all the Franks. I could deliver my province, the whole western part of Pannonia, to his protection, and we might then avoid the destruction I fear may soon be upon us."

The boldness and import of the tudun's whispered confidence shocked both Eric and Sebastian into silence for a moment. The tudun hastened to assure them, "When you return to your camp, you will have my two sons with you as a guarantee of my good faith. They will be able to explain in detail what I have risked my life to reveal to you just now. Will you accept my offer?"

Eric recovered himself quickly. "I thank you sincerely, good lord tudun, for your candor. And I will tell you this in answer: I can promise you that we will report to the king at once all that we have heard, and we will say to him that we believe you are absolutely sincere. Your promise of sending your sons with us will be an excellent sign of that. But I cannot guarantee what answer the king will give in response. My companion, Count Sebastian, is closer to the king even than I and has his ear. What say you, Sebastian? What can you add?"

Sebastian hesitated a long moment, wondering if he should speak at all. He did not wish to give the tudun false hope, but it seemed the tudun's offer represented a golden moment, one in which the king's desire to secure his eastern borders might be achieved and war might be avoided. "I think," he ventured, "your offer is most wise. Our king is deeply concerned with securing his borders with the Avar nation. If there is a chance to achieve that goal, the king would be quick to choose it."

After these assurances, the tudun was enormously relieved. He returned to his normal persona of magnanimous host and smiling, confident leader. He led Eric and Sebastian around to all the tables, briefly introducing each of the headmen and offering toasts of reverence for the code of the warrior, whether Frank or Avar, and mutual respect for each other as faithful followers of that sacred code. The strong drink and spellbinding effect of the rhythmic musical cadences disarmed for the moment all latent hostility, and the evening ended peaceably.

***

"I'll tell you frankly, Eric, I feel lucky to have got out of there tonight," Sebastian commented once they had returned to their quarters.

"And I!" the duke breathed emphatically. "But we can't leave here too soon, I'm thinking. We've got the message we came for, and the rotten situation in Avarland seems clear, for whatever that may mean to us Franks. It's enough, however. Now the trick is going to be getting out of here with a whole skin and bringing the word back to the king.

I'm sure you realized that not all those war captains we met were under the tudun's command."

In the early hours of the morning, the duke's forebodings proved justified. The sounds of sharp conflict rose from the courtyard outside of the lodge. Sebastian was awakened by the loud crash of splintering wood, men shouting, and the clang of swords. He sprang from his bed, rushed past the guards in the main hall, and flung open the door to the courtyard. In the dim light, he could see a crowd of angry Avars bearing torches, their swords drawn in front of the ruined door of the stable. In the breach stood Liudolf with three other men, swords flashing, shields locked together before the entrance. Others stood in a second rank behind the shattered wood. Already one Avar lay bloodied on the ground before the door.

"Tudun! We must get the tudun." Sebastian shouted as Eric came running up. He ran back to rouse the sleeping interpreter and set him straightaway to find the tudun. Meanwhile, both Eric and Sebastian got hastily into their chain mail and retrieved their weapons. Just as they were about to charge out into the fray in the courtyard, the tudun bustled up frantically with a squad of armed guards. He burst out into the courtyard and, in a surprisingly booming voice for such a small man, cried out "Stop at once! Or die by my hand!" The attackers at the door jumped back as before a snake, and the tudun inserted himself between his men and Liudolf's defenders.

"What is the meaning of this?" he demanded. "These are our honored guests! For shame! Back away. Disperse—if you value your heads. And take this filth with you," he said, gesturing to their fallen comrade. He then revealed the curved sword he held beneath his cloak and took a menacing step toward the torchbearers. They faded reluctantly into the night.

As Eric and Sebastian came up, the tudun bowed low and apologized profusely through the interpreter. "My friends, I am mortified. You cannot know how ashamed this makes me. How can I ever atone to you for this insult? I assure you only the strong drink and the late hour are to blame. There will be no further unpleasantness during your visit here."

"That may be, sir," the duke said, gesturing to the men to lower their swords and stand down. "But this incident affirms what you told us at dinner. Unfortunately, there is ill will toward us among some of your people. We may no longer be entirely safe here. I think it is best that we take our leave as soon as possible. With your permission, my lord tudun, I will give orders for the troop to prepare to leave at once—well before dawn."

"But my friends, we have had no chance to discuss sufficiently the importance of the possibilities I proposed to you. How can I know if there is some hope of their fulfillment?"

"I can assure you, sir, without further reflection on the matter that we take your proposals most seriously, and we are disposed to present them favorably before our king. Sebastian here will be the messenger. He will fly with all haste and will swear on his life to bring them as soon as possible before King Karl with our witness of your good faith. Do you swear this, Sebastian?"

"I do indeed, my lord."

"Then we must be gone. Please give the order, my lord tudun, to clear a way for us through the fortress gates and grant us safe passage from your lands."

"I do as you ask, Duke Eric, and gladly—with the hope you will present me and my proposals for alliance and baptism favorably before your king."

"There's good hope that we can do as you ask. But we must go—and now!"

True to his word, the tudun obliged and the way was cleared in surprisingly quick time. The dark streets remained empty, and the gates opened magically as they passed through one ring after the other until all ten were behind them and the road to the west opened before them.

As they cantered through the last gate, Sebastian turned to Eric. "I'm sorry to say it, but I have the distinct feeling we may be out of the woodshed but definitely not out of the woods."

"I wish I could say I don't agree," Eric laughed. "But it's been a fine lark, has it not? What is life without a little excitement? It's exhilarating! But you're right, my dear friend, we may be truly in for it before this journey's done."

***

They traveled night and day, but on the last day, just as they were reaching the camp where they had left the rest of Eric's soldiers, their trailing scouts spotted a sizable Avar column following on the road behind in haste. They spurred into the camp at a gallop, shouting to the men to arm themselves and mount up at once.

As they watched the fast-approaching column, Eric grunted. "*Ach*, they've got three times our number. What now, Sebastian? Run or fight?"

"The Avars are born horsemen and superb horse breeders. Their warhorses are incredibly hardy and tireless. I think we'd better not let them catch us on the run."

"My thoughts exactly. See that steep hill a short distance behind us? It looks like there's a brook in front of it and to one side. If we can manage to get onto it and arrange our battle order before they're upon us, we've got a good chance."

They raced for the hill, and having gained it, Sebastian ordered the troop to dismount on the other side of the small rill. While some held the horses, other soldiers strung their bows and knelt. The Avars did not even hesitate; they attacked at once, peeling straight out of their column into a broad front three lines deep and taking the hill at a gallop.

"Look at that, Sebastian," Eric cried. "It's a beautiful thing to watch."

"A bit scary, I'd say. They're using those stirrups I told you about. Look at the control it gives them! Extraordinary discipline!"

But the hill was too steep and the ditch through which the small stream ran too deep. It narrowed the Avar front and funneled the riders into a cramped passage in the middle, slowing their charge critically. When they were in range, Sebastian gave the order, and the bowmen cut down the horses of the front line with arrows before they were halfway up the hill. As more horses fell, the Avars struggled to push the rest of the cavalry through the gap. When they reached the ditch, the horses faltered completely, and their leader called them back, dismounted the squadron, and came at the Franks again, this time on foot. Behind a stout shield wall, the Franks put up a prickly fence of spears and javelins, turning the Avars back twice.

"I would say they fight much better on horseback," Eric called as the enemy again backed down the hill.

"That may be, but now they're all coming at once. Steady, men! Keep the shield wall tight."

The Avars ran up the hill in a mass, crazed and howling like wolves, and it was down to the swords. The Huns used a wicked looking curved sword with a single edge, very sharp but not as long or as heavy as the famous Frankish *gladius*. Their armor was also not as good, with many of them wearing only thick leather coats and turbans instead of chain mail and iron helmets.

During a pause in the fighting, the duke yelled to Sebastian, "Cutting them up pretty badly, wouldn't you say?

"Right, my lord, but they're bleeding us, too. We're losing too many men. Let's mount and ride them down."

Eric simply gave the order, "To the horses," and they drove downhill into the Avars while they were reorganizing. For a brief while it was madness, but the Franks waded into them furiously, killing horses and men alike. The blood and noise finally unnerved the Avars, and they broke and ran, some on horseback, but many just footing it hastily down the road.

Liudolf drew up beside Sebastian, Avar blood covering his face and right arm. "I would say that was a bit desperate.

And a considerable gamble, if I may say so. Is this what being a paladin is going to mean from now on?"

"Well, it worked, didn't it? Took the heart right out of them. And yes, I suppose this is what we're meant to do, damn it. Do you want to live forever? Come on, let's get out of here."

Chapter 14

The Seeds of Greed

The King's Court at Worms, Winter 790

Pannonia, Spring 791

"Well, what did you find out?" The king demanded as soon as Sebastian entered his receiving room. Charlemagne was edgy and somewhat distracted. The rumors and bad reports about the Avars had been growing, and he did not as yet know what to do about it.

"Duke Eric sends you his greetings, my lord king, and regrets he could not ride here with me. But we were a long time away from Friuli, and he had much to do upon our return."

"Yes, yes. I'm sure he did. But get to it; what did you find out about the Huns? Are they going to be another blasted problem for me?"

"Eventually, perhaps, sire, but the most important thing we learned was that the Avars appear to be on the verge of a civil war right now and don't seem to pose as serious a threat to us as we thought, at least for the moment."

"Well, that's a relief! But how can you know that? Did you get in there?"

"We did, sire, I can say that Duke Eric and I and some of our soldiers may have been the first Franks ever to have been inside the Ring City."

"Good Lord! You went that far and you still have your heads? Sit down. Tell me, tell me!"

"The good news is there's an interim commander in Pannonia called the tudun. He's the local governor in the west, and for now he's in command of their capital, the Ring City—

the Hringum, as they call it, just to the east of the lower Danube River. Apparently this tudun is afraid of what might happen to him if there is a civil war. He feels in danger and wants to offer himself to you, sire, as an ally and friend. He said he's even ready to be baptized a Christian."

"Oh, wonderful, another bloody pagan like the Saxons who thinks one can take a religion on and off as if it were some kind of cloak. Well, go on."

"The first thing to know, perhaps, is that the Avars are not the invincible horde we once thought them to be. They've been beaten in the east by the Bulgars and are being pushed westward. They no longer threaten Constantinople, and the Greeks have refused to pay them their annual bribe."

"Well, fancy that—the Greeks actually being able to hang onto some of their gold for a change."

"Afraid not, sire. We heard the emperor is now having to pay the Bulgars or fight them, and he's doing no better at that than he did against the Avars."

"Ah, of course. It's to be expected from that dotty beggar. Go on."

"The second important thing is that the Avars are deeply divided among themselves. Their leader, the great khagan, still controls the kingdom, but he finds himself confronted by a potential successor, a fellow called the jugur. The tudun hinted to us that this man is the reason for the confusion that's immobilizing the Avars. The jugur seems to be the heir to the khaganate. He's somehow related to the present khagan, and he doesn't want to wait until his kinsman dies. The tudun thinks the man is the spark that will ignite a civil war among the Avars.

"We heard the fight over the succession will be soon. When that's decided, there's a good chance the Avars will resume their raids on our territory. They live by raiding and plundering, and our southern provinces are their best choice now."

"Well, what do you and Eric think of this tudun?"

"I think we can use him, sire. He gave us his sons as hostages. They're still with the duke now. The tudun wants to send emissaries to meet with you. It's possible he might even smooth our way into Avarland if you should choose to exploit their weakness."

"No, thank you. I don't want anything to do with any more wild pagans. It's enough we've had to fight the Saxons for thirty years. What we need to do is build up a strong march between us and them. Only go against them if we have to punish them for some reason and then get back out as soon as possible. I certainly don't need any more territory. Besides, if we try to take over Avarland, we'll be up against the Bulgars and Greeks in no time. Where does it end?"

"Sire, there's another factor you may wish to consider. As I said, the Avars are divided. Half of them want to make war on you. We barely escaped with our lives when some of the tudun's enemies attacked us on the road home. His sons said they were the jugur's men, and they're the ones who've been raiding into Bavaria and Friuli. The tudun also said he thinks they actually made an informal agreement for alliance with Duke Tassilo against Friuli and the Franks in general."

"I knew it! There's already plenty of proof against that confounded scoundrel. Now we have more. We were right to bury Tassilo in a monastery with his head shaved. How could he have had anything to do with those brutes? I should have relieved him of his head, cousin or no."

"One more thing, sire: Duke Eric and I have seen the Avar treasure."

"What? How'd you do that? Does it really exist?"

"My lord king," Sebastian said, shaking his head at the memory of the enormous horde, "the treasure from just one of their storehouses would fill most of this great room with more gold, silver, and jewels than you have ever seen. It far surpasses the Saxon treasure we found under their Irminsul holy tree. It's impossible to imagine unless one sees it."

The king fell silent, mouth agog. Sebastian continued. "But even should one want to take it, we're not actually at war with the Avars, and even if we were, they are still very formidable fighters, my king. I'm sure those were elite troops we fought on the way back, and if there are many more like them, we would have our hands full, especially if the khagan settles his quarrel with the jugur and is free to move against Friuli or Bavaria.

"And the Ring City itself is a mighty stronghold. Once one gets past the outer wall, there are nine more layers of circular earthworks to overcome. It will be no easy matter to take it."

"Hmm," the king mused, stroking his mustaches, his gaze turned toward the window. "Something to think about, though, isn't it, old son?"

Sebastian could almost feel the wheels turning in the king's head. From his original hard position, the king was beginning to wrap his mind around the possibilities of a completely different course in Pannonia. It struck Sebastian that he had never seen the king with such a hungry look in his eye.

***

It did not take long for Charlemagne to make a decision. After Christmas, he began making plans to use the Avar conspiracy with Tassilo and the "outrage" of their raids into Friuli as justification for war. By early summer, he had launched a full-scale invasion of Pannonia.

Once more, the king sent Sebastian south to meet with Duke Eric. This time, however, they rode at the head of a mixed force of five hundred Frankish and Lombard soldiers, all heavily armed mounted warriors, picked from the best men available in the duchy. And they were not riding to gather information. They were the advance guard of a much larger army led by Charlemagne's third son, King Pepin of Italy.

Sebastian was not happy with the king's decision to invade Pannonia. He couldn't avoid a nagging sense of guilt that he and Eric had promised the tudun to make a good case for him to the king, but Charlemagne had never mentioned the tudun's offer again, and when Sebastian brought it up, he brushed it off, saying that he would consider it later.

"Here we go again, Sebastian," Eric said casually as they rode through the Dolomites toward the Pannonian Plain. "This time we'll be looking for a fight, and I expect we shall find it."

"It makes me wonder if the king even listened to me when we came back last time with the tudun's offer. Instead of seeing this as a sign of Avar weakness, he's claiming it's some kind of ruse the Avars are cooking up to deflect our concerns about them. When I objected, he said he'd come to think 'those Hunnic savages' just might be the greatest threat he's ever faced. I don't know if he really believes that or if it's something else. I suspect it may be the Avar treasure he wants more than anything. Why else would he assemble three armies to attack Pannonia along the Danube and send us, a fourth army, to do the same from the south?"

"Well, they *are* the Avars. At one time, their empire stretched from the Mare Balticum to the steppes of Slavic Rus. Once, they even attacked Constantinople itself."

"I'm not convinced they still have that kind of power. But the king insists on magnifying the threat. All winter he's been calling in troops from all over the kingdom to the assembly in Regensburg. It's the largest force he's ever gathered. You wouldn't believe the noise and commotion. I couldn't wait to get out of there—even if it means another fight in Pannonia."

"Hopefully, we can avoid a pitched battle. Our job is only to create a diversion here in the south. If we do a quick job, we can cause some panic, make them think it's the main attack, and then get away before they respond in too much force."

"We'll be lucky to do that, Eric; you saw what horsemen they are. They won't be slow to respond."

"Perhaps not; it's in God's hands."

The way was long and tense with expectation. But Eric and Sebastian had become good friends. As on many a road to battle, they shared their personal stories. Eric had led a life of privilege and had always been expected to inherit leadership in the duchy. Still, it was no life of leisure. It was the Pannonian

March, and there was always struggle there, either with Avars or with the Slavs in the mountains to the south, who were forever trying to edge themselves onto better land by the sea or on the plains to the north. In all his ten years as duke, he had never spent a summer in peace. But he had held his ground, and the king knew his worth.

Sebastian was reluctant to share war stories with Eric. He found he could not be dispassionate about all the killing he had done in the cause of expanding the realm and defeating godless paganism. Eric, on the other hand, found it easy to believe that pagans were the devil's spawn and it was a Christian's duty to stamp them out.

Eric changed the subject. "I can't believe you haven't found yourself a new wife, Sebastian. You could, you know. If one's wife chooses the convent, a man is free to choose another."

"I don't want another."

"Well, yes, I understand that you loved her deeply. But is it good for you to be alone? No one to comfort you, no one to share your burdens? No one to give you pleasure?"

"There is pleasure to be found anywhere, Eric. If I succumb to a need for it from time to time, it's not something I really care about or even remember."

"I see. But you could have many fine ladies if you wanted. Who knows, one of them might fill the void Adela has left in you. Even the queen was interested in you, I've heard."

Sebastian started and said nothing for a long moment. "I'm not sure what you have heard, my lord. But I never overstepped my bounds with her despite what some people may have said. I did encounter her from time to time, and once or twice she tried to know me better. But I never responded."

"I'm sure you didn't, my friend. Take no note. I am only concerned about your welfare. In the work that you and I do, without some support or human comfort, it would be easy to succumb to the loneliness and violence and become more like an animal than a Christian man."

"What about you, Eric, don't you feel the same need for a woman to give you comfort and assuage your loneliness?"

"No. I am close to my God, as I told you. That's enough for me. Besides, I don't expect to live a long time."

Later Sebastian reflected at length on this conversation, pondering his role as a king's paladin. He already felt he had been too long at it. The king pulled him like a sword whenever he needed answers to thorny questions or a bold spokesman in a strange environment. It was true that he had had precious little time to feel sorry for himself about Adela or spend much time thinking of vengeance on Konrad. But the long missions, filled with strife and violence, did not make for an ordinary life. He needed always to be on guard, it seemed, never able to relax. Liudolf and Heimdal could see it; they often told him that he was too edgy and quiet. Archambald had almost stopped trying to cheer him up with funny stories or jests. The other day he had even scolded Sebastian for being "stiff and cynical." Sebastian wondered how he had come to be that way and how he might find his way back to what he had been when they were boys. They were his closest friends, and he mourned that he could not seem to recover the carefree camaraderie that he once had with them.

He did occasionally see his sons. Adela had tearfully released the younger boys from her care in the convent at Bischoffsheim, and they were now immersed in their grandfather's school for warriors at Andernach.

Milo, now a tall, strong young lad of sixteen years, was by far the top scholar of Alcuin's pupils in the famous palace school at Aachen. Even the king knew his quality and praised him often to Sebastian. He said that Alcuin told him the lad knew more and reasoned better than many of his teachers. Milo had Alcuin's gift of cutting through the complexity of academic questions to the heart of the matter, often providing the simplest of answers. His peers and teachers held him in high esteem. But Milo never failed to remind his father of the promise that they would one day journey "to see the world" together.

***

As they rode through the hills and low mountains of western Pannonia, they noted much evidence of Slavic settlement.

"What do you make of all these Slavic villages we've been passing through, Eric? There don't seem to be any Avar settlements so far."

"I'm told the Croats are gradually moving down from the mountains looking for rich soil in Pannonia. They've paid for their access through alliance with the Avars and are largely subject to them. But I know they don't like them. I have some good contacts among the Slavs. We may be able to use them eventually."

But the course of Eric's brigade had not gone unreported. Four days later, they spotted the first Avar horsemen.

"Uh-oh, Sebastian, it appears we're not going to get much farther. I'd better start looking for a good place to fight while you scout the roads to the north. We don't want to be surprised."

Sebastian took a small troop and was not gone half a day before they came thundering back.

"They're coming! Hundreds of them. We'll be outnumbered, and they'll be on us soon. If I know them, they'll come right at us, right out of their columns into attack formation."

Eric had not had time to set up fortifications, but he had found a reasonable defensive position. He butted the baggage train and spare horses up against a rare evergreen forest growing by a deep brook and positioned the mounted warriors in close ranks, three lines deep, in front of it.

"I think, my esteemed comrade," he said calmly as Sebastian finished turning his troop about, "that it's time to try your famous stirrups in actual battle. Thank God you insisted that we practice with them. When they get within bow range, we'll charge right down on them. We won't wait. They will prick us full of arrows from a distance if we give them half a chance."

Eric and Sebastian went among the men, admonishing every troop leader and sergeant to hold a tight, shoulder-to-shoulder formation in the charge. If a horse went down or a rider fell, another from a rear rank was to fill the gap immediately. They insisted the lines must remain intact and solid.

A cloud of dust announced the arrival of the Avar host. True to Sebastian's prediction, the long line of horsemen transitioned smoothly from column to battle formation. Then the Avars did what they were famous for and filled the air with arrows, fired at full gallop from the backs of their horses.

Sebastian wasted no time in sounding the charge. What the Huns saw next was iron clad men on huge horses pounding down upon them in close-packed lines, their long spears bristling in front like so many deadly thorns. Despite the shower of arrows, the Franks, riding downhill, closed the gap in seconds, skewering riders and bowling horses over as by a boulder rolling through grass. Wave after wave of Frankish horsemen crashed into the Avar mass of warriors, finally splitting and scattering them.

Eric, with a troop of two hundred men in reserve, watched the collapse and split his force to each side of the battle arena to begin the mop up of the sundered enemy. The fight had lasted less than half an hour.

"Praise God!" Eric shouted, laughing exuberantly. "That was a lark. We hardly lost a man!"

And that was the way their campaign went throughout the southern part of Pannonia, all the way up to the great Lake of Balaton. They burned Avar villages and crops, fought when an enemy appeared, and laid waste to the countryside. Oddly, no other large forces came against them. It was as if there was no coherent response to the Frankish invasion.

The tudun's predictions kept running through Sebastian's brain as he considered how comparatively easy the campaign had been so far. The Avars seemed to have given up after a halfhearted fight. They seemed completely demoralized. And yet messages from the king ordered them to continue laying waste to the countryside. There had to be a larger reason behind the general Frankish success, Sebastian thought. One evening around a campfire after a four-day lull without any fighting, he voiced his concerns.

"Do you wonder if this is right, Eric? I mean, do we really need to destroy everything to defeat them? So far, aside from a few lopsided engagements with cavalry, we've only seen poor peasants."

"I've given up long ago questioning the king. I only know he's making life better for Christian Franks. If these miserable pagans oppose him, so much the worse for them. I don't think about them. I just do what the king wants. And he must want this badly; he's gathered the largest army he's ever assembled. I hear he brought troops all the way from Frisia and Aquitania. He's even conscripted those Saxon units that came over to us. And the dispatch rider who came in this morning from Italy says the king is moving east on both sides of the Danube and that he's even got barges in the river so he can transfer troops easily from one side to the other."

"Yes," Sebastian added, "and did you hear him say that King Karl stopped the army for three days at the Enns River border to celebrate Mass and pray for God's blessing? He even led a barefoot procession before Mass, with all the troops singing the Kyrie Eleison. He made all his war captains go to confession and decreed that the troops should fast and pray fervently. He's never done all that before a campaign, as far as I know."

"To answer your question, Sebastian, I don't think the king is thinking about the right or wrong here. He's just bloody determined to trounce the Avars, whatever it takes."

Yes, and why? Sebastian thought—it's the bloody treasure that's behind all this bloodshed. He regretted he'd ever seen it or told the king about it.

***

With Eric and Sebastian leading the way, King Pepin's southern army enjoyed staggering success. Whatever sporadic resistance appeared was quickly vanquished. Hundreds of prisoners were taken as Avar outposts, and their Slavic allies simply threw down their arms. The vaunted Hunnic war machine seemed broken.

Pepin sent word at once to the king about the success of the southern column and that they had reached Lake Balaton, halfway through the Pannonian Plain. It provided Charlemagne with the impetus he needed to inspire the army for a decisive battle.

As it turned out, he hardly needed it. As in the south, everywhere the king's army went, the Avars faded before him. The army penetrated as far as the River Raab, deep into the Avar homeland. But then an inexplicable phenomenon occurred. The horses all throughout Charlemagne's army began to die.

Eric's advance force was camped upon the shores of the lake awaiting further orders when the disaster struck. "Good Lord! What's wrong with your horse, Sebastian?" the duke inquired as Sebastian knelt beside Joyeuse's prostrate body.

"I don't know, but he's dying." The stallion lay covered with sweat, every breath a labored moan. Sebastian's face was a wretched map of grief. "I've had him for more than twenty years. I've never had a better friend. He's saved my life countless times—never failed me. What can I do?"

"I have no idea, Sebastian. How can it be? He's such a strong old boy."

"That's just it. He's old, and we've been using our mounts heavily these last few weeks, but I think it's more than that. I've tried everything; he doesn't respond. There's something else wrong."

Joyeuse died the next day with Sebastian still by his side. Eric's horse also died. Suddenly, more than half the horses of King Pepin's entire force were either sick or dying.

"It's a pestilence, Sebastian. The northern army has fared even worse. The last courier said the king has already lost ninety percent of his warhorses, and he's using the barges on the Danube and forced marches to pull the whole army out of Pannonia as soon as possible—before the Avars get wind of what's happened.

"You must leave the horse. We've got to go. We've no idea where the enemy is and whether he's still capable of attacking us."

"You don't understand, Eric. My father gave me this horse when I was little more than a boy. He's been with me through everything. I care for him more than I do for most people, and I can't suffer to leave him for the crows. I want to bury him."

"Listen, my friend, there's no time. "We must go now."

"I'm sorry, Eric; you go. I'm going to bury my horse. I can't just walk away; I must do something to honor him. You go on; I'll catch up, I promise."

When Eric reluctantly led the Lombard men away, four men remained with Sebastian.

"Well, what did you expect?" Liudolf said casually. "We knew this old warrior as well as you."

"We did, Lord Sebastian," Bardulf chimed in. "Why, it was him what saved our lives that time them bandits wanted to make robbers of me and Drogo or kill us instead. We'll help ye bury him, m'lord. And with a good will."

And so Liudolf and Archambald, his oldest friends, and his steadfast servants, Bardulf and Drogo, shoveled through the night, making a hole big enough for the great stallion. Then they jerked and pulled Joyeuse's body an inch at a time into the grave and covered him up. As they trudged away to find cover and rest, Sebastian said a prayer of thanksgiving for the gift of the wonderful animal. He found himself profoundly sad but warmly comforted by the act.

As Sebastian and his men caught up with the southern army, they discovered that their survival was due to the same disease that paralyzed the Franks; the horses of the whole Avar nation were dying with the same incredible suddenness.

Thus Charlemagne's grand design was dashed by an mysterious equine disease, and the Avar campaign that had begun so auspiciously for the Franks came abruptly and ignominiously to an end. Sebastian could not help but think that it might be God's judgment on the king.

Chapter 15

Pepin the Hunchback

The King's Court at Regensberg and Worms

Fernshanz 792 – 794

Charlemagne retreated to Regensburg in Bavaria to lick his wounds and plan another foray into Pannonia for the coming year. During their occasional meetings, Sebastian realized with chagrin that the king had not been put off at all by the failure of his campaign. He was even more obsessed with the Avar treasure. He could talk of little else.

Sebastian usually had precious little information to pass on to his sovereign about the situation in Pannonia, but recently he had received a letter from Duke Eric, and the king was keen to know what was in it.

"Well, what's the word? What's Eric say about how the civil war's going? Damn it, I'd love to get back in there before the khagan patches things up with that jugur fella."

"Sire, the tudun's men say the Avars have been hit with the horse disease just as badly as we were. It's a huge epidemic, and it's brought the fighting to a standstill. The khagan has never returned to the Ring City, not even for a visit."

The king roared with approval. "That *is* good news! Now if we can just recover before they do. I'm staying put here, Sebastian—not wintering in Worms this year. We're going back to Pannonia as soon as we can get enough horses. Can't go down and fight cavalry without warhorses. We want to get down there to the Ring City before someone else walks off with that treasure. What do you think, old lad? Can we pull it off?"

Sebastian shifted uncomfortably on his feet and looked out of the window before replying. He had been in this position many times before: not happy with the course Charlemagne was taking but having to move very carefully to avoid stepping on the king's toes. In this case, it was fairly clear that the king's mind was made up. But Sebastian plunged in nevertheless in the hope that he might temper the king's sanguinary approach to the Avar nation.

"My lord king, have you had a chance to see the Avar emissaries from our friend the tudun?

"Not yet. No time. I'm not sure I want to see them."

"Sire, if we gave the tudun a chance, he might pull half the Avars over to an alliance with us. And we wouldn't have to lay waste to the countryside or lose men fighting unnecessarily. He certainly seems very eager for it."

"That might be, Sebastian, but the bugger would want me to stay out of Pannonia, and we'd lose our chance to capture that treasure you found. Do you realize how much that great pile of plunder would mean to us? I could pay everything I owe, build my great capital at Aix, and give a boost to the army, too!

"Besides, they're only one faction. How do we know we can trust them? They're all bloody pagans anyway. The Avars would probably be no better at keeping their word than the Saxons. Enough about that now. We're going, and that's all there is to it—and as soon as we can muster the men and horses."

Sebastian took a deep breath and tried a different tack. "Sire," he said in a low voice, easing into the subject carefully. "I hate to mention it, but I'm sure your counselors have told you how bad last year's harvest was."

"Well, what of it?" the king replied irritably. "We've had bad harvests before."

"Yes, sire, but if it's as bad as they say, there'll be famine. And if there's famine, there will be precious few horses for a campaign."

"Bugger all, Sebastian! Why do you always have to be so pessimistic? We don't know yet if there will be famine. Or how bad it'll be."

"I'm sorry to be the bringer of bad news, my liege, but couriers from my own lands at Fernshanz and Adalgray tell me the villagers are already near starving, and they're begging at the manor house for grain. If it's that way all over the land, you won't be facing just starvation; you'll be looking at upheavals and possibly revolt."

"I know, I know," the king conceded. "There's always strife when there's famine. I'm already getting reports that the Saxons are restless again, and there are even nasty incidents occurring down in Italy. It's that damned Duke of Benevento again. He uses any excuse to draw away from me. He knows I can't come down there right now. If I could, I'd stick a sword up his arse and shave his ruddy beard for him. I'd like to do just that—will, too, someday."

The king paused for a long moment, staring absentmindedly into the fireplace. He finally turned and said in a low voice, "Listen, old son, what I'm about to tell you I don't want anyone else knowing—no one, you hear?"

"Certainly, my lord king."

"You're probably right, much as I hate to admit it. We may not be able to return to Pannonia this year or next year either, devil take it. I know these are already looking like bad times. And bad times breed evil. There are some ugly rumors floating about concerning my son, Pepin. You know—Pepin the Hunchback, my first son—the illegitimate one? You've noticed he's not here with me in Bavaria?"

"I hadn't remarked it, sire, but now that you mention it, I realize I haven't seen him. I know he's usually with you at court."

"Right, but he didn't come with me this time—said he was ill and wanted to stay in Worms where he could recover better. Hmph! Thing is—a mongrel set of nobles from Thuringia and Upper Franconia have stayed behind as well, for various suspect reasons. This isn't the first time. I let them stay because that lot's never much good on the battlefield anyhow, and I hate having them around me. But now I hear they've been chumming up to Pepin. I want to know what that's about." He paused again, slowly beating a fist into the other hand. "Can you go up there to Worms and find out for me, Sebastian? I mean, you can't go up there as yourself— you'd have to be invisible somehow. You think you could do that?"

Sebastian hesitated, realizing with a sinking heart that this new mission would mean he wouldn't be able to go home and take care of his people at Fernshanz and Adalgray, with whom he felt the deepest attachment. Finally, he gave in, as always. He would send Liudolf and Archambald back with strict orders to feed the peasants as long as the surplus in the barns lasted and then to head down to Andernach and get more help from Duke Gonduin, whose barns were many and always full.

"Well, sire, I make a fairly good monk, I suppose. I went all over Brittany in a robe and cowl with my head shaved, remember? Perhaps I might do that again."

"Splendid! Do that. There are plenty of monks at my palace at Worms. They say they're there to study and pray for me, etcetera. But I think they just like their meals a bit tastier than at the monastery. Anyway, go up there for me and listen in. Keep your eyes open. Watch my son and who he talks to. If there's a hint of smoke, we'll know there's a flame somewhere."

"I'll leave in the morning, sire."

"One more thing, Sebastian." The king looked away and cleared his throat. "It's Fastrada."

"The queen, sire?"

"Yes, damn it! I'm getting reports about her, too. Many of my nobles don't like her. They say she's disruptive— always trying to wriggle herself into their confidences, promising wildly inappropriate things. And when they pointedly back away from her, she turns against them and spreads the damnedest rumors about them. Fastrada has always been ambitious and a bit conniving. But now. . ." he paused again to look earnestly at Sebastian. "Now I've heard she's talking to those same nobles Pepin is. Go up there and find out what's going on, all right? See if it's true—about either one of them."

***

"Count Sebastian? My God, is that you? I almost didn't recognize you through that beard—and in monk's clothing? What on earth are you doing?"

"Hush, Fra Fardulf. Come with me."

Sebastian had spent an hour peering through a narrow window onto the colonnade passage from the palace to the chapel. He wanted to make sure none of the monks passing by would know him. In Worms, he had little to do with the clerics' community and less with the many monks who came and went when the king's court was in Worms. But he needed to be certain.

Finally, he did recognize one. It was Fardulf, a Lombard Benedictine who had been visiting Duke Eric's community in Friuli. The duke liked Fardulf for his earnest faith and his insight into the contemplative life. They had spent one whole evening in his company talking about mystical transformation. Sebastian had been surprised at how interested Eric had been to hear Fardulf's account of such experiences. For his part, Sebastian doubted he could find the patience for such exercises.

"Listen, Fardulf. I'm really glad to see you. I'm here on special charge from the king. He has commanded me to look into the affairs of Prince Pepin and learn more about the men who surround him here. And I need your help. Do you trust me?"

"Of course, my lord Sebastian. But how can I be of any service?"

"I want you to deflect the attention of the other monks away from me. Tell them I'm a devout contemplative you met down in Friuli—which is at least partly true. Tell them I am on silent retreat and do not wish to distract myself through the company of others. I will probably spend a good deal of time in the chapel, 'praying,' as it were. I may obtain information that I will need to pass on to you in case something happens to me, or I may want to send a message. Will you do this for me? It's actually for the king, whom you also serve, right?"

"Well, of course, my lord, but I'm not..."

"Never mind, you'll do fine. I'll see you don't get into any trouble. Just look for me in the chapel from time to time and come and sit or kneel beside me."

Sebastian felt fairly secure taking Fardulf into his confidence. He was not a young or inexperienced monk. He had traveled a good deal seeking wisdom and had conferred with many of the best minds in the world of the Church. He had even met Alcuin and had spent a day sitting at his feet in the academy at Aix. Sebastian felt reasonably sure Fardulf would make a good ally.

"Where should I look, Fardulf? You've been here longer than I."

"Oh, it's not hard to find the prince, my lord. He always moves amidst a considerable entourage of hangers-on. He doesn't hunt. Nor does he drink much. What I think he likes to do is hold court, as if he were the king. He invites anyone to come and see him and tell him their concerns. He even uses the throne room. The rest of the time he has receptions and wine parties in his own quarters and has his so-called friends come to him. If the king is not here, they meet in the throne room. But I've also seen them in the great hall and often in the chapel."

"And the queen—where do you see her?"

"Oh, she's everywhere. She likes to be seen, though she's not keen on talking to just anybody. It's mostly high-ranking visitors or young war captains. I've seen her several times with Prince Pepin and his friends."

"Really? Do you have any idea what they may be discussing?"

"Absolutely none, Count Sebastian. But they always seem very serious."

"Listen, Fra Fardulf. It's very important that the king knows what is being discussed by the prince and his friends just now. Even more so, what reason does the queen have to share their company? If you can find out somehow, the king would be very much in your debt. He would reward you handsomely, I know."

"Oh, I certainly will do as you say, my lord. But not for any gain; I do so because he is the king."

"Of course, my friend. I meant no offense. Just keep your eyes and ears open, then, and come to me as soon as you know anything. I think I shall be much in the chapel, experimenting with those, ah, contemplation methods we discussed that time in Friuli with Duke Eric."

"Ah, then, even if we learn nothing, your time will have been well spent," the monk said with just the hint of a smile.

Sebastian steeled himself for a long and possibly tedious watch. His base was the chapel, where everyone came at one time or another. He got used to spending a lot of time sitting on a bench or painfully kneeling for extended periods in a corner by the back wall.

He saw the prince often and in various places and studied him carefully, thinking to define his character enough to get a hint of what he might be doing. Sebastian was gratified to see that Pepin and his associates came often to the chapel when it was relatively quiet. They became used to seeing the monkish recluse praying in the far corner.

The king's son was not particularly personable, given to brooding moods and a perpetual sense of calumny and injustice. The hump on his back was not gross, but it was noticeable, even through the heavy cloak he always wore, winter or summer. He walked with a long face and disliked being looked at directly. Sebastian wondered how the king could love him. But apparently he did, for Charlemagne always spoke kindly of Pepin and defended him from insults and slights.

The breakthrough came suddenly one day when Pepin and his friends from the north burst into the chapel talking animatedly. They saw that the place was empty except for the solitary monk praying on his knees in the far back corner of the chapel.

"Who is that fool back there?" one of the men said. "He's always in here."

"Oh, it's only an old monk," another said. "He just sleeps and prays. Not to worry."

A tall, thin man with long hair and mustaches stepped forward as the prince came in. Bowing low, he said in a clear voice, "Your Grace, it is time we act. And we must know that you are with us."

Another interrupted loudly, "Your Grace, it is an outrage. Have you seen what your father has just decreed regarding the nobility? He has announced that he intends to 'check the abuses of the local nobility,' and that's not all— every count, every land owner, must take a new oath, not only to the king but to his sons. But not yourself, my lord prince, I'm sorry to say. He means the sons of Hildegard only."

The complaints and solicitations continued by others: "He means to castrate us, take away our right to control our own lands!"

"He wants too much from us. We can no longer follow him to his endless wars or support them."

"There is famine in the land. We must look to our own affairs."

"Your Grace, these are desperate times. We must remove the king if he will not hear us."

Pepin drew in his breath sharply at this last comment and took a step backward. The chapel fell into dead silence. At length, the shaken prince turned his back and started to walk away from the group, one hand over his mouth.

A voice called after him in calmer tones, "Your Grace, you must think of yourself. The king intends to remove you permanently from any chance of succession. You will remain forever on the outside. And we, my lord prince, will be forced to shoulder an even greater burden to support his wars. We cannot do so, sir! We are already faced with revolt in our own lands. We must do something!"

"Yes, yes. I understand," Pepin exclaimed, pacing up and down between the door and the front of the altar. "But. . ."

"Your Grace, we are not alone. There are many, many of us. All we need is a stronger legitimacy—a royal connection . . . yourself—or the queen."

Silence hung over the room. Finally, another voice spoke up, "Prince, it is true, even the queen is sympathetic to the idea."

Pepin's mouth fell open, and he drew in his breath again sharply, as if steeling himself against pain. "I cannot say. I don't know. I must think. Let me think. I will tell you tomorrow," he said and rushed out of the room.

***

Sebastian was afraid to move a muscle for a quarter hour after all had left the chapel. He could not believe what he had heard. This cannot be true. Whether it was or not, the queen was in grave danger. He had to find her at once.

He set himself to watching through the little window off the busy colonnade walkway. Finally, the queen passed by on her daily stroll through the palace, but she was not alone. He had to follow her from a distance until she finished the walk with her ladies and entered a central garden. He watched as the ladies chatted, wandering from one bed of flowers to another. Then he slipped into the garden and hid himself in a small grove of birch trees. Eventually, Fastrada moved away from the chatter of the group and came near the birch grove. Sebastian stepped out quickly and revealed his bearded face beneath the cowl.

"You," she gasped. "What on earth?"

Sebastian motioned for her to be silent and follow him into the grove. When she did, he grasped her by the hands and whispered, "My lady queen, you are in great danger. I must warn you. I must meet with you. It is of the utmost importance."

The queen looked around nervously, sensing the other women might at any moment break into the grove.

180

"Come to my quarters tonight," she said. "Do you know where they are?"

"I will find you. I will come when all is quiet."

Later, feigning a need to bring a message to the queen, Sebastian gave some coins to a servant girl and learned which rooms in the royal apartments were the queen's. He then sequestered himself behind a large decorative trunk in the corner of the waiting room of the apartments. When it was dark, and long after all activity had ceased in the hall, he made his way to the queen's rooms and furtively slid through her unlocked door.

The room was lit by a single candle. Fastrada was fully dressed this time. "Oh, Sebastian, I'm so glad to see you," she breathed as she took his hands. "But you have me in such a state. I don't know what to think. Come. Sit." She led him to a low couch, and sitting down with him, she continued to hold his hands. "Tell me now. Why do you say I'm in danger?"

"Your Grace, I have good reason to believe there is a plot to kill the king or somehow remove him as sovereign in Francia. Your name has been mentioned in connection with the plot."

"No!" She jumped back in horror. "Are you talking about the prince? That ugly crowd that's always around him? I'm not with them. Oh God! I was only there to visit the prince. I hardly know any of those other people. Sebastian, what must I do?"

"Tell me everything, Your Grace. Perhaps I can help. I want to help."

"Oh, Sebastian, it's true, I have been with the prince when he's had those men around him—those conniving sycophants! He likes their company because they flatter him. He invites them often for wine and talk. It's true. . . those men did disparage the king and belittle his accomplishments—even in my presence. I know that they grate under his control and wish themselves free of it. But you must believe me, I only thought it was their usual way of grumbling about things they cannot change. I laughed at them and dismissed their complaints as empty air. I never once thought they were serious."

"Did you ever. . . my queen, did you ever encourage them or agree with them? Did you sympathize with them or somehow give them the idea that you might approve?"

"Never!" She realized the import of Sebastian's questions and began to cry. "Sebastian, oh, my sweet Sebastian, please. What have I done? What must I do? I never meant to harm the king." She reached out and threw herself against him, wrapping her arms around his neck, sobbing into his robe and pressing her body against him. Sebastian had to brace himself just to remain upright. It was as if she wanted to get inside him and hide. If she was lying, it was a very convincing performance.

"You must believe me, Sebastian. I only went to those wine parties because I was angry and disappointed. The king has been paying less attention to me. He even shuns me sometimes. Not long ago, I discovered he has been sleeping with one his concubines. They say she even gave him another bastard. I have taken to traveling about more often because I hate to be at court and not see him or be ignored by him. I cannot bear his rejection and neglect." She began to weep uncontrollably once more and fastened herself more tightly to Sebastian.

So that was it, Sebastian concluded with relief. She was innocent. The king had simply grown tired of her, or was fed up with her petty meddling, and he had looked elsewhere for female companionship. It was enough. Sebastian was convinced.

"My queen, you mustn't. It will be all right. I will help. I'm sure you've done no real wrong. You just were seen with some evil men. We will deal with them, and you will be all right. I promise you. The king would never believe that you could be part of a conspiracy against him. I will assure him of that. I will do everything I can to deflect any blame from you. Please calm yourself. All will be well."

"Oh, Sebastian! How can I thank you? You are so good, so true." She pulled back slightly to look him in the eyes. "Do you know, my dear friend, I've always loved you—since the day we met. You are so kind, so brave. The king is often so indifferent to me. I wanted to be special. But he has never loved me the way he loved Hildegard—or the way you loved your Lady Adela once. I so envied her and your love for her. Couldn't you have a little love for me? I need someone to love me so much. I always wanted you so."

She wrapped her arms around him once again and fell backward, pulling him down upon her. She began kissing his face, neck, and mouth and thrusting her body into him. At first, he tried to disentangle himself, but then he felt himself losing control, almost as if intoxicated. It had been such a long time since he'd had a woman, especially one like Fastrada. Her closeness, her perfume, her hands upon his body made him weak but at the same time tremendously excited. He wanted her. He wanted to let himself go. After all, she needed him, she loved him—the queen loved him!

A bell rang in the nearby chapel. Its single clear peal snapped him back to awareness of what he was doing. The king's image burst into his head. "You are my paladin," the face said. "I trust you with my life."

Sebastian jumped back and quickly stood up.

"No, no, Sebastian, don't! Don't reject me again. I have nothing now." She began to cry again. "Please be here for me. Please let me love you. I need you so much. I need someone. . . someone who cares for me. Please say you do."

"My dear lady," Sebastian protested, holding up a hand and backing farther away from the couch. She was such a mercurial woman, always going too far. But he could see Fastrada was on the verge of falling apart. She was profoundly frightened, and she wanted to bind him to her, to ensure his help. He realized that if he was going to be able to get out of her quarters without a scene, he would have to calm her down and tell her whatever she needed to hear.

"I do," he stammered. "I do care for you—very much. There is nothing I'd rather do at this moment than love you—fully, with no reservations." He paused to let his words sink in. He even went back to her to hold her in his arms, feeling acutely uncomfortable with the subterfuge but knowing that it was the only way to keep her from panicking and making a serious mistake.

"But you know I cannot. I am sworn to the king, your husband. I can think of no greater crime than to betray him with his own wife. I'm sorry, but I cannot. But let me tell you this," he whispered into her ear, "if you were not the queen, I would fasten myself to you. I would love you completely. You are a remarkable woman. In my whole life, I have felt an attraction for only one other woman as strong as I feel for you. And she was my wife.

"Still, there is the king," he said, continuing to hold her and looking into her eyes as sincerely as he could manage. "I cannot betray him. I cannot fail him. You must understand. If I did, I could never again look him in the eyes. I would be less than nothing.

"I must go," he said, breaking away but continuing to hold onto one of her hands. "But let me warn you once again, my queen—you must distance yourself at once from the prince and his friends. I have seen and heard enough to know that they are dangerously close to treason, if they have not already committed it by their treacherous talk. If they go one step further and begin to organize, the king will know it. I am not his only eyes and ears here. Many are watching Pepin. Move away from him. Do not see him at all, my queen. If you can, leave here at once."

He stood a moment longer, looking into her eyes. Impulsively, he took both her hands, pulled her up to him, and wiped the tears from her eyes. Then he kissed both her hands, backed away with a bow, and left the room, guiltily acknowledging to himself that most of what he had said to her was lies but realizing that he did have genuine feelings for her—of physical attraction, of sympathy for her plight, and of gratitude that she seemed to genuinely care for him.

The next morning, Sebastian conferred briefly with Fardulf. He passed on all that he had heard in the chapel but confided that he had found no evidence whatsoever linking the queen with the conspirators. He enjoined the monk to continue to monitor the prince and his associates and wait until a courier came from the king ordering him to court.

Then Sebastian simply walked barefoot to the gate and out of the palace like a mendicant monk so as to raise no suspicions. He went into the town, bought a farm horse at the first market he saw, and rode the clumsy animal until he reached the village outside Worms where Liudolf and the others of his band awaited him. From there, they set off again to Regensburg and the king.

***

"Are you sure the queen was not involved?" the king said, rising out of his seat like a thundercloud and towering over Sebastian. "You said she was seen with them."

"Yes, Your Grace. She did go to some gatherings the prince had for his friends. But you know the queen, she goes wherever she likes and is at ease in almost any venue. She enjoys the company of men and loves to hear talk of their doings. But I am absolutely sure, sire, she is not part of the plot."

"That's not what your man, that monk Fardulf, says. He says she left Worms in a fluster one morning. She could not leave fast enough. Later he heard those men bringing her name up in their conversations. But, like you, he was not certain she was involved."

"Sire, I am certain she was not. They may have spoken her name; they may even have approached her, and that could be why she left so quickly. But there's absolutely no proof she was in league with them."

"Ah, we'll see. She's coming here soon. I'll find out one way or another. Meanwhile, I want to thank you, Sebastian, for exposing this rotten thing. It was a very great service to me, and I want to reward you handsomely. What would you like—another holding perhaps, something in Saxony, maybe? I already owe you so much. I'd be happy to give you half of Pannonia after we beat them."

"No thank you, my lord king. But there is one thing you can give me. It's all I want."

"And what is that, lad?"

Sebastian seized the moment. He couldn't wait to get the bitter taste of court intrigue and betrayal out of his mouth and go home to simpler, cleaner tasks. He was missing formative time in the growth of his boys. Milo was almost eighteen and ready to go out on his own. The younger boys were thriving and he wanted to connect with them again. And the plight of his people in the midst of this period of famine bedeviled him constantly.

"I want a leave of absence again, sire. I need to go home for a good while, see to my lands, especially in this time of famine. And I need to see my sons. For the most part, they've been growing up without me."

"Oh, that's it, is it? Well, I'm a bit disappointed. But of course you can have some time. Take as much as you want. There's nothing so urgent at the moment. Before you go, however, I want you to let me celebrate you, at least among my leaders. You're a splendid example of service and loyalty to your king."

"Please don't, my liege. If you want to thank someone, thank Fardulf. He helped me find out what we needed to know, and he brought additional proof after I left. He's the one who should be rewarded. Besides, if you tell everyone what I do for you, it'll be harder for me to do such things again."

"I suppose you're right about that, old son. Good thinking. Go ahead, then, and come back to me when you're ready. And mind you don't go looking for that scoundrel Konrad. I strictly forbid it!"

"No, my lord king."

"I'm sure it will be a year or more before we can go back to Pannonia. But I'm not giving up. We'll have that treasure if it's God's will. And I intend to make it easy for God to grant it to us," the king said with a boisterous laugh.

***

Surprisingly, Sebastian enjoyed a singular leave of absence from the court for a year and half. It was a godsend.

But it was no lark from the outset. When he returned in early autumn, first to Fernshanz and then to Adalgray, he found that the famine had begun the previous winter when the stores of wheat from the year before ran out before the warm weather. The previous year's wheat crop had been damaged severely by a heavy rain only a few days after the sowing, followed by a devastating frost. When they harvested in the summer, the yield was far too little. The harvest of barley in late summer was also damaged by floods of rain. Lintels and vegetables provided some winter stores, and the villagers tramped all over the nearby woods for mushrooms, wild apples and berries, acorns and other nuts, but it was still not enough to make up for the loss of wheat. Old people and children were the first to die, but the two manors also lost men and women in the prime of life from hunger and sickness caused by deprivation.

"Baumgard!" Sebastian shouted as he spotted the old man getting off the boat at the landing. He ran to meet the long-time former steward of Fernshanz who had retired to the Rhine port of Lippeham several years earlier. He returned now at Sebastian's special request, having lost none of his old flamboyant panache or bombastic speech.

"My gracious Lord Sebastian," the crimson-faced old man began, "count of two manors by the grace of God and the gift of our glorious king, legendary hero of the Frankish host, who are conquerors of the world! Well met, my lord! I come in great haste at your command, anxious to know how your humble servant might have the great honor to serve you once again." He ended, hands outspread and eyes to the sky, as if thanking God for a special gift.

Sebastian was so glad to see the hairy old fat man that he embraced him as soon as he stepped off the boat, much to the embarrassment of Baumgard.

"Baumgard, my old friend, I am so glad to see you! I thought you might be dead."

"Not so, my good lord! Not by half. 'Tis true I am retired after three score years of service, and I live modestly in a small room over an inn in Lippeham, where I lend my services and vast knowledge to one and all, whoever has need. Ah, it is a modest life, not so glorious as being steward of this wonderful and sublimely successful place, which, I might say, I had a small part in building."

"Ah, Baumgard, I wish it were as you describe. But Fershanz has fallen on very hard times. There's been a terrible famine, the crops have failed for the last two years, and people have died. We must do something before winter if we are not to face absolute disaster. Can you stay and help me? I know you might be. . . ah . . . a bit past your prime, but we could still use your famous knowledge of peasant husbandry to rescue us and bring us back to that former glory you mentioned—which, I might add, was indeed due to you in no small measure."

The old man was vastly pleased to be appealed to by his lord in such glowing terms and in front of a crowd of his former peasant underlings, and he agreed gleefully to serve temporarily as steward-emeritus of both Fernshanz and Adalgray until the crisis had been overcome. He rubbed his hairy old hands with glee and announced that he would "bring things aright or die in the pursuit!"

The first thing Sebastian and Baumgard did was travel to Andernach. Liudolf and Archambald, along with the stewards of both manors, had tried to get help from Count Gonduin, Sebastian's father-in-law. But Gonduin had been away with the king on campaign, and the Andernach steward had vehemently denied any help at all, claiming that Andernach itself was suffering terribly from the famine.

This time the old duke was in residence, and Sebastian quickly received almost everything he asked for. Gonduin had been exceptionally fond of Sebastian ever since he knew him as a boy, and he was particularly grateful to him for rescuing his only daughter from the clutches of the madman Konrad. He opened his barns and gave freely of both animals and grain, much to the consternation of his steward. But Andernach was one of the largest estates in Charlemagne's realm and still, even in hard times, a wealthy place with barns stuffed with reserves.

Baumgard provided most helpful advice. "Ask for pigs, my lord! Sows, as many as they'll give us. Healthy sows farrow twice a year, and they'll present us with as many as fourteen, perhaps even nineteen, delicious little piggies a year. And we could use some sheep if they have them. They are wonderful for their fleece, their milk, their meat, and their skins. Get a flock of 'em, if you can. Then ask for some geese—or at least geese eggs. A goose will give you at least five goslings a season, many eggs, too. And they are superbly tasty!

"And, my lord," he continued in a conspiratorial whisper, "I know it is much to ask, but seek to get the duke to give us some oxen. Ours have been severely weakened by two winters of poor diet. They can scarcely pull a plow. And, finally, my lord, we need seed. The peasants, bless 'em, have eaten into the sowing seed, and we won't have enough for the winter wheat this year."

It was a very large order, but Count Gonduin, too old now to care about amassing more riches, easily agreed to everything Sebastian asked. He even provided the barges and bargemen to transport the items downriver to Fernshanz and upriver to Adalgray. His generosity went a long way toward saving both estates.

But Sebastian and Baumgard performed some minor miracles of their own. Before leaving Andernach, and once again at Lippeham on the way home, they went along the waterfront wharves and inns recruiting cotters and farm laborers who had lost their farms or abandoned a failing manor. They congregated in the ports along the Rhine, desperately seeking any kind of work. Sebastian engaged two score of freemen for each estate because there was so much work to be done before winter and so few hands. He and Bardulf and the blacksmiths of both manors devised wheels for the deep plows, using iron obtained from Duke Gonduin. The innovation enabled the peasants to control the depth of each furrow by adjusting the wheels, thereby saving much labor time.

Once back at home, Baumgard drove the peasants, working them many nights past the vespers quitting time. But Sebastian ordered a whole sheep butchered and roasted once a week and fed the peasants directly in the fields around a bonfire each day after the work was done. And he often organized feast days, providing meager fare but adding much to the dreary life of the peasants. It was drudgery for a long time, but Sebastian and his comrades worked as hard as the peasants, alternating between Fernshanz and Adalgray. They created an atmosphere of justice, hope, and progress, and after one year, it was clear they had begun to reverse their fortunes.

Sebastian brought his sons up to Fernshanz whenever he could pry them away from their grandfather at Andernach. He relaxed. Life returned almost to normal. The images of his violent life as a paladin began to pale. Still, in the night, or on Sundays when there was no work, his loneliness returned, and he felt incomplete in spite of the presence of his children and friends.

***

During his time away from court, he kept abreast of the news through couriers and travelers who often stopped at Fernshanz or Adalgray. His friend Simon stayed with him a few days whenever he was in the north. On one occasion he learned the fate of Queen Fastrada.

Their meeting in Worms was the last time Sebastian saw the queen. But he heard of her from time to time, and he learned from Simon that from that time of crisis in Worms, she simply faded away. She no longer held a place of high regard at court and was rarely seen in the king's company.

The Lombard monk Fra Fardulf maintained his doubts about her, and when the conspirators were finally brought to account, they blamed the queen for their misfortune, claiming she encouraged them and then abandoned them with false accusations. They said her cruelty was what brought about their downfall.

Most of the authors of the plot were executed by the sword or by hanging, but Charlemagne spared his son. The unfortunate hunchback was tonsured and committed to a monastery for the rest of his life. Fardulf received the credit for exposing the conspiracy. As a reward, he was appointed abbot of the prestigious monastery of Saint Denis near Paris. Sebastian was never called to appear at the trial.

As for Fastrada, the king excluded her from all his councils and apparently from his affections as well. She wandered about for a time, visiting the villas of the few friends she had left, but most of the nobility distanced themselves from her.

Shortly before he returned to court, Sebastian learned that Queen Fastrada was dead. She was not even interred in the Basilica of Saint Denis, the burial site of almost all the other Frankish queens.

As he went about the mundane business of seeing to his estates, Sebastian mourned for her with great remorse because he had been unable to save her from disgrace. He often remembered the last time he had seen her. She had been such a beautiful woman, so alive, so full of enthusiasm and energy, so passionate about everything she did. In spite of himself, he sometimes dreamed of her. But he eventually concluded sadly that Fastrada had simply gotten too close to the flame of power and reckoned wrongly that she could endure it and become part of it. Her ambition had destroyed her.

Chapter 16
Twilight of the Avars

Pannonia, 796

Revolt in Saxony plagued the king once more. For two years in a row he felt compelled to invade the Saxon lands and bring them to heel for breaking their treaties and renouncing their promises to become Christians. The Saracens had suddenly poured north over the Spanish mountains to raid and plunder in Septimania, and the Greek empress and her feeble son Constantine were attempting to dominate and change Church doctrine.

With so many concerns from multiple directions in his kingdom, Charlemagne resigned himself to pursue his objectives in Pannonia through other agents, particularly his son King Pepin in Italy and Duke Eric in Friuli. Once again he sent Sebastian to Friuli to be his agent and provide the spark for a new effort.

This time Sebastian traveled first to Rome with his usual band of comrades: Liudolf, Archambald, Bardulf and Drogo, and the faithful, silent old soldier Bernard. The king was always talking about Rome, and he wanted Sebastian to see it for himself and learn something about the pope and the politics of the place. To that end, Heimdal rode with them as far as the city, and as they strolled around it investigating the famous sites, the blind man instructed them. Though he had never actually seen the city, he had been there many times and had soaked up the special atmosphere and spiritual importance of the capital of Roman Christianity.

After a few days, they left Heimdal to enjoy himself until the return trip. Sebastian rode away from the ancient city feeling that it was indeed an extraordinary place, a magnificent spectacle, even in its ruins. Charlemagne had given him contacts with a few highly placed clerics and some Frankish officers of the military garrison surrounding the pope. His conversations with them had left him with a troubling conviction that Rome was a city of contradictions, full of controversy among factions and bogged down by an internal administration in the papacy that was not always on the pope's side in those controversies. He was glad that he did not have to live there, its glorious history and key place in the dynamic Christian world notwithstanding.

In a few days, they arrived at Duke Eric's fortress on the edge of his duchy. "Ah! There you are. Welcome back to Friuli, my good friend," Eric said, embracing Sebastian. "What a pleasure to see you again! You're just in time to meet Prince Wonimir of our new Croatian allies. We are very lucky. They are Christians and have offered to help us against the Avars. The prince has some very interesting ideas."

"A pleasure to meet you, Your Grace," Sebastian said with a low bow.

The prince bowed graciously as Eric continued, "Wonomir thinks the time has come to move again into Pannonia. Please, Prince, share what you have told me with my friend Sebastian."

"My pleasure entirely, Count Sebastian. Many tales of your accomplishments have preceded you. If they are true, you are indeed worthy to be counted, along with Duke Eric, among King Karl's greatest paladins."

"Ah," Eric interrupted. "You're too kind, my lord. But I'm afraid most of what you've heard about either of us is, as you might say, folklore—stories told by peasants around the hearth fire at night to make their lives more interesting. We'd best move on to your news. Please repeat what you've told me."

"It is this way, my lord Sebastian, you know that we Slavs have been under the yoke of the Avars for generations. We're allowed to live and rule ourselves only as long as we stay primarily in the mountains, pay tribute, and humble ourselves before our overlords. That miserable circumstance may be ending. As you also know, there is chaos amongst the

Huns—the civil war continues, and the time has never been better for us to throw off their yoke. I think we can do it, but we need help from you Franks to destroy these wretched pagans once and for all time."

"Why is it the right time now, Prince?" Sebastian ventured, trying to remain casual. What has changed?"

"Everything. What the king saw five years ago was only the beginning. But he succeeded even then because of the discord between the khagan and his kinsman, the jugur. Since then, they've waged nearly continuous full-scale war against each other. Providentially for us, and most surprisingly, both of them have recently been murdered by their own people."

"My God! Who rules, then?" Sebastian burst in. "Have they chosen a new khagan?"

"No one, my lord, at least as far as I know. Your old friend the tudun is beside himself with fear."

"We know," Sebastian interjected. "We've heard from him. He sent a large embassy all the way to Saxony to submit himself and all his people to the king. He even proposed that he should be baptized a Christian. I think he wants to be the new khagan. The king was astonished, but he was in the middle of trying to put down another Saxon revolt, and so we didn't take the time to deal with the tudun's proposal as seriously as we might have. King Karl sent the emissaries back to Pannonia. Now he regrets that he did not take advantage of the offer. That's why he has sent me down here—to see if an opportunity still exists."

"It most certainly does, sir. The war continues, but the fighting is mainly at the eastern end of the Pannonian Plain. In the west, the tudun is the only real power, and his tax collectors tell me he worries daily about what will happen when the war ends. One or the other side is likely to come for him because he took no part in it—unless he can count on a very strong ally."

"Well, obviously," Eric said. "Wonomir, you've a plan?"

"I do, my lord. I think we should strike now—right into the heart of Pannonia. My scouts tell me there are no significant Avar forces west of the Ring City. We could be there in ten days. I doubt the tudun would even oppose us. If we could take the city, Avar power might be broken forever."

As the prince expounded, he demonstrated his ardor for the fight with elaborate gestures and a passionate countenance. Sebastian got the impression Wonomir would fight heroically but might also get them into trouble with his naked zeal and intensity. His nature was in sharp contrast to the cool, almost casual temperament of his friend Eric.

***

Charlemagne's boast that Eric of Friuli was a bold leader was resoundingly confirmed when he raised, with Sebastian's help, a substantial cavalry army in less than a month. Franks, Lombards, and Bavarians swept into Pannonia to join Prince Wonomir's small army of Slavic Croats. He met them partway and swelled the force by half.

"I don't like it," grumbled Liudolf. "We've hardly seen any Avars—just small bands of riders who run off as soon as they see us. I'm worried it's a trap."

"You may be right," Sebastian agreed. "It makes me edgy, too. I'm going to suggest that you and I and a few others go ahead as scouts. We'll take extra horses. In case we run into trouble, we can outlast any pursuers."

When they came within a day of the Ring City, the Franks halted and prepared to wait until the scouting party returned. Sebastian was not surprised when Eric insisted on going with him.

The ride to the Ring City was bizarre. They began by traveling at night, but they encountered no one. When they came to the rise above the city, Liudolf complained, "There aren't any riders; there are no people. It's as if the land's been cursed and everyone's gone."

Determined to unravel the mystery, they rode right up to the outskirts of the city—no resistance, no movement, no life, nothing. They dared to ride straight into the city.

To everyone's profound astonishment, when they reached the fortress, they found it undefended. The gates lay open. Even the tudun was gone. Riding through the empty streets of the great fortress, Sebastian felt a chill running up and down his spine. The mighty fortress was inviolate, no evidence of burning or slaughter. Yet the inner city and town around it, once full of life, was abandoned. They were drawn immediately to the area of the treasure storehouses and dared to enter one.

"Look at this, Sebastian!" Archambald cried. "There's enough gold and jewels in this place to rival the treasure of Solomon! Why did they just leave it? It's unbelievable! And this is only one storehouse. There are at least a dozen more, chock full of the riches of all the world."

They sat in the middle of a pile of golden *solidi*, running their fingers absentmindedly through the coins. "It makes me beastly uncomfortable," Liudolf announced to no one in particular. "Where is the tudun? Why was the city not defended? This has been entirely too easy."

"Yes," Sebastian answered, "but we've sent scouts in every direction. There's still no sign of any large enemy force."

"Perhaps not now," Liudolf argued, "but Wonomir thinks they will come. And we've found out the hard way that it doesn't take an army of plains horsemen long to cover a substantial distance. If we ride very hard, we might cover ten leagues a day—with our armor and big horses. Their light cavalry can do twenty in the same time. We never planned to come this far, did we? We were just going to test the waters, I thought. We don't have nearly enough men to face the whole Avar horde."

"What if there is no Avar horde?" Eric suggested quietly. "What if the few who were left here saw us coming and cleared the city rather than fight us? Even Wonomir says they are ruinously divided and still killing each other. No one else has emerged."

"Well, you are the commander, my lord," Sebastian said as he stood up and threw a sack of coins back on the pile.

"But it is my humble opinion that we don't have enough men to hold this city if we are besieged. And it will take King Pepin a month or more to bring reinforcements from Italy, even if he will do it. We don't know that he will. And at the moment, King Karl is in Aachen at the far end of the kingdom."

"You're right, of course, Sebastian. We must go back. But, damn all! Not empty-handed. I'll be bollocksed if I don't take some of this incredible gleaming hoard back for the king. He won't believe it. I hardly do, and I'm sitting on it."

The decision left Sebastian with a painful feeling in the pit of his stomach. In spite of the agreement he and Eric had made with the tudun, and the idea that they could deal with the Avars peaceably, they were going to rob the Ring City. And it also appeared that once the king had a piece of the treasure, he would want it all, and he would agree to let Wonomir and Duke Eric begin the annihilation of the Avars.

***

It took Sebastian several months to get the clumsy carts all the way to Aachen. As before, Duke Eric sent his best regards to the king but stayed behind in Friuli, fearing a late retaliation from the Avars. But he sent a small army with Sebastian to safeguard the fantastic cargo.

It was past the harvest and on the cusp of winter when he reached Aachen. Charlemagne was in the new chapel inspecting the huge marble pillars from Rome that would support the heavy cupola.

"Look at them, Sebastian! They've just arrived. Aren't they beautiful? Can't you imagine how they will look? The throne will be right up there between those pillars on the second level. It will look down upon the altar where Mass will be said first thing every morning! I can hardly wait. But come, tell me everything. I've heard some incredible rumors. Are they true?"

"More than you know, sire." Sebastian drew out a heavy pouch from under his cloak, waited deliberately for a moment, and then upended the contents upon the stone floor. Scores of gold *solidi* clanged down around the king's feet."

"God's blood!" The king bent to inspect the glittering coins. "It is true, then. The gold of the Greeks!"

"Sire, if you would care to walk with me to the stable area, you will see a sight you may never have seen before or will again."

The king was speechless; he kept opening chests and peering inside, running his hands through coins and stroking bars of gold, all the while muttering, "*Um Gottes Willen*! He was so wildly pleased that he immediately granted a goodly portion to both Eric and Sebastian. And, as he had done throughout his long reign, he demonstrated that he was not only a generous ruler but a shrewd one. A large part of the "treasure of the ancient kings" was pledged to his magnates, and another ample part was soon carted off by his steward to Rome, including items of fine art and artistry as well as precious metals and jewels.

"But, sire, I must tell you. . . there is more," Sebastian disclosed as they gazed at the treasure trove in one of the carts. "We didn't have the time or enough heavy carts to carry off even half of the treasure. There were still several storehouses packed to the ceiling with gold and silver."

"It's still there?" the king erupted incredulously. "How could they just leave it like that? I don't believe it. No one would abandon riches like that! Give me one reason why they would do such a thing?"

"Sire, I spent the whole way back from Pannonia thinking about that very mystery. I've come to the conclusion that they simply don't see gold the same way we do. They don't look at it as a means to acquire something else. From what little I know of them, I think they regard that gold and silver treasure as a testimony to their glory—to the courage and prowess of their people. That's why they pile it up in great storehouses and don't use it. It stands for their might, for their glorious past, for the defeat of their enemies. After all, they wrested it away by their might from everyone they ever fought. It represents their triumphs and superiority over all their enemies. But now. . . now that the glory is fading and they've been ripped into mere pieces of what they once were, they no longer value the gold. It's worthless to them."

"Fancy that! How very queer of them. Well, it's bloody well not worthless to me! I will have it—all of it."

The king's shining eyes betrayed his latent greed. He turned away, opening his hands wide toward the palace. "Do you know what I could do with the rest of that treasure, Sebastian? I could make this place the envy of every king in the world. I could make it greater than Rome, greater even than Constantinople. I could make Aachen my capital, by the great God and all the saints! And all the world would come here to see the power and glory of the Franks!"

So, it's what I feared, Sebastian thought bitterly. He turned away and stared blankly out of the window. Now he'll do whatever he has to, even if it means slaughtering every last Avar.

If Charlemagne was a generous man, he was also an immanently practical one. He wasted no time. His first act after seeing the treasure was to send an order to his son King Pepin to gather an army, go back into Pannonia, and do whatever he needed to bring out the rest of the treasure.

Sebastian chose that moment to ask the king for another leave of absence for the purpose of seeing to his sons. He was glad to have a ready excuse not to go back to Pannonia. The king was so exuberantly pleased with the incredible outcome of the Avar war that he granted the request. "Of course. Go, my good old son, go! And with my blessing. You've done enough and more. Go and teach those sons what it means to be a paladin for the king. I expect one day I'll need them just as well."

***

Sebastian went back to Fernshanz and brought up the younger boys for a long visit. Occasionally Milo came up from Aachen. They took many walks, talking about all manner of things. On one of those long walks, they had a particularly meaningful conversation. Sebastian was surprised to find that Milo was interested in the affairs of state.

"You're a spiritual person, Milo. Why on earth do you care about what happened in Pannonia? Or anywhere else in the realm, for that matter?"

"I am interested, Father, in all things that impact the lives of men. What you do on the sword edge of the king's policies affects what happens in the lives of his ordinary people—all his people.

"For example, look what he's doing with all that Avar gold you brought him. He's building a glittering edifice to the power and might of the Franks. Of course, that makes everyone proud, even the little ones. They strut around saying, 'Look at me, I'm a Frank. I am one of a conquering race. Fear us! Fear me, world! We are the greatest people on earth. I'm a Frank, and I am great, too!' Lots of bravado, but it doesn't improve their lives. Most of them still wallow in sickness, ignorance, and poverty. Military power is just a painkiller that makes them forget their woes."

"Whoa. It's not as bad as all that. If we weren't strong, others would oppress us or make us their slaves. Would you want that for your precious 'ordinary people'? Perhaps if you saw how people live in the rest of the world, you might thank God for King Karl and his power. At least he's started to improve things. He has cathedral schools now for the sons of anybody who's capable. He's encouraged landowners to foster pilgrim inns, and he even hopes to have hospitals for the poor one day. His counts and landowners have been inspired by him, so much so that they are building, sponsoring learning, and paying more attention to their people. On the whole, the king is making change. Granted, it's slow, but compared to anything at all that went before, it is colossal."

"You'll pardon me, Father, if I don't think he's doing enough. But I am glad for whatever changes do occur. On another subject, you still haven't told me what happened in Pannonia after you returned."

"Ah! The king's son Pepin is not the general his father is, but he was successful in retrieving the rest of the Avar treasure, quite an enormous hoard, far bigger than what Duke Eric and I came back with. But his success had more to do with the complete collapse of the Avars than with his skills as a general. The civil wars and multiple enemies they've been facing have drained the blood out of them. They're now less a nation than a ragbag of disparate peoples—Huns, Slavs, Teutons, and Turkic tribes from the steppes, held together weakly by an appointed Avar strong man.

"Do you remember that friendly tudun I told you about? Well, he's never been one to misinterpret signs. He showed up at the king's court yet again and surrendered all the people of his part of Pannonia to King Karl and himself to baptism. But after he left, a new khagan emerged and put our tudun in his place. That new khagan also presented himself before King Pepin's army, and of course Pepin welcomed him magnanimously and declared 'a new and lasting peace,' but then he proceeded to pack up the rest of the treasure in the Ring City storehouses and cart it away while the new khagan watched!"

"But won't the Avars recover now that the civil war is over? They'll be out for vengeance against us, won't they?"

"Oh, they've already made a show of trying to bring their nation together again, and they've even tried a few raids against us in the south, but their efforts were woeful. They don't have the numbers they need any more—or the arms or the leadership. I'm afraid the once-feared Avars have just become only a strange, shrinking mongrel race and their kingdom not much more than a wild field, a largely empty basin, which King Karl is happy to use as a buffer against the Greeks and Bulgars in the east."

"That's a terribly tragic story, Father. I'm afraid I shall never be able to look at this grand palace we're building without thinking that it's all been paid for by the blood of those poor Avars. Once, they were a great kingdom, but now, if you're right, soon the last of them will simply disappear."

Sebastian paused for a moment and remembered ruefully his promise to aid the tudun of the Ring City and his hopes that their adventure in Pannonia might end without war or devastation. But then he thought of his own part in the fall of the Avars. He had gone along with the king's intentions. Who was he to assert any moral judgment? The truth was that the Avars were no innocents either, far from it. The treasure was smeared with blood from the wars they had waged to obtain it.

"I'm not so sure they don't deserve it, Milo. Now they're reaping what they sowed," he said with regret. "They were a ferocious lot of bloody killers in their time. But I suppose no race of people deserves to be completely wiped out, and, if it's any consolation to you, I'm not proud of my part in their extinction. Be glad you're not a soldier and bound by your oath."

Chapter 17

Isaac

The King's Court at Aachen, Summer 798

"That's him, Sebastian," Simon said, inclining his head toward a dark, thin man in a black robe and turban standing before the king in the council room of the palace. "That's the man I've been telling you about. He's one of us—a Radhanite. And he's been everywhere and knows all the world's great kings personally. He must be the most famous Jew in the world."

"What makes him such a famous man? Does he turn water into wine?"

"He's just the best-known trader in the entire merchant network of the Radhanite Jews. That unassuming old gentleman can procure almost anything you want, no matter how precious or rare, regardless of the difficulty or risk. And he can get a message through to the ends of the earth. For more than thirty years, he has plowed the sea and trudged on horse or camelback from one great empire to another, welcomed equally by the popes and kings of the west as well as the emperors of Byzantium and the caliphs of Baghdad."

"How is it that he can be received in safety in so many different and dangerous places?"

"He's a Jew, my friend, like me. He's a neutral quantity; he takes no sides, voices no preferences or opinions. He is strictly business. If he accepts a particular task or goal or journey, he asks no questions and makes no demands other than that the price he asks must be paid. And, of course, his services are not cheap. Somehow that makes him even more attractive to those who can pay. They say, 'Well, he must be worth it.'"

"Well, he doesn't look like so much. He's already an old man. Look at that long gray beard. And he's as gaunt as a wraith."

"I've been on one long journey with that man, Sebastian. And you're right; he doesn't ever seem to eat much and drinks even less—no wine or spirits of any kind. And he isn't strong at all. But he is durable; that's a fact. We landed on the Syrian shore with a mission to the court of the Arab Empire in Baghdad. To get there by the shortest route, we had to cross a desert. It took seven days of riding on camels in the blazing sun. Day and night we rode. You would have thought it was a matter of life and death, but it turned out to be just another uncomplicated trading journey—Spanish leather and Frankish metalwork for Persian jewels. Of course, it was worth a fortune."

"I must say, he doesn't look like a famous man, Simon. More like a humble beggar. He hardly raises his head to look at the king. "

"Well, he is a humble man. He does very little for himself. If he has spare time, he studies; he must know a dozen foreign languages. And he prays a great deal. If it's a quiet moment, you'll find him kneeling on a rug like an Arab or sitting cross-legged, eyes closed in prayer, or reading one of the sacred scrolls of Hebrew scripture he always packs in his baggage.

"And he always speaks quietly and in a low voice, saying no more than he needs to and always deferring to those he considers above him, which is almost everyone with whom he speaks. But all that humble demeanor and the reluctance to say much just gives him an odd aura of wisdom. When he does speak, everyone leans forward to listen. I've never seen him express emotions or deeply held feelings, but he's been to the far ends of the earth and possibly knows more than anyone about the world and its variety of peoples."

"And yet, old son," Sebastian gibed, "not all the words said about him are good, are they? I've heard the Jewish traders—yourself excepted, of course—have no scruples about whom they trade with or what things they trade. There are

204

stories that they are famous suppliers of blond Saxon and Slavic girls to the slave markets in Baghdad."

"You're right again, and that is true of Isaac as well. He does not concern himself with Christian values. He will tell you it's not his business. He has his own moral code, and it is thoroughly Jewish. None of us can be concerned with how the Christians think or act—or the Mussulmen, for that matter. It's how we survive.

"However, I can give you a better insight into Isaac: the next time you're traveling through the Loire Valley, stop in a town such as Orleans or Claremont and talk to any Jewish young man. Chances are that boy will be able to read and tell you about the world better than any comparable Christian youth. The Jewish communities of the Rhine and the Loire have immensely profited from Isaac's enterprises. His money finds its way into scores of Jewish schools, and he has assembled teachers from all over the world. Even King Karl is envious of those schools and is using them as a model for the cathedral schools he's founding right now.

"I doubt, however, that's what he's talking to Isaac about at present. You and I have been summoned to the king as well, and I see some of the king's favorite envoys, men high up in his own family, the kind he likes to send abroad when he has a particularly important matter to attend to beyond his own borders. I think, my friend, we are on the verge of a momentous change in our lives."

Sebastian paused for a moment to reflect. After the episodes in Brittany, Denmark, and Pannonia, he had come to feel a bit like Sisyphus, condemned eternally for his sins to push a huge boulder up a hill only to watch it roll back down. Now he had a gloomy premonition that this would be another one of those Herculean tasks conjured up by the king's boundless ambitions. But then, what else was there for him to do? There were no larger ties, no greater demands. He was a soldier, and he had sworn an oath to the king.

His flippant answer belied his inner thoughts. "Splendid! I sincerely hope so. I could use a change from all this hopping about from one bloody crisis to another that I've been doing for the king for the past ten years or so."

"Well, you'd better find a quick source of renewal, Brother, because this does not appear to be an invitation to a holiday."

***

"Good morning, gentlemen!" the king cried out lustily as he waved Sebastian and Simon over to him. "Sebastian, this is Isaac. Welcome, Simon. I think you already know Isaac, don't you?"

"I have had the pleasure of a long acquaintance with him, my king. We traveled together once before to the Orient. The trip was memorable. We could not have a better shepherd for the journey I believe you are about to suggest."

"Aha, I see you've done some preparatory snooping about."

"Sire, Master Isaac was kind enough to alert me that you might need my services."

"I do indeed, Simon, and yours as well, Sebastian, most particularly. But let me warn you at the outset, this may be a rattling good adventure, the roughest I've ever given you. It'll take you to places you've only dreamed of and into situations far more perplexing than any you've ever faced. Simon knows, and I am sure he'll confirm what I say. That's why I'm sending you, Sebastian. You're the best suited of my paladins for this singular enterprise. I shall need you to defend Master Isaac if necessary and to go places where Jews cannot. My official emissaries, Counts Lantfrid and Sigismund, are high-ranking enough and good leaders at home, but they'll be toothless lions, I fear, in the places I want to send you. You will be my ambassador *ex officio* and take care of them as well as Isaac when necessary. I know they will all need you to solve puzzles and unlock doors, so to speak. That's what you're so good at.

"I shall miss you greatly, for I'm afraid you could be gone a good while." The king paused a moment to study

Sebastian's face for a reaction to this sobering news. There was no visible response, except in Sebastian's mind, where he received the news stoically, thinking he had been right to expect the worst. Well, what did it matter? At least he would have his good friend Simon along for company. His main concern, as always, was whether he would be equal to the king's expectations.

"Mind you," the king offered halfheartedly, "I don't insist that you do this, old lad. If you feel that the task is beyond you or you have any pressing personal reasons for declining. . ."

Sebastian hesitated for only a second and then said with a smile, "My king, I believe it might be a bit more stimulating than farming. I'm honored to oblige you."

The king guffawed with approval and pounded Sebastian on the back. "That's my lad; that's what I expected. Nothing less. Right! That's settled. You will go, then?"

"Of course, my lord king."

"Splendid! But let me tell you the good and the bad of it. Perhaps you won't be so keen to go once you've heard it all. Let's get out of here—too many bloody people, all wanting attention. Let's walk outside where I can see my beautiful buildings going up!"

As they walked, the king pointing out enthusiastically from time to time aspects of the construction of the new complex, he explained the journey offhandedly, just as if it were a trip to Rome or Paris.

"I want you to make your way to three great cities, each occupying a place in the world that will be completely strange to you. And in each place, I will ask you to help me achieve some highly difficult goals. You'll have no army at your back and you won't even travel with a large contingent. We don't want to frighten anybody. In fact, it's best if you travel as inconspicuously as possible and keep your purpose to yourself until you reveal it to the right person at the right time." The king paused again to observe Sebastian's response. "I'm well aware it's a very big undertaking."

Sebastian responded impassively, having already reconciled himself to whatever fate waited. "I'm ready, my liege. There's nothing to keep me here. Just tell me what you want me to accomplish in these three grand cities."

"Good. Let me put it very simply, and then I shall elaborate. The first city is Constantinople. I've received an unusual offer from the Empire, and I want to work out what I should do about it. I also want you to find out if the ruler there, the Empress Irene, has a firm grip on power and if I can trust her.

"The second city is Jerusalem. I'm told that Christians living in the city and pilgrims wishing to visit there are being persecuted by the Arabs. The city is no longer under the control of any Christian power. The Caliph of Baghdad owns it now, though local Arabs administer the city day-to-day and manage access to our Christian holy sites. For a while, Constantinople was able to bribe the Arabs to let the pilgrims in and not do harm to the city's Christians. But Empress Irene is at war with the caliph, and she can do nothing now to rescue the situation. I want you to find out if they would allow *me* to give them their bribe and become the Christian patron of the city.

"The third city is Baghdad itself. There are three things I want from Harun al-Rashid, who is the Grand Caliph of the whole Abbasid Arab Empire. I want to know if I should make an agreement with him, instead of with Irene and the Greeks in Constantinople. I want you to convince him to give the word to stop the persecution of Christians in Jerusalem and allow me to be their protector instead of Irene. Finally, I want to know if he will help me against my enemies, the Umayyad Moors in Spain. As you know, we have a toehold south of the mountains—Barcelona, Pamplona, and some others. I want to keep those holdings, and I think Harun al-Rashid, who is an Abbasid Muslim, can help me. He hates the Umayyads, calls 'em heretic dogs."

As the king went from one bewildering task to another, his words conjured up Sebastian's oldest enemy: fear of failure. How could he do all that? He was a warrior, not an envoy. He was not comfortable in the company of kings and queens, let alone emperors and caliphs. He did not feel he had a quick wit and was surely not clever enough to think through the daunting ventures the king was commanding.

"What's the matter, my old son?" the king laughed, stopping in front of the unfinished basilica. "Your mouth is wide open. I suppose you find all this a bit intimidating."

"Uh. . . just a bit, sire," Sebastian stuttered, feeling like a rabbit in a snare. "But I think I. . . uh. . . do understand most of it. And you said you would elaborate."

"Good. Well, here it is: you must go first to Constantinople and ferret out what to make of the Emperor Constantine's mother—this Irene. She was booted out of power by her son two years ago, but now she's managed to wiggle her way back into the capital city, and she's the co-emperor again, believe it or not. No wonder, though, because that idiot son of hers has made a proper muddle of things; he was sent running with his whole army the first time he tried to fight the Bulgars, and now he's the laughing stock of the capital. So Irene is cobbling the Greek realm together again as if she herself were the emperor.

"I don't quite know what to think of her. For one thing, she's already stung me once by calling a bloody council of Christian bishops without bothering to invite me or even the Bishop of Rome! And do you know what they did? She got them to bring back icon worship! Bloody synod of nobody but the Greeks, it was. I wouldn't have it, and I told the pope to negate it.

"But she's worried now; the Bulgars are threatening in the north, and the Arabs are nipping at her heels in the south. What's worse, I hear, is that the capital is a steaming cesspool of factions, impossible to fathom. It's a wonder there's any order at all left in Byzantium.

"So I'm pouring you and Simon right into that poisonous soup, Sebastian, and I want you to make sense of it. What's brewing? How long can that woman hold on? And most preposterously—did you know that she's actually sent secret word to me that she might like to marry me? Imagine that! God's blood, it wasn't very long ago she was negotiating with me to marry off her son to one of my daughters. It's astonishing. The old girl must be past forty years by now, and God knows what she looks like, as if I would ever really entertain thoughts of actually marrying her!"

"I didn't know that, my liege. Is she really serious, do you think?"

"I haven't a bloody clue. That's what I want you to find out. If I play along, is there anything to gain? If you go there and put a wet finger in the air, you might discover which way the wind is really blowing. Can you do that, old son?"

"But, sire, what about Counts Sigismund and Lantfrid? They are your official ambassadors, not I."

"Oh, they won't be going to Constantinople. For one thing, they despise the Greeks, and for another, they wouldn't have the very first clue how to handle Irene. They'd be more likely to get us into a war than an alliance. They'll meet you on the road to Baghdad somewhere. Isaac will arrange it. So. . . not discouraged yet?"

"Let's see, my lord," Sebastian said ironically, "you just want me to seek an audience with the Empress of Byzantium and suggest you might possibly put a bit of pressure on the Bulgars for her because you are mightily flattered by the suggestion of a conjugal union with her and that you have been thinking on the idea most ardently."

"Don't be cheeky, Sebastian. I'm your king, remember. And don't get too borne away by the *conjugal* part. Ahem! Just suggest to her I *might* be interested—for reasons of state, of course. And then send a report back before you pack on for Jerusalem."

"I will, sire. And is Master Isaac to go along with Simon and me?"

"No. Only Simon, at least as far as Constantinople. Isaac has business in Spain and in Egypt, after which he will join you in Jerusalem sometime after the summer. When he gets there, you can consult together about how best to protect the Christians."

"Aye, my liege."

"The Christian patriarch of Jerusalem is a very old man named Elias, I think. I've heard he's a good man, and I want to support him in any way I can. If he needs money, I'll send him some on a regular basis. You can tell him that. In fact, Isaac will carry a goodly amount to give him on the spot. Tell him, too, that I have an idea of how to help him get some relief from the Arabs. And that, my good lad, ties in with the third great city."

"Baghdad."

"Right. Baghdad and the new caliph may be the key to many of our problems. From what I've heard, he's quite a man. When he was only in his early twenties, he led two campaigns against Byzantium. In one of them, he almost reached the walls of Constantinople.

"He's a man after my own heart," the king went on exuberantly as they resumed the walk around the complex. "He's not just a brilliant general, he's a scholar as well. And they say his capital is the richest, most civilized place in the world. It's not only an enormous center of trade—maybe even more so than Constantinople—it's a center of knowledge and culture like none other. Art, architecture, books, medicine! He's already done what I've been trying to do with Alcuin— he's assembled the best minds to be found in his part of the world, and they are changing his people and the world itself in the process!"

"Sounds most impressive, sire. I shall hope to meet him."

"Well, you'd better. I'm sending Lantfrid and Sigismund as my royal emissaries to his court. They're not going to Jerusalem. They'll travel by ship from Venice and meet you in the Syrian port of Antioch once Isaac has joined you and you're done in Jerusalem. Isaac will know where to find them.

"Then you'll go on to Baghdad with them. But I doubt they'll be much good in that strange environment, so they are going mainly to represent the crown. In the end, it's down to you, and you will certainly be the sharp end. Keep them safe while Isaac gets them where they need to be. Here, let Isaac tell you about the caliph." He nodded to the quiet man walking modestly behind them, arms behind his back, head down in thought, almost as if he had no part in the conversation.

"Thank you, your exalted highness," Isaac began quietly, coming abreast of them. "I do indeed know something of this man. I have seen him twice. Both times he was singularly impressive. He does not think as other men do. His mind flies above them. He has so many ideas and plans that no one can keep up with him. And he listens far more than he speaks—hears everyone, rich or poor, noble or not. It is the mark, I think, of a great monarch.

"He is the son of al-Mahdi, third caliph of the Abbasid dynasty, and a slave girl. But she was an extraordinary mother to the boy, I'm told. It is also said of her that no one in the palace had a stronger or more noble character. I saw her once and heard her words as she spoke to her son at court. In that single moment, I came to believe she was the most intelligent woman I have ever seen. It is my humble opinion that Harun al-Rashid inherited his great creativity from her. She is the wellspring and spirit of his wisdom."

Sebastian seized on the idea of somehow winning the favor of the caliph's mother. "Does she still live, or do you know?"

"I do not, Lord Sebastian. It has been several years since I last saw her." Having finished what he wished to say, Isaac bowed, as was his custom, and fell behind again.

Sebastian began to see Isaac with new eyes, realizing as the old man spoke that he was much more than he seemed—completely unimpressive on the surface but a vast reservoir of information, in intimate detail, about the people and places they would visit in the East. Sizing him up, he thought most people going past him in the road would fail to notice a decrepit, worn-out old Jew with a face like all the roads he ever traveled. Yet King Karl listened to him as if he were the Oracle of Delphi. So, apparently, did the Caliph of Baghdad. Oddly, after an hour or so with this inconspicuous, clever old man, Sebastian took some comfort in the thought that if they were to succeed against the considerable odds, Isaac would be the key.

***

The next day, in a private meeting, Isaac and Sebastian pored over the goals and details of their journey to the court of Harun al-Rashid.

"As the king mentioned, Lord Sebastian, I must first go on his business to Spain, to the Umayyad court in Cordoba. Are you aware of what King Karl wishes to achieve in Spain?"

"I have an idea: he wants to protect the city of Barcelona and the rest of the Frankish foothold on the other side of the Spanish mountains against the Umayyad Arabs. Barcelona, Pamplona, and other key strongholds there also have Mussulman rulers, or their lords are of the Basque people—all of whom resist Umayyad control in the rest of Spain. They sympathize strongly with the Abbasid dynasty of Harun al-Rashid. Am I correct?"

"You are, my lord, most accurately. Our king wishes to reinforce his allies in northern Spain, and to do that he needs Harun. If he can boast of an alliance with the Abbasids and their great caliph in Baghdad, it will help him greatly to keep the Umayyads in Cordoba at bay. That is why I must go to Spain first—to see clearly what the Umayyads plan and to bring that information and our proposal for alliance with King Karl to the caliph."

"When and where shall we meet in Jerusalem?" Sebastian asked.

"I have much to do in Spain—the king's business as well as my own commerce. I must collect fine Spanish horses for Harun as gifts from King Karl. And I must find goods for myself to trade in Jerusalem and Baghdad. After all, I am a trader, am I not? I'm not sure how much time all that will take. It will certainly be most of the summer. But I will give Simon the names of my Radhanite colleagues in Jerusalem. You can stay with them in the Jewish sector. You will be safe there.

And they will know when I arrive and give you the time and place where we can meet."

"I'm somewhat concerned about my part in all this, Isaac. I'm not the king's ambassador. He's told me he wants us to escort Counts Lantfrid and Sigismund. They're his royal vassals, great lords from his own house, with the proper rank to meet with any king or caliph. And I have no idea of how to accomplish what the king wants in Jerusalem."

"Have no fear. The king would not send you if he did not have special confidence in you. In Jerusalem, my people will help you. We know everyone and have good ties with Elias, the Christian patriarch. As for the king's royal consuls, it will be our duty to guide and help them. I am told they know nothing of the world to the east, and we will certainly find ourselves speaking for them, for they only speak the Frankish tongue. I speak fluent Arabic and a couple of Persian dialects as well.

"There's no need for the two counts to go to Jerusalem; it would only be an extra trip for them, and they would likely not be able to help us greatly there. We will meet them in Antioch. We can prepare them there for what they will encounter.

"But Jerusalem is the right place for you and I to meet. We must tend to the king's business with Patriarch Elias. And it will give us a chance to compare our information from Constantinople and Spain, forge a plan, and proceed together to Antioch. Do you think this scheme will do, Lord Sebastian?"

Sebastian knew both of the royal counts. They were arrogant, obstreperous noblemen, used to almost as much power and prestige as the king enjoyed. He breathed a sigh of relief to know he would be spending less time in their company. But he did not betray his misgivings about them to Isaac.

"I defer to your judgment and experience, Master Isaac. I must confess, however, that this is all a very scary and wildly complicated business for me."

Isaac flashed a rare smile. "You are right, my esteemed colleague, if I may call you such. We have quite an impossible job to do, you and I." He paused a moment to close his eyes and sigh deeply, and then he simply shrugged his bony shoulders. "But, as always, everything is in God's hands. We are merely his instruments, no? If he wills it, we shall succeed."

Sebastian envied the old man's confidence and apparent peace of mind. Reflecting on it that evening before he slept, he had a sudden insight: Isaac's serenity in the face of a daunting mission was most probably due to his willingness to die. Every time he set out on such a dangerous journey, he had to know that his life would often be at risk. It was the same acceptance and resignation that he himself had felt several times just before a battle. One had to accept that death was a likely outcome and disregard it, saying to himself, "There's no choice. If I die, I will have done what I had to do, and I am past worrying." In a way, Isaac was a kindred spirit. The thought was comforting.

***

A month after the king had given them the mission, Sebastian and his comrades took the road again, this time south along the Rhine. There were only ten of them. The king did not want them to bring attention to themselves, and they traveled in the style that Isaac suggested for them, simply dressed, concealing insofar as possible any resemblance to Frankish noblemen or soldiers. Simon brought two servants—a Danish bodyguard and an Arab horse master. Sebastian could not convince Archambald, Bardulf, and Drogo to stay behind, and he sent for Liudolf and the old soldier Bernard as well. And then there was Milo.

The court at Aachen was abuzz with the news of the great venture, and there was no way that Milo would be left behind. He had simply threatened his father.

"You told me that one day you would let me go with you to see the world. I have seen twenty-one years now, and I

215

have been here in this place long enough." He paused to fix Sebastian with his eyes. "I mean to make you keep your promise. If you do not, sir, the day you leave, I shall walk out of here and you will never see me again."

Sebastian remembered the time when he had said almost the same thing to his own father when the king led the Fernshanz men off to war. As before that first battle, when he faced the Saxons for the first time, Sebastian knew that there was no choice.

They followed the Rhine as far as Mayence and then the Neckar through dense, dark forests to Bavaria, crossing the Enns River into the foothills of the great Alps. Picking their way through narrow passes and across a score of treacherous gorges, the journey was arduous but otherwise uneventful. Eventually they emerged into the valley of the Po in Lombardy. From there it was an easy ride to the coast of the Adriatic, near Venice, where they took a Venetian ship for the long and hazardous voyage to Constantinople.

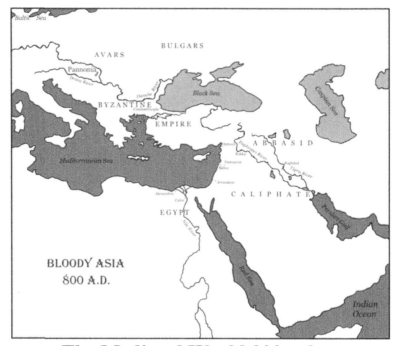

The Medieval World 800 a.d.

Chapter 18

The Road to Constantinople

Autumn 798

"They're coming fast!" Sebastian observed. "They seem to be flying over the water. What is that thing?"

"I'm afraid it's a cursed Arab raider, my lord," replied Barbero, the captain of their Venetian cargo vessel. "It's a pirate ship," he continued uneasily. "I'm fairly sure—accountable to no particular city or master. Otherwise, there would be a fleet of them."

"But what are those sails? I've never seen such slanted ones. Is that the reason they're gaining on us?"

"That is correct, Count Sebastian. That's what is known as 'the Arab sail.' Some call it the Latin, or *lateen*, sail. The old Romans knew how to use it on some of their big warships, but it was not widespread until the Muslims came to dominate the Roman Sea. Now such ships are like fleas on the water. They have crippled trade from Italy to Byzantium and made it too dangerous even to try a voyage to Egypt unless you have a fleet of warships as escorts. God send a plague upon them!"

"What can we do? Can you not go faster—put on more sail or more men on the oars?"

"No, my lord. This ship is only a small improvement on the old Roman *bireme*. We have only the big square sail and that little one on the bow. We can only use them effectively when there's a good following wind. As for rowing, we only have ten oars on each side, and they are fully manned already. I fear it may be all up for us if we cannot stay ahead of them before night falls. We will simply have to beach the ship and run for it on one of these islands. If they board us, they will kill us all."

"What? Nonsense! There must be something else we can do. Can we not buy them off?"

"Sir, it is likely they are very ignorant. Such ships are from northern Africa. Most of their sailors are Copts from Egypt, but their fighters will likely be Bedouin Arabs, who speak a language that is hardly intelligible. If you try to negotiate, they will simply come at us quicker, sensing our weakness. No, when they catch up, they will use grappling hooks. If they succeed in boarding us, they will cut us into pieces and throw us to the fishes." The captain shuddered.

"How many do you think there are on that boat?"

"It's hard to say, my lord. From the size of her, I would say there are at least thirty oarsmen. That's why they're coming so fast. They can manipulate those triangular sails to catch even the lightest wind, whether it comes from fore or aft, and the oarsmen provide double the speed. I have no idea how many fighters they will have."

The captain was bravely trying to hide his fears, but it was clear he was losing his nerve and would likely ground the ship. He was already heading for the nearest island.

Sebastian stepped to the rail once more to think as he watched the fast-approaching corsair. If he chose to fight, he risked everyone's life, even that of his precious son. If he agreed to beach the ship and run for their lives, they would lose everything on the ship and still might not be able to escape. One thing was certain, if they chose the latter course, they would certainly have to abort the mission.

Everything in his nature, everything he had ever been taught to do since he was a boy—even the ghost of his father—screamed at him to fight. And yet there was Milo. He hesitated. The young man was special. Sebastian was sure that one day he would become a man of great consequence, able perhaps to stop wars instead of start them, surely destined to contribute greatly to change the raucous world in which they lived. Perhaps Milo was worth saving no matter what the cost.

At this point, Simon stepped in.

"I saw such ships once before, Sebastian. Three of them attacked us just off the coast of the Peloponnesus. But I was on a much bigger ship—a Byzantine war galley—and we had Greek fire on board. We drove them off easily."

"What was their strength? What arms and armor?"

"The captain is right; there may be as many as thirty oarsmen. But they will only be slaves or serfs, like our own oarsmen. However, there may be twenty or thirty fighters if the Copts will fight, too."

"Why wouldn't they?"

"I suspect they will have been pressed into service because of their skills in using the lateen sail. But they may not wish to die fighting for the Arabs."

"What of arms and armor?"

"I saw plenty of swords and spears. Some shields. But no armor besides the odd helmet or two. They will likely give us a barrage of arrows before they try to board."

Sebastian felt a wave of relief—they had a fair chance of winning! That was what he needed to know to make the decision.

"We will fight!" he announced emphatically. "Captain Barbero, keep pushing the ship. I'd rather escape them, but if we must, we'll make them sorry they have set upon us."

He conferred briefly with Simon and then gathered the men. "We're in for a fight, lads. And I don't know how many there are—twenty, perhaps thirty, against us. They are Saracen pirates, and the captain says we can't outrun them. But I believe we can outfight them. Simon thinks they are not regular soldiers and they will have little armor. They will likely get up close to count our numbers, and then they will attack if they think they can take us.

"We will use a bit of surprise. I want everyone to throw a cloak over his armor and then conceal yourselves behind the stacks of cargo on this deck or below deck with the oarsmen. We don't want them to see how many of us there are or know that we have shields and armor. Only the Venetian sailors should be visible on deck."

Sensing a bit of hope in Sebastian's confidence, the captain plucked up his courage. "Some of my men are good archers, sir. We can try to cause as much damage as possible before they try to board."

"Good. Do it, but fall back as soon as they throw the grappling hooks. When they try to board, my friends, the nine of us will come together and form a shield wall behind our spears. Milo, you will go below with the oarsmen. You're not trained for this. Do you understand?"

"Yes, Father," the young man answered with noticeable reluctance.

"Good, when I give the signal, the rest of us will form the wall behind the small guard rail on this deck. We'll spit them as they try to come across. If they succeed in getting aboard our ship, then it's swords. Stay close together behind the shield wall. If they get behind us, bend the wall into a circle. If it comes to it, choose a partner and fight back-to-back.

"We'll have surprise on our side. And once they get the feel of a good Frankish long sword and see that we won't back down, they may give it up. They are likely to have no armor and few real fighting skills. I believe we can hurt them badly. With luck, we'll batter them right over the side. For God and King, then! What say you?"

"For God and the King!" they shouted and ran to get their weapons and take their positions.

It soon became clear they could not outrun the Arab ship. Sebastian's men hid themselves among the cargo, ready to come forward on signal. Sebastian stood on deck with Simon and the captain, helmets off and cloaks over their armor, as the long black ship, adorned with Arabic symbols painted on the sails and hull, closed the distance. A huge Arab with a great black beard and an ugly scar down one side of his face stood amidst a crowd of yelling warriors waving a long, curved sword over his head. It was more a mob than a fighting formation, and the big leader was the only one with a shield. The rest waved swords or axes.

When the Arab ship drew within bowshot, Barbero's sailors launched a flurry of arrows just as the attackers prepared to fling the grappling hooks. The assault faltered as their wounded fell back, and the big Arab called for his own archers. While Sebastian and Simon threw off their cloaks and crouched behind shields, the Venetians and their captain retreated to the rear deck. The Arabs fired several weak volleys, shipped oars, and then threw the hooks as the raider craft slid smoothly alongside.

Sebastian shouted the signal, and his men emerged and raced forward to form the shield wall, Sebastian and Simon in the middle, Liudolf and Bernard on each end, Archambald, Bardulf, and Drogo in the middle on one side, and Simon's two bodyguards beside Simon on the other. Only Milo, unarmored and weaponless, was spared the line, but he would not stay below decks and stood instead with the captain and the Venetian sailors on the raised aft deck, watching with trepidation as the fight was joined.

The big bearded Arab took his place in the middle of his screaming fighters and made his leap between the two ships. His moment of glory was absurdly quick. Sebastian speared him in the throat in mid-leap, and he fell back into the water between the hulls. Half a dozen others met the same sharp resolve and fate. But the Arab onslaught carried many fighters onto the deck of the Venetian trader, and they fought desperately to turn the tide.

The Franks gave way gradually, bending the ends of the line until it was almost a circle, and hacked away at the unarmored, undisciplined mob. The Arabs slipped on the blood of their brothers as they tried again and again to penetrate the wall, but their swords fell on hard wood and leather, and each attempt drew a deadly response. Bodies piled up between the shield wall and the attackers, and it became increasingly hard for them to spring close enough to land an effective blow. Their attack became a sporadic nipping at the edges of the wall instead of a coordinated assault. Without their leader, the Arabs quickly lost heart and one by one disengaged from the fight and ran leaping for their own boat.

Sebastian gave the word for the line to straighten, and the wall moved forward steadily to the edge of the ship. As the attackers retreated, the Venetian captain called for renewed showers of arrows, causing more casualties. The Arabs slashed the ropes binding the two vessels, and their ship fell away quickly, its rowers pulling with a will. A huge shout of triumph rose up from the Franks. Captain Barbero and his crew echoed Sebastian's fighters with lusty cheers as the black ship pulled rapidly away.

"Who is hurt?" Sebastian shouted, peering anxiously up and down the line. "Who is wounded?" he repeated. Suddenly, all eyes turned toward the rear deck, where several Venetian sailors had been struck by arrows. Amongst them, Milo lay crumpled on the deck with an arrow through his arm.

**

It took two weeks for the heavily laden Venetian trading ship to thread its way cautiously through the labyrinth of islands off the Dalmatian coast. They made at once for Corinth, fearing each day a new attack by Arab raiders. The Venetian captain had trade opportunities in the famous city, and he assured Sebastian they could find a competent surgeon to treat Milo's increasingly festering wound.

The arrow had embedded itself in the bone of the youth's upper arm. They broke off the shaft, but no one aboard ship felt competent or willing to dig out the arrowhead. Milo suffered agony when he was not dosed with potions to keep him in a semiconscious state. Sebastian was beside himself over the excruciating delay as they made their way slowly around the coast of Greece into the long fjord-like Corinthian seaway.

Arriving at last in the bustling port city, they were able at once to find a Greek surgeon, but the man immediately insisted, in the face of Sebastian's vehement objections, that the arm must come off or the lad was certain to die. In the end, Sebastian had to concede, for the wound was on the edge of gangrene. The surgeon took off most of the arm above the elbow.

They began an agonizing period of doubt, and Milo's sickness caused them to linger extra weeks in Corinth.

Sebastian stayed with his son almost every waking moment, bathing the wound, patiently ladling a strong broth into his mouth, and making him as comfortable as possible. Several times he despaired of saving Milo's life.

He prayed often, blaming himself in remorse for his neglect. He thought of the times he could have seen Milo more when he was growing up and blamed himself for always letting his duties take precedence. For once, he had time to see Milo's virtues clearly. He could see that his son was vastly different from most young men. Milo thought little of himself and seemed to be without the vaulting egotism of the young warriors that filled Charlemagne's army. He was a kind-hearted, compassionate soul—just like his mother, Sebastian reflected—just like sweet Gersvind, who had loved everybody. Oh God, he pleaded, just let him live. He's so much better than me. He'll be a great man. He's what you need here in this tortured world, not me. Take me! Take me instead.

Eventually the lad's youth and blooming health redeemed him, and he began to get better rapidly. Sebastian spent almost a whole night on his knees in thanksgiving. When Milo was past the crisis, he was strangely unconcerned about the loss of his arm.

"Oh, Father, it's not my head or my heart. It's just an arm, and not even the one with which I write. I can still think, can't I? I can still have a happy and holy life. God remains with me, no matter what occurs."

On a different occasion, Milo's comments were less comforting. He took his father to task about the fight with the Arab raiders.

"So many of them died. The deck was literally washed in their blood. I saw you kill five men by yourself alone."

"It was necessary, Milo. You know that. If we had not killed them, they most assuredly would have done for us. All of us would have been dead now, including you."

"But it was as if you didn't even think of them as men. You just sliced them up like so many animals—without a thought."

224

"They were evil, my son. How can you not see that? They meant to rob and murder us. They didn't deserve compassion or mercy. Besides, they were godforsaken pagans."

"But they were men, Father, created by God, the same as you and me. The least we could have done was bury them with some kind of respect and prayer. You just had the men shovel them over the side like so much offal. It was cruel and unfeeling. What has happened to you? You weren't always this way. You used to care about people."

Sebastian felt his temper rising, and he fought to contain it. He took a deep breath, closed his eyes, and waited. He looked up at Milo's beseeching face and opened his mouth to speak in argument, but in the end, he closed it again and dropped his head. Finally, he rose and quietly left the small room in the surgeon's house and made his way back to the ship.

Milo is right, Sebastian thought as he made his way back to the harbor. *I have changed.* Except for the aching hole in his heart where the ghost of Adela dwelt, he hardly cared about anything—perhaps only Milo and the younger boys, and of course the king and the men who served alongside him. He used to love life. No place was dearer to him than his home at Fernshanz. Now even that seemed trivial and empty. *What has happened to me? Has God abandoned me? No, that wasn't it. It was what he had become—he'd seen too much blood, too much loss. He'd become an instrument of death—a naked sword only. More likely, it is I who have abandoned God.*

Chapter 19

Byzantium

The "Queen City" and the Imperial Court of the Byzantine Empire, Winter 798-799

Like a great triangular ship, the spectacular bluff upon which the great city sat seemed to plow its way inexorably into the Sea of Marmara—all old gold and green and deep purple in the fading twilight. Night fell gently as they passed through the Bosphorus on the way to anchorage in the estuary of the Golden Horn. Even in the low light, they could see the outline of the magnificent dome of Hagia Sophia, Emperor Justinian's incomparable church of churches, known formally as the Shrine of Holy Wisdom. "My God," Sebastian marveled to Simon, "there's nothing like it in all the world. It's true what someone told me, even at night, that fantastic cathedral broods over the city like its very soul and shield."

Simon was elated to be back in the great city in late December. He explained to Sebastian, "We're just in time for the most elaborate celebration you will have ever seen—a Byzantine Christmas, more than two weeks of feasting lasting until Epiphany. It's a perfect opportunity for us to observe the court of the Second Rome in its most brilliant form. Imperial banquets will happen almost every day, and every other day a flag will go up at the entrance of the Grand Palace as a sign that there will be chariot racing that day in the legendary Hippodrome. I, for one, intend to make a little money on these famous races, my friend. I'm quite good at it, you know. I'll help you bet, if you like."

"Hmph," Sebastian snorted. "I doubt we'll have much time for such trifles. Besides, I haven't a clue about chariot racing."

"The races are no trifles, my friend. Huge fortunes have been made and lost on them. They are run by two famous clubs in Constantinople, the Greens and the Blues. Those clubs are like powerful guilds. They are political, and they have almost as much influence with the people of Constantinople as the emperor. They're certainly a lot closer to them. The outcome of the races can start riots and turn the city upside down occasionally."

"Let's hope that doesn't happen. We don't need complications; we just need to see the emperor and get out of here as soon as possible."

"Well, it will be after the Christmas season, I can tell you that. The emperor won't see you at all till all the celebrating is over."

After anchoring the ship in the Golden Horn, their plans of remaining unrecognized were dashed when Captain Barbero wasted no time, even in the late night, informing the port authorities that a Frankish ambassador was on board carrying tidings from the King of the Franks. He explained to Sebastian that he was required to announce any foreign representative on board on pain of having his ship confiscated.

Early the next morning, a committee of brightly dressed court officials, accompanied by servants and a trumpeter, arrived from the palace in a carriage pulled by matching gray horses. The trumpeter hailed the ship, and the committee waited patiently on shore while a dinghy was put into service to bring a summons from the imperial palace to the ambassador from King Karl.

Sebastian and Simon returned at once in the dinghy to present credentials and a request for an audience with the sovereign of the empire. After an elaborate welcome with much bowing and saluting, the senior official regretfully announced that it would not be possible to see the emperor until after the celebration of the Holy Season but that the ambassador was to dress himself in special festive clothing, which they forthwith produced for him—a long, garish, rust-colored tunic embroidered with intricate flower designs, a heavy red cloak, and a gold-and-silver hat shaped like the blade of a huge scythe. This is ridiculous, Sebastian moaned to himself. I'll look like a jester—or a complete idiot!

He was instructed to be prepared that afternoon to ride through the city, escorted by horse guards in full-dress uniform, to be seen and greeted by the people, as befitted the emissary of a great king. On reaching the palace, he would then be escorted to quarters appropriate to an important dignitary and attended by servants, two of whom were to accompany him back to the boat in order to dress him properly.

After the holidays, as befitted his rank, he would be given a royal audience and a banquet in his honor. It was all a bit overwhelming for Sebastian, who began to feel uncomfortable just to learn of the pomp and ceremony being prepared for him.

"Go with me, Simon, damn it. I don't know how to act among all these peacocks."

"No, my friend, the Christmas season here is no place for a Jew, I'm afraid. I'll attend a few races, and then I'll find passage across the straits to the Asian part of Constantinople. I have community there, and I shall be glad to see them. We need a small, fast ship to take us on to Jerusalem and beyond, and they might help me buy one with the same kind of sails the Arabs use. But I shall return after the feasting and accompany you when formal meetings with the crown begin. Meanwhile, you need do nothing or speak to anyone unless you wish to.

"I'm sure you will receive many invitations to the daily church services and various festivities. Believe me, they will be spectacular. But you need not go. You will be completely free to do as you please, and everywhere you will be treated like a very great man indeed, almost as if you were King Karl himself."

"I don't wish to be treated in such a manner. It would be completely strange and awkward for me."

"Stay on the ship, then."

"No thanks. I've had enough of that foul-smelling tub. Besides, Barbero plans to finish his business here and then make a quick trip to Athens. He'll return after the festival days, and since you will be getting us a new ship, I'll be able to send him back to Venice with messages for King Karl.

"So I will go with those bloody officials if I must. But you must be back here the minute all this nonsense is over. You can't leave me to face the magnates of Byzantium alone."

"I shall, Sebastian, not to worry. Meanwhile, why don't you just let yourself enjoy what happens? You may never get such an opportunity again. You have immunity, you know. You may do anything you like without fear of penalty. Learn something! Experience something different!"

***

A dozen fully armed and armored imperial guards on jet-black horses were waiting in the early afternoon sun of a beautiful day to accompany Sebastian to the sprawling complex of the Great Palace on the acropolis of Constantinople.

As he climbed clumsily out of the dinghy, encumbered by his new, voluminous procession dress, Sebastian was greeted at once by a smiling young Greek dressed in an equally elaborate costume. He was a short man, but he made up for it by a cocksure, cynical attitude bordering on impudence. He bowed low and introduced himself formally.

"Good sir, a thousand welcomes to the Queen City of the world, the center of knowledge, power, and greatness, ruled by the most enlightened ruler of the world, by which I mean Her August Highness, Her Serenity, the incomparably intelligent and beautiful Emperor Irene, the Joy of the World and Glory of the Purple.

"I have the honor to be Leo, son of Heraklonas, an honored senior member of the Senate of Constantinople and the Empire. I have been given the very great privilege to serve as your escort while you are visiting our wonderful capital. As the estimable and most worthy representative of His Excellency, the exalted and mighty King of the Franks, you are most welcome and shall be treated while you are here as if you were the king himself."

He finished with an elaborate flourish and a deep bow and then looked up, grinning broadly at Sebastian as if to say, "It's all ridiculous, of course, but isn't it great fun!" He then came over and shocked Sebastian speechless by giving him an exuberant hug.

"You are Count Sebastian, are you not? We shall be best friends. Come on, then, mount up! Let me show you my wondrous city."

"Steady on there, Leo, or whatever your name is. It's true I've been sent here to see the Empress Irene, since we understand she now rules. But we have heard nothing of why that is so. What has happened to her son, the Emperor Constantine? And why do you call her 'Emperor'?"

"Ah yes, I'm sure it must be confusing to your king who is used to dealing only with male rulers. In Byzantium, however, we are not so constrained. You see, count, we have managed to survive so long as a great power because we are wonderfully resilient. We readily adapt to change when it is necessary and we choose as our rulers from the best persons available. We give that person the full power of the empire. That is what we have done in this case. I have the honor to inform you that Her Grace and Glorious Wonderment, Irene, has taken the title of supreme ruler. She is no longer the *basillissa*; she is the *basileus*, the *autokrator*, the one and only absolute monarch of all Byzantium. Ergo, she is to be addressed, if you please, as *Emperor* Irene."

"What happened to Constantine?"

"I regret to inform you of the sad news that the former emperor can no longer see; therefore, if he cannot see, he cannot, of course, be our emperor. He has decided to pursue a life of peace and solitude in a monastery, where he will, no doubt, pray for his mother."

"You mean he is blind?"

"Precisely, esteemed sir."

"How in the world could that have happened?"

"My good count, I fear the answers to such questions are beyond the competency of a poor minor official such as myself. It may be best, I think, if we concentrate on the tasks before us this day. They may actually prove to be quite taxing, and we have a long way to go."

With that, he presented Sebastian with the reins of a superb white stallion with a golden saddle decorated with colorful ribbons, and then he mounted its twin with a bound and a "Hi-yup!"

Milo and the others were waved into a brightly colored, ribbon-bedecked carriage pulled by mules, which brought up the rear of the column.

Sebastian and his effusive guide rode to the front of the guard and prepared to commence the procession. Leo dropped his flowery speech and, in a lower voice, suddenly assumed the role of friend and confidant.

"I say, old lad, I'm sorry they gave you that ugly hat to wear. It's traditional. But you don't have to wear the ridiculous thing. You can say you lost it on the way, riding on that frisky animal you've got there. Hope you can handle him. He's barely broken. I'm not sure why they gave him to you. Perhaps it's to see if you really are who they say you are. Or perhaps," he added with a raised eyebrow, "they wish to see you put in your place. In any case, I should truly hate to see you embarrass yourself trying to hold on when we get to the people."

Sebastian deftly turned the stallion and flipped the hat to Archambald in the carriage, instructing him to wear it instead. He continued the ride bareheaded, his long black hair streaming down his back. "What people?" he asked with a note of concern.

"*The* people, the citizens of Constantinople! They are always in the streets, especially when there's somebody visiting who really is somebody. They love all the pomp and commotion. And they love to examine the foreigners and make a bit of fun of them as they ride by. Don't worry, they won't hurt you. They don't dare; that's why we've got some soldiers."

Just then, a large troop of musicians, some dressed all in blue and others in green, appeared and began lining up in front of the horses, jostling and joking with one another, anticipating the march.

"Those fellows are from the famous Blues and Greens," Leo explained, "the plebeian factions who organize all the events of the Hippodrome and most of the city's gala affairs and celebrations. They draw the crowds into the streets with their music whenever a new celebrity is in the city."

"Thanks for the warning," Sebastian said as he stroked the neck of the magnificent stallion. "I think I'll be able to handle this horse."

They rode north along the shore of the Golden Horn until they reached the first great defensive barrier of the city, the Wall of Constantine. There they went through the gate and rode west toward the *Mese,* or Middle Street, the city's wide central artery, and then south from the great outer Wall of Theodosius through the heart of the city to the Augustaion, the main public square.

Sebastian had seen a bit of Rome on his way to Friuli, and it had been a disappointment. Unavoidably, he compared the dilapidated state of the First Rome he had seen with the vitality of this Second Rome. "What a dazzling metropolis this city is!" he remarked to Leo. "So many people everywhere— gold-domed churches, tree-lined streets, marble paving in the squares. Magnificent!"

"Yes," Leo replied proudly. "And don't forget all those statues in every square! Heroes and emperors—generations of them—and pagan gods next to Christian saints. You won't see that in Rome, will you?"

He pointed to a tall, delicately curved aqueduct threading its way through the city. "That's the grand Aqueduct of Valens. Look at the architecture. It's already centuries old and still beautiful and quite functional. It brings water from the mountains over some thirty miles to replenish the reservoirs of our city and fill its baths and fountains.

"By the way," Leo warned, "be a bit on your guard now. Here are the people." Crowds began lining up on both sides of the street and pushing out into it to see the distinguished visitor. Soon there was hardly room for the horses to pass. Bolder spectators reached out to touch Sebastian or his horse, causing the stallion to shy away and rear several times. Whenever that occurred, the crowd ducked away and cheered and then cheered again when Sebastian brought the beast back under control. Many pointed and made impertinent comments about "the barbarian's bare head" and the length of his silky black hair. Not a few pretty young women ran up to offer Sebastian flowers and touch his knee or arm.

The crowd thickened when they reached the bazaar area with its myriad rows of shops where one could buy almost anything from every kind of food to precious silks and jewels and works of exquisite artisanship in glass, wood, and gold. They were obliged to slow to a walk.

"Well, what do you think of our glorious city, Lord Sebastian?"

"I think it is indeed beautiful, Master Leo, breathtaking. But I'm astonished at all this fanfare and attention. I'm nobody, just a messenger. It's extremely disconcerting. And God knows if I'll be able to say anything at all to your empress. . . ah, emperor."

"Nonsense, my friend, and please call me Leo. You certainly *are* somebody. We know of you. You are Count Sebastian, a favorite of your king, one of his trusted paladins. You have been a leading figure in his wars with the Saxons and the Avars. Your reputation is already legendary. They say you are a great fighter and that you cannot be killed, yes?"

"I'm afraid all that is terribly exaggerated. But how in the world would you know about me?"

"Oh, my dear Sebastian, you underestimate us. We have informants everywhere. We are famous for it. Besides, we have a mutual acquaintance. I myself know your good friend Duke Eric of Friuli." Alarm signals went off in Sebastian's brain. Why all this pick and shovel work for a minor official? he wondered.

"One could say the duke is also my good friend, and he told me much about you. You shall certainly be a favorite at court. Ah, and here we are—the Augustaion, and just beyond, as you see, the Grand Palace of the emperor!"

***

"Right, lads. Here's the game. We're here as King Karl's eyes and ears. He wants to know many things about this very impressive place. He isn't sure whether we should count the Greeks as friends or enemies. They are certainly our rivals in Italy, they don't like our pope, and they think their religion is a good deal truer than ours.

"Still, it is a Christian land, and they believe in the same God we do. The king has been offered an opportunity to forge an alliance—or at least closer ties with them. It's our job to find out whether he should or should not. It's a daunting task. And I need your help—all of you."

"Oh, of course, Sebastian. We'll just go and hobnob with the high and mighty. Nothing to it, right?" Archambald remarked in an offhand manner.

"No, you probably won't even get a chance to see the inside of the throne room where the empress conducts her business. They call it the Golden Room, so it's apt to be a bit on the grand side. I dread seeing it myself. But there it is.

"But all of you can contribute something. Liudolf, I want you and Bernard to see if you can find a way into the barracks area. There are guardsmen everywhere. If you can get in with them, we might learn a great deal about the state of their army. I'll provide you with enough gold to loosen some tongues at a tavern or two.

"You, Archambald, don't sell yourself short; you might be able to chat up some chambermaids or serving wenches who work in the palace and see if you can pick up some inside stories about the old girl herself. From what I've heard so far, she might be a lady of questionable morals. If she is, I want to know it. And I particularly want to know why Constantine is no longer the emperor. What is *that* story? How could Irene get away with deposing her own son? Why is he blind? Did someone put his eyes out? Who—and why?

"Milo, you can help with that, if you've a will. I think you said you want to spend some time in one of their monasteries and learn a bit more of the Greek tongue. Good luck in choosing one. I've been told there are dozens of them in the city or within a morning's ride. The place is overrun with long-bearded monks. You might look into their great churches. I know you want to see the inside of the Hagia Sophia. I want to myself. They say it's very beautiful, inside as well as out, and it is one of the great seats of learning in the world—a renowned college of wise men and such, much like Alcuin's academy in Aachen, only more so. Go there. Poke about. See how the Church feels about a woman emperor. Is there any stress there? And why would they let her become the supreme ruler?

"Bardulf, you and Drogo can see what's going on amongst the folk of the city. What do *they* think of the empress? Are they content with her? Do they feel she's a usurper? Anything—whatever you hear—can be important."

"Uh. . . m'lord," Bardulf suggested, "are we to have a bit of that gold yer handin' out so freely, as well? Ye know one can hear a great deal if one is buyin' the ale."

"Well, I suppose you must have a few coins, too, but you are to spend it wisely and listen more than you talk. And don't be giving out information about me while you're at it, or about any of us, for that matter. Just act the barbarian bumpkin and listen."

"Why, I *be* a barbarian bumpkin—me and Drogo—ain't we? But we'll do the best we can, for all that."

***

Once Sebastian had settled himself into a visiting diplomat's spacious and luxurious quarters in one wing of the sprawling royal palace, he found he had little to do. As the ambassador of the Frankish king, he could not just walk inconspicuously around the city. With his long hair, drooping black mustache, and rough Frankish clothes, he was immediately labeled a "tribal barbarian," especially since most Byzantine men wore neatly clipped beards as a sign of masculinity and to distinguish themselves from the many beardless eunuchs in the city. After a day of wandering about the gardens and chapels of the Grand Palace, he was already beside himself with impatience.

Leo saved him. The high-spirited young nobleman was interested in everything about Sebastian and seemed to feel it was his duty to be his constant companion. He personally conducted Sebastian on a grand tour of every great edifice in the city, beginning, appropriately, with the greatest of them all, the Hagia Sophia.

Leo took Sebastian to a spot near the wall where they could observe the magnificent cathedral from a distance. "See how it completely dominates the acropolis of Constantinople, along with the Hippodrome and the adjoining palace complex. It's already two hundred and fifty years old. Nine doors lead into the cathedral, but only the emperor may come in through the main entrance, known as the Imperial Gate."

Once inside, Sebastian stood open-mouthed and awestruck by the unbelievable free space under the enormous dome and the aura of light that suffused the whole cathedral, reflected everywhere from the forty windows at the base of the dome. "The light. . ." he mumbled, staring straight up.

"Ah, yes," Leo agreed, "that flowing light reflected off the walls is the renowned mystery of the cathedral. See how it seems to separate the dome from the rest of the church?"

"It looks like the dome is floating somehow. . . actually floating high above the floor!"

Sebastian spent at least an hour wandering through the great church, marveling at its towering columns, its polished marble floors, the huge golden cross over the altar, and the blazing colors of the giant mosaics on some of the walls. "You're right, Leo, it truly is, as you say, a vision of heaven."

The great church was only the first of the events on Leo's crowded agenda. Next he took Sebastian to the first of the famous Hippodrome races, which occurred on every important feast day during the twelve days between Christmas and Epiphany. Crowding into the stadium along with the masses, they passed under triumphal arches topped by the symbolic bronze sculpture of four enormous horses.

"Nothing can compare to the excitement, noise, and energy of these major sporting events," Leo bragged.

"There must be tens of thousands of people here. I've never seen so many in one place together."

"They fill the stadium on every race day, from early morning to nightfall. Look there, my lord, there she comes!" Sebastian got his first glimpse of the Emperor Irene when she appeared in the royal box at the first of the festival races, waving and smiling at the crowds.

Her voluminous purple-and-silver gown and the light golden cape she wore concealed her body. A jewel-encrusted crown completely covered her hair. Even her hands were encased in silk gloves. Her face alone was uncovered, and Sebastian could barely make out her features from where he sat. Yet her mere arrival seemed to cause vibrations throughout the crowd. All of her movements were slow and deliberate, full of dignity and privilege. It occurred to Sebastian that she was playing a very important role, and she was doing it to perfection.

"Does she do this often?" he asked Leo, who was clapping and calling out for the emperor as enthusiastically as the rest of the crowd.

"Oh yes. She comes to every race. They're quite exciting, as you will soon see. Even she wouldn't miss them. You saw all that bread being handed out in the square before we came in? Well, that's Irene gifting the huge crowd at the beginning of each race. She commands that thousands of loaves of free bread be handed out. Many of them contain gold coins baked inside. And wait until you see the elaborate entertainment organized by the Blues and Greens. There will be multiple performances of music and dancing between the different heats of the race."

With a nod from the emperor, the first race began, accompanied by a thunderous roar from the crowd as four chariots, each with four horses, burst from the starting line. Seven ostrich eggs were set upon a stand high above the track. After each of seven laps, an egg was removed. The noise was deafening for the duration of the race. At its conclusion, the winning driver was awarded with a wreath from the emperor—until the last race, when the grand champion would receive a wreath of gold and a box of golden *solidi*, the coin of the realm. Later, at subsequent races, Sebastian decided he would make sure that all his men, including Milo, were prominently seated in the stadium. None of them had ever seen anything like it, and he was sure the races would become a topic of animated conversation.

The holy season provided Leo with an ideal opportunity to show Sebastian not only the splendor of the seasonal pageantry and brilliant ceremonial occasions, but he also took it upon himself to introduce Sebastian to the underbelly of the capital city: the *tavernas,* where Greek food was at its most exotic and delicious, the tawdry public houses, filled with raucous singing and gambling, and brothels for the upper sector of society, replete with women of every age, color, and race and adorned like so many tropical birds in long, colorful, sleeveless tunics of thin silk and revealing bodices, their feet tucked into gold-colored sandals with straps of silk. Silver serpents encircled their arms and long, heavy jewelry of pearls and precious stones hung from their necks and earlobes.

Sebastian realized as soon as such tours began that Leo was testing him with the seamy side of Constantinople, not only his character but his vulnerability. It occurred to him that Leo might be working his wiles for someone else who might be very interested to know if there were chinks in the armor of the royal Frankish ambassador that might be exploited. Sebastian determined to use the opportunity to turn the tables on his host. He would see how far Leo would go in such environments, and while he kept his own equilibrium, he might watch Leo lose his and learn from it.

***

"How about that one, Sebastian? Have you ever seen such silky skin, such soft raven hair, such sultry eyes, like a fire was lit in her belly and the smoke comes right out of her eyes."

This was no ordinary pleasure house. It was in a part of Constantinople near the marketplace, not hidden away in some alley but boldly placed among other reputable establishments. Inside, extravagant furnishings filled the main hall, and softly burning torches provided low light to the room. The women who entertained there were all exquisitely dressed. And they were skillful, even famous, dancers who performed before the guests periodically and then mixed with them in the drinking area in an ambience of luxurious sensuality, nothing tawdry or blatant. It proclaimed itself a house of entertainment and music.

A riot of colorful pillows provided seats for the guests behind low tables filled with fruit bowls and silver flasks of excellent wine. The walls were adorned with red velvet and silk. Intricately designed Persian rugs covered the floors.

"She's certainly beautiful. They all are," Sebastian replied. "But they don't seem to be pleasure women. I see no assignations being made. It's all very genteel, it seems."

"Well, they are certainly not common whores, if that's what you mean," protested Leo. "These are courtesans, my friend, many from prominent houses in the city. They do not hire their bodies out, but they are often called upon, and generously reimbursed, as they are here, to share their beauty and talent before men of good position in the city."

He added hastily, "That is not to say that one could not find himself a companion among a lot such as this. But it would have to be an arrangement on a very high and semi-permanent level. These women are in huge demand for many of the great celebrations of the city. They are the ones you saw dancing in the Hippodrome during the races—to the delight of the populace, as you must have noticed."

Abruptly, the sound of a flute summoned the women out of the room to a dressing chamber, and in a few minutes they returned, adorned in elaborate dancing clothes, mostly thin silks and veils of transparent cloth over their faces, arms, and bosoms. They paused momentarily before beginning the dance, dead still, heads down, an entrancing tableau. Then they burst into life and movement as the music began, their soft silk skirts billowing out as they turned and whirled, revealing bare legs up to the thighs. The music slowed, and they began to sway, beckoning to the watchers, imitating an embrace and then quickening again as they whirled and turned, their backs alternately arching and then deeply bending, fingers brushing the floor. The music became hypnotic as the dancers spun gracefully, dipped, and rose again, moving about the room so that each dancer appeared enticingly for a moment or so before each guest. At one point, they undid their veils to reveal the beauty of their faces, causing the men to catch their breath in delight. If a man reached out to a dancer, she melted quickly away from him, only to be replaced by the next dancer, one lovely face following another beguilingly. Yet no man stepped over the invisible line.

Sebastian told himself there was no harm in watching, but he soon fell under the spell of the dance as much as any of the other onlookers, utterly charmed by the combination of grace and beauty. One of the dancers paused, swaying before him a moment more than most.

Through the haze of burning torches and voluptuous bodies, he recognized a familiar face. She had changed the color of her thick auburn hair to a luxurious red, and it hung down over both shoulders, partly covering her ample bosom, which she hardly bothered to conceal. Everything about her exuded sexuality. He recognized her at once, not just by her libidinous face and classic form, but by the flawless fettle of her skin and the siren smell of her. It was Adelaide.

As she swept away from him in the flow of the dance, he was staggered by the completely unanticipated apparition of a woman whom he had once thought to marry. She was the daughter of Count Leudegar, a rich and powerful landlord on the middle Rhine, one of Charlemagne's generals.

But even when he first met her, she had been so different from other young Frankish women, recklessly headstrong, and from an early age in the habit of pleasing herself in whatever way she chose. She was incredibly alluring and just as intelligent, but she was also outspoken and unruly. She drank and mated like a lord, as she pleased, and with whomever she pleased, gallivanting up and down the Rhine as if she, and not her father, were the master of Kostheim manor.

Inevitably, when it became clear that no young gentleman of name or high place would marry her because of her reputation, Count Leudegar banished her from the manor and disowned her. She had come to Sebastian as a last resort, at a time when he was especially vulnerable. He had just lost Adela when she was forced to marry Konrad by the king's decree. He was at a low ebb of confidence and hope. Adelaide had used all her wiles and beauty to seduce him and had beguiled him in his loneliness into a promise of marriage. Only the timely appearance of Simon had saved him.

Adelaide had seen immediately that the dashing trader Simon was not only more the kind of man she was used to but was also her way out of the very limited life of a typical Frankish wife and mother. She had cavalierly abandoned her pledge to Sebastian and ensconced herself on Simon's boat when he departed, all the while plaintively proclaiming her still undying love for Sebastian and her abject sorrow that she simply could never live in the middle of a wilderness on the wild Saxon frontier.

Now, out of the blue, at this surpassingly extravagant celebratory feast, in a completely bizarre and foreign place, here she was, the last person he ever expected to see again, undiminished in her elegance and allure. He could scarcely believe it.

He watched her as she finished the dance, passing several times before him, each time with an unmistakable glint of recognition and excitement in her eyes. When the dancers finally retired to the dressing room, Sebastian turned to Leo.

"You said it was possible to make an arrangement with some of these ladies. Do you happen to have one?"

"That is a very bold question, my friend. A nobleman of Constantinople would never ask it," Leo said with a grin. "But since you are an innocent fellow and one from, ahem, perhaps a less refined land, I shall confide in you. As a matter of fact, I do happen to be enriched by a liaison with one of these fascinating sirens. It is, of course, not information that one widely disseminates in this society, but it is quite an ordinary, if unacknowledged, practice." He paused to study Sebastian sardonically. "Why? Do you find yourself sorely tempted? It's quite all right, old fella, all the best men of the city indulge in such diversions."

Sebastian cleared his throat again and avoided looking at the smirking Leo. "Ah, it's just that I thought I recognized someone, a woman I knew many years ago in Francia."

"Oho, how intriguing!" Leo proclaimed, warming to the opportunity. "Well, we will see about this surprising phenomenon. The ladies will return in a moment, and you may be able to renew your acquaintance, if you like. I will, of course, be discreet and allow you to speak to her alone. If something further should develop, you have only to let me know. You would be astonished at what I can arrange in our fair city. No one else need know." With that, he moved away to another table and began exchanging pleasantries with acquaintances.

Sebastian was not surprised that she came at once to his table, sat down beside him, and poured herself a bowl of wine. It was clear she was absolutely flummoxed by his presence and could not tear her eyes away from his. A rosy blush of color had risen in her neck and bosom, and she leaned eagerly toward him, as if she were on the verge of devouring a delicious treat.

"Sebastian!" she breathed. "Is it really *my* Sebastian? I can't believe it's you! How can it be? Did you come looking for me? Oh, please tell me you did. You are still such a beautiful man. You take my breath away. Tell me! Tell me everything. I'm dying to know all about you and my poor forsaken homeland. I'm so glad to hear the sound of my own tongue again and lose myself in your company! What are you doing here? Tell me you will stay here a while. I must see you. I must be with you. I will die if I cannot be." She leaned her face so close to his own that he drew back involuntarily.

"I am King Karl's ambassador to your empress, Adelaide. I will be here until I can see her and convey to her the king's business." He hesitated and then admitted, "Of course, I want to see you as well."

The subdued sound of a gong abruptly interrupted further conversation. Adelaide hastened to tell him, "That man, that Leo you are with, he's a dangerous, secretive man—and very rich. I don't trust him. But he can tell you where to find me. Come to me, my dear Sebastian. I presume you're staying at the palace. I'm there, too—in a different wing, of course. Leo can direct you. If there are no celebrations, we are free on most evenings after nightfall. At least send me a message. But do not fail me. I can't wait to see you—as soon as possible. Come to me," she whispered.

And she was gone, a vision of gleaming gold jewelry, perfume, and silk, joining the others as they swept out of the door and into waiting carriages.

***

Two nights later, thanks to Leo, he met her again. Leo brought him in the middle of the night to a room somewhere close to the women's quarters in the palace. "Wait here," Leo said, "it may take a while. Meanwhile, there's some good wine. Indulge, but be careful, it's quite strong. Enjoy yourself, my friend." He slipped silently out of the little room.

The trysting place was located near a garden. It was filled with the sweet smell of gardenia and wisteria. There were breezeways near the ceiling, and the floor of the room was strewn with pillows. A small torch burned on one wall. For a long time, he lay on the bed of pillows, drinking the thick, strong wine, eventually drifting in and out of a gentle, fanciful slumber.

Suddenly, there she was again, a vision of red and gold and orange silk, her beaming face aglow with excitement and passion.

"My dearest love," she breathed as she laid herself down upon him. "I have so long dreamed of seeing you again." She came at him, an eruption of color and heat and passion. Without thinking, he simply melted into it.

Eventually, toward the morning, lying face-to-face, inches apart, breathing each other's breath, they began to talk. She wanted to know about home, her father, the people she knew, what Sebastian had done since she last saw him, about Adela and his family, and about the king. She even inquired, in a detached way, about Simon.

"Oh, Simon was pretty and fun and all that, exciting for a time. But all he really cared about was collecting information and gold wherever he went. He never missed an opportunity for business, and he was a master at discovering secrets. I believe he must be the most informed man in the world. If what he knew could be measured in weight, he would need a great ship to carry it all."

Sebastian grunted in agreement. "Yes, that's Simon all right. Still, he's a very valuable man to know, and he's been a good friend to me."

"He certainly cared more about all that accumulation than he did about me. It was deadly boring after a while— nothing to do but ride about on his boat with those ghastly, foul-smelling Danes and wait for him to come back from his business. I nearly went mad. So I left him in Barcelona and took the next ship I could find to Constantinople. Simon talked about it so much—called it the most interesting place in the world. I decided that was where I was meant to be, and I left him. He was right, it *is* the most exciting place I've ever been. I love it here."

She paused a moment, thoughtfully gazing into Sebastian's eyes and caressing his face. Suddenly, she sat upright and declared, "Why don't you stay here, my darling, when your business is done? Sell your sword to the emperor.

We can live together here. I am famous. So are you. We can have a good life amidst all this splendor."

Sebastian was confounded. "How can you ask that, Adelaide? I'm a Frank. This place is foreign to me. I serve the king. I have sons. I could never do such a thing. It's out of the question."

"Listen, my love," she said, clasping his head in both hands. "You can do anything you like. You're a great warrior. Everyone knows it, including Her Grace, the emperor. You could find a high place here. King Karl has used you enough. From the looks of the scars on your body, he's almost used you up. Your wife is in a convent. You're not even really married anymore. Even the Church would concede that. And your boys are being trained apart from you anyway. At least Milo is here. He can find a thousand places to study and learn, far better than anything in poor, ignorant Francia. Stay with me, my sweet, lovely man. I will make you insanely happy."

Adelaide was nothing if not a consummate lover. During the next three weeks, they made love constantly. She revealed herself tantalizingly, bit by bit, surprising Sebastian with new delights each day. I know what she is, he told himself. But she is much more than I thought.

She made him laugh, and he could not remember the last time he had really laughed. Her stories about life in Constantinople and the silly, vain people she often had to deal with were clever and hilarious. She sang to him, in a low, husky voice late at night after their lovemaking. She rubbed his back and massaged his hands and feet and ran her long fingers endlessly over his skin. And she listened. She wanted to know everything he had done since they had last seen each other. He spent hours recounting his adventures, revealing his mistakes, his doubts, his regrets. She was like his confessor except that, instead of penance, she gave him only absolution.

"Oh, my dear, dear Sebastian, you've done nothing wrong, poor lamb. Everything you have done has been for someone else—for the king, for your wife or your family, for your friends and for the people of your land. Nothing for yourself. So look at me, come to me. I am your reward."

When they were not together, his thoughts slipped back to her persistently. She had bragged to him long ago that she could give him such pleasure he would think he was an angel in heaven. Well, there was no question about that. She was a stunning wonder. It was easy to remind himself that he had been a very long time without love, without a woman to care for him. An inner voice cautioned him, however, that she was casting a spell over him. That may be, he conceded, but at this crisis point in his life, he wanted to think she might be right—she might actually be able to teach him to be happy again.

Chapter 20

The Emperor Irene

Winter 799

More than a month had passed since they had arrived in Constantinople, and still there had been no formal word about an audience with the emperor. Finally, on the Sunday of Epiphany, the holy season of the celebration of Christ's birth was ending, and Sebastian was invited to the concluding Divine Liturgy in the Hagia Sophia. From the same messenger, Sebastian received a summons to appear before Irene in the Golden Room on the following day.

Irene, the first-ever female emperor, processed through the great church's Imperial Gate in her most elaborate ceremonial robes. She was clad in a brilliant white silk tunic with a bejeweled mantle of royal purple embroidered in gold and draped around her shoulders, her crown a skullcap of solid gold, sparkling with precious stones and hung with pendants of jewels.

Leo, Sebastian's annoying and ever-present escort, almost fell over himself praising the emperor as she walked slowly, like a great swan through a shimmering pond of water lilies, between rows of elegantly dressed clergy, officials, and courtiers toward the enormous cross over the high altar where the Patriarch of Constantinople awaited.

"Listen, Sebastian," Leo gushed, "there are five choirs chanting her praise. Isn't she magnificent? See those two thrones she's headed for? The patriarch will seat her in the left throne of the two, the one just before the altar. The empty one on the right represents God, and the one on the left represents God's representative on earth—her!"

"Leo, I don't know what to do. This is a very different kind of Mass."

"Of course it is. This is Byzantium. This is the Hagia Sophia. This is where God resides. This is his throne on earth. Don't worry. Just do what I do. Listen to the choirs. They're singing now about Theotokos, the Mother of God, and comparing her to Irene. Next they'll be singing about Saint John Chrysostom, the patron saint of Constantinople. Aren't the voices magnificent! Ah, now we will walk a bit."

Everyone except the seated emperor and the patriarch began to process around the church for the next two hours, alternately paying homage to the many favorite saints of the city and returning to the altar for another part of the Mass. Sebastian was bemused to find the onlookers endlessly crossing themselves with broad gestures and abruptly kneeling to press their foreheads against the cold marble floor. The long ceremony was marvelously grand and impressive, but Sebastian was completely mystified and felt himself more than ever lost in a new and very strange world.

***

Early the next morning a committee of high officials in formal dress came forth to escort Sebastian to the throne room for his audience with the emperor. Among them was a tall, distinguished patrician who introduced himself only as John, the Eparch of Constantinople. The eparch was the second most powerful person in the city. It was he who controlled the city's enormous commerce and its legion of foreign traders, assisted by a staff of thousands. Even the military garrison and local peacekeepers were under his power.

With only a terse greeting and little prelude, John presented Sebastian with the suit of formal dress he was to wear to meet with the emperor, including a pair of bright yellow leather shoes. When Sebastian had dressed, the eparch launched immediately into a confidential conversation, preceded by a very short apology. "Sorry you had to wait so long to see the emperor, Lord Sebastian. You must forgive us, but nothing gets done in this bloody city during the Nativity season. It's the same with Easter. Bit of a bother, actually, but

I suppose there's nothing for it. In any case, you're at the top of the list now, and with luck, we'll get you through the formal nonsense quick and lively.

"You come highly recommended, my lord. Your reputation is impressive even here, and the letter from your king which accompanied your credentials could not have been more laudatory. We are pleased to make your acquaintance."

"Thank you, my lord eparch. You do me honor."

"I happen to be here right now only to help you understand exactly what it is that the emperor wishes to accomplish in your visit. It will be much easier when you meet her if you clearly understand her desires. She may not speak a great deal, but I hope to give you a chance to prepare what you will say to her. Before I begin, would you be so kind as to tell me what the vital interests of your king are in this visit? What does *he* wish to accomplish?"

"I shall speak candidly, my lord, as you do," Sebastian said, laying down his first gambit. "My liege, King Karl, finds himself wondering why the throne of the Greeks is suddenly occupied by a female ruler. We do not know what has happened to the Emperor Constantine. You must know that many in Francia and in Rome do not understand how a woman may call herself by a man's title and assume the orb of supreme ruler. Some claim the Byzantine throne is empty."

Sebastian paused for a moment to watch the eparch's eyes carefully to see if his words might be regarded as a provocation. There was no reaction, not even the blink of an eye. The eparch sat stone-faced, hands clasped together in his lap. Sebastian forged on, determined to be completely honest. It seemed better to be as open as possible with this wary, powerful man.

"Secondly, Empress Irene—or perhaps better in the moment, Emperor Irene—is the one who suggested this embassy. I am here at her request. We are intrigued by her suggestion that she and our king might marry and forge an alliance. We should like to know, frankly, what she considers to be gained by such a match.

"We should also like to learn what might be the costs of such an alliance. Would the king be asked to come here to Constantinople and rule both West and East jointly with the emperor? Would we be expected to give up territory or provide troops for a Byzantine war? These might strike you as bold, even outlandish questions, my lord, but they represent the weightiest consequences of an alliance of any nature."

"I thank you, Lord Sebastian, for your candor. It is refreshing to come right to the point. I'm afraid in this city we hardly ever do. I shall speak just as openly. We call Irene our emperor because it is vital that the throne be filled by an emperor, an absolute ruler, God's representative on earth. Irene's son, Constantine, unfortunately experienced a stunning military defeat against the Bulgars and subsequently was unable to function well as army commander or supreme ruler afterward. He has also found himself at odds with our Church. Sadly, he lost confidence in the face of these unhappy developments. That, of course, affects everyone. In the end, unfortunately, he became blind and decided to retire to a monastery. Thus, it is absolutely essential that Irene, a very strong, decisive woman, should take the crown in his stead. So far, she has done admirably well and hopes to do even more with the suggested alliance.

"Our intentions regarding your king are nothing less than to restore the power of the Roman Empire when it was united and to preserve the Christian world against the depredations of the savage pagans who surround us on all sides. Our Emperor Irene needs a strong man to rule here at her side so that all of us—East and West—may better serve the Most High God we share in common.

"When you meet with her in a few minutes, you must assure her that you understand completely what is expected. Please tell her that you will faithfully transmit our wishes to your lord, the king. Will you do that?"

"I will, and gladly, lord eparch."

"Then let us proceed, and may God bless our hopes and plans."

The interview had been mercifully short, but the eparch had spoken without emotion or feeling, almost as if he were reciting a rehearsed speech. He had spoken plainly but without revealing much. And yet Sebastian came away sensing a veiled threat of negative consequences should the meeting with the emperor go badly. The clearest message had been the concern that the empire felt itself at present to be surrounded by pagan enemies, ergo Irene's desire to have King Karl rule "at her side."

***

As Sebastian approached alone, down the long throne room hall toward the imposing porphyry stairs leading to the throne, he was prepared to see an impressive woman. Leo had spoken to him at length about her personal qualities. For one thing, he had related that twenty-five years earlier she had been selected by Constantine's father, Leo IV, after an exhaustive search from among the most promising women in the empire. All brides of heirs to the throne, he said, were chosen in elaborate beauty contests. They were judged not just for their looks, but also for their poise and intelligence. Irene had been an easy choice.

Sebastian was surprised that he could not see the emperor as he approached. The throne was concealed behind purple silk hangings adorned with jewels. He paused and knelt on one knee in the purple marble circle directly beneath the stairs leading up to the throne, his head bent in homage. When he raised his eyes, the curtain had been lifted, and Irene sat on the right side of the double throne in all her splendor, clad in purple-and-gold ceremonial robes with a heavy bejeweled crown perched on her thick black hair.

"Rise, Count Sebastian," she pronounced, extending a hand as if to lift him to his feet. "Do you know," she said slowly, elaborately enunciating the syllables, "why I have summoned you? Please speak freely."

Sebastian noted that Leo had spoken truly; Irene was indeed still a handsome woman but with a distinctly cool and distant demeanor. He began with flowery flattery, as he had been coached to do by Leo. "O great mysterious Wonder of the East, I thank you for this audience, and I assure you I understand thoroughly what it is you wish from my king."

Irene smiled faintly and bent forward, as if to penetrate into Sebastian's head through his eyes. "And do you think your king may be amenable to my suggestions?"

"I do not know, Your Serenity. I am only the messenger. King Karl is an inscrutable monarch. But I do know that he is also a reasonable man, and if he sees advantage in alliance, he is very likely to look favorably upon it."

"I see." She paused and leaned even farther toward Sebastian. "And what do you think he will make of my personal proposal? What will you tell him of me?"

"I must tell him the truth, Illustrious Ruler. And the truth is you must be truly remarkable to have dominion over such a rich and powerful land, and you are, I make bold to say, a most compelling and attractive woman." Sebastian bowed low toward the throne, praying he had not overstepped his bounds.

But Irene was visibly pleased. She smiled broadly and even nodded slightly. "Count Sebastian, you have made me quite happy. I believe a union between myself and your king would be most fortunate for both our realms. We might even succeed in reconstituting the unity the first Constantine established here almost five hundred years ago. Would that not be a most wondrous accomplishment?"

"It would indeed, Your Sublimity, if it is indeed possible and proves beneficial for both our peoples."

"Then go, Lord Sebastian. You have won my approval and my friendship. I think we have an understanding. The eparch and others will work out with you the specifics. For now, suffice it to say you will ask your king to look favorably on an alliance, both of our lands and of ourselves.

"Tonight we shall have a banquet in your honor in the Hall of Nineteen Tables. In the meantime, you may have whatever you wish in our city. It is yours only for the asking."

Sebastian backed away, wondering if he had said too much—or not enough. He was sure he had not actually agreed to anything, but the emperor may have assumed a different conclusion. It worried him a bit, but he was just the messenger. Let her think what she liked. In the end, he would tell the king what he truly thought of this devious place. He bowed until he reached his escort and quickly retired from the court.

That night he sat in the Hall of Nineteen Tables, very near to the table where Emperor Irene was seated alone on a slightly raised platform. As she ate, daintily and sparingly, a constant stream of courtiers, clergy, and noblemen approached and knelt before her to pay their respects. When she was not formally responding to them, she was observing the people at the rest of the tables, her gaze keenly taking in every detail.

Sebastian was allowed to have several of his entourage at his table, including Milo, Liudolf, and Archambald. All were required to wear formal clothes, and all were considerably discomfited by them but very happy indeed to partake of the culinary fare, which included a half dozen kinds of fish, the succulent flesh of young lamb, and a cornucopia of exotic fruit, which none had ever tasted before.

"Look at this orange!" Archambald giggled, his mouth dripping with juice. "This is a delicious wonder! I've never eaten anything like it. And look at these plates. . . we're actually eating off gold plates! Milo, taste some of this wine. I know you don't drink, but you may later, and you'll never taste any wine like this again. It's. . . what do the lords call it? Ambrosia! That's it, the nectar of the gods. And there's more than one kind, and we're drinking it all out of cups made out of pure gold and that agate stuff that looks like marble."

Sebastian had tried to find Simon in time for the banquet, but the trader was nowhere to be seen. In fact, Sebastian realized uneasily that he had not seen Simon since the early days of their arrival. He vowed to go down to the Golden Horn and track him down on the morrow.

Leo was one of the guests at the banquet, and he made a point of joining Sebastian briefly to inquire how the embassy with Irene had gone. "Well, my friend, what did you think of her? Isn't she magnificent?" He leaned in close and whispered, "And what do you think of her as a woman, eh? She's not bad, right? Your King Karl could do far worse, I reckon. Do you think he might fancy her?"

Leo was already well on his way to intoxication, and Sebastian found his effusive outburst highly embarrassing and offensive. It only served to heighten his suspicions of this ambitious young courtier. He fended off the questions with feigned detachment. "Ach, Leo, don't ask me such questions now. . . far too serious. And I've had far too much to drink. I want to enjoy the moment. Later, my friend. Look, the dancers!"

Sebastian was not surprised to see Adelaide first among the dancers appearing. They were the same troupe he had enjoyed so much at the house of entertainment in the market area. The difference this time was their modest dress— no bare legs or flashes of bare bosom. They wore long gowns of black and red and gold silk with broad hems and sleeves embroidered with ornate and elaborate designs. Wide gold bands adorned their waists, and their heads were crowned with tall, elaborate hats shaped like fans.

Leo interjected himself again. "There they are, our famous courtesans. They are the premier entertainers of the city, the same ones we saw in town and performing at the Hippodrome. And they're at every other important occasion, I can assure you. Ah, there's the redhead you fancy. I can see why, old chap. She's quite lovely. You have very good taste. I hope she's as good in bed as she looks."

Sebastian was greatly relieved when the cloddish dandy lurched away to another table, all the while leering at the women with undisguised lust.

Musicians with flutes, lyres, tambourines, and bells preceded the dancers as they weaved their way among the tables, finally forming a wide circle enclosing Sebastian's table and the emperor's. In this first dance, they held each other by the shoulders and moved gracefully back and forth around the tables in time to the music, gradually increasing their speed until they seemed a spinning blur before breaking off and weaving once again throughout the room. Sebastian was singled out for their attention as each beautiful dancer paused several times before him to hold out a hand to touch his face or shoulder. Some paused to run their fingers through Milo's golden hair, their eyes sparkling in delight as they took in the handsome one-armed youth.

The banquet was a high point for everyone. As they made their way back to their sleeping quarters, the men couldn't stop talking about it, and Sebastian wondered why he had feared coming to Constantinople. So far, everything—Adelaide, the Emperor Irene, the beautiful, festive city—had far exceeded all his expectations. He couldn't help feeling a bit triumphant.

***

Late that evening after the banquet, Sebastian met with Adelaide as usual in the small room off the flower garden. He was elated and could not wait to sweep her up into his arms. They made love passionately at first and then gently, as if to calm the inner fire into comforting, restful warmth.

Sebastian made up his mind. Clearly, Adela had given him up for good. He could hardly believe it had been twelve whole years since they had lived as man and wife. Every attempt to win her back had become a dead end. He was tired of the lonely life he led, filled with endless duty and travel. Over that long time, he had lived constantly between anger and regret. He was sick of it. He desperately wanted to feel again the love of a woman, the comfort of sharing the same thoughts and circumstances, the balm of intimacy.

"Adelaide," he said, turning to look into her eyes. "We have a long history, do we not? I remember that once you wanted me more than any other man. I hope you still have the same feelings. My dear Adelaide, I want you to share my life. But I must finish my embassy for the king. There is still Jerusalem and Baghdad before I can return to Francia. I would like you to come with me. But if for some reason you cannot, I will return for you here when we're done. Will you come with me?"

Adelaide said nothing and looked away. Surprised, Sebastian watched as she got out of bed and began to dress. When she finished, she sat back down on edge of the bed. "Oh, my love, I was afraid you would say this. I had hoped you would agree to stay here with me. We could be happy here. But I cannot go back to Francia—ever. I hated my life there. I had no freedom; I could never be anybody there—it's a man's world. You know that. Here I'm a famous courtesan and dancer. Even the people of the city know me and celebrate me in the Hippodrome."

"Yes, and all the men look at you as if they want to tear your clothes off and ravage you."

"Well, what of it? I am beautiful, am I not? What is beauty for if not to show it—and use it for my own benefit? Besides, I like it when men look at me. I revel in it. It's thrilling to be the object of everyone's desire. They know they cannot have me—unless I wish it. And I am very careful about whom I choose to be with. Don't you see? This is an exciting life. Here I am free. I can do everything that I was censured for in Francia. Bah! Who wants to go back to that suffocating life?"

He couldn't believe she was actually turning him down. She had sworn she loved him many times and proved it with her body over and over again. She seemed fulfilled. He was a famous count in Francia and a favorite of the high king. What more could she want?

"But you would have *me*. You said you loved me. You said it many times these last few weeks. What we've had here has been wondrous—an enchantment. If we could hold onto that, it would be enough for me."

"I *do* love you, Sebastian. So much my stomach hurts to think of you leaving. Still, it is not enough. Don't you see? If I went back with you to that life, I might just dry up and die. And it's very likely our relationship would turn bitter and die as well because of it."

"Not if we could keep what we've had here. Besides, how long do you think you can stay here and keep your beauty and the attention you crave? In Francia, I would always be there for you. Think! If you give any thought to the future, you *must* choose to come with me."

"No, my heart, it is you who must choose. You can stay here—with me—or you can serve your king. Choose. . . and let me know. Now I must go."

***

Grievously disappointed and hurt by Adelaide's decision, Sebastian felt a terrible urgency to get out of Constantinople as soon as possible. He realized bitterly that she had deceived him, probably not intentionally—she was not a cruel person; she could be compassionate, kind, and loving one moment but fiercely independent in the next and hedonistic to a fault. He faced the truth: Adelaide was completely incapable of being satisfied for long by only one person or circumstance. He thought ruefully that her love was just like the biblical seed that falls on rocky ground; it sprouts up quickly and intensely, but its roots are so shallow they're easily plucked out.

It dawned on him that Adelaide had changed very little since he had first met her. Her love for him, as intense as it had been, was bound to be impermanent. It was her nature. The realization, however, did not dull the pain of her rejection.

Suddenly, Sebastian was shocked to realize that he had been blind while with Adelaide almost constantly these past weeks and that, aside from the banquet, he had hardly had time to talk to Milo or the men in all that time. He felt out of touch with them and strangely apprehensive. Wild with concern, he sent a messenger at once to Captain Barbero, whose ship had returned from Athens and was in the harbor of the Golden Horn. The captain reported back that he was ready to sail at any time.

Then Sebastian quickly called the small company together to plan how to send an accounting of the embassy to Charlemagne and to affect their departure at once.

"Has anyone seen Simon? We must get out of this place straightaway!"

"Aye, m'lord," Bernard answered. "I saw him yesterday down by the harbor. He's got a new ship. He told me to tell you he's been hearing that something's up about us Franks. Many of them Greeks don't want no alliance with us. He said we ought to be getting out of this place as soon as may be. I would have told you before, but I couldn't find you."

"What harbor, Bernard? The Golden Horn?"

"He ain't in the Golden Horn, m'lord. He's got the ship moored in the Harbor of Julian. It's where the woman emperor comes in, right down the hill below us."

"Did he say anything else?"

"He said he's ready to go when you are, but we should hurry 'cause he can't keep the ship fixed there for long."

"Good! We'll send word to him at once. But first we have to decide what to tell the king about Irene and the Greeks. Tell me quickly, what have you learned?"

Liudolf was the first to speak up. "I know this, Sebastian, the morale in their army is not good. They've suffered some punishing defeats lately against the Bulgars. And the Arab armies keep pushing into Anatolia from the south. They can't seem to fight them off either. That's why they want our king to make the alliance; they hope our strength, together with what's left of theirs, will stave off their enemies. And it may be we shall even be asked to send troops to help them. Anyway, that's the talk around the water cask in the barracks."

"That's what I've heard, too, Liudolf," Sebastian said. "But it's only half. The young blue-bloods I've been associating with these past few weeks want nothing to do with us. When they've been deep into their cups, they're derisive about our people, and they ridicule our king. I don't know how many times I heard them call him a barbarian. Among the decision makers, however, there are several powerful generals who would love to see the match. They're truly worried, but they're divided somewhat too.

"Milo, what have you heard amongst the clergy? They seem to be as powerful an influence on the emperor as anyone."

"I believe they are, Father. They talk constantly about this subject. Some definitely do not wish to see a union between our king and Emperor Irene. They call him a papist, and they say he would bring our brand of Christianity—and our pope—to Constantinople. Others, like the generals, say they must support the union if they hope for Byzantium to survive. You're right, they are deeply divided."

"Did you discover what happened to Constantine?"

"I did, sir. The young emperor was blinded by order of his mother. The clergy concurred because no one wanted him to rule any longer. He had almost no supporters among the clergy. It seems Constantine divorced his first wife, and the Church could not condone it. He flaunted his second wife and completely disaffected them. Apparently, he's in a monastery now. Their law says his blindness means he's unfit and ineligible to rule."

"Hmm. So that's why they didn't kill him. What else? Anyone?"

Bardulf spoke up hesitatingly. "Well, sir. I don't know if it makes much difference, but what I heared amongst the folks who cooks and cleans and runs this palace was that this emperor they got now is a crazy woman. She don't like nobody, they says. She won't let nobody but a very few folk attend her. They say she's feared to death that somebody's goin' to murder her. That's why she makes everythin' so formal and such, and don't hardly go nowhere. I reckon that must be why she would like our king to come live with her, so maybe she might could sleep at night."

"All right. I have enough. Most of what you've said confirms what I've learned as well.

I'll write a letter to the king. When it's done, we must go on at once to Jerusalem, but someone must bring the letter back to the king. Here's what I think is best: Archambald, you will take the parchment and answer to the king. Bernard, you'll go with him. It's down to you to find the way back and get you both home with the parchment. Can you do it?"

"I reckon I know the way, if you get me a ship back to It-arly and some silver to buy some horses from there."

"Right. Captain Barbero has sent me word that he has returned from Athens. I will send orders to him to take you back to Venice. Barbero's a good captain, and we're paying him plenty, so he will get you there safely enough. But from there, you'll be on your own. I'm worried that you won't have any help getting all that way to Aachen."

"We will find us a way, m'lord," the taciturn old soldier replied.

"All right, then. I will have the parchment ready by tonight. Barbero reports he's ready to sail at any time. We'll try for the early tide tomorrow. Liudolf, you hie down to the royal harbor as fast as you can and tell Simon he must be ready to leave before first light. Everyone else, stay close. We may have to leave quickly. Say nothing to anyone about our going."

Late that evening, Sebastian turned the parchment over to Archambald with instructions to proceed at once to Captain Barbero for the departure on the morrow.

"I don't like this, Sebastian. I'm supposed to stay with you. We're always together, ain't we? Besides, I want to see Jerusalem and Baghdad and all that. It's not fair."

"Listen, my old friend, someone has to go. We must let the king know what we're thinking about this alliance business before it gets out of hand. It's best for you to go now while we've got the chance. We don't know what troubles we're likely to encounter down the road."

Sebastian gave his long-time comrade a fond embrace and looked into his eyes to say farewell. "You know I hate to send you back, my brother. What'll I do for a jest or two or some fun on the road? It'll be a dull road for sure without you. But it has to be someone the king knows and trusts, and you know him and know all the details of our trip. Just pass them on and tell him we're doing all right so far. Be safe, Archambald. I can't do without you."

***

As it turned out, Simon's reservations were well founded. In the middle of the night, as Sebastian was packing hurriedly, Leo burst triumphantly into his room, recklessly drunk and wearing a serpent's smile. Sebastian could tell from the ugly smirk on his face that this was not likely to be a friendly invitation to one of Leo's nights of carousing. The man was positively panting to launch some terrible news like a weapon at Sebastian's unsuspecting head.

"Well, my good *Lord* Sebastian, I see you're ready to leave us. I wonder if you will be able to do so," he taunted, clearly enjoying himself. "I fear the eparch may have something to say about that. It seems the message you wrote to your king has been intercepted. The emperor was not pleased by what you said about her. Apparently, you feel she is unstable, and you think her hold on power here is tenuous. Tsk, tsk. You should never have written that, my careless friend.

"And you also do not think your king should marry her. My, my! That is not what you told the emperor at your audience. You said you would recommend the alliance."

"I never said that. I never told her I would recommend the marriage, only that I would tell him what she said and how she looked and that it would be up to him entirely to decide."

"Well, you must have led her to think you would make the recommendation. You certainly should have, but it doesn't matter now. I'm so sorry, Sebastian, but I'm afraid that mistake will cost you dearly. The emperor likes to prescribe torture for those who insult her personally."

As Sebastian stood up, thunderstruck, and searched for words to respond, Leo continued. He was relishing the moment, sniggering and almost swooning with pleasure as he heaped on more bad news.

"And what's more, my woolly barbarian, your friend Adelaide. . . you know, the voluptuous redhead. . ." He paused to watch Sebastian's face. "She has consented to be my consort. She was quite flattered that I asked her. You see, my father is one of the leading members of our nobility, and I am certain to take his place eventually, which means I will have the emperor's ear and a very high place in this realm. Adelaide was quite taken with the prospects of rising with me. What do you think of that?"

As Leo gleefully delivered one blow after another, Sebastian's emotions changed rapidly from alarm and fear to rage and hate. It was suddenly clear that this man, this weasel-faced, conniving little fool, had been plotting all along to sabotage the mission and bring them all to grief. Sebastian could feel his gorge rising, the blood beginning to pound in his temples, as if before a battle. He gritted his teeth; his fingernails dug into his palms.

"Oh, I see you're disappointed. Poor bumpkin! Well, she was too much woman for you anyway, old fella. You couldn't have kept her satisfied for very long."

And then Leo delivered the final blow. "One last thing, old boy, I'm so sorry to tell you, but one of your men, Archambald, I think you called him, resisted our constables when we arrested him there on the Venetian boat. We had to kill him. The other one, the old fellow, jumped overboard. We did not see him emerge.

"I'm sure you understand we could never have allowed that parchment to get back to your king." Leo stiffened, and the taunting smile was replaced by a look of naked malice. "And I have the great satisfaction to tell you neither will you or any of your men. I only tell you this because I wanted the pleasure of seeing your face." He narrowed his eyes and sneered. "How could you ever think you were on a level with me?"

With a final triumphant smile, Leo turned to go. But there was no way he would ever get out. The full impact of the disaster flooded into Sebastian's brain and filled his body with uncontrollable fury. Realizing that all was lost, including, most likely, his own life and the lives of his beloved son and the rest of his friends, he turned his wrath fully on the man responsible.

"You piece of *scheisse*, you bloody, conniving schemer, sneaking murderous rotter—you shall pay!"

Sebastian caught him by the hair and pulled him back. "You did this, you snake," he whispered into Leo's ear. "You said you were my friend. But it was you who spied on us and told them everything. You even went with them to kill Archambald. You. . . you. . ." Leo's face turned purple as Sebastian's pulled his head back violently. He screamed like a woman as Sebastian drew his dagger and slit the little man's throat.

Chapter 21

Jerusalem

Spring 799 and Winter, 800

Sebastian burst in on the sleeping Liudolf in the next room. "Get the others—now! Run! Leave everything except your weapons and the money bag and get down at once to the emperor's harbor, the Julian. Tell Simon to man the oars and set the sails. Go! I've got to find Milo. Do you know where he is?"

"Try the palace chapel," Liudolf shouted, buckling on his sword belt. "He goes there every morning early."

Sebastian raced for the chapel and frantically flung open the door just as Mass was beginning. He grabbed the astonished Milo, who was standing in the last row of monks and clergy. "Shh! Don't say anything. Just come. Hurry!" He led the lad out of the chapel with as little stir as possible and shut the door quietly. Once outside, they began to run at breakneck speed out of the palace and down the narrow stone stairs toward the wall. Beyond it lay the Julian Harbor and Simon's waiting ship.

The palace bells began to ring the alarm just as the morning sun cast a halo of light around the tallest tower. No doubt the eparch's constables had discovered the empty rooms of the Franks, and perhaps someone had already spotted Leo's bloody corpse in the garden.

There was no time. Someone must have seen them racing out of the palace. More bells began to ring, and the sound of voices could be heard from the direction they had come. They reached the wall—and there stood two guards barring the gate to the harbor.

Sebastian drew his sword as they descended on the guards. "You have a choice, men," he said in his primitive

Greek, holding the sword out to one side. "You can die now, or you can take this gift and let us through the gate." With his left hand, he drew a small pouch of gold from his belt and emptied it onto the ground.

The guards were low-level sentries pulling the graveyard watch. Not exactly their best fighting men, Sebastian considered. He could kill them both easily if he had to. God, make them choose the money!

They did. A single look passed between them, and then they turned to open the gate. Sebastian warned them as he and Milo passed through, "Lock the gate. When the eparch's men come, tell them you've seen no one. Hide the gold, or they'll find you out."

As they ran up the plank onto Simon's ship, they could hear shouts from the gate and the sounds of running men. But Simon had only to give the command and the oarsmen pulled the craft rapidly away from the shore and toward the channel leading to the harbor entrance. His lean new ship quickly sprouted sails, and just at daybreak, they slipped smoothly through the entrance and set sail into the open Sea of Marmara.

The ship Simon had purchased on the Asian side of Constantinople was equipped with lateen sails, which, with a fair wind, quickly bore them out of sight before chase vessels could assemble crews and break sail. However, Sebastian kept everyone on high alert until nightfall and never truly relaxed until they had passed through the narrow straits of the Dardanelles and completely out of Byzantine territory.

***

"Does it really matter how many men you've killed, Sebastian?" Simon suggested offhandedly while they paced the deck of the pitching ship as it plowed its way toward the Levant. Sebastian had been in a brown funk ever since they got out of Constantinople. Everything had gone wrong, and they had barely escaped with their lives, but Archambald and Bernard had not. Sebastian was in mourning for them—and for himself as well. He mourned for the man he had been, despising more and more the one he had become. Suddenly, as he walked unsteadily with Simon back and forth across the boat, gazing out to the horizon, he felt the need to confess what he was feeling to someone lest it poison him from within. He poured it all out to Simon, who was as discerning and forgiving a friend as he had at the moment.

"You don't know, Simon. I just cut the throat of that serpent Leo. And before him I murdered Ivor the Bold in cold blood. But I killed scores of others, too—in battles and for the king. I stopped counting long ago. I tell myself it's war— killing is justifiable in war, right? At least that's what we tell ourselves. The Bible we Christians hold so dear does not say that, however; quite the contrary. I don't really know how we came to reconcile all the killing we do with what we profess to believe as Christians—and often, God forgive us, in the name of Christianity!"

"One has to defend oneself, no?" Simon ventured. "And what would happen to our children, our families, all of our people if we didn't defend ourselves? Can you imagine what the Saxons would do to us Franks if the king suddenly stopped fighting them?"

"Well, he steadfastly refuses to believe there *is* another way. I suppose you're glad you're a Jew instead of a Christian, right? 'An eye for an eye.' Isn't that what you believe? It's an easy rule to understand."

"I wish it were that simple, my friend. But ever since the Romans nearly exterminated us in the years after your Jesus was executed, we've been a homeless people, too few in number, condemned to wander about the earth depending on the tolerance of everyone else—Christian, Muslim, you name it—for a place to live and the permission to try and earn a living somehow.

"Oh, I've had to do my share of killing, no mistake. But I do it only in my defense, and I'm very careful who I kill and where I do it. It certainly is the last resort for a Jew. You never know who is going to decide to seek revenge and whether they might well take it out on any Jew who happens to be passing by—or even on our whole people."

"But it's so easy to justify the killing I've done. It's all in the name of the king, isn't it? And that makes it all right. I don't understand the logic of it, considering we're Christians, but it's war, and so we accept it!

"But there have been too many killings, Simon. I'm sick of it. My hands are drenched in blood. I often can't sleep at night without dreaming of the men I've killed. So many! It's become like a bloody habit. I don't even think now about using violence to solve a problem. And now I've killed two men in cold blood. I never even gave them a chance."

"It's my understanding, Brother, that those two deserved killing more than any of the others. Ivor the Bold was a bloodthirsty pirate, a scourge, no better than a diseased rat. He only spared you because he wanted to torture you by letting you live without Adela and in a crippled state.

"And that weasel Leo sabotaged your mission for the king and was more than happy to see you die because you refused to kiss his patrician arse. Then he added insult to injury by literally buying that woman you were so enamored of there at the end. What was her name?"

"Don't be ridiculous. You know it was Adelaide—and everyone knows she was once your mistress. And don't say anything bad about her. She was just doing what she could. She's a woman alone in a very intimidating place—and a brave one at that. Do you blame her for seizing what security and opportunity she can?"

"No, I don't. But I was never as close to her as you were. And, as it turned out, she was just using me to get out of Francia. I'm sorry, old comrade. I don't want to add to your misery. You just have the most infernal luck with love of any man I've ever seen. You know what your problem is, Sebastian?"

"Oh, pray tell me. I'm sure you'll be able to demonstrate what I've been doing wrong with women all along and miraculously use your discovery to cure me."

"Well, you do have a disease. It's called 'addiction.' You're addicted to certain women. You gravitate to them as if it were inevitable, ordained by God himself. You love them so completely and passionately that you get your heart completely smashed into pieces. I've told you before—women are everywhere. All it takes for most of them is a winning smile, a hearty laugh, and a jingle in one's pocket. You can have even the most beautiful women if you don't seem to care whether you do or not. Don't you know the rule about men and women? The man wants the woman—mostly physically, but what the woman wants is for the man to want *her*. All one has to do is show a healthy interest, but make it clear you can take it or leave it and it won't matter a tinker's damn either way."

"What a disgusting philosophy. Where's the love in all that?"

"Love? Love is in the moment, my friend. And you can have such moments over and over again. They're inexhaustible—just not for very long with the same woman. . . for the most part."

"I can't be satisfied with that, Simon. It seems so impersonal. As soon as I'm done with a woman, I start to feel guilty and sorry for her. What is left for her?"

"A silver coin or two, if you're generous. Perhaps more if she's special. Believe me, she'd rather have it than not—even if you don't stay."

"It's all bollocks. I'm beginning to think I'm not good enough for any woman. Adela said she would love me to the end of time. But a heartless and impersonal Church decree could make her leave me forever. And then even a woman such as Adelaide, a courtesan and a free thinker if there ever was one, won't have me, though she, too, said that she loved me desperately.

"I have no peace. I feel I've become someone I don't even know. I have neither love nor virtue left. I'm haunted by the men I've killed and the women I've loved. I see no point to this insane life.

"Leave it now," Sebastian said, holding up a hand to stop further comment. "I cannot reconcile anything. And I don't think more talk about it will help. I'm grateful for your concern, friend Simon, but you can't help either. I seem to have lost my way. . . or I don't even care. I fear I may even have lost my soul." He walked away abruptly to the other end of the ship to stand at the prow and look out over the sea.

The voyage across the Mediterranean was a time of penance for most of the Franks. Even Sebastian felt physically sick some of the time when the ship bucked and pitched against an aroused sea. During such turbulence, he walked back and forth, from one end of the ship to the other, looking straight ahead and not at the roiling waters.

He continued to spend much of his time mourning his murdered boyhood friend. Like Liudolf, Archambald had been with him at every significant moment in his life—the death of his father, the burning of Fernshanz by the Saxons, his marriage to Adela, and almost every battle he'd ever been in. The lighthearted, carefree lover of music and jests had been as close as any brother. Archambald had his weaknesses, he remembered sadly. He was a bumbler and a terrible soldier. But everyone loved him for his weaknesses nonetheless. He never made excuses for them; he just poked fun at himself and laughed them off.

He recalled with sympathy how Archambald had been the sickest of them all on the way to Constantinople, even though the ship stayed between the islands or close to shore, and he thought with some comfort that at least Archambald didn't have to endure the present rough crossing.

And how could one ever forget or replace Bernard, his mother's own personal guardian and the most faithful and distinguished soldier he'd ever had in his command? Bernard was like an oak tree; he could go through fire and storm and still be strong and steady. And he never breathed a word about how hard anything was. He was ageless. It was hard to believe he was gone. Sebastian knew he would never stop missing the old fellow.

He had not wanted any of his closest companions to join him on this mission for the king, knowing its dangers and how long it would take. But he could not deter any of them, even his son Milo, who was no warrior and woefully ignorant of the realities of the world outside Francia. Now, after the tragedy of Archambald's and Bernard's deaths, he feared more than ever for Milo and the others but could think of no way to turn any of them back toward home. The thought of inevitable future perils added to the burden of guilt he felt about so much of his life so far. By the time they reached Ashdod, the ancient coastal village that was the gateway to Jerusalem, Sebastian was truly sick at heart, lethargic, and nearly inarticulate.

***

Simon bought horses enough for their small company and for the scant baggage that remained after the escape from Constantinople. He also arranged to have each man fitted out with Arab clothing for the drier, hotter desert climate, though they arrived to an unusually mild and pleasant spring. They spent one more night aboard ship while Simon saw to the transport of his commercial cargo to Jerusalem, then set off with the group at dawn the next day, covering the dozen leagues to the city before nightfall.

All felt the excitement of approaching the holy city, but Milo was alive with fervor. His face radiated joy when he got his first glimpse of the sand-colored stones of the walls and towers of the ancient holy place, transformed into gold and purple by the late afternoon sun. Milo was sure it looked no different from that long-ago Palm Sunday when Jesus rode in on a donkey. He kept riding up to Simon with questions about the city and its holy sites.

"Tell me about the Via Dolorosa, Simon. I want to walk it myself as soon as we arrive. Is it true what they say, that one can actually visit the tomb where Christ was buried and even see the hole where his cross stood on Golgotha? Will I be able to walk freely about the city so I can see everything?"

"Well, Master Milo, I believe you will be able to do most of what you wish. But keep in mind this is an Arab city now. Its ultimate ruler is Harun al-Rashid, whom we mean to see in Baghdad; he is the supreme authority in every place we intend to travel."

Milo was fascinated by the change in the pervading culture of the new land. He had never seen so many dark-skinned people, and he longed to talk to them to see how they might be different from the Frankish people he was used to. Constantinople had been very different as well, a bustling city with crowds of Greeks. But it was a rich and boisterous city, sanguine and proud, in spite of the perils that lurked beyond its borders.

Here in Palestine, there were also many people everywhere, but they were strikingly poorer, more gaunt and serious, sere, and used to hard conditions, like the desiccated land they lived in. Milo was greatly surprised by their dress: for the men, turbans and long, loose robes called *thobes*, mostly white and reaching to their feet; for the women *hijab* head scarves and loose enveloping cloaks covering almost all of their skin. And everywhere, even in Ashdod, the modest coastal town where they disembarked, there were signs of religious fervor—chanting from minarets and prayer moments throughout the day when all life seemed to pause. He questioned Simon relentlessly about everything he saw.

"Actually, the rule of the Mussulmen has not been so bad for us Jews. We were allowed to move back into the city after the Greeks under Constantine kicked us out a few hundred years or so ago. We move fairly freely in the old city and have our own quarter there. That's where I'll do most of my trading while we're here."

"What about the Christians? Can't we also move about freely?"

"I'm afraid, young Milo, that lately, since the wars Harun has been fighting with the Greeks, the Arabs have tightened their grip on the Christian population of the city. Greek and Armenian Christians still comprise the largest populations in Jerusalem, and the Byzantine Church still oversees most of the Christian sites, but there are a great many more Arabs in the city now, and I've been told the Christians find it more and more difficult and expensive to live there."

Simon gave Milo a sympathetic look and then reached out to squeeze his shoulder. "You're not in the Christian world anymore. You will soon find out what it's like to be in the minority in a hostile environment. It won't be pleasant. Christians are required to wear identifying clothing. They can only worship in certain specified places. They must make way for any Arab passing by and must bow every time they pass a mosque. But the worst thing is that the Arabs have imposed a heavy tax on all Christians living in or entering the city, so much so that the number of Christian pilgrims has dried up to a trickle, and many Christians who have lived here all their lives are becoming Muslims or leaving. It's just become too costly and dangerous for them."

"What about us? Will we have trouble entering the city?" Milo asked with alarm.

"I don't think so, lad. Your father is an ambassador from King Karl to Harun al-Rashid himself. If he has to, he can make himself known and present official credentials from Baghdad inviting him to the court of the Abbasid Empire. But we should have no problem. Once we're in the city, we'll keep a low profile as long as we can. I've arranged for us to stay in the Jewish quarter with some of my associates. If we dress inconspicuously, we should bring no attention to ourselves."

"But what about me? If I have to dress like an Arab but with some clothing that identifies me as a Christian, and if I have to live in the Jewish quarter, how will I be able to see the Christian holy places?"

"Have no fear, Milo. Once you're in the city, you'll be able to move about fairly freely. There are many others who will look like you. All you need do is remain inconspicuous and stay out of trouble. You can do that, can't you?"

"Of course. I only want to see and experience where Jesus walked and preached. I want to feel his spirit here, in this holy place, where he died and rose again. It's important to me to take advantage of this incredible opportunity. I would rather be here now and have this experience than anything else in the world."

"Well, you shall have it. I will see to it personally, if nothing else. While you're at it, it might be a very good thing if you could get your father to go along with you on your little pilgrimage in the city. His spirits are very low at the moment."

"Why is that, Simon? No one will tell me why he's so down. He won't even speak to me beyond one-word answers. I know it has something to do with why we had to run for our lives out of Constantinople, but no one will say more to me than 'there was some trouble with the Greeks.' Everyone seems to think I'm still a child who mustn't be frightened by anything."

"It's really not my place to tell you what happened. One day I hope your father will. Let me say only that our mission to the emperor was put into jeopardy by contemptible men. Our lives were in danger, and your father did what was necessary to get us out of there alive. He will fill in the blanks in the story when he's able. Right now I believe he's feeling the consequences of the hard life he has led thus far and the many disappointments he has experienced. He desperately needs renewal, which I'm hoping he can find here. Be alert. You may be able to help him."

Milo was now seriously worried about his father, who had hardly spoken at all since they left the ship and seemed to take little interest in the phenomena occurring around him. He spent the rest of the journey to Jerusalem racking his brain and vowing to find a way to help his father.

***

"There it is, my friends," Simon pointed out as they paused on a low rise to gaze upon the holy city before entering. "There to the right of the western gate, you can see the ancient Tower of David. It's the highest point and overlooks the whole city. It's the Citadel of the city, and there before the walls is a wide and deep moat. Look farther and more to the other side of the city and you can see the gold sheeting of the Muslim Dome of the Rock. From the Temple Mount where that mosque stands, Mohammed is said to have ascended into heaven. See those tall, narrow towers around it and in other parts of the city? Those are minarets. Every morning the whole city is called to prayer by mullahs chanting from the tops of those towers."

"Right, Muslim prayers," Liudolf grumbled.

"Of course, my dear Liudolf, but the city is holy to the peoples of three different religions, all of whom worship the same God. Don't you think that it's appropriate that all should be called to prayer?"

Surprising everybody, Sebastian interjected with the first words he had spoken since they left Ashdod, "Listen, all of you. We haven't heard from Isaac yet. It may be a while before he comes. But he's the key to our success in Baghdad, and maybe here as well. We cannot go on without him. He knows exactly how to get to the caliph, whom he knows personally. And he will also help us find our royal ambassadors in Antioch. We'll have to wait here in Jerusalem for as long as it takes.

"We've important things to do here. Simon and I need to meet with the Jewish leaders who will help us, and we need to get an audience with the Christian patriarch of Jerusalem. In both cases, we will need Isaac.

"Meanwhile, it's extremely important that we make no stir whatsoever here in Jerusalem. Except where absolutely necessary, I won't reveal who I am, and we'll all try to pass ourselves as part of Simon's trading community, the Radhanites. Simon, what else do we need to tell them?"

Simon was somewhat taken aback by Sebastian's sudden resumption of command, but he was nonetheless relieved to hear the old decisiveness he knew so well. He continued the tutorial. "There are two large Christian communities here, one Greek and one Armenian. They're both in the western side of the city. You shouldn't worry about not experiencing the Christian holy sites, even though many of them are in the Arab sector. But stay away from everything else in that part of the city. The Arabs are forbidden to drink alcohol, so you might find it difficult to find any beer or wine, but it's there nonetheless—so no drinking or storytelling in the back alley taverns there, Bardulf. Do you understand?"

"I do, Master Simon. But it's all right if we can find a pint or two in the Jewish part, ain't it?"

"Yes, but don't draw attention to yourselves. If you keep your ears open, you might see or get a whiff of something that might be very important to us. Don't fail to let us know."

***

Simon got them into Jerusalem without incident as part of the Radhanite trading circle, and they disappeared into the Jewish quarter before any word from Constantinople could have reached the city. Sebastian was grateful to have some time just to keep low and think of what to do next. However, his thoughts kept returning to the fiasco in Constantinople.

As far as Sebastian knew, Irene and the eparch had not even known that he planned to go on to Jerusalem and Baghdad rather than immediately back to Francia.

Only Adelaide knew. And Sebastian's first thought was to pray that she would not be interrogated for what had happened to Leo.

But he was having second thoughts. On the night Leo was killed, he had said that Adelaide consented that same evening to become his consort. How could she have done that so soon after swearing that she would love him forever? Had the whole affair been a huge lie, a plan to influence him and seduce him into sending a favorable report to King Karl? Had she been in league with Leo the entire time? No, he thought, that would have made Adelaide a depraved monster, and everything in him told him her love, shallow though it may have been, had been real. But if it hadn't, Adelaide knew he was going to Jerusalem, and she would most likely betray him again.

The questions nearly drove him mad. If Adelaide was innocent, she was in grave danger. If she was not, she could jeopardize the whole mission and all their lives.

To distract himself once they were settled in the Jewish Quarter, Sebastian set to wandering around the city at all hours. He meandered into bazaars where all kinds of food and wares were available, no matter which quarter of the city. After a while, he tired of bowing at every mosque he passed in the Arab quarter and ripped off the telltale cloths that designated him as a Christian, blending instead into the constant flow of people on the streets and paths.

He noted with some interest that Arab men tended to walk or work together in groups, their clothes and turbans identifying them as members of the various tribes of Palestine. It was obvious that such identification was vital even in the city. He eschewed visiting the mosques and even avoided the Christian holy places, which were many. For one thing, he felt totally unworthy, and for another he felt far from any kind of spirituality.

It was clear that Jerusalem was a garrison town of significant proportions. Outside the city, a large cluster of baked brick barracks had blossomed, complete with bazaars, mosques, and artisan shops. He estimated it could house as many as a thousand soldiers, many of whom were on the streets of Jerusalem at any hour of the day or night, either on duty or on leave. He also noted large areas for livestock and stables for horses. And the city walls and roads leading into the city were in good condition, or at least under repair with many laborers. If Jerusalem was any indication, the Abbasids were serious about keeping a strong military grip on their far-flung empire.

Eventually, he tired of the bustle of the city and began walking out into the desolate country beyond the walls, hoping to make peace with his gnawing doubts and somehow find new meaning to his damaged life.

Chapter 22

Magdala the Mystic

Milo was the happiest about their stay in Jerusalem. He felt that everything in his life thus far had been leading to this experience. He spent all day every day in the Christian quarter of the old city or along the narrow dirt road in the Arab part of the city called the Via Dolorosa, the route Jesus took to his crucifixion. For the most part, he was oblivious to the latent hostility of the Arabs and politely stepped out of their way and bowed. However, his bright hair drew everyone's attention, and he had to cover it with a cowl.

He wandered through the Golden Gate and spent hours on the Mount of Olives or in the Kidron Valley. His Latin and Greek language skills improved dramatically as he used every means to find out all he could about the holy sites from monks or priest custodians. He tagged along with solitary pilgrims as they prayed their way systematically from one famous shrine to another. With some apprehension, he even visited the beautiful Dome of the Rock and Al-Aqsa mosques and stayed a whole afternoon joining his prayers to those of Jewish worshippers at the Wailing Wall, the last remaining vestige of their precious temple.

It was on one of these rambling expeditions that he met Magdala.

She was a young woman about his own age. He first saw her with a beggar's bowl in her lap sitting near the ancient Pool of Bethesda near the Via Dolorosa. There were only a few coins in the bowl, for she made no effort to hold it out to passersby or to beg aloud. She simply sat and watched keenly all those who passed, saying nothing but boldly meeting the eyes of anyone who looked her way, as if to discover behind their eyes something important that lay within them.

Drawn to her, Milo stopped before her, having met her gaze as he approached. He drew a small purse from within his tunic and dropped a coin into her bowl. The girl did not respond but continued to gaze intently into his eyes. Finally, she stood up and said in the common Greek tongue, "Come."

Milo hesitated and thought of turning on his heel and avoiding her. But her eyes compelled him, and he followed her dumbly as she made her way purposefully toward the eastern wall of the old city. There she turned and led him out through the old Golden Gate into the Kidron Valley. He watched her as she moved before him, trying to discern who or what she was and what she might want.

She was slight with unassuming features and olive skin, like most of the people in the city. She was neither beautiful nor ugly—a poor woman by the look of her, in a plain, colorless Arab tunic, belted at the waist, and shod in simple rope sandals. She wore no adornments of any kind. Her hair was covered by a cap, over which she wore a loose hood but no *hijab* or veil over her face, a sure sign she was either a Jewish or Christian woman.

When they arrived at the small stream that ran through the valley floor, she sat down on a flat rock and bade him sit beside her. Turning to him, she asked calmly, "What is it you seek?"

"I—what do *I* seek?" he stammered. "Why, nothing, I only look."

"No," she said firmly, laying a small hand on his arm. "Perhaps you don't know exactly what you seek. But you do seek something. I see it in your eyes. You look unfulfilled—not at peace." She waited a moment. "Tell me, do you look for God?"

Startled a bit by her frankness, he hesitated, then replied, surprising himself, "Why, yes. . . yes, I do seek God . . . I think."

"Do you know why?"

"What? Doesn't every Christian seek God? I'm no different."

278

"Yes, you are. I can see it in your eyes. You have a purpose. I think you want to be a holy man."

"What? I've never even thought of that. I'm no saint! I suppose I do want to follow my faith—if that's what you mean. I want to be a good Christian. But that's not being a holy man, like some saint or something."

"Ah, of course. That's what I saw in your eyes; you want to be of use as a Christian." After another silence, she said, "I can tell you this; you will one day become this holy man you seek to be, but not soon. One day you may do great things in the name of our faith. And you will achieve wisdom. One day your wisdom may be sought by many, even by kings." She hesitated. "But not soon. You have yet a very long journey before you with many hardships and dangers. You must be burnt by fire and tempted sorely. You will see many die and will know fear and suffer torment. But all of that will make you strong, determined, and wise."

"How do you know these things?" Milo demanded, shocked by her unnerving predictions.

"I don't know for sure. I only see dimly. Such things often lie behind the eyes of the people I meet. It's a gift." She paused. "But tell me, there is something else, something immediate that steals your peace . . . *someone* else, perhaps?"

"It's my father," Milo said, stunned that she had perceived his foremost concern so easily. "He's ill. . . sick at heart. He's been a warrior for King Karl of Francia for a long time. He's killed many men, and he's lost many people who were very dear to him. He has no peace; he believes that God has abandoned him."

"God abandons no one. God is the faithful one. It is people who abandon God."

"Once he was such a good man, fair to all and striving to do good things. But his losses have been great, and a hard and lonely life has made him change. I think he will die of his sorrows. Tell me, please, if you know. What can I do?"

"Do you believe it is possible to heal him—to give him new life?"

"I certainly hope it might be, but I don't know."

"All things are possible if God wills it." She held up her hand to stop his reply and looked away. Finally, she said, "Bring him here—tomorrow, at the same time. I will speak with him."

"But who are you? How can I trust you? Even if I trust you, how can I get my father to come when I tell him about you? What can I tell him?"

"Summon your faith. Do you not believe that God can do all? If you do, you will find a way. Then we shall see. I must go."

"Tell me, who are you?"

"I am called Magdala, after the village where I was born. My mother was a Jew, the daughter of a rabbi, my father a Christian priest, a Greek. Their love caused them much pain and nearly destroyed them. They had to leave Jerusalem. For many years, we lived in the desert tending sheep. They taught me to read and speak many tongues. When they died, I returned to the city to beg. . . and heal. Sometimes I am able to use what I know to heal people."

"But how is it that you know such strange things? How can you see into the future?"

"I don't know. I cannot see everything—only an outline. But what I have is a gift, as I said. Perhaps it came to me out of the desert. . . from the emptiness and silence, from so many nights watching the stars in the immense night sky. Eventually, God showed me a way to live, and I live accordingly. I think that's what you wish to do."

***

Milo was beside himself as he made his way back to the small inn where they stayed in the Jewish quarter. He agonized about what to say to his father. How could he make Sebastian come with him to see the girl?

After all, he reflected, she was just a common street girl, a poor Jewish Greek. His father was a Frankish count, a famous warrior, and a Christian. They had nothing in common. What could she possibly say that would be meaningful to him?

No, he reasoned anew. His father was once a very good man, full of love and faith. Deep down, Milo believed he still was. He was sure that Sebastian wanted to return to the man he once was but just could not see how. The life he had led had twisted his soul.

Master Alcuin would know what to do, he thought. What would Alcuin tell his father? Time after time the great scholar had emphasized to his pupils that it was a sin against God to despair of life because life was a gift and was filled with great grandeur. Somehow he must make his father see how precious life was and that he must learn to be grateful for it and use it well. He longed to believe that this young woman might be the key. She certainly was astonishingly different and special. She was a seer. He had never met one. But she had known him at once—better than he had known himself.

When Milo returned that afternoon to the inn, he was relieved to see his father sitting on the side of his rude bed in the common sleeping room, head down as if lost in thought. He looked tired and despondent. Milo took a deep breath and sat down on the floor at his father's feet.

"Father," he began, "do you know that I love you?"

Sebastian sat straight up. Milo took another deep breath, fearing his father's reaction. He had never said such a thing to him before. His father might not welcome such intimacies. "Wh-what?" Sebastian stammered.

"I may not have told you how much I admire you and care for you. You've always been a kind and generous father to me. I tell you now because I'm worried about you. I used to think of you as invincible, a rock of strength and courage. Nothing could touch you. I almost feared to approach you because you were so regal. When I look at you now, I see a sick and discouraged man. It makes me heartsick and desperate to help you."

Milo held his breath. For a moment, he thought he had gone too far. His father looked shocked. He was afraid he would be angry. But then Sebastian smiled wanly and dropped his head again.

"Milo. . . oh, my son. You needn't worry. It's all right. It will pass. I just need some rest and time to forget some things. I'll be fine."

"Well, you don't look fine. Please, Father, hear me out. I have a great favor to ask of you. Will you grant me this favor if you know it is what I desire right now more than anything in the world?"

Milo was taken aback by the quick response. Sebastian hesitated only a moment and then said, "Of course, Milo. If it's something you really want and it won't compromise our mission or my honor, I will do it."

Milo breathed a sigh of relief. "Thank God. . . and thank you, Father. Actually, it's a simple thing. I don't even know as yet why it's so important to me. I just want you to meet someone."

"Who? Have you met someone important?"

"No, no, it's only a girl I met who impressed me very much. She's a native person, a Jewish girl, actually, a young woman. But she might be a Christian Jewish girl. . . I think. She is very different. . . strange. Though she is poor, she speaks Greek and even Latin. She sees things, things in the future. I want you to talk to her. I've never met anyone like her. Her insight is so wise and on the mark, it's almost as if she were some kind of oracle."

"All right, I'll go since you wish it. But why do you want *me* to see her? What meaning has such a meeting for me?"

"You'll see. Just come with me tomorrow."

***

They met on the stone bench by the little stream below the Mount of Olives. She sat with a small, silent boy of six or seven years at her feet. After a brief, halting introduction, Milo asked Magdala if she'd like him to stay. Without lifting her eyes from Sebastian's face, she simply said no. So Milo excused himself quietly and left Sebastian with the girl. His quick departure startled Sebastian, but he was curious, so he decided to see it through, if for no other reason than to make sure Milo wasn't being deceived by this strange young woman.

When Milo had gone, the girl gently lifted a hand to point to the bench beside her. Sebastian sat down, feeling uncomfortable and a bit foolish but inexplicably interested in what mystique this woman possessed that she could charm Milo into trusting her. He could see at once that the girl was out of the ordinary. She was completely calm and unafraid. She looked him straight in the eyes and exuded a sense of confidence and inner conviction.

Magdala smiled briefly when he sat down. When she did, he noticed her face changed dramatically from plain to quite lovely, like the moon breaking through clouds. She was silent a moment more, looking down the valley. Then she began abruptly, speaking in a passable, if unrefined, Latin.

"Your son has told me little of you, only that you are in pain and full of sorrow and regret. He hoped I might say something to you that would ease your burden."

"And what would a poor young woman know of a stranger's burdens? Why would you even want to help such a man?"

She looked away and remained silent for a moment. "I saw something in your son. He will be special to God. He is destined to do much good in his life—if he lives. If he is such a man, then his father must also matter in a special way. I see in your eyes that you are such a man."

"Pardon me if I have my doubts, but if you were a true seer, you would see that the man before you is broken and sick—used up, no longer good for anything."

"One can see that you are wounded, but wounds, both of the body and the spirit, can be healed. They can also be used to heal oneself."

"How, pray, is that supposed to happen?" Sebastian said in a derisive tone. "Tell me simply how I am supposed to heal myself."

"I cannot help you if you do not wish to be healed."

"Ah, you are also a healer, then?"

"I can sometimes help people and also tell them how they can heal themselves."

"All right, then, tell me."

She sighed and looked away again. "First you must believe that it is possible to heal yourself. You must also want to be whole again. Do you?"

Now Sebastian hesitated. Did he? For what? So that he could go and kill again for the king, like some unthinking beast? So he would have to endure the loss of someone else he'd loved and somehow caused to die? Why shouldn't he die instead? He felt worn out, sickened. He just wanted to say, "No more, no more."

Finally, he said, "I don't know. At the moment, I find it hard to want anything—except perhaps oblivion."

She took a deep breath and turned to him again with the full force of her compelling eyes. "I will tell you two things. Don't ask me to explain them. If you wish to understand, you must go somewhere and find a place to be silent. Be still and listen. When you have contemplated these things, come and see me again, if you wish.

"There are two most important things about life. They are love and death." She paused for a moment for him to consider her words. "About love. . . it is not enough to love passionately or deeply. There is more; you must understand how love is connected."

"To what?"

"To everything."

She paused for a moment to let him consider what she had said. "And about death...if you wish to truly live, you must die."

"What? I don't understand."

"Go, then, if you wish to understand. Go and find a place of silence. Be still and listen. It may take a while. Be patient. Wait for the answers."

With that, she got up abruptly, took the small boy by the hand, and walked away.

***

At first, Sebastian was irritated as he trudged back to the Jewish quarter. He felt a fool for listening to this slip of a peasant girl with the mute child at her feet. But he could not get her out of his head. He pondered the riddle about love and death. How could death be as important as love? Perhaps *he* was death—or death's agent. And as such, he must forsake love. Was that it?

Eventually, he decided to give the girl's counsel fair trial. What could he lose? He had nothing better to do. So that evening he walked out of the city again and up to the Mount of Olives. He found a solitary hollow among some rocks from which he had protection from the wind and could see the whole city. As dusk fell, the hill became silent, and the sky gradually blossomed with a million stars. He stayed the whole night, taking in the beauty of the sky and filling himself with the silence and peace of the place. But no answers came.

Since they had little to do until Isaac arrived, Sebastian began to spend every night in the same place near Gethsemane, under that wide-open sky. At first, he struggled to go and to stay for long. He could admire the abundant beauty around him, but after a while he found it almost impossible to continue sitting in the silence, urging some significant thought to come, some astonishing answer to Magdala's riddle.

He fretted at his inability to concentrate, got up, and wandered about. The silence became oppressive. Blast! It's another night's sleep wasted. She was probably a fraud in any case. The next thing he knew, she would be asking for money.

But the next night, he went back and sat down in the silence. This time he ordered himself to just stop fighting and surrender to the night. He decided not to think at all but to let his mind drift pointlessly, without design or destination. He lay on his back for a long time, drifting in and out of sleep. Deep into the night, he began to have the illusion that each time he awoke the star-filled sky was somehow closer, until it surrounded him.

It was then that he began to feel transported. He seemed to hover above the earth and slowly float into the depths of the sky. He was not alarmed, not even surprised. He simply let himself go until it seemed he had become part of the vast sky.

Later, in the early morning light, he came fully awake and suddenly an answer…or at least a piece of an answer…to the first part of Magdala's riddle came to him. In his dream, if that's what it was, he felt he had become part of the great night sky, which seemed to go on forever—eternally. He felt he had become part of that eternity, part of everything that had ever been created, the bad as well as the good.

At first light, he went back into the city and waited until he saw Magdala coming down the Via Dolorosa with the wordless boy and her begging cup. "I must talk to you," he said almost furtively, trying to avoid attracting any attention.

"I must work. There are people who need me," she said without stopping. Then she turned, as if having second thoughts, and gestured to him. "Come. You may go with us and see what we do." He hesitated, feeling awkward and a bit humiliated to be seeking the company of a peasant woman. She smiled knowingly and nodded her head. "It's all right. Where we're going, no one will know you."

He fell in behind her, and there he stayed for the rest of the morning and much of the afternoon as Magdala made her way amongst the poor of Jerusalem. It didn't matter what quarter the people lived in; she visited them all, Christian, Arab, Jewish. She was little more than a girl, and yet they all treated her with the greatest respect. They even talked of her miracles!

But Sebastian could see from the beginning that there was nothing magical about her; it was her wide knowledge of disease and remedies that made her miraculous. She was a native healer who used the herbs and desert skills her mother had taught her to treat common illnesses among the poor and to bind up their wounds and deliver their babies. Nevertheless, the people regarded her as a saint with extraordinary powers.

Sebastian witnessed that same day a vivid illustration of how Magdala won her stature as a healer and miracle worker. They were in the Christian sector when the boy who accompanied her experienced an epileptic fit after watching Magdala reset the bone of an older peasant worker. The man had fallen from a church building under construction and was screaming at the top of his voice as Magdala realigned his leg and bound a rigid piece of wood to it. The boy was so overcome by the screaming that he fell to the dirt floor of the small house in convulsions. Magdala shooed everyone from the room except Sebastian and the injured man. She dragged the boy to a corner of the room and, cradling him in her arms, began to sing softly to him in a rhythmic voice while slowly dangling a small shiny coin on a string before his eyes. Before long, the boy stopped struggling and fell into a trance. Then he fell asleep. Absorbed in watching the process, the injured man stopped groaning and also slept.

That afternoon Magdala spent hours begging in the streets, sitting silently and watching. Many knew her and stopped to say a word or two, but she had little time for pleasantries and simply dropped her head and fell silent as a means of ending conversation. The boy stayed beside her the whole time, his eyes hardly ever leaving her face.

Sebastian left several times to wander about the holy shrines of the neighborhood. Gradually, he found his interest in them quickening. But he returned to Magdala after short absences and was finally rewarded when she stood up and beckoned to him to follow. They went to the same place below the Mount of Olives, where she and the boy produced bread and olives and began to eat. "Speak," she said. "What did you learn?"

Haltingly, he told her about the vision. "I don't know if it really was a vision. Perhaps it was a dream. But I felt I had become part of the sky, part of everything that ever was. It was so vivid that I felt I couldn't have been asleep."

"What of love? Did you learn the meaning of love?"

"I'm not sure. I understood with all clarity that the Creator has made the earth and the sky and all that's in it, down to the smallest detail, and that this Creator is like a father who is delighted with everything he has created—and loves it all, bad and good alike. It seemed that I, too, was called to love like that father."

"Ah," Magdala sighed and gave him a radiant smile. "It *was* a vision. You have found a great truth. It's only one step from there to know that you—and I, and everyone else—are called to love, leaving no one out, even our enemies. As you perceived, we must value the good as gift, the bad as lesson.

"If you know that—and even strive to do that—you will be on the path to peace. If you know that, you can dispense with hate. Everyone becomes important. Everyone is worthy of forgiveness and mercy."

Sebastian paused to consider what she had said and then slowly shook his head. "I don't think I can do that. I've made too many enemies. There are too many people who have harmed me and wish to kill me, and some very important ones who have disappointed and abandoned me."

"Well, then, perhaps it's time you began to try and reduce their number," she said with an impish laugh. "Start by considering your worst enemy. Make a decision to stop hating him."

"What?" Sebastian was stunned by the thought. How could he stop hating Konrad? That evil man was responsible for everything bad in his life, for the misery he felt in the depths of his soul. "Impossible," he blurted abruptly.

She sighed. "I knew you would say that. But you must try. To the extent that you can do this, you will find peace. Mark my words—eventually you will come to a point where the offenses of your enemies will no longer matter."

She waited for a moment while he pondered her words again. Then she asked, "And what of death? What have you learned of death?"

"I cannot say I have any new thoughts about death. It's a frightening thing, often accompanied by terrible pain and anguish. Though one knows it's inevitable, one shuns it and does not dwell upon it."

"Ah... well, then, you must go back to a place of silence and look for another answer. That is not the kind of death I meant. You have learned that you are part of all—everything that has been created, bad or good. Now you must go and learn what you must do about it."

She started to move away but turned back. "But this time I want you to go out into the desert. Go out for three days and nights. Take no food and only a small flask of water. Do not drink it if you can resist. Think of it as a temptation from the devil. Only drink of it when you feel you might die if you don't. Pray that you have another vision—this time about death—the kind of death you need to embrace. Seek the Spirit within. It is always with you." She turned and walked away, leaving him with yet another mystery to ponder.

***

He woke Milo before dawn the next morning to tell him he would be going on a short journey at the behest of Magdala. "Not to worry, son; it's only for three days and not dangerous." He gave Milo a quick embrace and then decided to begin the journey by walking up to the Via Dolorosa and out the Golden Gate toward the semi-desert wilderness to the east of the Mount of Olives.

He walked briskly at first. In the relatively high ground around Jerusalem, the morning air felt clean and fresh. But gradually the day grew hot, the countryside less hospitable as the land sloped downward. Vegetation became sparse, and only the occasional isolated sheepfold spoke of human activity. He decided to find what shade there was and make his camp. He found a lone terebinth tree and settled under its spindly branches.

The first night was almost pleasant. He built a small fire, more for comfort than for warmth, and enjoyed once again the sweeping glory of the starry panorama. But no answers came. Eventually he slept.

The ordeal began the next morning when he awoke with a parched throat, stiff joints, and a dull headache. And then the day's heat hit him. For a while, he resisted the suddenly stunning allure of the water flask. He tried to distract himself by looking around for firewood or searching for berries or roots. There was nothing, and the sun finally drove him to the meager shade of the tree. As the day wore on and night approached, his head throbbed and he could think of nothing but relief. At last, he gave in and guiltily took a few sips. He drank more. The precious water seemed to him like elixir of the gods, an instant magical medicine that cured almost at once the pounding in his head. He got through the day and was again able to sleep, though fitfully.

The next day, the hallucinations began. He drank the rest of the water, but it was not enough to slake his desire. To take his mind off his thirst, he began to review his life. He began with a complaint: Why am I still here? Why am I still alive? He looked back over the violent life he had led so far. He could have died in any one of a hundred fights. People had begun to say that he could not be killed. But he had become the angel of death. How could he die?

That was his role, and that was why he was inviolable, he reasoned. But the role had killed his soul.

He was empty now, only a shell—nothing left of the boy who wanted to learn to read the Bible, nothing of the young man who dared to stand before the king and insist that he exchange his violent methods for a different path to peace. "Sebastian's Way," the king had once called it. Ha! Absurd now. Only a memory. How naïve that youth had been. How simple. He realized bitterly that it was the king who had changed him, not the reverse. Now both of them were committed to do anything in order to succeed.

What had happened to that virtue he once had? What had happened to that faith that was once so strong in him?

It was war, he concluded. It was the killing, the constant violence. It had ruined him beyond redemption. It had made him a brute, a monster. How could God forgive him now? The memories had made him crazed.

Around midday, he began to imagine things. People who had filled his life so far—both those he had loved and those he had not—appeared before him, ethereal, wavering in the ripples of heat that rose from the desert floor, but life-size and as real as when he knew them.

The first he encountered was his father. As early as he could remember, Attalus had always been a part of his life, had always been there for him, teaching him, helping him to become a man.

Sebastian was sure that Attalus could have been much more than the constable of Adalgray for most of his life. It was his love for Ermengard, his mother—and for himself—that kept him there. Everything he ever did was ultimately for them.

And then the form of Father Louis appeared, shimmering in the heat. The fat, exuberant priest had been the one who had changed Sebastian's life by teaching him to read and thus opening so many new and fateful doors. Louis came the closest to what Magdala was talking about, he mused. He loved everyone with abandon, even the Saxons. He often said, "Oh, they're just poor and ignorant. They need to come out of those dark woods into the light. If we give 'em good land and teach 'em a bit about life, they will come around. God made them too, didn't he?"

Adela appeared briefly, with tears in her eyes and the word "no" on her lips. Adelaide was also there, tossing her hair and blowing a kiss to him with a merry laugh. Eventually, there was Konrad, scowling, sneering, his face turning purple with rage.

Suddenly, this illusion of Konrad drew his sword and began to advance. Sebastian instinctively reached for his own sword. The effort jerked him back into reality. And there, not four feet away, was a huge snake, coiled and ready to strike, staring into Sebastian's eyes, its ugly head moving slowly, ominously, from side to side.

There might have been room and time for Sebastian to draw his sword and strike. But no, he reckoned, it would be a bad wager. The snake was ready. He could barely even see to strike it, let alone draw quickly enough. Perhaps this was the

end, then. Perhaps this was why he had come into the desert—
to have an end to his misery.

He did not draw. Why continue to give himself to
killing? No! It had already done enough injury to his soul. At
least he could make a final gesture of protest, even if it cost
him his life.

He relaxed the tension in his arms, took a deep breath,
and let it out slowly, waiting for the snake to strike. There was
no accounting for the time Sebastian and the snake spent
considering each other. In Sebastian's mind, the snake was
clearly Konrad. So, Sebastian thought, his old enemy had won
out after all. The violence, the evil he represented was
destined to continue. He would never be able to stop him.
Then why? Why did God let him live this long if only to show
him that it is evil which must triumph in this world?

But then the snake moved. A lone jackal had trotted
into view and was now carefully assessing the situation. It
took a few tentative steps forward. The snake turned
completely to face the new danger.

He could strike it now, Sebastian realized. He could
kill it.

But he held his hand, observing the tableau of the
snake and the jackal with wonder. He considered through the
fog in his brain: God had made them too, had he not? They
were beautiful in their might and prowess. It was not for him
to change that. Why should he interfere?

The jackal had seen enough. He turned and loped off to
find easier prey. The snake looked back once at Sebastian,
who had not moved, and then uncoiled and slithered out of
sight.

Sebastian stared for a moment afterward and then
vowed he would never again seek to kill a living thing. If he
had to fight, it would be in self-defense, and he would not kill
anyone if it was possible to spare him. Then he got up,
gathered his things, and stumbled, disoriented and almost
delirious, downhill toward what he sensed must surely be
water somewhere below.

As he staggered along, he suddenly remembered the dream he had after the fight with Konrad in Denmark, when he had lain wounded and sick and fantasizing. He recalled walking with Adela through a golden wheat field. They had walked waist-deep into a clear pond by the edge of the forest. He had felt then that the pond was magical and that it had the power to draw out the pain and regret in his heart. "The pond, the magic pond!" he shouted out loud. "I've found it. I can begin again!"

Before long his intuition proved correct, the ground leveled off, and he came into a patch of rich vegetation. His spirits soared at the thought of water. His whole being yearned for it, and he pushed harder through the brush. Unexpectedly, the ground gave way beneath him, and he fell headlong into a small river. He came up gasping and sputtering.

A voice cried out to him in perfect Greek, "Hallo, don't drink of that dirty water, my friend. Come out, and I will give you your fill of sweet well water."

"Where am I?" Sebastian croaked.

"Why, my good sir, I have the honor to tell you that you are sitting neck deep in the River Jordan."

***

Sebastian's rescuers turned out to be two Armenian merchants making their way back to Jerusalem from a trading expedition to Mosul on the Euphrates with a caravan of donkeys. Like their contemporaries, the Jewish Radhanites, they were enterprising, intrepid men who survived by their wits and knowledge, and after a long, dangerous journey, they were delighted and mystified to find a sunbaked Frank in the middle of the wilderness. They treated him like a brother and brought him safely back to Jerusalem on the back of a donkey.

Sebastian spent two days sleeping and drinking as much water as he could hold. Liudolf clucked and complained about Sebastian's unannounced absence but doctored his blistered lips and peeling skin just the same. At length, Sebastian felt well enough to go and seek out Magdala.

He found her on the Via Dolorosa. As before, she made him wait until she had finished her rounds. This time he did not follow her but went instead to visit the Christian holy sites, seeing them anew and experiencing some of Milo's awe. Then he found her again, begging in the street. This time she went with him at once to their spot by the brook under the Mount of Olives.

"I have solved the riddle," he said without preamble. "I know the answer about death."

"And what it is, Lord Sebastian? Have you spoken to God?" she said with a lighthearted laugh.

"No, of course not! Well, not exactly. But in the desert, I did have a vision. I saw the face of my mortal enemy and I could not kill him, though I had the chance. And I saw the faces of the two men who helped me most to become who I am, my own father and a priest who was kind to me. Both gave up everything for me, and for others. I suppose one could say it was a kind of death for them."

In answer, Magdala remained silent for a time but then took his hand in hers. "Ah, you see, Sebastian, the riddle is nothing more than the biblical lesson—'the seed must fall to the ground and die if it is to reach its most meaningful life.' It is you who must die—to your ambitions and desires—and become, if you can, like your father and your priest friend. Give yourself to others if you want peace. You can be free of your burden of guilt and loss, and you can win back your soul."

"I *can* see that, Magdala. And I'm grateful for that understanding. But I'm a soldier. The king depends on me. I can't just walk away from him. So how can this 'seed' story apply to me?"

She took a long time to think of her answer. Finally, she said, "If your duty to the king must be your main focus, then you must make that duty as virtuous and useful as possible. Your 'death' will be in subordinating your life to that purpose. If your master is the king, then you must be his prophet. You must suggest to him how he can best serve God as king.

"To do this, you will probably have to tell him what he does not wish to hear. But you have done that before, have you not? It is possible you will suffer again if you do it; you could even lose your life. But from what I perceive in you, I think it is the only way you can live and be satisfied with your life. It is the only way you can be happy, no matter what occurs."

"But how am I always to know what to tell the king?"

"You're a good man, Sebastian. Tell him the truth, as you see it. Tell him what is in your heart. If you need help to understand, you must make time to listen in the silence, as I have taught you."

***

They had been in Jerusalem several months already. Having little to do, Sebastian's small band passed the time as best they could. Bardulf was often the source of their entertainment. In the late afternoon, he could be found in a small Jewish tavern adjacent to their inn. There he was in his element; a crowd of fellow lodgers staying at the inn had gathered to hear him tell one of his ribald stories, for which he was already famous. He looked around at his grinning, expectant audience and began.

"Well, ye know there has always been a lot of virgins in this here Jerusalem town—some holier than others." He waited for the laughter and whistling to die down. "Many of these here virgins was powerful pious—and some not so pious, let me say. Well, one day this here be-ute-e-ful virgin was walkin' around them hills outside the city, and she was carryin' this stone in both hands, prayin' as she went. Well, the stone was a very old one, and it had seen a passel of hard weather and hot sun. Causin' of that, the stone had a image on one side of it, and believe it or not, that image was the face of our very Lord Jesus!" This produced much sighing and signing of the cross.

"Well, there was this here soldier comin' down the path from the other direction, and just as the two met, the girl

295

looks up and then trips her foot against a rock and drops the holy stone. The soldier, he lunges out to grab it, but—too late—he misses the stone and grabs the girl's bosoms instead."

After much hooting and guffawing, Bardulf continued, "Well, he jerks back and she jerks back, and they kinda looks at each other wide-eyed, as ye can imagine.

"'I'm so sorry, my lady,' he says. 'I meant to catch the stone. I do hope I ain't offended ye.' And he bows real low.

"And she says, 'Oh, good sir, pay it no mind. I know ye was only tryin' to help me. And I thanks ye for it with a right good will. Oh my,' she says, lookin' down. The stone with the face of dear Jesus was very old, and it had broke right in two. 'Tsk, tsk,' she says, 'what a terrible shame. I am distraught.' And she puts the palms of her hands to her bosoms and looks about to faint away.

"Then the soldier hauls off and says, 'Well, ye know, sweet lady, I have heared that there be many such stones a-lyin' just over the hill there in that apple orchard. We might could find us another one just like this here one that ye dropped—lyin' on the ground. Er. . . I mean to say, the stones would be lyin' on the ground.'" More hooting and raucous laughter ensued.

"There ye go, Bardulf," someone shouted, "ye'll be wantin' to go to confession after this one, by the blessed rood."

"What?" Bardulf protested. "Why, it's all true, I'm tellin' ye. And what's more is that the girl done took the soldier's arm that he offered her, and they walks off, all chummed-up-like, toward the apple orchard. And what's more than that, I'm tellin' ye, I reckon they lived happy ever after, don't ye know."

The laughter and clapping died abruptly as Sebastian burst into the room to announce, "Look alive, lads. Isaac has come."

Chapter 23

"Bloody Asia"

Jerusalem and Antioch, Spring 800

The Jewish sector of the city buzzed with the news of a huge train of camels coming into Jerusalem from the port of Ashdod, led by a small squad of Radhanite traders and accompanied by a heavy guard of Bedouin horsemen. Such a large train always created excitement in the city as it usually meant work to be had and trade profits to be made. Sebastian caught the drift of it in the late afternoon and hurried down to the caravanserai on the edge of the Jewish sector.

It was a rich collection of expensive merchandise: horses and leather goods from Spain, grain from Egypt, metal tools and weapons from Francia, and precious oak lumber from the forests of Europe for the wood-starved desert people of Jerusalem.

Sebastian looked in vain for Isaac, but though he learned it was indeed Isaac's caravan, no one seemed to know where the old merchant was. Finally, Sebastian decided to go back to the inn and wait for word. When he returned, there were a half dozen heavily loaded camels in the courtyard of the inn, looked after by a modest, unimposing mounted guard. And it was Isaac himself who greeted him.

"Ah, there you are, my friend," he said, bowing low to Sebastian. "They said you had gone to seek me at the caravanserai. I'm so sorry for my little deception. We sent the larger caravan ahead as a diversion. The road from Ashdod, I fear, is notorious for its bandits. And we came a less traveled way."

"No matter. Welcome, Isaac! And thank God," Sebastian said, bowing slightly to the wiry old man. "I was beginning to worry."

"My humble apologies, Count Sebastian. There is always too much delay in Egypt. Many hands, all demanding a piece of gold."

They sat together over a cup of wine and dried fruits as Isaac recovered from the journey. But, spent as he was, he would not sit for long.

"We must hurry, my lord. Sigismund and Lantfrid may already be in Antioch waiting our arrival. I received word in Egypt that they left Italy over a month ago. And there is something else, I'm afraid. Word came to me that you are being sought by the Byzantines. It is rumored that you killed a man in Constantinople—a man of high rank, close to the throne. The Greeks have put a price on your head, ambassador from King Karl or not. I was relieved to find you still alive, but you will not remain unnoticed for long. Jerusalem is full of Greeks. They will know where to find a Frank when the reward becomes known here. We must leave at once, or as soon as may be. I suggest, after our business tonight, that you go straightaway to Simon's ship and await my coming. My commerce will take only a few days."

"But what about the patriarch? We must at least try to gain his approval for King Karl's offer of protection. I would have approached him earlier, but he knows you, and I have no connection and no guarantee he would recognize my authority from King Karl."

"I have not forgotten, Lord Sebastian. There are six camels outside with packs full to bursting with Avar gold—a gift to the patriarch from King Karl himself. We must go this very night to see him. It is being arranged as we speak."

"Did you say *Avar* gold? I had a little something to do with the winning of that treasure."

"You did indeed, my lord. We are all well aware of the bold expedition you and Duke Eric made into Pannonia. It was a legendary feat. But now King Karl is pleased to share from his plenty by giving alms to suffering Christians and their Church in this Holy City as well as in Palestine and Syria at large."

"Well, I certainly approve. What better use could there be for it? I'm sure there was plenty more the king retained for his grand project in Aachen. But even if we win over the Patriarch of Jerusalem, we still must convince the Caliph of the Mussulman Empire to let us protect and aid the Christians here, in place of the Emperor of Byzantium."

"Of course it will be no easy job. But you know from our last council with King Karl that we have something potentially valuable to offer."

"You're speaking of our possible double alliance with Harun, are you not? The one against the Umayyads in Spain and the Byzantines in Constantinople."

"Exactly, sir, and it may be just the thing to interest the caliph. Unfortunately, my experience at Harun's court is that he has little or no regard for Francia. In fact, he has only a vague inkling of its present king, our master. For the caliph, as for many in the East, the Franks are just another motley band of rough German barbarians. We must somehow convince him otherwise."

***

Later that evening, Sebastian appeared with Isaac at the church complex of Elias II, the Patriarch of Jerusalem, from which that eminence presided over the spiritual welfare of all Christians in Palestine and Syria.

"He is a venerable prelate," Isaac advised as they approached the complex. "He has given long and faithful service to the Christian Church throughout war and occupation. He has managed to endure and survive under the most trying circumstances. But you will see it has left him unable to hear and even to walk. His affairs are being handled by his syncellus, George, a much younger man of talent and foresight. The rumor is that he is destined to be the next patriarch upon the death of Elias. So you may find him a bit pretentious."

As they entered the patriarch's residence, George came forward to greet them as the old man sat quietly and vacantly in a corner of the room.

George began immediately, speaking in a formal and dramatic voice. "Welcome, Your Excellencies! Welcome, Count Sebastian, ambassador of the great King Karl of Francia. Welcome, Isaac, our Jewish friend. You could not have come at a more providential moment, a time most perilous for us. We are under the greatest stress here, and we hold much hope that you have come to help us. Please pay your respects now to our illustrious patriarch."

Sebastian and Isaac bowed low to the old man in the corner, who lifted two fingers from the chair arm in acknowledgement but said nothing.

As King Karl's ambassador, Sebastian began. "We come bearing the highest esteem and love for you, O esteemed patriarch, and to all the Christian community of Jerusalem— from our liege lord, King Karl of Francia, who wishes to assure you of his love and great concern for the well-being of all the Christian souls under the protection of your shepherd's crook.

"We also come bearing precious gifts by which King Karl wishes to prove his love and sincerity." With that, Isaac motioned to the door, and a company of youths from the Jewish quarter trooped in bearing bulging sacks, which they stacked in the middle of the room. Isaac opened one of the sacks, revealing a gleaming hoard of gold coins.

The old patriarch barely acknowledged the gift, but the syncellus was stupefied by the unexpected windfall, so much so that he could not speak. At length, he caught his breath and stammered, "My friends, it is. . . I cannot think. . . I cannot thank you enough—on behalf of the patriarch, that is. Your king's gifts come at a desperate time. We are in such need. Christians are starving; many are leaving the faith to join the pagans. Constantinople is at war with Baghdad and is no longer able to help us. You. . . you are nothing less than God's messengers. He has sent you to save us."

"Please, my good syncellus, we are only King Karl's servants. But he will be very pleased indeed to know that his gifts have brought you comfort. I'm sorry to ask, but this is a great deal of gold. Are you able to provide safeguards for it? If not, we can spare some guards until you can secure or redistribute it."

In answer, the syncellus clapped his hands, and a dozen armed and muscular young men came in and took places at the door and around the walls of the room.

"My friends," George began, "I don't know what to say. How can we ever thank you? We had no idea. You cannot know how important such alms can be for us. But, before I accept formally on behalf of the patriarch, please tell me what lies behind this wonderful gift from your king."

"I wish that you could know our king," Sebastian replied. "If you did, sir, you would understand that King Karl is a very devout Christian monarch who feels most strongly his obligation to protect and succor the faith insofar as he is able. He sends this largesse, part of a treasure taken in war from godless pagans, to help sustain you here in the heart of our Christian faith. I assure you, his efforts are sincere."

"I see," George said, "and he wishes nothing further than our thanks in return?"

"You do not entirely understand how deeply King Karl is devoted to our Lord Jesus and to his Church. He has heard of late that Christians in this region find themselves in dire need and in some danger. Is that not true?"

"It is, most certainly," George said emphatically. "We find ourselves increasingly unprotected and in need."

"I must ask, my lord," Isaac broke in apologetically, "if that is true because the Emperor Irene is no longer able to come to your aid?"

George hesitated, squirming uncomfortably. "I regret to say our benefactors in Constantinople have for several years been able to render only very meager support. They are in conflict with the caliph, who has successfully cut them off from us."

"I see," Isaac continued. "That is precisely what King Karl has heard and why he sends these gifts to you. Under the circumstances, he wishes to offer himself as your protector and benefactor, and he would ask that you acknowledge to Caliph Harun that you approve of this transition."

When George hesitated again, Sebastian stepped in to press the case. "We find ourselves, my lord syncellus, in some urgency to continue our mission—to Baghdad—where we intend to suggest this very turn of events to the caliph, among other things. We ask only that you write a letter to Harun al-Rashid attesting to your agreement. We must have that document, on parchment or papyrus, before we leave in a few days for Baghdad."

"What makes you think that King Karl will be able to protect us any better than Emperor Irene? Both are Christian monarchs."

"As you see, we have gold to give. We are also not at war with your overlord, and we have reason to believe that mutual interests will convince the caliph to protect you in the name of our king. That is what we want."

After another long moment of silence, during which more bags of gold were carried in and piled before him, George cleared his throat and announced his decision with conviction. "I cannot, of course, agree without first gaining approval from our beloved patriarch here. I must convince him that this is a course we must make bold to take. I believe, gentlemen, that I can do that and have our decision to you in writing in a few days, certainly before you leave."

In other times, obtaining such a binding commitment from the Patriarch of Jerusalem might have taken months. But the Arab sword hung perilously over Jerusalem's Christians, and the promise of more gold from Francia accelerated the proceedings marvelously. In a few days, George was as good as his word, and the little embassy proceeded on to Simon's ship and set sail, the historic papyrus letter with the patriarchal seal in hand.

*****

As the ship pulled away from the shores of Palestine, Isaac and Sebastian stood on the deck looking back at the historic land. "Do you realize what we have accomplished, Lord Sebastian?"

"And what is that, Master Isaac?"

"With this slight bit of papyrus paper, we have single-handedly strengthened the position of the Bishop of Rome as the principal authority of the Christian Church—that is, if we can get the Caliph of the Empire of the Mohammedans to approve it."

"That is a very bold statement, my friend. How so?"

"You Christians look to Jerusalem as the shrine of your Messiah, Jesus, do you not?"

"We do."

"With this decree, if Harun al-Rashid agrees to it, the Arabs, who are the secular authority of Jerusalem, will transfer the *spiritual* authority for Christians in the Holy City from the Greek Church in Constantinople to the Franco-Roman Church in Rome. It will make your pope unbelievably more important throughout Christendom. He will cease to be merely the Bishop of Rome and become the pope of most of the Christian world."

"What about Constantinople? They will never accept the pope as head of their Church."

"No, but Constantinople is being savaged slowly by the Bulgars and the armies of Harun into isolation. Now, with a 'friendly agreement' between King Karl and Harun, this trend will continue while the influence of Rome will only grow."

"Well, it does make sense, Isaac. Even sounds prophetic. If that's how it turns out, how will your people feel about it?"

"Ah, my good count, we Jews are like the little lizard which changes colors depending on wherever he happens to sit. We will simply adapt. We are able to live in all worlds, though we are never really a part of any. That, I fear, is the price of refusing to give up our very singular identity. Things may change, but for now we enjoy a period of relatively free enterprise."

"I see," mused Sebastian. "Well, I wish your people well. You have certainly done us Franks a good turn. I was astonished by the note from George when he agreed to send the letter to Harun. He gave us everything we asked. And I left him with a written report from me to the king concerning our mission in Constantinople and what we recommend regarding Emperor Irene. He promised to send it with a special delegation to the king in Aachen. He is even sending Elias's blessings to King Karl, along with actual relics from the Resurrection of Our Lord Jesus. We could have asked for nothing better."

"Yes—but it all depends on getting Harun to agree. As I mentioned, he has a rather low opinion of Francia, if he thinks of it at all. Somehow we must find a way to impress him. They say he gets bored rather easily. So if we are able to pique his curiosity, we may gain his ear—and his good graces. By the way, Harun al-Rashid is Persian, not Arab, so we may find him more open-minded and not so colossally stubborn and dogmatic.

"One more thing, Lord Sebastian, I have recently learned that Harun is not in Baghdad. For the moment, he has changed his imperial residence to Raqqah, which is on the upper Euphrates, considerably closer for us than Baghdad. Apparently, as supreme army commander of the empire, he wishes to be closer to his enemy, the Byzantines, and at the crossroads of any military necessity."

"Pity, Isaac, I was looking forward to the experience of Baghdad. They say it's the world's most illustrious city, even grander than Constantinople."

"Well, I expect we will have occasion to go there in any case. I must certainly go because I have business there. And the caliph may have occasion to go downriver while we're there. Who knows? He travels a great deal around his great empire.

"But one really doesn't want to go to Baghdad in summer. It is a perfectly circular city, surrounded by huge walls. It swelters in the heat. I think that's one reason Harun moved his capital temporarily. Raqqah is much more temperate. Still, Baghdad is at the heart of the empire and the hub of its commerce. You should certainly see it if we get the opportunity."

"We shall see," Sebastian yawned, looking lazily out to sea. "I have a feeling we will see Baghdad one way or the other. The very name—Baghdad—sticks in my brain and draws me like a sorceress."

***

The ship plied up the coast of the Levant, finding itself boarded several times by naval ships of the Muslim empire and once by an Arab corsair. But Simon had taken the precaution of flying a flag blazoned with the colors and insignia of Harun al-Rashid. In all cases, even the pirates honored their credentials as emissaries to Miramolin, the Commander of the Faithful, the Hand of God on earth.

At last they passed safely into Antioch, the principal city for travel to the East from the Mediterranean. From there, it was a relatively short overland journey through Aleppo to Raqqah and then downriver by barge to a point on the Euphrates directly across from Baghdad on the Tigris.

But their goal was Harun al-Rashid, and he was in Raqqah.

Once in the small city, they easily found Counts Sigismund and Lantfrid, who had been languishing there for two weeks in great discomfort and apprehension. Their Frankish apparel was woefully unsuitable for the climate, their quarters in the middle of the market district were cramped, noisy, and hot, and the only interpreter they had spoke only Greek and badly—no Arabic at all. They were understandably in high dudgeon when Sebastian arrived with Isaac and Simon.

"By God, Sebastian, where in hell have you been?" Count Sigismund raged as soon as he saw them. "You were supposed to have been here *before* us. And where is that bloody Jew who's supposed to interpret for us and help us find the way?"

Sebastian bit his lip at the offhand manner of Sigismund. After all, he was also a count, the same as Sigismund, and as such should be addressed as one. Ach, he reasoned, Sigismund is just a figurehead here, not likely to help accomplish their goal with Harun al-Rashid. In fact, he would most likely turn out to be a liability. But as part of King Karl's own family, his cantankerous guff had to be tolerated, at least for a while.

"I beg your pardon, my lord, for any inconvenience. We were unavoidably delayed on the king's business in Jerusalem."

"Jerusalem! What in blazes would you be doing in Jerusalem? You were supposed to have been in Constantinople."

"I was there, my lord. But the king also gave us important work to do with the Patriarch of Jerusalem. And we did manage to accomplish some good things for Christians in that city on behalf of King Karl."

"Well, no one told *me*! You listen to me now. I am the chief ambassador of this mission, and I'm telling you I want to get out of this confounded city at once and get down to Baghdad as soon as may be. No more delays, you hear? I am apt to go mad in this filthy, steaming place if we stay here one day more. And I want some better clothes, by thunder, you hear me? That confounded interpreter we brought with us can't seem to make himself understood by anybody. He's not even a real Greek. And I'd swear he's cheating us every time he goes out to buy food. I want to murder him now that you're here."

"Please, my lord, we don't need any more trouble, nor do we want to draw any attention to ourselves. I assure you we will go on as soon as Isaac over there—that 'bloody Jew' you mentioned—can purchase a string of camels and get our gifts packed up and ready."

"Camels! I'm not riding on the back of any bloody camel. I don't know how. Get me a horse."

"I, too, refuse to ride on such an ignoble beast," Count Lantfrid piped up, looking very nervous at the thought.

What have I got myself into here? Sebastian lamented. Count Sigismund was an arrogant popinjay who presumed he could have his way simply through bluster and intimidation. Count Lantfrid was completely out of his element, and the more exotic the circumstances, the more frightened he became of the whole enterprise. No help either, Sebastian concluded.

"Let me assure you, gentlemen, you don't want to ride a horse in the desert we must cross. For one thing, you would need a great deal more water than we are prepared to bring along. For another, I think you will find the camel a much more comfortable ride in this kind of country."

"And by the way, Count Sebastian," Lantfrid continued apologetically, "we also have gifts for the caliph. We. . .ah . . . we have brought dogs."

"Dogs, sir?"

"Yes, hunting dogs. The king thought it would be nice if the caliph could see what Frankish fighting dogs are like. It might give him a bit of insight into how formidable the Franks themselves might be."

"How many have you brought?"

"Thirty. They are still down at the docks, making a considerable row. And they need to be fed. We've had the devil's own time buying food for them."

Sebastian cleared his throat and looked at Isaac, who took a deep breath and replied calmly. "We shall need more carts—and more camels."

After a frustrating delay, they managed to outfit the two counts appropriately and arrange for their things—and the dogs—to be loaded into carts pulled by oxen. An hour's training on camel riding, amidst much complaining and cursing, sufficed to make them ready for the trip. Sebastian considered his fellow countrymen as they sat swearing aboard the camels while attendants led them around in a circle. For a fact, he thought, they are likely to be our biggest handicap.

"It'll be a miracle if the oxen ever get to Raqqah, Isaac," Sebastian remarked. "What are they going to do for water?"

"There are wells along the route. If they are not pushed and do not travel in the heat of day, they may eventually arrive, but much behind us. We must continue on. If the dogs die, so be it."

Both counts were big, red-faced, red-bearded war captains, accustomed to authority and strict obedience. In their own country, they were passably effective. They were not incompetent, lazy, or cowardly. At one time or another, both had been generals in Charlemagne's army. At least, as members of the royal house, the Arnulfings, the king could trust them completely. But in this strange environment, what they liked to call 'Bloody Asia,' they were entirely at sea, totally ignorant of the people, their language, and their customs. As it were, they were simply extra baggage on the journey and considerably more trouble for Sebastian and Isaac than even the dogs. The only saving thing so far was that they did not have to go all the way to Baghdad with them.

***

In Raqqah, there was no celebration or fanfare for the Frankish embassy when it arrived in the late afternoon of the third day. They were surrounded by mounted soldiers as soon as they approached the double walls of the caliph's fortified palace on the Euphrates. They were made to wait for hours into the night while their credentials were examined and finally approved. Then they were escorted by the guards to an area of open fields beyond the city and informed they could establish a camp there until the morning, when they would be contacted by agents of the caliph.

Milo, who had been in a contemplative mood ever since they left Jerusalem, came alert again as soon as they became immersed in this exotic new culture. Since their arrival in Antioch, he had been using his Arabic at every opportunity and spent his time wandering around the streets and bazaars watching the people and learning their customs. Sebastian was glad of the delay so that he could spend more time with him.

"Well, son, you seem to be adjusting well. Good thing, too, because I don't know when we'll get to see the great man—if at all. Isaac says foreign delegations sometimes have to wait weeks for an audience, and then it might be only with the caliph's vizier. In the meantime, we are to camp out on this open plain outside the city, where armed guards can keep a close eye on us. We aren't even allowed to go into the city except to buy food at the bazaar and bathe occasionally at one of the public baths. It's not going to be at all like Constantinople and not even much like Jerusalem. Are you going to be all right with that?"

"Of course, Father. What do you take me for, a pet cat? You might find I'm as tough as you—in some ways. Besides, I find this place fascinating. It's quite different from the Arab culture in Jerusalem. I sense there's a tremendous energy here. I don't know what to think of it yet."

For the first time, Sebastian felt glad that Milo was part of this grand expedition. He had wanted to come along "to see the world," and he had seen enough already to last a lifetime. It even looked as if they might be through with the hardest part of the trip if only they could gain the attention of the caliph. If they could somehow succeed with him, they could go home, and the way home seemed infinitely easier than the journey they had endured so far. Milo had come through it all heroically and had profoundly matured. Sebastian was enormously proud of him.

"You're right, there is a different energy here," Sebastian continued. "Isaac told me these soldiers you see everywhere are not Arabs, at least not here in Raqqah and around the palace. They are Persians, and they are the caliph's personal army. Most of them can speak the language of the majority Arabs, but there's no doubt who's wielding the power. We just have to watch our step and bide our time. Watching and waiting is the game right now. Sorry."

"I'm looking forward to it, Father. Have no fear. In fact, I welcome the delay. It might give you time to tell me of your experience in Jerusalem and your time with Magdala. I'm very anxious for you to share it with me, especially since you seem to be in a better place now. Please, Father, I really need to know—for my peace of mind."

"I will, son. I learned much from that amazing young woman, and I will share it with you, just not yet. I'm not ready. I'm not sure myself yet. But I will tell you this, I am hopeful. Let us leave it at that until I've had some time. I promise I will tell you everything once I've had time to think it through."

***

One morning at the end of a fortnight of waiting, as the Frankish camp awakened to another day on the dull plain outside the city and began to prepare the morning meal. Counts Sigismund and Lantfrid were beside themselves with indignation and raged at Sebastian and Isaac. "Listen here, Sebastian. Can't you do something? Are we to waste away and die on this godforsaken field? We can't even get a decent jug of wine or beer," grumbled Sigismund. "I'm for riding right up to the palace and pounding on the gate."

"Do not, Count Sigismund!" Sebastian commanded in a threatening, if subdued, voice. "That would jeopardize our mission and could cost you your life. For one thing, you would never get to the gate before they cut you down. Our guards, it seems, have very explicit orders regarding us. I'm afraid their caliph has little regard for or interest in us."

"Count Sebastian is correct, esteemed Lord Sigismund," Isaac said, hurrying to head off a confrontation that had been brewing for some time between the two counts and Sebastian.

"As a merchant who has made several trips to the city of the caliph," he continued, "I may say that one must often wait for several weeks before being invited to enter the city to trade. Twice I have been admitted into the presence of the

310

caliph, and once he came to inspect my wares at our encampment. He is very informal and does not waste his time with much ceremony. But one never knows when he will respond. He is an extremely busy man, as you might imagine."

"Plague take the bastard, I say," Sigismund said vehemently. "What kind of king is that?"

"A very unique one, I think, my lord. He is quite unpredictable. He may not even be in his palace. I fear our only recourse is to wait."

Chapter 24

Harun al-Rashid

The Court of the Caliph at Raqqah on the Euphrates, Syria

Autumn 800

Early on, Sebastian determined to fill his time as profitably as possible under the circumstances. In the mornings, he would take a camel and ride to the nearby river to bathe and swim for the exercise, always escorted by a mounted guard or two.

To keep fit, he fell into the habit of rigorous exercise with the sword against Liudolf or Simon and, occasionally, even against Counts Sigismund and Lantfrid, neither of whom could provide much of a challenge for him. But it gave Sebastian pleasure to reduce Sigismund to sweating exhaustion within a few minutes, having in the process given him a few lumps on the shoulders and head with the practice swords. It made the frustrated count livid, but he said nothing. He had come to a point where he recognized Sebastian would no longer tolerate his bullying and was definitely no longer his subordinate.

With all but Liudolf, Sebastian practiced with heavy wooden swords carved from rare pieces of driftwood found along the river. But he and Liudolf used their real swords in a dangerous ballet each morning in which they came within a hair's breadth of drawing blood. It was heady exercise, exhilarating to all, but especially to those who were masters of the craft. Such duels always left them sweating profusely and laughing like boys on a lark.

At night, he began to walk out with Milo to sit somewhere under the myriad of desert stars. "I'm not yet the man I used to be," he confessed to his son on the first night, "and farther still from the man I once felt I was meant to be. But I have made some progress. I no longer feel so heartsick and guilty. It's true, I learned much from the girl, from the questions she asked, and from the things she taught me to do. I had some astonishing visions in the desert and under the night sky. People came to me in the visions, people who gave me much throughout my life. They came to teach me again, one more time. I saw my enemies as well and lost my dread of them.

"Toward the end of my experience in the desert, I was delirious and I had this vision about a healing pond. It was a recurrence of an old dream about a magical pond that could cure all my ills and sadness. I know it was a fantasy, but the next thing I knew, when I was charging through the wilderness, mad to find water, I literally fell into what we Christians believe is the holiest river in the world. I fell into the Jordan.

"I know it's a bit laughable, and I don't consider it some kind of second baptism. Nevertheless, it was a calming thing that somehow cleared my head. I came to feel that in time perhaps I'd be reconciled—to my losses as well as to my enemies. In the end, the whole strange encounter with Magdala and the experience in the desert helped me gain a balance between what I feel I have to do for the king and how I must do it. I've no other ambitions. I can sacrifice whatever is left of me if I have to."

"I don't understand, Father. What sacrifice? You've already given everything to the king. I think it's been far too much. You've exhausted yourself with the effort. No man could have done as much. In my humble opinion, once this trip is over, you need do no more."

"I'm afraid I'm the kind of man who can never really rest. If I should just retire to my lands, I'd find myself bored within a fortnight. And who would share those golden years with me? You're a man now, and Attalus is seventeen.

Gonduin has already sent him to the army as attendant to Prince Charles when he's on campaign. Karl will be sent to the army this coming year as well. And I have no partner," he concluded sadly.

Sebastian's memories of Adela flooded him, and he paused to review them briefly once again, his eyes wandering up into the night sky. For the thousandth time, he felt the pain of her loss in the pit of his stomach. No matter what he had done or how he had tried to forget her, it was always Adela who sprang into his mind when he thought about his life— past, present, or future.

"Besides," he said, coming out of his reverie, "now I have only one ambition; I'm determined more than ever to change the way the king thinks, no matter what price I have to pay. There's a better way to rule than constant warfare against those who live on one's borders."

"I can't tell you how happy it makes me to hear you say such things, Father," Milo said exuberantly. "It's exactly what I learned at the feet of Alcuin. He says the time has come. We can build now. We can make a new awakening. We can make life better for our people."

"Ah, well, I'm reluctant to go too far, knowing how lustful and avaricious men can be, even those we know and love. Look at the king. He still thinks like his pagan enemies—life is a brutal contest of arms, winner take all. That's the attitude we must change. We must make sweeping laws that benefit everybody and convince even our enemies to abide by them."

"I am with you, Father. That's what I looked for from this journey, nothing less than an answer as to how I should spend my life. If you devote yourself to that ideal, then so will I. I can think of no better course."

"It's not so easy, Milo. I can say these things in the peace of such a moment as this. But life is full of obstacles— trials, sorrows, afflictions. It's easy to lose sight of one's goal.

"Right now I still need a great deal of healing. I'm content for the present just to continue the practice of meditation I learned with Magdala in Jerusalem. I find great satisfaction just sitting still and allowing my mind to empty itself into the quiet night. It gives me peace, helps me forget my past and not worry about tomorrow, which will, in any case, be full of its own trials."

***

One morning, when Sebastian and Liudolf were intent on their dangerous game with the swords, a troop of six horsemen rode by and stopped to watch the pair at a distance. From the looks of their fine clothing and tall, beautifully embroidered turbans, they were of the Persian Abbasid aristocracy. Finally, they dismounted and came forward. Everything about them spoke of authority—the spirited stallions they rode, their elegant dress, and the confident stride with which they approached. Sebastian and Liudolf stopped immediately and sheathed their swords, awaiting the visit.

Sebastian bowed low as they approached, and a tall, handsome man of military bearing spoke to him in Arabic from the middle of the group. Sebastian bowed again and uttered a few words of greeting in his limited Greek. He made a gesture of welcome toward the small fire in the middle of the encampment and called for Isaac.

As soon as the old man saw the group and the tall individual in the center, he fell to his knees and touched his forehead to the ground. The other half dozen Jews in his entourage followed his example, as did Simon. In Arabic, the tall man bade him rise and approach. Then he turned to Sebastian. Isaac fluently translated their subsequent dialogue.

"My friend," said the tall man in a clear, deep voice, "allow me to compliment you on your skill at arms. One rarely sees such elegant swordplay, especially with weapons as sharp as those I see that you use."

Sebastian bowed again. "You are too kind, sir, we do but practice our skills to while away our time while we wait."

"And who might you be, good sir, and on whom do you await, if I may be so bold?"

"I am called Sebastian. Where I live, I am a count and I have a bit of land in service to the King of Francia. We are a delegation of Franks from that king, and he has sent us to bring his greetings and heartfelt best wishes to the illustrious caliph of that great realm, known everywhere as the Shadow of God and King of Kings."

The tall Persian smiled broadly and said, "I know him rather well, and I shall be sure to pass on to him your gracious remarks. Perhaps he will soon wish to see you."

From the man's princely bearing and the obvious deference given to him by everyone, including Isaac, who seemed to know exactly who the man was, Sebastian was beginning to get the feeling that here was a most fortuitous moment, one he definitely should make the most of. "I sincerely hope so, my lord. We are most anxious to see this great man to convey to him the urgent business of our king. Meanwhile, could I offer you some tea, perhaps—and fruit or melons?"

"Thank you, no. I must confess I do not know many Frankish folk. And I am intrigued by your swordsmanship. You are obviously a great champion. I wonder if you would be so kind as to match your skills against one of our fine swordsmen—in fact, he is one of our best. I doubt you could match him, but if you could manage to give him a good bout for a bit, it would tell me much about Frankish warriors."

When Sebastian bowed in assent, the Persian sent to his saddlebags for finely carved and balanced wooden practice swords and presented him to his champion. He was a man of wiry build, much like Sebastian, with well-toned muscles in every part of him, no hint of extra weight, and as light on his feet as a dancer. From the time he held the sword in his hands, his flashing black eyes never left Sebastian's face. Each bowed to the other and took a sword.

There followed a furious quarter hour of superb and even breathtaking swordplay, lightning-fast from start to finish, with each man managing to score a few hits on the other, none of which would have been lethal. Finally, the tall man raised a hand, calling a halt, as both combatants, pouring with sweat, breathed deeply in relief.

"I thank you, kind sir, for that beautiful display of skill. I don't know if I have ever seen better. Unfortunately, we must be on our way, but I would very much like to see you again. Would you be willing to visit me tomorrow at my own quarters in the palace?"

"I should be delighted, my lord," Sebastian said, bowing deeply again.

"Till then," the man said, turning on his heel toward the horses without further comment. As he strode away, he turned and shouted, "I am glad it was not I who had to face you in such an exquisite struggle. Marvelous! Many thanks."

As the Persians rode off, Isaac, the two counts, and all the others gathered around Sebastian. "Do you know who that was, Lord Sebastian?" Isaac asked in an almost reverent voice.

"I can guess, but I'm sure you already know," Sebastian said, watching the back of the riders. "Correct me, then, if I'm wrong, but I believe we've just been visited by none other than himself—the Caliph of Baghdad."

***

The next day, the delegation was invited to the palace; this time an honor guard and an escort of court officials waited at the main gate. They were led without fanfare past spiral towers, graceful, domed apartments, through seductively aromatic gardens along paths of marble and corridors of glazed tiles exhibiting Abbasid art at its finest. They arrived eventually into a lovely courtyard shaded by palms and the graceful spreading branches of mimosa trees. There, beside a bubbling fountain of pure spring water, was the tall man from the day before, lounging on a bench and having lunch served by four strikingly beautiful harem women. There was no doubt that he was indeed Harun al-Rashid, caliph and master of the world's largest and richest empire.

He smiled and waved but continued to converse earnestly with an advisor. Finally, he rose to welcome them.

"Ah, it is See-bas-tee-yan, the swordsman," he exclaimed, and Isaac translated, "he of the blade of light and the winged feet." Welcome indeed. And who are these other fine gentlemen—also Franks by the looks of them." He sniffed a bit as he said this.

Sigismund and Lantfrid had been fussing with their clothing for hours before the meeting, choosing, even though the day was warm, to wear their finest cloaks, dirty nonetheless from the long journey. Sebastian wore a simple clean tunic over his usual linen shirt and woolen trousers. No one wore chain mail or carried arms.

Sebastian bowed low, as did the others, except for Isaac and Simon, who prostrated themselves, foreheads to the floor. "We hail you, great Star of the East, Father of Half the World. We thank you for this audience, and we bring you warm greetings from our own illustrious King of the West, His Excellency King Karl, who is master of a realm almost as wide and worthy as your own. These are his ambassadors, members of his own royal house, Counts Sigismund and Lantfrid—and this is Liudolf, who is my blood brother and companion in arms, and my son Milo, who is a scholar. I believe you already know Masters Isaac and Simon, with whom you have traded before and who are our trusted guides and advisors."

"Welcome, all!" the caliph said enthusiastically, and he turned to a short, dark man whose empty, inscrutable face belied his lofty status. "This is my chief advisor, Jafar al-Barmaki, son of the illustrious Yahya al-Barmaki, who was for years the grand vizier of the empire and right hand of the caliph. Jafar has earned his father's place. We have been friends since our youth. Come, sit, eat with us." He clapped his hands for more food and drink.

Thus, over a savory stew of lamb's meat and cups of pomegranate juice, the embassy was finally able to broach the subject of their visit. Strangely, Sigismund and Lantfrid, who at home in Francia or anywhere near the Frankish realm could speak confidently and with authority in the king's name, found

318

themselves intimidated by the foreign circumstances and the strangeness of interpretation through an old Jewish medium.

After a few attempts at communication, Sigismund stepped back and said under his breath, "You talk to the bugger, Sebastian. The way that bloody Jew translates, I don't know whether it's my turn or his, and he seems to like you more than me anyway, the ruddy heathen."

Sebastian stood up, bowed low, and spoke, "Great Sovereign, let me be as plain in speech as I am honest in my heart regarding our state visit here to your great empire. My king is a great man in his realm, and it is a beautiful, prosperous land. He also has a large army—the largest in the western world. He is wise, and in his wisdom he recognizes you as a ruler of exceptional power and enlightenment. He admires you greatly and seeks to know you through our embassy. He sends gifts to you—unworthy of your great splendor, of course—but sincere tokens of his esteem.

"He wishes you to know that he, like you, is a man who loves to hunt and swim and hear poetry and music. He is a king, like you, who leads his own army and creates just laws within his realm. He is a father who loves his children and raises them up righteously. He offers you his friendship and declares that you and any of your people will always be welcome in his land."

Lantfrid, excited and relieved by the recent safe arrival of the hunting dogs, could not contain himself and interrupted the conversation. "And dogs! Tell him about the dogs," Lantfrid hissed to Isaac.

Sebastian continued, "Our king wishes you to know that he hates the Umayyads of Cordoba and deplores the antics of the Greeks, who have caused so much war between your empire and theirs. He hopes by this embassy that you will see in him a reflection of your own virtue and power and that it will be possible to forge between you and us 'a friendly understanding,' which will prove mutually beneficial to both our realms."

With that, Sebastian bowed low and stepped back. Lantfrid hissed again, "The dogs, damn it. Tell him about the hunting dogs."

Harun smiled broadly after Sebastian had finished and motioned with a broad sweep of his arm for Sebastian and the others to sit on the colorful pillows provided for them as the caliph himself sat down facing them. Isaac remained standing to translate. He said to the whole delegation, "You Franks begin to intrigue me. You are a young people while we Persians are of an ancient race. Your energy and candor are refreshing, and you bring some very enticing ideas to my court. We shall have to ponder what you suggest. When I have met with my counselors, perhaps we will have some wisdom regarding your suggestions. Meanwhile, what is it that that gentleman seems so anxious for me to know?"

Sebastian rose again. "Ahem," he began uncomfortably, "Great Lord, as I mentioned, we have made bold to bring you some humble gifts. They are representative of our native land—of course, very modest indeed compared to the wonders we have seen here. Yet we offer them with sincerity and with great thanks for your gracious hospitality. What Count Lantfrid wishes me to mention is that we have brought you some Frankish hunting dogs that we hope you might enjoy since hunting is one of your chief passions, we hear, as it is with our own king."

"I should be delighted to see these dogs. We do indeed love to hunt. And tell your man there we shall see about arranging a hunt with this fine gift of dogs as soon as may be. Tell him we have prey here in my land that should be worthy of a pack of good hounds and may surprise even such brave men as yourselves. Tell him. . . we shall hunt lions."

***

Two days later, they rode out with the caliph and his entourage in the morning twilight. The dogs had been a major problem for the two counts throughout their long journey, and Sebastian feared they would be a disaster in a hunt for lions.

They had not brought nearly enough handlers. But the day before the hunt, a battalion or so of Arab dog handlers appeared at the kennels and demonstrated beyond doubt that they had more than enough experience.

Count Lantfrid had brought thirty of the best hounds from Charlemagne's kennel: big lumbering tracking hounds with a superb sense of smell, tall, thin greyhounds, excellent in the chase, and huge fighting mastiffs with powerful shoulders and jaws.

The first hunt was an unqualified success, thanks to Count Lantfrid, who at last had found something he could do for the mission. He was a consummate master of hounds, and he took charge of the Arab handlers and commanded them like a general, all the while working through Isaac's interpreting.

"Look!" The caliph pointed eagerly to a copse of low brush near the river. "Vultures! The lions have a kill!" There were three lionesses and a big male with a thick black mane feeding on the carcass of a large antelope.

There were twenty horsemen in Harun's hunting party, each armed with spears, javelins, axes, and hunting bows. Sigismund, Sebastian, and Liudolf rode with the caliph. As expected, Milo had declined an invitation to the hunt. As they approached the lions, the dogs put up a cacophony of ferocious howling, straining against their leather leashes. It was all the handlers could do to restrain them until they got close enough to the kill. The lions were all up, pacing nervously back and forth in front of the kill.

Finally, the caliph gave the signal, and Lantfrid released the nimble sight hounds. In no time they were on the lions, leaping in and out, nipping at the flanks of the raging cats and dancing back when they whirled around or charged. Several of the mastiffs burst right in, unfortunately to their destruction. One swipe from the big male was enough to break their necks. Sebastian could see at a glance that lions were unlike anything they ever hunted at home. Even the giant forest auroch could not match their power or ferocity.

The riders closed quickly, too, whooping with excitement. Some held a javelin high above the shoulder, looking for a chance to hurl it into a lion. Others held back, seeking a clear shot with the bow. Sebastian hesitated, suddenly remembering his vow in the Palestinian desert that he would never again seek to kill a living thing.

The caliph rode boldly right into the middle of the fight. For a few tense moments, the melee was in limbo, with the lions putting up a savage battle. Soon, however, two females lay dead, pierced by javelins hurled from close quarters. The third female limped off, an arrow in her hip.

"Not so close, my lord!" Sebastian yelled as Harun rode straight in toward the big male, a javelin above his head. The lion broke free of the yapping hounds and went for the horse, rearing up on its hind legs to rake the horse and rider with its claws. The caliph's thigh ran red with blood. Sebastian spurred his nervous horse in as close as he dared and instinctively flung his own javelin just as the lion prepared to leap again. The throw was true and caught the lion in the throat in mid-leap. It fell back, clawing at the javelin. Several other riders closed in and finished off the big cat with spear thrusts.

It had been a very near thing. The caliph was wounded, but not seriously. He was laughing exuberantly, delighted with the outcome and even with his own wound, which he exhibited proudly.

Sebastian did not smile. Instead, when the big lion was dead, he dismounted and knelt over the majestic beast. "I'm sorry," he whispered, not knowing whether he said it to himself, the lion, or the source of life itself. But he felt genuine sadness that he had been unable to be true to his vow. Is this the way it's always to be? he asked himself. Will there always be something that stains my hands, no matter how much I resist? God help me.

Suddenly, the caliph was standing beside him, quietly considering the slain animal. He put his hand lightly on Sebastian's shoulder and called for Isaac. Through the old man, he offered his thanks. "By the prophet's beard, See-bas-tee-yan, I believe you have saved my life!"

Sebastian rose and replied with a smile, "What matters most, Your Grace, is that I was there in time—which is only as it should be. In a dangerous game, all must be there for each other, is it not so? Praise God."

"Too right, my friend. But you were there first, and I shan't forget it."

***

Hunting was not the only sport the caliph loved. He was a Persian, so of course he loved to indulge in *pulo*, a game that originated long ago in his home country. The caliph was accustomed to playing two or three times a week. He did not hesitate to invite Sebastian to play on his team.

"Right, then, See-bas-tee-yan!" Harun said through Isaac. "The game is played by teams of seven on horseback. It is very fast and can be quite rough. One might need several horses during a morning's play. I will, of course, provide some of my best mounts for you, my friend."

Sebastian believed himself to be a good rider, but the *pulo* players rode circles around him in every game. They raced back and forth between two goals while attempting with a long-handled mallet to knock a small wooden ball through the opposing team's goal, two simple poles driven into the ground a few feet apart.

Sebastian found himself at once too slow and clumsy. He had a difficult time trying to smack the ball toward the goal at full speed, especially with opposing players crowding and nudging him, even blocking his way. They pummeled and rammed his horse with more than a little glee, enjoying punishing the upstart Frank.

The caliph was highly amused. He laughed at Sebastian's consternation, urging him on with hand gestures and shouting at the top of his voice. Caliph or no, he played the game with abandon, almost always at full gallop.

During a rest between games, he brought Isaac up and tutored Sebastian. "You must charge after the ball, See-bas-tee-yan. You must be willing to bowl over any horseman who rides into your path. It is not a game of manners and certainly not for the faint of heart. Oh no. It is quite serious, I must say. In fact, several Persian princes, even a caliph here and there, have died playing this ridiculous game. But I love it," he concluded, as if that justified everything.

Sebastian soon lost his sense of fair play and courtesy and began to play as his opponents did, spurring his horse wildly and yelling like a maniac. He never came close to matching the skills of the other riders, but the caliph was nevertheless greatly satisfied when his team managed to win the victory—and with no major casualties.

At length, Sebastian realized that in such surprising ways he and the caliph had managed to forge a bond which had seemed impossible at the outset. But each came to respect the other for his talents and courage. They even came to spend long evenings together in the company of the tireless Isaac, discussing philosophy, poetry, music, and even religion.

***

"My sentinels tell me, See-bas-tee-yan, that you remain awake late into the night, sitting motionless in a quiet place, gazing up at the heavens. What do you see there, my friend?"

"Eternity, my lord caliph; I search for the face of God."

"Ah! But I am not surprised, actually. Our discussions on so many subjects give me to know there is a deep spiritual side to you. Everything you say tells me of your belief in a higher power. God, you call it, is it not?"

"Yes, Your Grace. But it is the same God you worship, I believe. We simply use different names."

"Of course. But such faith as you demonstrate with your long hours of prayer and meditation is rare among men. Did you always have such devotion?"

"No, Your Grace, I have only recently come to this level of awareness. You see, I've led a violent life as warrior and servant for my king. I have done many things which I

324

wish I could undo. And I have had grievous losses, of people and places I loved. The worst is the loss of my wife, the mother of my children, who for important spiritual reasons has decided to live apart from me and expiate the sins she supposes she has committed. She lives in a convent now as a celibate nun. Since the day of her decision, I've found my life increasingly devoid of meaning, and I became somewhat hard and unfeeling—and empty."

"How is it that you have changed so dramatically?"

"I had an experience in Jerusalem before we came here. I met an uncommon woman—a seer and a wise healer despite her young age. I believe she was a saint, or at least a person clearly living in the spiritual world. She taught me to seek a place of peace—and there I would find God. I believe that I have made some small progress in that way. But I struggle still."

"We have much in common, Sebastian. I seek the same things. I have already made eight pilgrimages to Mecca. It is three hundred leagues from here. Twice I have done it on foot. This is how a caliph manages to stay in touch with the most important realities of life. I, too, feel I have enjoyed a modest success. So we are indeed kindred spirits."

He paused for a long moment of silence, then said, "It is late now, my good friend, but I must tell you it grieves me that you should be so alone—with no companion to give you comfort. Tomorrow I will have a small feast in your honor here at the palace. But bring only Master Isaac, who is our mouth. We cannot do without him."

***

The next evening, Sebastian entered the palace with Isaac. As he walked into the inner garden, he was surprised to see torches lending a warm light to a heavily-laden banquet table and a small band of musicians who filled the air with the sweet sounds of lute and lyre. A boy of ten or twelve years, with a face as pretty as any girl's, lent a pure soprano voice to the tableau.

As Sebastian sat down at the caliph's bidding, a troop of young women dressed in diaphanous red silk tunics and nothing else entertained them as they ate with the undulating, hip-swaying dances of the region. Each was exceptionally beautiful, chosen for the perfection of her form and face, her long black hair adorned with flowers and jewels, her eyes darkened from brow to eyelids, adding much to her compelling allure.

When they had finished eating, Harun dismissed the lovely dancers and all others except Isaac, through whom he said, "I have been thinking about you, See-bas-tee-yan. And I think it is not good for you to be so long without a woman. Why, it is Allah himself who gifts us with beautiful women. They are an indispensable delight and comfort amid the difficulties of this life."

He paused and clapped his hands. "I propose to gift you now with something you clearly need—and most assuredly deserve. Call it a reward for giving me your friendship."

"But, my lord, I want for nothing. You have certainly been most generous already. I need nothing more."

"Of course you have a need. All men have such needs. You need a beautiful woman to take you out of this taxing world and for a time bring you to an earthly paradise."

As he said this, an exquisitely attractive woman appeared, framing herself for a moment in an archway, ravishing in the soft glow of the torches. She was neither young nor old but certainly at the peak of her feminine charms. She glided gracefully into the room and stood before them, eyes lowered modestly, poised as still as a statue, as if inviting them to study her classic beauty. She was clad in thin, lustrous silk so that it was possible to define every curve and fold of her lissome body. And she smelled of jasmine.

"She is from my own harem," Harun said in a low voice. "You may have her for tonight—if you like."

With effort, Sebastian pulled his eyes away from the lovely vision, afraid lest she raise her eyes and capture his soul.

He cleared his throat and said in an almost inaudible voice, "I humbly beg your pardon, my most generous host and benefactor, but I cannot take her. For one thing, she is from your harem. God would surely punish me if I took what is so intimately yours. Beyond that, my lord, I must tell you—I have experienced love so deeply that I thought I would die from the loss of it. It does not satisfy me to be with a woman I only want but do not love. Now I try to fill that space in my heart with my God and with devotion to my king. I thank you, most generous sovereign, with all my heart. You are truly a great king in all ways. But since my experience in Jerusalem, I have been thinking of following a certain life style practiced by some of the warriors in my country. It is called the path of the 'warrior monk,' as they say. I can find peace and honor by devoting myself entirely to my God and my king."

"A warrior monk! Hmm, interesting. How did you come by such a decision?"

"I have a good friend, Your Grace, the Duke of Friuli. He is a *markgraf*—a guardian of the march between us and our potential enemies in Pannonia, one of the most dangerous approaches to our realm. He believes one cannot be a perfect soldier if he is not free to face death without concerns for wife and family, or anything else. He is totally devoted to the service of the king and our God. He also believes it is not important when or how one dies—a perfectly dedicated man is assured a perfect life in the next world."

The caliph went silent for a long time. Then he clapped his hands softly, and the lovely person before them disappeared as quickly as she had come. Finally, Harun broke the silence, "I never thought any man capable of resisting that one. She's absolutely the best I've got. She is not only beautiful, but she is remarkably intelligent, even educated. She can read and write in several languages. And she is a marvelous storyteller. She keeps me up all night, telling me the most marvelous tales, whose endings I can never guess. She has a thousand and one of them."

He sighed and went on, "But you know, See-bas-tee-yan, I'm glad you refused her. I like her so much I might have been jealous for you to have her. And then I would have had to lop off your head."

Sebastian looked up in alarm. The caliph laughed, and so did Sebastian. They finished the evening drinking good wine and singing native songs to one another.

Chapter 25

Baghdad

The Land Between the Rivers, Winter 800

"Listen to me, you old Jew—Isaac, I mean!" Sigismund exploded in exasperation, grabbing the fragile old merchant by his tunic. "I want you to go tell that bugger Harun that we must go home. It's time for him to make a decision."

Sebastian stepped in at once and pried the irate count's fingers apart. "You listen to me, Count Bullyboy! I don't care if you are King Karl's kinsman. He would not thank you for treating Isaac in this manner. Nor do I. If it weren't for this 'old Jew,' we wouldn't have had a chance of succeeding here. For one thing, we need his languages. For another, he's got a lot more sense and tact than any of us. That's how we've gotten this far. If you use him badly, he just might disappear some dark night. And then where we would be? I'm sorry, but you've just got to sit and wait like the rest of us. We're not in Francia anymore, or didn't you notice?"

Sigismund looked stunned. He stepped back, mouth agape. "Wh-what!"

Isaac wisely inserted himself, stepping between them. Clearing his throat, he offered some advice to calm the waters. "Esteemed counts, I must tell you another thing we must be careful of. It is extremely unwise to call the caliph by his name. If someone who understands your language should tell the caliph, you would lose your head. After all, he is the Defender of the Faithful, the so-called Shadow of God on Earth. They believe he rules by divine right. He is all-powerful."

"That's what I'm talking about, Count Sigismund," Sebastian echoed. "I mean you no harm. But you must watch your tongue—and your actions. The caliph has no limits to his power. As you remarked, this is 'Bloody Asia,' and our friend the caliph is what men call 'an Oriental despot.' He can do exactly what he likes—including chopping off your head for any perceived insult, real or imagined."

"Oh, all right, then, bugger all!" the count said irritably. "But for God's sake, tell his royal nibs, the caliph, that we must go home. Our king—who also rules by divine right—needs to have his decision."

"Very good, my lord," Isaac replied. "I will try to see his vizier at once, and hopefully we shall have an answer soon."

Two days later, the caliph sent for the Frankish delegation. Even Milo, Liudolf, and Simon were allowed to go. This time the meeting was held in a part of the palace reserved for state affairs. Isaac warned them it would be a formal occasion and they should pay appropriate homage at the very least by bending the knee before the caliph if they could not bring themselves to press their heads against the floor in his presence. All elected simply to kneel.

Harun was seated upon a raised and pillowed couch, over which a silken canopy was stretched. He was attired in a purple robe stitched with gold thread. Over it, he wore the formal black cloak and large black turban of the royal house of the Abbasids. He raised a hand for them to rise, but they were required to remain standing in a line before him for the duration of the meeting.

"You may speak," he said formally.

Sigismund stepped forward, boldly this time, cleared his throat conspicuously, and declared, "Your Grace, we Franks are practical people. We must always be about our important business, and it is most important that we go home to our king." He stopped, cleared his throat, and waited while Isaac translated his words. The caliph answered casually and somewhat disdainfully.

"You can go home whenever you like, Count See-jes-moon. You do not need my permission."

Sigismund sputtered and seemed to forget what he wanted to say next. He cleared his throat again, getting more and more nervous. "I mean, sir, we need. . . we need a decision!" With that, he stepped hastily back in line with the others. Sebastian stepped up beside him.

Harun eyed the group somewhat irritably for a moment and then turned to Sebastian. "See-bas-tee-yan, your friend is an important man in your country, no? Perhaps you will inform me why he is so important. He does not seem to like my hospitality. I don't know if I should be offended or not."

Sebastian bowed and replied, "Your Exalted Excellency, you have been a most generous host. We have wanted for nothing. Count Sigismund owns a lot of land in my country and has much responsibility. He is accustomed to having things his own way, and he is not used to speaking to one who is so far above him and in such unfamiliar circumstances. It has been a bit much for him, I'm afraid.

"But the count does speak with some urgency because our king is most concerned to know if you favor an alliance with us Franks against the Greeks at Constantinople and the Umayyads in Spain—and if you would allow him to support and protect our fellow Christians in Jerusalem."

"Yes, we have spoken of all this before," Harun said dismissively. "So I will tell you now since you insist and you are my friend, I have no objection to what you suggest. I have never had an objection. It is a perfectly good arrangement for both of us. I assumed you understood. I have only delayed your mission out of love for *you*, my Christian brother. Yes, that is it! I have come to love you like a brother, and I do not wish to let you go. Do you agree with your count that you must go?"

"I do, Excellency—sadly. But our king has serious concerns. And we are his loyal servants."

"Ah, well, then. . ." The caliph broke out in a broad smile. "I suppose I must allow it—but not without gifts!" he shouted jubilantly, jabbing a finger into the air and clapping his hands. At once, a company of servants entered carrying a wealth of elaborate gifts: formal robes for Charlemagne, a golden plate and goblet, beautiful enameled glass, a large trunk full of spices and perfumes made from the attar of roses, and roll after roll of fine silk cloth, the whole worth a fortune. The Franks stood in speechless wonder.

Sigismund again cleared his throat loudly. As Sebastian eyed him askance, the ungainly count fumbled with a bag at his feet, pulled out a large ivory drinking horn, and handed it to Sebastian.

Embarrassed by this awkward intervention and uncertain how to explain it, Sebastian turned back to the caliph, "Ah, Great Lord of Half the World, our king will never forget your kindness and magnanimity. We could ask for no finer gifts than these. King Karl will hold them in highest esteem, I can assure you. And yet—I apologize in advance— there is one small favor we must beg to request.

"You see, my lord emperor, our king received this item in my hands as a gift from your father, Caliph al-Mahdi. We were told it is the tooth of a beast that lives somewhere in your realm. Our king, being an avid hunter, is also very fond of wild animals. He has a garden at his palace in Aachen, in which are contained many captured wild beasts—great bisons, bears, and even a few wolves. He loves to look on them. Before we left, he charged us to ask you if you know of an animal with such teeth."

Abruptly, the caliph burst out laughing.

"Your Grace?" Sebastian ventured. "Am I missing something?"

"No, no, my friend," the caliph said, still chuckling to himself. "It's just that I have suddenly had a grand idea. I must take you with me to Baghdad," he said suddenly and decisively, "you and your Hebrew friend here—and your son, of course. The rest may depart immediately if they like—with my blessing. And they may take with them all these gifts to your king, along with my consent to everything you wish. I will have a pronouncement drawn up with my seal.

"But I must keep you with me, my good friend, for just a while longer. There is another gift I would give your king, which will dramatically seal our understanding and please him beyond all expectations. But it is in Baghdad. In any case, it would be a pity if you left my realm without seeing my fabulous capital city. I must show it to you. It is truly the envy of the world. Do you agree?"

"As you command, great caliph. I will inform the others, and Isaac, Milo, and I—and my personal men, if you agree—will be ready to leave at your convenience."

"Of course. Splendid, then! I am delighted to have your company for just a while longer. I must go to Baghdad in any case to raise the army; there is trouble with the Byzantines in Anatolia. We will leave the day after tomorrow."

All the Franks bowed as one and backed slowly out of the room, as Isaac had coached them to do. As they left the palace, instead of elation at their success, Sebastian felt a growing dejection. It was flattering that the caliph had made such a fuss over him and had personally asked him to stay, but he found himself wishing he had not. He was homesick for Francia. It had already been two long and very hard years. And he longed to see Adela again, even if it were only to talk for a little while. There was no telling how long this new delay would be.

On the way back to the camp, Sigismund raged aloud, "By God, Sebastian, how the devil are we supposed to get home without you and Isaac?" It was all Sebastian could do not to strike the man. But what good would that do? It would only make matters more difficult. At least the legion of intense happenings over the past two years had cemented his conviction that he must contain his frustrations and remain calm if he wished to survive.

"You will be in very good hands, my lord. Simon will return with you as far as the Rhineland. You could find no better pilot. He has one of the fastest ships on the seas, and he has made this journey many times before. Once you are in Francia, you will be able to find the king, wherever he is, and tell him yourself of our success. We have achieved everything King Karl desired. So you will be very welcome indeed."

"Right, then," the big man snorted, clearing his throat pompously several times, "if that's all there is to it. I can't wait to get out of this place. I've had quite enough of Bloody Asia! You can keep it, thank you very much. Can't understand a bloody word the buggers are saying, don't like their awful food or anything they drink—bloody fruit all the time and pomegranate juice! Lord, it gives me the flaming runs. I'd give a fortune for some good roast meat and a flagon of beer!"

***

"I hate to say good-bye to you, Simon," Sebastian said as the caravan prepared to return to Antioch. "You've done so much for the success of our mission. It wouldn't have been possible without you."

"Nonsense, Sebastian, it's been a lark. I wouldn't have missed such an adventure for the world. Besides, I only had a very small part."

"Now you're fishing for compliments, you fox. But it's true, your part was indispensable. You fought back-to-back with me against the pirates. You saved all our necks by getting us out of Constantinople in the nick of time. You shared our every hardship. And you gave up at least a year of your life to boot. All through it, I couldn't have asked for a more faithful friend. God knows what it's cost you personally."

"Oh, come now, Sebastian. You know me better than that. I've been busy with my own affairs the whole time. Do you think I was idle while we were in Jerusalem? I was making a fortune in trade there while you were mucking about in the desert and consorting with young girls in alleyways."

"Stop! Or I'll take back everything I said about you. Seriously, I'd like nothing better than for you to come with us to Baghdad and then home. Milo will go on with us. I wouldn't want him to miss it now that we've come so far. But the royal counts would never get back without your help, and I could never convince them to go to Baghdad now that they've got what they want. Besides, I know you have urgent business of your own to attend to. So go on, then. . . with my profound thanks and blessing.

"And here, these are the two letters for the king I stayed up all last night preparing. One attests to the success of the mission, in case something happens to Sigismund and

Lantfrid; the other is about you. Don't open it, you wily bugger, but get it to the king by whatever means you can. If you do, you will find that you have earned a great deal more than just his thanks. Good-bye, my good friend," he said with a warm embrace. "We will see each other again, God willing."

On the second day, as the caliph promised, they boarded a barge and fell in line behind the caliph's own royal boat to begin a comparatively easy float with the current downriver to Baghdad. For the first time in a long while, Sebastian was able to relax and enjoy the feeling of completion. He leaned back on a bench against the side of the barge, savoring the leisure to spend some time with his close companions. He knew that Bardulf and Drogo had enjoyed some of their best moments of the journey drinking unlawfully in the company of the rough soldiers of the caliph's palace guard, and he looked forward to hearing Bardulf regale the company with some new outrageous tales.

"We had us a fine interpreter. He was this here young blond Saxon slave which the A-rabs had tooken in war, and he was sold to a Jewish trader and then to the caliph's house. Through him, I learnt a good deal about the way them soldiers of the caliph fights. And I got some good tales from 'em as well.

"Ye see, gentlemens, it seems there was this other caliph—before Harun, there—who was every bit as lively and important as him. He was out huntin' one day and he found hisself lost in the desert somewheres—on foot. Now he didn't have no food nor water, and he got very weary and hungry. Finally, he comes upon this poor old village A-rab settin' by a tent in the middle of nowheres.

"Now this caliph was a great man, he was, and he hated to ask anythin' of the poor beggar who was just out there tryin' to herd some goats. But he comes up and sets hisself down by the poor fella's fire, and he says, 'Have ye got anythin' to eat?' The poor devil straightaway gives him some coarse bread. He gobbles it up and says, 'Now have ye got somethin' to drink?' The man don't hesitate, he brings up a whole big skin of wine outta his bag, and he gives the caliph a brimmin' cup of it. He takes a big drink, and then he asks the peasant, 'Do ye know who I be?' The peasant says, 'I do not, sir, and it don't matter. Ye are welcome to what I have.'

"The caliph says, 'Well, I serve in the court of the Commander of the Faithful!'

"'Well,' says the poor man, 'ye must have a very fine work to do. I hopes ye are grateful for your good fortunes.'

"Then the caliph holds out the cup and gets it filled up again. He drinks it all down in a shot and says, 'Do ye know now who I be?'

"The peasant replies, 'Ye done tole me already.'

"'Well, that ain't exactly all. I am actually a high general in the army of the caliph.' And he holds out the cup again. The peasant promptly fills her up once more, and the caliph drinks her down in a big gulp. Then he says to the poor A-rab, 'Well, if ye still don't know who I be, I'll tell ye, then; I am the Commander of the Faithful hisself!' And he holds out the cup again. With that, the peasant snatches back the cup and hides away his skin of wine, sayin', 'Ye ain't gettin' another drop. If I give ye another cup, ye'll be telling me ye be the Prophet Mohammed hisself.'"

***

The trip downriver was uneventful except for the myriad of stories with which Bardulf filled the hours. Sebastian spent much of the voyage observing Arab life along the river's course and discussing it with Liudolf. He had expected the land to be empty and arid. Instead, he discovered that it was green and fruitful, with many canals and irrigation ditches.

Sebastian was surprised to find the usually imperturbable Liudolf so impressed by the land. "You remember how hard we had to work to hack good farmland out of our wild forests? Here they hardly have to do anything. These farms here along this big river remind me of the Rhineland—rich soil, full of plenty."

"Yes. I can easily see why the region could be called part of the biblical Fertile Crescent. It must have been this way for thousands of years."

At last, they reached the point on the river nearest to Bagdad and found horses and a royal escort awaiting them. They took the so-called Damascus Road for a short journey to Baghdad on the Tigris. The system of roads that Harun and his father Mahdi had created throughout the realm allowed riders to bring messages over three hundred leagues in less than a week. Riders from Raqqah had already reached the city and spread the word of the caliph's return. When they reached the outskirts of Baghdad, a huge crowd lined the road leading into the city. Harun was met by a delegation of dignitaries and a squadron of the palace guard in brilliant uniforms. He crossed the river on a floating bridge and entered the city on a great white stallion, clad in black Abbasid ceremonial robes and a high, round Persian turban with a black scarf down his back to cover his neck. Over his shoulders, he wore the double-bladed sword of the Prophet.

As they reached the city, thousands came out to greet him. Women on the rooftops under which he passed trilled the high-pitched ululations of joy that typified Arab celebrations. Everywhere there were shouts of, *"Allahu Akbar."* Sebastian realized at once the caliph was not only the all-powerful secular leader of a people but the spiritual leader of all Islam as well.

Harun was the picture of a great emperor. At age thirty-seven or so, he was strong and in full health with the vigor of a younger man. He sat tall and erect on the stallion, handsome with a perfectly trimmed black beard and mustache and flashing white teeth in contrast to his dark olive skin. He controlled the stallion with his legs and smiled back at the crowds, waving both hands high above his head in joy.

They rode with difficulty through the throngs in the marketplace with its ubiquitous bazaars and shops. Finally, they passed through the enormous gate of the western wall into the "Round City," named by Harun's grandfather, Caliph al-Mansur, Madinat as-Salam—the City of Peace.

When Caliph Mansur founded the city, Bagdad had been a sleepy Arab village on the great river. Now it was a city of tens of thousands, a hub of commerce and manufacturing, two miles in diameter. It was renowned for its fine metalwork, enameled glass, leather, and beautiful ceramics. It had special shops filled only with books, and the shopkeepers sold a new and strange writing surface from China called "paper." Everywhere the city seemed prosperous and clean, a city of hundreds of public baths and an equal number of mosques, large and small.

The procession made its way slowly through the crowds to the city center, where stood the caliph's grand palace, the Golden Gate, so called for its huge central entryway. It was a fortified citadel with high walls and towers. Inside, it contained the royal residence and hundreds of administrative buildings for the military and civilian government. But there were also many gardens and trees of all kinds, giving the whole place an aura of peace and quiet. The noise of the city was almost completely shut out.

The Franks were escorted at once to comfortable quarters adjacent to aromatic gardens shaded by cypress trees, where hundreds of colorful fish filled artfully designed ponds and waterfalls. They were treated to every kind of food and drink, their every need satisfied.

Sebastian did not meet again with Harun for almost a fortnight after arriving in the city, but they could see the reason in the endless delegations of officials and military officers who came and went through the corridors and porticoes of the palace. Meanwhile, the Franks were treated day-to-day with tours through the huge city, visiting bazaars filled with wares from all over the world and sampling food cooked for every appetite. They noticed with wonder the many aqueducts bringing fresh water into the city, so much that they could even use the water to clean the streets.

And of course they spent time in the teahouses, taverns, gaming rooms, and theaters, where they were entertained by poets, singers, and storytellers. The Franks had never seen a place where there was so much to do and so varied a collection of peoples. They came away believing that Baghdad was truly an enchanted, fanciful city, mysteriously unreal in its color, excitement, and variety.

On the second Friday after their arrival, Sebastian and his company were invited to the great mosque adjacent to the palace. There they witnessed Harun al-Rashid leading the prayers of the faithful, dressed in the robes worn at one time by the Prophet himself. They were astonished at how many times during the ceremony Harun prostrated himself in prayer. They came away understanding why the people considered the caliph the "Shadow of God."

Two days after the ceremony in the great mosque, Harun sent for Sebastian and Isaac. As in their first meeting in Raqqah, Harun met them informally in a garden. He looked exhausted from the past two weeks, but he was relaxed and smiling.

"See-bas-tee-yan! How good to see you! I am so sorry there has been no time to be together. I have missed you."

"And I you, great caliph. But we have been treated in magnificent fashion, and we are most grateful."

"Listen, my friend," Harun said, taking Sebastian by the arm to a small bench by a tiny waterfall. "I'm afraid from now on I shall be very busy indeed. I must call up the army. And I know you are anxious to be away on your journey back to your king.

"But I want to tell you personally of my great regard for you and for your king—through you. I wish to give him a very unusual gift to express my regard—an unforgettable gift, which will not only delight him but give him an idea of the power and grandeur of the monarch who sends it. My gift is called Abul-Abbas."

Without another word, Harun led Sebastian through a small alley into another larger garden to a small pavilion enclosed by flowering trees. There, standing quietly by a lovely pond filled with goldfish and munching on succulent leaves, was Harun's gift, Abul-Abbas—an enormous light gray Indian elephant.

Chapter 26
Abul-Abbas

None of them but Isaac had ever seen an elephant before. It was quite the largest beast any had seen or could imagine. Even the great auroch that ruled the deep forests of northern Francia was nowhere near as big and formidable. Sebastian's first response was total amazement. He had never even seen a drawing of such an animal. His second response was absolute dread.

"How in the world are we ever going to get him home?" Sebastian groaned after they left the caliph's presence and settled in a private garden near their quarters. "He's almost as tall as two men and longer than two horses! He's enormous! And probably very dangerous. Did you see those horns on his face?"

"Those are called tusks, Lord Sebastian. Every male elephant has them," Isaac replied, blowing his nose into a rag. "Ach, I still can't get the smell of the beast out of my nose. But I believe he has been quite well trained. Did you notice the young man standing nearby holding a stick with a hook on the end of it? That's the mahout. He's the elephant's master, so to speak. I have seen such people before; they sit right on the elephant's neck and use that hook to make the animal move wherever they wish. Elephants are extremely strong, but they behave for the mahout like a dog."

"They're also extremely big! I say again, how can we possibly get him home? I can't believe the caliph really expects us to do that. I mean, we have to cross an ocean. Is there a ship big enough? I've never seen one, and even if we could find one, how could we load him onto it? Ye gods! Do you think the caliph might just be having us on a bit? I suppose he enjoys a good jest as well as the next man. Right?"

"Sebastian, my friend, let me assure you, the caliph is not joking. He gave us a gift for our king. He fully intends that we will faithfully present that gift to King Karl with his compliments. What this caliph does is always beyond what an ordinary man would do. He expects everyone to take him most seriously. In a way, it's quite a compliment to us that he feels we can actually do this."

"Can we, Isaac? I don't even know where to start. And, good Lord, how long would it take?"

"I think, sir, we must do it at all costs if you expect the caliph to honor a pact with our king. There's no telling how long the journey will take. Much depends on whether we can find a Noah's Ark, or something like it. As for a beginning, I think we must start with the animal's mahout. He should be here any minute."

Almost before Isaac finished speaking, two Indian men came quietly into the garden. Keeping their eyes downcast and their hands clasped before them as if in prayer, they bowed deeply before Sebastian and Isaac. *"Namaste,"* they exclaimed softly. They were clad in simple peasant clothes with sandals on their feet. Both wore ragged turbans. One carried the hooked stick Isaac had mentioned as well as a long bush knife in a sheath around his waist. Isaac spoke to him in Arabic, asking his name.

"I am called Rahul, master. I am mahout to Abul-Abbas. This is my apprentice, Amit," the man spoke in passable, if very simple, Arabic. Amit did not look like an apprentice. He was at least as old as Rahul, perhaps in his late twenties. He kept his eyes on the ground during the entire interview. Sizing them up, Sebastian noted how slight they both were and how unassuming. He wondered ruefully how in heaven's name they could possibly be of any help in moving an elephant across the deserts, mountains, and seas of two continents.

"Rahul," Isaac went on in a kindly voice, "have you been told what future lies in store for you and Abul-Abbas?"

"I have, master. I am told we must make a far journey to a place the like of which we have never seen. It will be long and dangerous, and it is very possible we shall never return."

"And how do you feel about that, Rahul? Are you willing to go with us and bring Abul-Abbas on such a journey?"

The young man took only a few seconds to choose his words. "Master, I have been given to you by the great caliph, who is the Shadow of God, I and Abul-Abbas, and also my friends who will travel with us. It is *kismet*, as they say. It is our fate. We now belong to you, and we will go where you go and do as you will bid us."

"Actually, Rahul, you belong to Lord Sebastian here. He is the servant of a great king on the other side of the world, a king like your caliph. He will be your new master until we bring Abul-Abbas to our king. Then you will become the servant of the king himself, and he will give you great honor if we succeed in bringing Abul-Abbas to him in safety. You are right, it is your destiny. But I shall be your guide. Together, we will make this *kismet* a most fortunate one."

Later in the day, Sebastian invited Milo and his comrades to the meeting to introduce them to their new situation. They were struck speechless as Rahul brought Abul-Abbas to the garden, riding on his neck. He deftly maneuvered the elephant to within ten paces of the group and, using the hook, induced Abul-Abbas to bring him gracefully to the ground while standing on the elephant's trunk. He then stood humbly, bowing before the group as if to apologize for his insignificance.

No one spoke for a long moment, then everyone tried to speak at once. Milo was full of questions. Bardulf wanted to touch the elephant and have Abul-Abbas lift him up onto his back. Drogo, mouth agog, merely sat rooted to the earth like a petrified tree.

"Gentlemen," Sebastian began rather formally, "this is Rahul. He is going to help us bring"—he took a deep breath— "this noble beast to the court of Karl der Grosse, our king and master. I have brought you here just now to help Isaac and myself plan how we are going to accomplish this feat. I want you to open your minds and let your imagination guide you. We're going to need every bit of wisdom and insight we can muster, not to mention a great deal of divine providence.

"Rahul," he said, gesturing to Isaac to translate, "who are these other young men behind you?"

Amit and three other smallish men had wafted silently into the garden while they were marveling at Abul-Abbas. They looked like copies of Rahul and must have been his brothers. They came forward shyly, eyes on the ground. Rahul introduced them formally: "Great sirs, you have met Amit. These others are Arjun, Kumar, and Prateek. They are my assistants."

"Whoa, Rahul," Sebastian said. "We have a very long way to go. And as you say, it is possible you may never return. Why do we need these others?"

"Sir, if I may be so bold, Abul-Abbas will need them."

Sebastian turned in consternation to Isaac and said, "You question him, Isaac. I have no idea if he knows what he's doing or not." And he sat down to wait for the outcome.

After several minutes of interrogation, Isaac made his report. "I believe he is right, my lord. We will need these men. Apparently, this worthy beast eats as much as ten horses every day. He will eat almost anything, but it must be procured for him, or he must be led wherever the food is and be watched constantly because he tends to do a lot of damage when he eats. He also must be bathed daily, especially when the weather is hot. And, ahem, since he eats so much every day, he tends to expel feces from his body quite frequently. This is quite messy, apparently, because the manure is barely digested. However, they say it's very good as a fertilizer."

"Wonderful! I'm so glad to know that last bit. So we have to take four other men just to tend to the beast and clean up his messes?"

"It appears so, my lord."

Sebastian sighed and wearily pronounced the news. "Well, my friends, it seems we're in for a long journey, perhaps the most fantastic of your lives. We must take this giant animal home to the king. How we are to do that is what we must decide next. I believe the caliph will lend us a military escort, at least as far as the coast of the Roman Sea. We can procure camels for us to ride on, but Abul-Abbas there must walk, and we must go at his pace, whatever that may be. Hopefully, God willing, we will be able to find a suitable vessel in Antioch by which we can all be transported back to Italy. But I fear it may be too much to hope for.

"The first question, then, is by what route must we proceed to the sea? As I see it, there are two possibilities; we can go back the way we came, along the river to Raqqah and then to Antioch. Or we can take the Damascus Road toward Jerusalem. From what I have seen on Harun's military maps, it is a much shorter route."

Luidolf answered quickly, as if he had already thought about it. "We must go back as quickly as possible. Soon it will be summer, and I've heard it's blazing hot from dawn to dusk. Can we not take the western road to Damascus and then to Jerusalem?"

"My dear sirs," Isaac spoke up. "The western route is one of the most desolate roads in the world. I have been over it many times. It is often hard enough to find water for camels and men, let alone for an animal which might drink its weight in water in one day, not to mention what it needs for his baths. Besides, I know of no shipbuilding capability near Jerusalem, and I doubt we could find any ship there big enough. I fear we must retrace our steps."

"All right, then," Sebastian decided. "We will go back on the river road to Raqqah and then across to Antioch."

"Father," Milo broke in, "what happens if we find there are no suitable ships in Antioch?"

"Well, we could possibly find a ship or have one built for us in the Asian part of Constantinople. But I'm afraid I'm a wanted man there. I cannot go back. We'll have to go south along the coast to Jerusalem. If nothing is available at the port of Ashdod, we will simply have to go on to Egypt. I've heard there is a large port at El Iskandariya, or Alexandria, as the Greeks call it. Perhaps we can find an appropriate ship there."

"That is wise, Count Sebastian. I think it is the only way," Isaac added. "I have friends in both Ashdod and Alexandria. Perhaps they will help us find what we need."

And so the die was cast, and a week later they left Baghdad with an entourage of thirty camels, fifteen camel drivers, five elephant attendants, and a military contingent from the caliph's own palace guard. Sebastian's only real comfort was the letters of safe passage bearing the golden seal of the Caliph of Baghdad.

Chapter 27
Muddling through to El Iskandariya

January 801

Following the river road, it was easier to feed and bathe the elephant, but the pace was agonizingly slow for Sebastian. He fretted daily that they could make no more than four or five leagues a day because the elephant insisted on stopping whenever he spied a copse of succulent young trees or an opportunity for a bath in the river or any convenient water hole or stream. But even Sebastian had to admit that the journey was pleasant and the countryside seductively attractive in the soft, clear air of the river region. He began to hope they might actually be able to bring the elephant home.

All was well enough until Abul-Abbas uprooted his tethering stake one night and silently padded off into the surrounding neighborhood of farms, foraging at will and sampling the vegetables and grain in a half dozen fields and a score of peasant gardens. The next morning, a crowd of angry peasants surrounded the encampment and demanded satisfaction, even calling for the elephant to be killed forthwith. Sebastian was obliged to ask Isaac to pay a handsome sum in order to persuade the irate farmers to depart and stop threatening the elephant. He was in a dark mood when he confronted Rahul.

"What is the meaning of this, Rahul?" he demanded through Isaac. "Can you not control the beast? What have you got to say for yourself?"

Rahul fell to his knees. "Kill me, O master, I am unworthy," he begged, touching his head to the ground. "I am a despicable servant. I am nothing."

"Oh, for heaven's sake, stand up. I just want you to tell me why this incident happened and what we can do to keep it from happening again."

"Sahib, it is only because we tethered Abul-Abbas too close to the campfire. At night, if there is a bright light nearby, he cannot resist staring into it. And then he cannot sleep. It makes him crazed, and he wants to eat."

"Well, how will you stop that? We must have a fire at night, and we cannot afford to have such trouble and cost."

"My lord, if you allow me to remain mahout, I promise you I will tether him tightly to a stout tree or heavy rock. I will hobble him." And he pulled from a sack at his side two loops of heavy ropes connected to a center ring. Imbedded in the inside of the ropes were short nails which would cause pain if the elephant moved too quickly while hobbled. "And I swear that every night we will tether him far enough away from the light, and one of my brothers will be required to sleep as near to him as it is safe to do. I promise you this will never happen again."

Rahul was as good as his word. But for several nights thereafter, they had to endure further disturbances as Abul-Abbas trumpeted his displeasure at being hobbled and contained. Rahul and the others eventually solved the problem by piling up leaves and vegetables before the elephant went to sleep and chanting to him in low, melodious voices. The routine worked, and there was peace. But the stubborn beast still insisted on stopping for his daily bath when they passed an attractive spot. He loved to wade into the water and then lie down on his side in mud or sand and let his handlers wash him, wriggling over now and then to scratch his back into the dirt. Progress remained maddeningly slow.

When they finally reached Antioch, the contingent of the caliph's guard immediately rode off in spite of Sebastian's arguments that they should stay until a ship was found. And though they scoured the port area and talked to every shipbuilder, no one had the capability of building the kind of ark that would be needed, nor had they ever seen a ship big enough for Abul-Abbas. "How could he be contained? What if he moved around from side to side? The ship would capsize with such a beast on board," they said.

Eventually, it became clear the journey would have to continue to Jerusalem and then possibly to El Iskandariya, the fabled city of Alexander the Great of ancient history. Sebastian steeled himself and the others for the challenge before them. "Listen, it might not be so bad. Isaac says the road along the sea is fairly safe; water and vegetation should be plentiful. I have writs of safe passage with the seal of the caliph himself. No one would dare interfere with us. If we do as well as we have so far, it need not be an ordeal."

In a subdued voice, Isaac added a corollary to the plan. "I do not believe, my friends, that we could find any kind of suitable ship in Ashdod. I propose therefore that we go straight on to Jerusalem. There we might find some men who could act as security for us on the continuing journey. I fear that the farther our march takes us from the caliph, the weaker his control may be."

Milo added another suggestion. "Perhaps we could find such men among the Christian community in Jerusalem. Didn't you say, Father, that the patriarch and his syncellus were very grateful to us?"

"You're right, Milo. It won't do any harm to see just how grateful they really are. We could do with a few extra guards we can trust. We'll stop off in Jerusalem."

***

The next leg of the journey was down the coastline of the Roman Sea, still in the province of Syria and still enjoying the protection of the caliph, through the famous biblical towns of Tyre and Sidon, which Sebastian was sorry to see were in a state of ruin. Wherever they went, the elephant was an instant sensation, and they had to keep a constant armed guard over him to prevent gawkers from upsetting Abul-Abbas or being trampled by him. At length, they arrived near Jerusalem, where they managed to buy tents and set up camp in a village within a small oasis where they could feed and water the elephant adequately without attracting too much attention. Sebastian and Milo left almost immediately for the city.

They found Magdala, as before, begging on the Via Dolorosa with the mute boy at her side. Given her accustomed reserve and serious nature, she surprised them both with a warm smile of genuine delight. She rose immediately and embraced Milo—to his great embarrassment, but she simply took Sebastian's hand and looked deeply into his eyes.

"You are well, then, my lord?" she asked, already sensing that Sebastian was in a better place.

"I am, Magdala. I am feeling very well, in fact, much thanks to you. You have made quite a difference in my life, and I am grateful for it. In fact, I have a proposal for you. Can we talk somewhere?"

As she led them once again out of the city to their old bench in the Kidron Valley, Sebastian briefly recounted their adventures since she last saw them. "We did manage to meet the caliph. He's quite incredible, and we even managed to become good friends. Such friends, in fact, that he has given us an extremely large gift."

"Ah, well, then. Did he make you a sultan? Did he give you much gold?" she asked, laughing puckishly.

"No, he gave us an elephant." Sebastian paused to enjoy her shocked expression. "Have you ever seen one?"

"No, no. But my father once did, and he described it to me. Can I see it? Where is it? I would love for my friend Damien here to see it," she said, placing her arm around the small boy's shoulders.

"We will take you to see it. In fact, I would like to give you a chance to see it a great deal. We want you to go back with us to Francia. You can travel with us."

"But why, Lord Sebastian?" she said, slipping back into her usual grave demeanor. "Why ever would I want to go? And what use would I be in such a distant strange place as Francia?"

"I've been thinking about this ever since we left. In Francia, there is great need for healers such as you. I don't mean miracle workers, though you do seem to perform some, but we have many poor in our land, and there are no hospitals for them, no orphanages besides the monasteries, and very few people who even know how to heal. I think you could do wonders there. You could teach others what you know.

"And it is a Christian land; you wouldn't have to worry about offending the authorities as you do here if you, as a woman, help a Muslim, for example. And one more thing, I am most grateful to you for the insight you gave to me. I would like to return your kindness by giving you great honor among my people and a place where you could be of even greater value than you are here."

"And what of the people who depend on me here, my good count? Shall I leave them simply because you offer me a better place, honor, and greater purpose? What makes you think your people are more worthy than mine?"

"I don't say that, Magdala. I don't mean to look down on your people here. I only say that there are other people who have great needs as well. I know you would not want to leave your people, but I offer this to you in case you would *need* to leave here to save yourself or someone else. If you have to, it's a new place where you could start again and be of much value. I guarantee that you would find fulfillment in Francia. We need people like you desperately. We are still barbarians compared to what you do in medicine and care here and what they do in Baghdad and Constantinople, on a much greater scale. I won't press you, but will you at least think on it?"

"I shall, Lord Sebastian. I can see your sincerity. And I honor it. But I have my place here. I must stay. Besides," she said on a lighter note, "who would care for my sweet Damien? He would miss me too much, wouldn't you, love?" She hugged the boy affectionately.

"Bring him with you. We would be glad to have him. And one more thing, Milo would be very glad to have you— both of you."

Later Milo complained of his father's subtle insinuations. "Did you really have to say *we* want you to come? You never told me what you planned to ask her. You took us all by surprise, not just Magdala."

350

"I'm sorry, son, I wasn't sure I should bring it up so suddenly, but it seemed like a good moment. I said *we* only to make my argument seem less selfish. Besides, I didn't think you would object, would you? She could do a world of good in Francia, don't you think? Besides, don't you like her?" Sebastian grinned as he observed his son's face turning bright red.

"Like her—what's that got to do with anything? Of course, she's a fine young woman and she definitely does wonderful work. But what I think doesn't really matter, does it?"

"Nonsense, of course it does. You're a man now, and you're my son. You will inherit whatever legacy I have. It may make you more important than you realize. In any case, what you think matters very much to me."

"Thank you, Father. And, no, I don't object," he said, turning away in an attempt to seem nonchalant. "If she should come, I would welcome her and even help her—in whatever way I could. But I'm fairly certain we shall never see her again."

***

The stay in Jerusalem was a short one. Syncellus George, anticipating further bounty from the King of the Franks, readily agreed to supply a company of twenty young Christian men to accompany the travelers as far as Alexandria. They were not exactly trained soldiers, but they had experience in providing a level of inconspicuous security for the Christian community in Jerusalem, and they were young and healthy and spoiling for a bizarre adventure such as Sebastian offered.

Sebastian and Milo saw Magdala one more time when she brought Damien to see the elephant. They were both thrilled. Damien even uttered a single Arabic word. *"Kalb-ee-ee,"* he said and beamed from ear to ear. Magdala said it meant "doggie." From that time on, Sebastian referred to the huge pachyderm as Doggie, especially when the animal had vexed or perplexed him, which was often.

As for Magdala, she again refused to go with them, claiming obligations to her people. This time, however, a large tear glistened in the corner of her eye. Taking her hands in his, Sebastian seized the moment to tell her how important she had become to them.

"Magdala, I wish with all my heart that you would come with us. You need to know how strongly you have influenced Milo and me." Milo shifted uneasily on his feet and kicked at a small rock but said nothing. Sebastian went on, groping for the right words. "Before I met you, I thought I was lost. Now I have hope again. As far as I'm concerned, I'm one of your miracles. I shall be forever grateful." He hurried on to hide his own emotions.

"Here is a small parchment with the names and places of people in Friuli, Rome, and Francia where you can find help if you ever change your mind. I guarantee you these people will welcome you and do whatever necessary to help you find us. They are among our closest friends. And here, my dear, are some silver coins for your ministry. There are some golden ones besides. I hope you will hold onto these and keep them in a safe place in case you ever change your mind about coming to us. Please do not refuse me. I am a king's minister and am justified in giving you this. It is, after all, only a small thing considering how profoundly you have helped us."

She said nothing but stepped forward and embraced him warmly, tears streaming down her face. He turned and walked away quickly toward the elephant and the rest of his entourage. He looked back once and saw Milo and Magdala locked in a long embrace. She broke away quickly, gathered up the still-excited Damien, and hurried down the dusty road back into the city. The caravan left Jerusalem at first light the next morning.

***

At Gaza, the last Syrian town, they were able to procure for several days a comfortable and obscure lodging for the elephant while they enjoyed the many bazaars of the city and bought supplies for the trip to Alexandria. A more serious reason for the delay was the customs post on the western edge of the town, at which they had to endure the first of several such border outposts, where the country being entered, in this case Egypt, did its best to gouge travelers with exorbitant tariffs before allowing entry.

Isaac was outraged by the demands made by the Egyptian officials. "They are simply filling their own coffers. It's an old story, even biblical. We Jews have always despised tax collectors. They are always the most corrupt members of any society. We must find someone, a man of influence and power. It's only a matter of finding the right person. Better to bribe a single individual and let him smooth the way than deal with a lot of scurvy petty officials. It might take a day or so." And he went off in search of such a man.

Grumbling mightily, Isaac finally procured their passage into Egypt with a significant bribe, but once cleared to continue the journey, their camel caravan found slow going along the arid Sinai coast. Abul-Abbas was not happy with the heat and lack of water and the food he was used to. He refused to travel in the oppressive heat of the day and could only be coaxed to move in the early morning and late afternoon. Finding a suitable place near water to camp each night became a huge burden. Sebastian had to send foragers out far and wide every night to find enough fodder for the elephant, who trumpeted loud and long when he did not get enough to eat. It took nearly a month to travel a distance that ordinarily might have taken the camels four or five days.

Riding along together in the early morning as they neared the Egyptian heartland, Isaac confided to Sebastian his worries about the next challenge to be faced. "You know that soon we'll have to cross the Nile River, don't you? Do you know anything about it?"

"Not much. I've only heard of it vaguely. They say it's the longest river in the world and that it is the source of

Egypt's wealth and power. But I don't see the problem. Don't elephant's swim, like most animals?"

"They do indeed, but I have spoken to Rahul at length about this matter, and he says that Abul-Abbas might swim across a small river. He might even walk along the bottom if it's shallow enough, breathing through his trunk while his entire body is under water. But he says Abul-Abbas might be afraid of a large river and refuse to swim across it. Besides that, I have spoken to several Egyptian travelers over the past few days, and they all say the river is teeming with crocodiles, huge water reptiles with powerful jaws and long rows of teeth."

"Are there no bridges?"

"None, the river is too wide. And along this coastal road, the river becomes a delta—it forks into five rivers that we must cross if we stay on this road. Abul-Abbas would have to swim each one. Rahul says he would not do it."

"Well, then, what is to be done?"

"I have no idea at this point, Sebastian. But obviously we must find a boat big enough—five boats, it seems. I suppose we shall just have to wait until we get there to find out what to do next."

The going got easier the nearer they came to the Nile. Vegetation was plentiful, and Abul-Abbas stopped complaining. When they finally came upon the great river, it was as Isaac had said, too wide to swim and too full of crocodiles. And there was nothing like a ferry that could handle an elephant. That evening, after they had pitched their tents, Sebastian called a war council, including Rahul and his brothers.

"Well, you know the problem: we must get across the river. Rahul says our Doggie will not swim it. Does anyone have any ideas? Think!"

Finally, Rahul cleared his throat and stepped forward. With downcast eyes, he suggested a plan. "Sahib, long ago when I was a boy, my father, who was also a mahout, found a way to bring an elephant to a big river and get him across."

"All right, then. That's what we need. How did he do it?"

"He built a raft."

"Good. We can do that. Describe how he did it."

"It must be a large enough raft to hold the elephant. What my father did was buy many very large jars with lids. He made them waterproof with resin. Then he tied them together to make a floating platform. On the top of them he lashed timbers together. But it was still not enough. The elephant was still alarmed by the water all around the raft. He would not walk onto it."

"All right, so what next?"

"He deceived the elephant, sahib. You know that Abul-Abbas has very poor eyesight, like all such beasts. He is easily fooled. My father covered the raft with dirt and the ramp leading onto it as well. Then he fixed small trees and farmyard items on the raft, such as bins, a chicken coop with live chickens, a goat or two, so that the elephant thought the raft was a small farmyard. Then my father got a donkey that the elephant was fond of to walk onto the raft before him. The elephant followed the donkey, and they crossed the river."

"Amazing! Do you think it will work, Isaac?"

"I believe it is certainly worth trying, Lord Sebastian. Alas, we have no donkey which our elephant likes."

"Sarah!" exclaimed Bardulf. "The elephant likes Sarah! He follows her around all the time. I think he's in love with her."

"What in the world is Sarah?"

"Why, she's my camel, m'lord. The camel I rides. I calls her Sarah. She's a sweet 'un, she is, and, like I say, ol' Abul thinks so, too."

"You've come a long way, Bardulf. I remember when we started this journey you said you 'would rather walk than ride one of them ugly, dangerous beasties.' I believe that's what you said, wasn't it?"

"Well, sir, we *was* a bit leery at first. But now it's a wonderment how good we rides 'em. Why, I almost likes camels better'n horses. For one thing, old Sarah is easier on me backside, and she's awful smart. I bet I can get ol' Abul to follow her onto the raft."

"Well, we've got to do something to get him across the Nile. It's worth a try."

"Wait a minute, Sebastian," Liudolf broke in, "we've got five rivers to cross. Isn't that what you said—about the river forking into a delta with five branches?"

"Ach, you're right. And I'm sure we couldn't portage the raft. We would have to take it apart and put it together four more times. It would take forever and cost a fortune in pack animals."

"Lord Sebastian, if I may," Isaac suggested, "we could go south to the ruins of the ancient city of Memphis. It is a fantastic place, the heart of one of the world's first great peoples. Near the ruins is the small town of Al-Jizah, or Giza, on the west bank of the Nile, where there are enormous pyramids, like mountains rising out of the sands. You will not believe until you see how wonderful they are. It would be a pity to be in Egypt and not see these marvels. It is a great mystery how those ancient people could have built them. There we will need to cross the river only once. The delta begins a few leagues north of the town."

Sebastian quickly decided to avoid further delay. They had already been underway for six months. So far during the journey, they had avoided disaster, but he worried that every passing day could hold a fatal hazard and that they should use every opportunity to push on before their luck changed. They moved south at once toward Al-Jizah.

As they approached the town, they could already see in the distance three looming triangular shapes rising out of the windswept desert sands. Rather than expose Abul-Abbas to the bustle and clamor of the town, they continued past it until they found a relatively quiet place to cross the Nile. All the while, no one could wrench his eyes away from the fantastic pyramids.

"This is the strangest place I've ever been, Isaac," Sebastian commented in an awed voice as the neared the plateau on which the great monuments stood. "It is so near the river, but there's nothing beyond but sand and no people whatsoever."

They stayed on the east bank for two weeks to collect all that was necessary to build the big raft—large jars, timbers, heavy ropes, poles, and oars. They hired gangs of natives to haul the materials and help in the building. Isaac found a ferryman and hired him away with an exorbitant sum. This man easily constructed a steering mechanism and saw to the raft's balance and navigability.

At last, they crossed. Sebastian held his breath as Bardulf led the camel named Sarah across the disguised ramp and onto the fake farmyard-raft with its little forest of camouflage trees blocking out any view of the river. Submissively, almost dutifully, Abul-Abbas followed behind with Rahul sitting on his neck, ready to insert the hook into whatever sensitive parts of the elephant's head that would direct him straight ahead.

"Quickly," Rahul hissed to his brothers as they came aboard, "bring the food!" Baskets of fresh vegetables and melons were quickly brought and dumped before Abul-Abbas as Rahul placed a light, transparent, scented silk wrap over his head and eyes. The brothers brought out pails of water and began to bathe the elephant's legs and belly while they softly sang together the hypnotic chants of their homeland. Liudolf and sixteen oarsmen slipped aboard silently and took their places to propel the raft across. All the others crossed in boats once the raft was underway.

Abul-Abbas settled down at once and began to munch the delicacies contentedly. He snorted only once and raised his trunk to sniff the air when the raft gave a lurch as it surged out into the river.

"Praise God and all the saints," Bardulf exclaimed nervously as he leaped off the raft onto the other shore and began to help the others bring up and connect a second ramp, placed beforehand at the landing point. "Arrgh! I ain't never been so affeared in all me life! Did ye see them ugly water beasts a-swimmin' round our raft? I swear some was big enough to eat me whole. And I can't even swim!"

357

Once Abul-Abbas, still behaving beautifully, was led ashore behind Sarah, the raft was sent back several times for the other animals and drivers and packs. Everyone breathed a sigh of relief, and Sebastian splurged to bring a surfeit of wine and plenty of spicy food from the town. They spent the early hours of the night singing and telling stories around the campfire.

In the morning, everyone rode out to see the pyramids. Milo was particularly unnerved by the eerie atmosphere. "What are those, Father—those other things in front of the big pyramids? They look like elaborate tombs. They're everywhere."

Isaac spoke up quietly, "They are tombs, lad. And so are the three big pyramids. This entire place is a huge graveyard. The pyramids were built to house the bones of kings, what the Egyptians called 'pharaohs.' The smaller tombs are for lesser nobles. It is truly a place of the dead, and they say it has been so for thousands of years."

"But who built them, Master Isaac? And how?"

"Ah, lad, that no one knows. Perhaps an ancient race of superior men who knew the laws of mathematics so well they could find ways to carve the stones to fit exactly into each other and then find ingenious ways to raise them to great heights. You will see for yourself when we reach them. You are welcome to climb up as far as you like and examine them. I guarantee you will not be able to imagine how they could have done it."

"Look! Look there," Bardulf shouted, pointing ahead. "There's a man's head stickin' up out of the sand. It's huge, and he's lookin' right at us."

"That is what the Egyptians call a 'sphinx,' good Bardulf. You are right, it is the stone head of an ancient king. See his elaborate headdress? Underneath the head, deep in the sand, they say there is the body of a lion. The monument is supposed to reflect the power and might of the pharaoh. I have seen smaller models of it in shops in Alexandria."

"It is so otherworldly, Master Isaac. It's like the king is looking out into the next life," Milo added in a subdued voice.

"Perhaps you are right, Milo. This whole place is what they call a *necropolis*, a site from which those buried here hope to ascend into the next world to meet their gods."

"Gods? Did they have more than one?"

"Oh yes, they had many. Some were supposed to be all-powerful. But many had the traits of ordinary men and could be as good or bad as any of us."

"How do you know all this? It's fascinating—in a rather frightening way," Milo added.

"I like to study the people and customs of the places I visit. It helps me to get along with them. And yes indeed, the otherworld of the Egyptians can be most frightening. But it is not so much different from your Christian beliefs. The ancient Egyptians believed that when they died their souls would be measured on scales. On one side of the scales was a feather. If a soul was heavy with sin, it would not balance against the feather, and the soul was doomed. Do you not also believe in a last judgment?"

"We do, Master Isaac, but I should hope that our God tends more toward mercy and forgiveness than to such stern judgment."

"Perhaps. We do not know. Still, we are all entitled to hope. Everyone is. It is only human."

They camped for another day and night in the haunted atmosphere of the great pyramids. Many of the company climbed up on them to look toward the river and the life it represented before turning their heads to the west to gaze out over the vast and empty desert.

Only Bardulf and Liudolf climbed to the pinnacle of the tallest pyramid. It took them nearly the whole of the day. But both were exultant when they climbed down, feeling they had somehow conquered the desolate place and could now return to the fullness of life.

As for Sebastian, he marveled once more in the night at the immensity of the star-filled heaven, comparing it in this sacred place of the dead to the insignificance and impermanence of human existence. Ah, well, he thought, these great kings tried here to guarantee themselves eternal life.

Now they were forgotten, their memorials sinking into the desert sand or being whittled away by the wind. The regal tragedy drove him to think of his own end. He promised himself fervently that whatever happened in the rest of his life, whenever he was faced with the choice between self-fulfillment and virtue, he would remember these somber monuments.

Chapter 28
Ifriqiya

Summer and Autumn 801

The caravan returned to the river and followed it north without further incident. After the lonely desert and the stress of the long journey, all felt an enormous sense of relief as they entered Alexandria, the seat of the Muslim government in Egypt. The famous old city was bursting with life and an exotic medley of peoples. Blue-domed mosques and stately minarets now vied with the great buildings, parks, and monuments left by the ancient Egyptians as well as the Romans and Greeks. It was a crowded, noisy, fascinating city, and the whole troop was full of excitement and hope.

After finding a suitable place to pitch their tents near the harbor, Sebastian and Isaac went at once to inquire among the several shipbuilding enterprises along the waterfront. Their high hopes of hiring or even building a ship for Abul-Abbas were dashed at once.

"But why? We can pay handsomely," Sebastian argued through Isaac with each owner. Every answer was the same. "We cannot build ships or hire our ships out to foreigners."

"But we have credentials! With the seal of the Great Caliph. He has given us safe passage through every land over which he has dominion. That includes this city."

"I see your permits, my lord, but they only allow you safe passage. They do not entitle you to build or buy a ship for your own use. The very same caliph who signed your papers has also given us a strict warning not to share the secrets of our shipbuilding with those who might someday be our enemies. I offer you my sincere apologies. You seem like good, honest men. But, no, we are forbidden by order of the caliph's new governor."

361

"Well, who is that? And where can we find him? Perhaps we can convince him."

"Sir, the present governor of Egypt is Abdallah ibn Takir. But you cannot see him; he governs from Baghdad. There is only a deputy here, who has no authority to countermand our orders to deny ships to foreigners. I am very sorry."

The message was the same from every shipbuilder or ship's captain in the large harbor: they were all forbidden from serving foreigners. After several days of trying, Sebastian again called a war council.

"We are unable to procure or build a ship here for the Doggie. It is forbidden to foreigners," Sebastian began. There was a chorus of moans. "Isaac says our best hope is to push on to Carthage, which is the closest point from this shore of the Roman Sea to Italy, and there is a wonderful harbor there. Somehow we must get King Karl to send us a ship there for Abul-Abbas." Louder moans. "And," Sebastian continued, looking straight at Milo, "I must send two of you home ahead of us to tell the king where to find us."

"Who?" Milo demanded. "Father, say it's not I!"

"It is you, my son. I'm sorry, but we don't know what to expect of the rest of the journey. Even Isaac has had very little experience in Ifriqiya. That's what they call the land we'll be traveling in next. It is ruled by a king who has only a token commitment to Harun al-Rashid. It's possible he could be hostile to us."

"But why me? Let Isaac go."

"We can't spare Isaac. You know he's our interpreter and guide. Even if he doesn't know Ifriqiya, he will be familiar with many of the people we're likely to meet. He is essential."

"Then go yourself. I'll go back with you. And we'll return together to pick up the elephant."

"No, Isaac will need me. The next part of the journey is likely to be very dangerous. He will need protection. It must be you, Milo. If I send my son, the king will be sure to respond. He may not even know we're still alive. You can make him see the urgency of our situation."

"But, Father, I don't even know the way."

Sebastian hesitated a moment and cleared his throat. "I'm sending Liudolf with you. If anyone can get you back safely, it is he." Sebastian avoided looking at Liudolf, for he knew how his old companion would feel. They had been together for most of their lives, through thick and thin, and Liudolf would not readily relinquish what he felt was his lifelong duty—to be at Sebastian's side and guard his life at all costs, as he had always done.

"You will go, Liudolf, won't you?"

Liudolf shifted uneasily from one foot to the other and looked away. Eventually, he spat in frustration and said in a low voice, "If I have to."

"It's the only way, my friend. I have no one else to send. You must tell the king what kind of ship we need and what kind of problems we are likely to have getting the elephant aboard it. And you must tell him to hurry. This trip has been unbelievably expensive. Our hoard of gold is all but gone. We may be able to borrow some from Isaac's trade contacts here in Alexandria. But that is not certain. In the meantime, what's left must be used to secure your passage on the next Radhanite or Frankish boat we can find. Pray God there will be one soon."

Isaac commissioned watchmen to inform them of the arrival of every ship coming into the harbor, regardless of its country of origin. They waited only a week until a Venetian trader sailed into the harbor in the middle of the night. The next morning, Isaac quickly hired a skiff, and Sebastian brought Milo and Liudolf along to go out to the ship before it had begun to unload. Leaning over the side of the ship as they came alongside was a familiar figure.

"Hallo, Count Sebastian, hallo, Milo, my friend, and Liudolf!" Captain Barbero shouted, the same intrepid captain who had brought them from Venice on the hazardous journey to Constantinople when Milo lost his arm. His red face beaming with delight, he yelled down to them. "Fancy meeting you here—indeed! This is the last place I would ever expect to see such friends. Welcome, welcome to my ship once more. Who would ever have thought we would see each other again, and under such circumstances? Quick, come up, and let me embrace you."

***

Milo and Liudolf sailed for Venice a week later, after Captain Barbero had completed his trade affairs. Sebastian promised to reward him with the price of a whole voyage's profits if he would head straight back to Venice and arrange for Milo and Liudolf to have horses and supplies for the trip home.

"Milo, just tell the king we must have a large enough ship and there must be a means to get the elephant aboard it. Surely there is a shipbuilder who can craft us such an ark somewhere in Italy. And tell him we must have it as soon as may be. We have no idea what may happen when we enter Ifriqiya. It's quite a different place than Egypt."

To Liudolf, he said, "You should be fairly safe once you reach Venice. Captain Barbero will see you right for your way home. Just make sure you don't travel alone. Join with other travelers until you get to Friuli, then go at once to Duke Eric. He will be sure to give you a troop of cavalry to bring you all the way to Aachen. Find the king, wherever he may be. Make sure he knows we will be out on the end of a limb in Carthage until the ship comes. Have no fear. I know you'll make it. And so will we, if you hurry. Godspeed, my brother! We will see you soon, if God wills it."

There was one more serious complication before the caravan could leave Alexandria; the twenty young men who had thus far served so well as guards announced their intention to return to Jerusalem. Sebastian had known the moment was coming ever since the plans for a ship went awry. He conferred anxiously with Isaac.

"We cannot let them go, my lord," Isaac counseled." The road to Carthage is along the coast. There will be towns and villages along the way, and it is not entirely a desert. But there will be parts of it that lead through very isolated country. There are Bedouin and Berber tribes, nomads for the most part, but little better than bandits. We must be able to defend ourselves; there are no laws where we are going. I think we should travel only with large caravans, and if we can find none, we must travel at night as much as possible and hide ourselves in a large village or town during the day so we can better defend ourselves. But we cannot travel with just camel drivers and the Indian men. We need these young men. Let me speak to them."

Accordingly, Isaac gathered the Jerusalem men and spoke to them in Greek as Sebastian stood nearby. "My friends," he began, "you have done us great service so far, and we are most grateful. But I wonder if you truly know what you serve and whom. Standing before you is one of the great champions of the King of Francia, a renowned warrior, known throughout that great realm. Both he and the king he serves are earnestly devout Christians. They wish to preserve the Christian holy sites and communities of Jerusalem and Syria. They, and men like them, are all that stand between your faith and the Muslim tide of conquest.

"It may seem strange that an elephant is an important part of the mission of the Christian king. But the animal is a gift from the Caliph of Baghdad. It symbolizes an important agreement which guarantees that Christianity will continue to exist and even flourish in Jerusalem. We must bring this elephant to the Christian king. And we cannot do it without your help. If you finish this trip with us, you will not only serve your beloved patriarch but your very faith itself.

"If you go on with us, to whatever destiny awaits us, you will be greatly rewarded, by us and by your God. In the meantime, you will see a part of the world you never expected. And when you return to Jerusalem, you will be experienced men of the world, men of consequence—not to mention the material rewards of silver and gold you will receive from our master, the King of Francia. What say you?"

It was quite a speech, and it worked. The men conferred only for a few minutes and then each approached Sebastian, bending a knee to offer him their continued fealty. Sebastian was so moved that he reached out and raised each one again, looking them in the eye and thanking them personally. Later he confided to Isaac that, thanks to him, they might really have a chance after all.

***

The next part of the trip was the worst. The coastal road was a dusty track, leading over ground that seemed never to have seen a drop of rain. Oases were few and far between. The summer heat was hellish. Abul-Abbas would not stir in the midday sun, so the caravan was forced to travel only at night, hiding themselves during the daytime as best as possible. When there was no shade, they pitched a tent over the elephant and brought as much water to him as possible. He complained loudly and began to look sickly.

Sebastian took a patrol of men each night to scout the road ahead and search for water, either in an oasis or a village with wells. It seemed to him he never slept except fitfully on the back of a camel. They paid dearly for what water they used wherever they went. The only blessing was that the oppressive heat and emptiness did not seem to suit whatever bandits might have lurked along the road, and they met none. But other travelers were few as well, and their fear grew larger in proportion to the emptiness of the land.

"We must be in Ifriqiya, Sebastian whispered hoarsely to Isaac upon returning from the latest night patrol. "There's a large oasis ahead, much more vegetation, signs of many travelers. Didn't you tell me Ifriqiya would be more hospitable than this bloody no-man's land?"

"It is, Sebastian, it is. I think the worst is over. I have heard there are towns, villages, cultivated land from now on, all the way to Carthage. And there will be rain, blessed rain. How long has it been since we have known it?"

"A very long time, my friend, and I, for one, could use a proper bath. I don't care if I have to do it upon the back of a camel as we ride. But we must go on. We have lost a month traveling so slowly at night."

Over Sebastian's objections, Isaac convinced him that they must spend several more days recovering in Tobruk, the first substantial town in Ifriqiya. "Sebastian, we cannot go on without the supplies we need. The men need to bathe and rest and burn their filthy clothes. Abul-Abbas must have a rest and be fed up to his old strength. You cannot jeopardize the elephant!"

"All right, all right," Sebastian relented. "But don't blame me if our ship decides we aren't coming and leaves without us."

"Nonsense, my good count, it will take far longer to build the ship we need than you imagine. If anything, we shall have to wait once we arrive in Carthage."

"You know, Isaac, I wish we had known about this place. This is a beautiful harbor, the best I've seen along the coast. We could have brought our ship in here. They even build a few ships here. Did you see those channels from the water they've cut into the land? Do you know what they are?"

"I do not, sir. Please inform me."

"Those are what shipbuilders call dry docks. They dig them right next to the sea, with only a bit of land to hold the water back. Then they build a ship in the dry dock, and when they are done, they dig the barrier of earth out, let in the sea, and up the boat floats!"

"Ingenious, my friend. And what does that have to do with our elephant?"

"Don't you see, it would solve the problem of how to get Abul-Abbas aboard the ship. If we could find a dry dock in Carthage, or build one, we could pull the ship in with ropes. The land sides of the dry dock will be even with the deck of the ship, and Abul-Abbas can walk over planks directly onto the deck. Of course, we may have to disguise the planks, as before, and bring Sarah to lead him. But I think we can do that now. He trusts us, finally." Sebastian laughed gleefully and

367

smacked his hands together at the thought of the plan. "So what do you think?"

"I think it will work, and if it does, we shall have solved the major problem of getting the beast on board. Now if only they are building into the ship a way to bring Abul-Abbas into the hold. If we have to tend to him on the open deck, it could be disastrous."

"That's a bridge we will cross when we must, my good friend," Sebastian chuckled as he rubbed his hands together. "Soon you will be back in business. In the meantime, I'm having some tea or something stronger, if we can find it, at the nearest *taverna*. Come and join me."

***

The rest of the journey was relatively easy. They were able to find other caravans to travel with for the most part, and they made good time during the day. Abul-Abbas was happy again, with plenty to eat, and he reveled in the occasional torrents of rain that spilled in off the sea. All seemed well, and Sebastian felt he could almost smell their destination at Carthage. He longed to put a swift end to their seemingly endless ordeal.

"We can save a great bit of time, Isaac, if we take the road to the southwest. The coast road will be much longer. It might even mean a week of extra travel. We can go with the small caravan of that sheik we met last night. He knows the way."

"Possibly, but can we trust him, Sebastian? We don't know him at all."

"Come, Isaac, we ate with him last evening. He seemed perfectly genuine to me. He has a normal cargo to trade, his men look ordinary—he even has women in his tent. Did you notice anything amiss last night?"

"No. But I still don't know him, and I'm more comfortable with the larger caravans—and a busier road."

At length, Sebastian prevailed, and they set off the next day, trailing behind the sheik's caravan. As they moved into less populated areas, Sebastian began to have doubts. Isaac is rarely wrong, he thought. I should have listened .When they paused for a midday rest, he brought the men together and admitted his doubts.

"I have no real reason to think something is amiss, but just to be safe, I want the Jerusalem men to ride, spears up, ten on each side of the elephant. Tell them to wear whatever armor they have. Rahul, I want you to place the box on the elephant, the one your princes ride in when hunting. Can you do that?"

"Certainly, sahib. We have it packed on a camel. We need only to assemble it."

"And I have seen you make the elephant rise up on his hind legs and trumpet loudly. Can you do that whenever you like?"

"I believe so, my lord. Only, Abul-Abbas is more likely to do it if he has had some wine. He is a great lover of wine."

"Well, give him some if you think you can still control him. And put those fancy blankets on him that make him look so big and grand."

"Yes, my lord."

"If we have to fight, I want the elephant in the middle with ten men on either side, spears and shields up and forward. Bardulf and I will be on the animal's back, in the box. We will use bows at first, and then I may ask Rahul to make the elephant charge if we have to. The Jerusalem men will advance with us. But stay out of the elephant's way." He had them practice the drill several times out of sight of the other caravan, and then they moved on.

They had almost reached their intended camping place just as the sun was going down when suddenly the road ahead was blocked by a motley band of Berber tribesmen, inserting their camels in between the two caravans. Sebastian and Bardulf dismounted at once and had Rahul lift them up on the elephant's trunk and onto his back. They scrambled into the carriage box and took up the bows. Meanwhile, the Jerusalem men fanned out on either side, ready to fight.

"How many do you figure, Bardulf?"

"About fifty, m'lord. And mean-lookin' buggers, they be as well."

Sebastian signaled for the men to keep moving slowly ahead. "Isaac," he called down to the trader riding behind the men on his camel, "tell the men to sing. Tell them to sing some of their chants, and as loud as they can."

Isaac rode among them, urging them to begin singing. "Anything, men, as long as it's loud," he shouted. The men began chanting a throaty, defiant Greek battle song at the top of their voices. All in all, it was an impressive show, and clearly the Berbers were not sure how to react.

When they were close enough to see the whites of their opponents' eyes, Sebastian whistled to Rahul, and suddenly the elephant rose up on his hind legs and trumpeted. It was all Sebastian and Bardulf could do to hang on and avoid being spilled to the ground. Over and over, Abul-Abbas made the air reverberate with his trumpeting and the ground shake with his massive feet as he reared. Then, goaded by Rahul perched on his neck, he began to run at the Berbers. The Jerusalem men proceeded apace, still singing their lusty song. Behind them, Rahul's brothers set up a high-pitched caterwauling straight out of the jungles of the Indus. The overall effect was formidable.

The Berber line broke well before the elephant reached it, and the undisciplined tribesmen scattered in every direction. Sebastian drove through, straight on into the middle of the caravan ahead of them as it waited for the outcome. The drivers and merchants were dismounted, and in the middle of them the sheik stood, mouth open in disbelief, stunned by the spectacle descending upon him.

But before he could have his camel brought up to make a run for it, Sebastian and Bardulf leaped down from the elephant's back, grabbed the sheik by the scruff of his neck, and threw him over the neck of Bardulf's camel. The whole troop then moved deliberately straight through the camp and into the gathering darkness.

They made a forced march well into the night. Finally, they veered off the road and into a small farmyard surrounded by fields and palm trees. Abul-Abbas and the camels were hidden away in the trees, and the men set up a defensive perimeter behind the rock wall surrounding the small farmhouse, its inhabitants remaining quietly inside the house.

Morning came without an attack. The sheik was livid, but he knew he survived only by the will of his captors, and so he begged for mercy, promising all manner of rewards. Sebastian sent out scouts, but there was no sign of the Berbers or the other caravan. By mid-afternoon, they were underway again, this time taking a fork in the road that led back to the coast. There they found several caravans moving westward together and fell in with them without further incident. The offending sheik was left afoot in the descending twilight after the last caravan was out of sight.

***

The road to Carthage led north, and they were finally able to leave the winding coast road and proceed straight up the Tunisian peninsula. The mood of the men was jubilant. Almost there, Sebastian thought. He scarcely dared to believe it. Now, if only there was a ship. . .

They had to pass through Kairouan, midway up the peninsula, and there they stopped to see one of the wonders of the Arab world, the Great Mosque of Uqba, famous for its wide marble paved courtyard, its colonnaded prayer hall, bedecked with luxurious Armenian rugs of all colors, and its massive square minaret.

An architectural masterpiece, it was one of the oldest places of worship in the Arab world. Sebastian and Isaac obtained permission to see the inside. Carefully they removed their boots and wandered tentatively through the beautiful complex. As they gazed at the intricate Arabic wall designs, they were suddenly surrounded by armed black men wearing high turbans and displaying slave tattoos on their bare arms. They said nothing but herded Sebastian and Isaac out of the

371

mosque with grim faces and abrupt gestures. They would not answer any of the questions Isaac put to them. There was nothing to do but obey their signals and follow them out of the building.

The entire caravan was forced to move under guard to the palace of the local governor. As the others waited in a small caravanserai adjacent to the palace, Sebastian and Isaac were led through the elaborate palace door and into a colorful, light-filled throne room. There, descending from his throne and coming to meet them, was the governor himself, ibn Ibrahim al-Aglab, Emir of Ifriqiya.

He was a cheerful, bald-headed man of about fifty years with a short forked beard and a pair of merry eyes. "Ah, I see from your serious faces, my friends, that you have been misled. I apologize. Sometimes the orders I give are misinterpreted. I meant to welcome you to my country, to Ifriqiya, where you will be my honored guests."

"We don't understand, Your Excellency," Isaac hastened to say. "We are simply Frankish travelers who wish to return to our homeland. We are going to Carthage to await a ship from our king."

"Fascinating! Wonderful! I am so glad to have finally met you. Come, sit, we shall have tea and refreshments. You see, I already know all about you. Everyone does. The news of your 'elephant caravan' is common knowledge. Have you not noticed the crowds who line the roads merely to see you pass?"

"We have, Your Grace, but we did not realize it was anything but curiosity."

"Nonsense. The stories about you grow with every passing day. I laughed till I cried over how you completely bamboozled poor Sheik Ahmed ibn al-Rifa when he led you into an ambush. I would punish him for that except that you have already humiliated him quite enough. Such a delightful story—and what a ferocious beast you have in your charge. Amazing!

"I even know how you crossed the Nile. Ingenious! Garden rafts—indeed! You see, my Frankish guests—and you are my honored guests—I wish to be your friend, not only because I admire you, but I also wish to make myself known to your King Karl as a friend."

He was interrupted by the arrival of refreshments served by a huge, bare-chested native the color of black ink. Everywhere throughout the palace such men were in evidence, all carrying heavy scimitars and sporting gold rings from their ears and around their biceps.

Ibrahim explained briefly, "Those are my Zanji slaves. Don't be alarmed. They are extremely loyal to me and protect me from some of my Arab associates. I have five thousand of them," he said gleefully.

"I must admit I also wish to be your friend because I have been instructed to do so by none other than the Shadow of God and Commander of the Faithful, Caliph Harun al-Rashid, may Allah give him long life and great good fortune."

Sebastian took the moment to pull from his tunic one of the parchment letters of safe passage with the caliph's seal. He offered it to Ibrahim, assuring him through Isaac that the caliph wished also to be friends with the King of the Franks.

"Yes, indeed, I already know. And I am most happy to echo my lord's intentions. You see, he has only recently appointed me as the first one of my family, the Aghlabids, to be Emir of Ifriqiya. And he gives me free rein to build this part of his empire into a shining example of Muslim wealth and power. I have already started an enormous project of irrigation, which in a few years will mean not only prosperity but an end to the cruel hunger that too often haunts my realm.

"But I need powerful friends to do all the things I wish to do. One of those things, I will tell you plainly, is to possess the island of Sicily, now ruled by the cursed Greek dogs. I know one thing about your king: he has no love for the minions of that imposter Irene. This is what Caliph Harun has told me, and he gives me full permission to pursue my ambitions in Sicily. I wish to have approval from your king as well. Can you assure me of that?"

As was his custom at moments of crisis, Sebastian took a deep breath and a long moment to reflect, realizing that their safety and eventual deliverance might depend on what he said now. He turned at last to Isaac with the answer. "My lord governor, I have not seen our king in over three years, not since we have been on this mission to visit your caliph. But I know this: King Karl certainly does not have any love for the Greeks, but he does wish to form an alliance with your caliph. I cannot speak for him at this time, however, since I have not seen him for so long. But I will promise you this: I will pass on your compliments to him and tell him that you have treated us well and as honored guests. I believe you may indeed find favor with him."

Ibrahim was more than pleased with the answer. He immediately ordered a feast for that evening for all in the caravan. At the end of it, as Sebastian and Isaac prepared to retire for the night, he had two slaves bring in two golden basins. He then stood on a small dais brought in for the purpose and pronounced in an official voice to the various officials who shared the feast that henceforth Ifriqiya would be ally to the King of Francia and that his emissaries were to be treated with honor wherever they went in the realm. With that, he took the golden bowls and solemnly poured a small fortune in gold coins over the heads of Sebastian and Isaac, which were later picked up and given to them by the slaves.

The rest of the journey up to Carthage was far less dramatic. They enjoyed an armed escort of Zanji slaves all the way to Carthage, and they were accommodated there in comfortable surroundings overlooking the great harbor. The pomp and circumstance of their celebrated arrival would have been the finest possible way to end their incredible journey.

Except that there was no ship.

Chapter 29

Homecoming

The Emperor's Court at Aachen, Summer802

Like thirsting for water in the desert and finding only a mirage, a sense of doom descended on the small company as they scrutinized the harbor for a hint of the promised ark. Sebastian immediately assumed the worst. Either it had not arrived or they had missed it and it had returned home. Perhaps it was never coming. Maybe Liudolf and Milo never made it home. It could be that Charlemagne had no idea they were still alive or that they were waiting in Carthage. It was possible the elephant would die before they could find another way. And at present they could do nothing about all that. They were just stuck in a God-forsaken African port, strangers in a land that could turn hostile any moment. Such were the thoughts that ran through the heads of everyone in the company.

It was Isaac who shook them out of their funk. Having survived a hundred dire circumstances in his long life, his practical mind told him to seek useful means to assuage their disappointment and assume a positive outcome. After the first grim day, he approached Sebastian, "Sir, do you not think we have wallowed enough in our disappointment? This is no good. We must assume the ship is coming and be in readiness to receive it. You must give the men something to do."

Isaac's words shook Sebastian out of his torpor and he realized at once that the old sage was right. He must do something to banish the fears of the men as well as his own dark thoughts. Accordingly, early the next morning, he called an assembly of the whole company. "Stand up everyone. Take a deep breath. Now, listen to me; the ship will come, I'm sure of it. Somehow Charlemagne will know we are here. Good

Lord, we've been a spectacle everywhere we went since we left Baghdad. He will find out where we are and send a ship. Believe it! He is not a great king for nothing.

"Meanwhile, we have to be ready and you are going to have to bow your necks and work your back sides off. Here's what we're going to do, We will set a watch on the harbor for the ship night and day. During every daylight hour, you will be building a dry dock, such as we saw in Tobruk harbor. Thanks to the generous gift of gold we received from the Emir, we can hire gangs of local people to help you dig, but everyone in the caravan must work generally just as hard as they do, digging and carrying, until we have shaped a large dry dock. The ship will doubtlessly be much bigger than an ordinary one. We need to be able to haul it into the dry dock so the elephant can step onto it without having to go up a ramp. He just wouldn't do that. And when the dock is ready, with just a few feet of earth keeping out the sea, we have to break the dam, let the water fill the dry dock, and haul the ship into it. We can do it! Never fear! And when it's done, the ship will be here." That last promise proved to be stingingly disheartening and embarrassing for Sebastian because the ship had still not arrived when they finished. They were still marooned in the ruins of old Carthage.

Sebastian had to stage an expensive celebratory feast on finishing the work and then every day after that he had to organize rough, elaborate games and races to keep the men occupied and exhausted during that stressful time.

But at last the ship did come! Early one morning it appeared on the horizon and was immediately spotted by the lookout. It was obvious, even to the untrained eye, that it was the ark. Even at a distance it looked like a great fat duck, wallowing in the waves as it slowly drew nearer. The lookout raised the whole camp and they watched in awe as it sloshed toward them through a heavy sea. Once closer to shore everyone could see the unmistakable colors of the monarch of Francia.

***

Sebastian and Isaac rode into the palace complex in Aachen on the back of the elephant. They dressed in robes of Persian silk and had Rahul make Abul-Abbas lift them up on his trunk to the carriage box on his back. On either side, the twenty Jerusalem men marched with spears and polished shields, once again singing at the top of their voices, this time a triumphant Greek church song. Ahead of them all, Rahul's brothers, also dressed in finery, repeatedly hoisted and waved large silk flags of red and green and yellow. Trailing behind the elephant, under the care of the drivers, came Sarah and ten of her sibling camels, all that remained of the caravan.

Following behind the animals were hordes of palace folk and villagers, laughing with delight and cheering the procession. The horse guard Charlemagne had sent to accompany Sebastian and his troop all the way up from Italy had all it could do to keep the mob from rushing in to crowd around the parade.

As they marched into Aachen amid the cacophony of bells, horns, and cheering crowds, Sebastian couldn't help but compare all the fanfare of their homecoming to the actual journey itself. It had taken four years, and the memories of the trials they had faced, the rigors, suffering, and deprivation of the trip, made him view all the celebrations somewhat sardonically. After all, bringing the elephant home, while exceedingly difficult for the most part, was by far the least important part of what they had accomplished.

But the people of Francia had never seen an elephant, and the stories of the journey began to assume the status of legend.

Sebastian spotted the king, who had been crowned emperor in Sebastian's absence, as soon as they came within the palace complex, all gates now wide open to the parade as well as to the huge crowd.

He might be a little heavier perhaps, Sebastian thought as he observed the emperor waiting excitedly on a small raised platform. They had heard that Charlemagne now spent most of his time in Aachen these days, but becoming emperor didn't seem to have changed him much at all—same small leather crown sitting precariously on that large round head of his, same old blue cloak. There he was, grinning and waving like a child—same exuberant delight in everything he did. Sebastian felt a wave of affection for him in spite of his deep-seated disapproval of the way the emperor chose to rule. Lord, it was good to see him.

"Sebastian!" the emperor shouted as soon as the caravan drew near, and he almost ran up to the elephant but backed away quickly when Abul-Abbas swung his head and trunk toward him. Sebastian quickly signaled Rahul to let him down on the trunk, and then he knelt before the emperor. "Your Imperial Highness," he said, head down, hand on sword.

"Oh, get up, Sebastian, and let me embrace you." And he literally lifted Sebastian up and off the ground in a crushing bear hug. "My God, let me have a look at you," he said, plunking Sebastian back to the earth. "I swear you've not changed a bit—a little weathered from the sun perhaps but still as fit as any youth. Good Lord, I've missed you! Why didn't you come up from Italy when you got there last October?"

"I'll explain later, Your Grace, but first one little thing. Please step this way." He led the emperor to Abul-Abbas, where Rahul stood waiting. "Put your hand on his trunk, my lord." He signaled Rahul. The elephant's trunk came right down into a curve before the emperor. "Now, sire, hold onto the elephant's trunk with both hands and put your foot on the curve of his trunk." Another signal and Charlemagne was suddenly sitting on the neck of Abul-Abbas with Bardulf holding him fast and helping him up into the ceremonial box. Sebastian quickly joined them. Then they proceeded to continue to parade around the entire palace with Charlemagne waving gleefully to the crowds.

***

Later in the royal apartments, they finally had a chance to talk. "Right then, old lad," Charlemagne said warmly as the two of them settled into his private quarters for the promised accounting. "I want you to tell me everything over a large flask of wine and some good food—the whole amazing story, every fantastic detail. We might take all night." He whooped and called for the wine.

After a first long draught and a toast to each other, Sebastian began. "First of all, sire, when we finally arrived at the bay of Carthage, there was no ship. I'll tell you frankly, after all we'd been through, when we didn't see the ark, we almost gave up. It was such a punishing journey, and everyone had given so much. It was a grim time for all of us.

"I set a watch on the harbor night and day and straightaway put everyone to work to take the men's minds off their disappointment. We got help from gangs of local people and built the dry dock. When it was done, we busied ourselves with games and races for another week. In spite of the make-work and games, that one week was as close as the men came to despair during the whole trek. But at last one early morning that blessed, ridiculous looking ark showed up. You never saw such relief and rejoicing."

"Well," Charlemagne countered a bit defensively, "we did have to build the bloody 'ark,' as you call it, and it wasn't easy. No one knew how to build a ship for an elephant. The shipbuilders didn't even know how big the beast was. I had to send for Milo and have him draw up some pictures and give us an idea of the size of the animal. But I did send the ship in August. From what Milo said, we thought you'd be there long before that. But go on with the story."

"We didn't even celebrate when the ship arrived but set to work at once to break the dike and pull the ship into the dry dock. We tricked the elephant into coming aboard the ship, but he absolutely balked at going down the ramp into the hold as planned. We had to keep him up on deck under a tent so he couldn't see the sea, along with a camel named Sarah, whom he apparently loved, thank God.

"He was hobbled and bound with heavy ropes to the mast and sides of the vessel. And that made our little Doggie, as we called him, very unhappy. The tight constraints and his fear of the movement of the sea made him by turns melancholy and unpredictably dangerous. He had to be watched night and day and soothed with much bathing and rhythmic chanting by his handlers.

"The crossing was a tense time for everybody, and thousands of prayers went up to God and the Virgin Mary for good weather. Luckily, the seas were calm, and we made good time. But once we got to Italy, our hopes of going straight on to Aachen were dashed. It was a totally new environment with its crowds of gawking people and its different soil and vegetation. Abul-Abbas refused to walk on. It was as if he decided he'd just had enough. It took two weeks to get him to walk away from the port area."

"And then?"

"When we got to the mountains and he sensed the growing cold of late October, he just refused to go any farther. We were delayed another six months until the thaw opened the Alpine passes."

"Good God, Sebastian, you could have come on by yourself and gone back for the elephant in the spring."

"Sire, I apologize for not coming home when we first landed at Porto Venere. But I hope you can understand how important the elephant was to all of us. When we first got him from Harun al-Rashid, I thought it would be impossible to walk such a large beast all the way to Aachen. To do so, we underwent a thousand adventures—one a day. It was the hardest thing I ever had to do, and I came to love the beast, as well as all the people who helped Isaac and me bring him to you. I couldn't leave him. He's a noble animal, indeed, one entirely fit for an emperor."

"Marvelous! I understand, old chap. It's all right. And I am absolutely delighted with Abul-Abbas. From now on, he'll go with me everywhere I go, and I will shower honor and riches on all those who helped you and Isaac. In fact, I want to celebrate your accomplishment at a grand fete in two weeks. I want your boys here and anyone else important to you."

"Sire, can we speak of that later? For now can you just tell me about Milo? I haven't seen him yet. Where is he? Is he all right?"

"Of course he is, man. He's better than ever. He's just not here yet. I didn't know when we could expect you. He's been traveling all over the realm, looking around and plotting ways to build some hospitals for the poor and sick. I'm a bit dubious about it, but I want to encourage him nonetheless."

"How did he fare once I sent him from Alexandria?"

"Wonderfully! He came through like a veteran—he and your comrade Liudolf, who's a good man to have beside you in any scrape, I'm thinking. They did have a rather rough time of it, though. And I hate to tell you this, old son, but when they did manage to get to Friuli, they found that Duke Eric was dead. I know you were great friends. What's left of the Avars managed to rise up against our reign, and he was killed in an ambush. We lost a great man. He was the image of the Christian warrior—an example to everyone." Charlemagne paused for a long moment as Sebastian turned away to hide his surprise and sorrow.

"At least he died fighting and in your service. He once told me it's what he wanted. I'll miss him greatly."

"So will we all. God rest his brave spirit."

"Amen."

After a moment the emperor continued. "Your man Liudolf pushed on with Milo anyway when the new duke hesitated about sending a troop with him. I shall have much to say about it to that wretched man the next time I see him. However, they survived and brought the news to me. I cannot tell you what a relief it was to hear you had gotten as far as Alexandria. But we weren't totally ignorant of your progress, you know. Every now and then I got a tantalizing report from this or that quarter. The first was from your old soldier Bernard."

"What! He's alive? We were told he was killed in Constantinople during our escape. They said he died trying to defend my old friend Archambald, whom they killed in cold blood."

"I'm so sorry about your friend, truly. I liked him very much as well. But Bernard apparently leaped off the ship and swam under it. In the dark, the emperor's guard didn't see him come up. Somehow he made his way amongst the peasant people out of the city, and once he was on the road, he did what he had to do. He told me he stole some horses. That's about all I was able to get out of him about his ordeal. But he made it. And he related what you thought about a pact with Irene, that saucy minx. She's still trying to get me to marry her—old bag. I have a good idea now how to deal with her.

"However, Bernard did not know that you had managed to escape from Irene's clutches. And he didn't know that Counts Sigismund and Lantfrid never made it back. Apparently, they never even got out of Syria. Your Jewish friend Simon reported that there was an altercation with Harun's Persian guards in Raqqah. The guards didn't recognize them. It became a muddle, and they were probably killed on the spot. They tried to take Simon, too, but he escaped. In any case, we never heard from them again. I'm sorry about that; they were of my own house. But I never should have sent them. I'm afraid they were quite out of their element, weren't they?"

"I'm afraid so, sire. But they were very devoted to you, all the way to the end. As was Duke Eric, God rest his soul. So many gone." For a minute, both the emperor and Sebastian rested their thoughts on old friends. Sebastian changed the mood.

"I swear, my king, uh, I mean, my emperor. I only found out when we got to Carthage that you had been elevated."

"Oh, that silly business in the church in Rome. I'll tell you about it. It was a bit of a muddle actually. It was Christmas Day, and I was only just back from some exhausting travel down in Benevento. I showed up late for Mass, and when I came up the steps of the cathedral, Pope Leo took me by the arm and almost dragged me to the altar. There he plunked a crown down on my head and started calling me the Holy Roman Emperor. Fancy that! He had half the counts of Italy and Francia already there, and I didn't know it. What could I do?"

"I certainly believe you deserve it, my lord emperor. Look at all you've done. You've restored the Roman Empire, after all. Look at the unity you've created—from the great sea in the West to the steppes of the pagan Rus. And we keep improving the whole realm, as far as I can see."

"Well, I hope so. But Holy Roman Empire? Heh! It may be an empire of sorts, but it's a bit of a distance from being holy, and it certainly ain't bloody Roman! Good God, what a muddle of things the Italians can make. Always either prancing around seeking favor or fighting amongst themselves. Some Roman noblemen even tried to kill the pope, didn't you know. Bloody sods!

"I'll tell you one thing, Sebastian, my lad, no matter what they call it, it's the same bloody business day after day— keeping it all together, I mean. I'm getting a bit tired of it all. That's why I stay up here in Aachen so much of the time now. I love the daily baths—and the hunting! Superb! Better to let my sons do some of the fighting from now on. I'd rather be on the chase!

"Say, I'm not campaigning this year. I'm going hunting. Why don't you come with me? You mentioned hunting lions with Harun al-Rashid. I can't wait to hear about that!"

"Sire, I'd love to come with you. But I must see my sons."

"They're already on their way here, man! They'd be here now except I wasn't sure when you'd manage to arrive.

"By the way, when you got to Ifriqiya, you apparently made another friend there, that fellow Ibrahim—emir or something. He sent me a letter of praise that made me believe you could walk on water. What did you do to deserve all that blather?"

"Well, lord, I promised him you probably wouldn't mind if he attacked the Greeks in Sicily and took over the island."

"Bloody hell! You didn't! I'll be damned if I'll let him have Sicily! Those bloody African beggars are probably just as bad as the Greeks."

"Sire, I'm afraid I might have used your name in vain quite frequently. We had to fudge things a bit in order to make our way. But I never signed anything, and in truth, I always said, 'He *might* become your friend' or 'It is *possible* he could agree with you.' I only hinted at what they wanted to hear. You're under no binding agreements."

"Well, fair enough, then, you sly dog. I suppose it's all right if you had to stretch the truth a bit now and again. Anyway, that Ibrahim fellow wasn't the only potentate to give us news of you. Last summer, an envoy from Harun al-Rashid himself came to Pisa and told me you and Isaac were wandering about all over Egypt and that you were bringing me 'large presents.' I already knew about the elephant from Milo and that you were headed to Carthage."

"Did you get anything from Jerusalem?"

"Indeed we did! A monk from Jerusalem showed up two years ago and brought me several of the most precious relics from the Holy Sepulchre—gifts from the patriarch. And he was mightily pleased with that Avar gold we gave him. The very next year, three more monks showed up and gifted me with the keys to the Holy Sepulchre itself and the very keys to the city of Jerusalem. They told me that if you succeeded in convincing Caliph Harun, we Franks would replace the bloody Greeks as protectors of the Christian holy places and people in Jerusalem and Syria."

"Well, we did succeed, Your Grace, praise God, and now you are that protector."

"I don't know what you did, Sebastian, you and Isaac, but you certainly must have charmed the caliph. How'd you do all that?"

"We became friends, Your Grace.

"Amazing. There's no one like you, Sebastian. You must let me celebrate you in front of everybody."

"Sire, please, I want no further honors. Celebrate Isaac instead; if he had not been such a wise and accomplished man, it would have been impossible. I would rather stand a bit to the side. I have my reasons. The journey has wrought a change in me, and I might ask you to let me live a quieter life now after all this. It's enough to know that I've served you well enough, and you are satisfied with your paladin."

"I certainly am, absolutely, but I don't understand. Most of my warriors would give anything to have the fame you've achieved." He paused, waiting for a response.

Sebastian said nothing, only gazed absentmindedly out of the window as the mournful image of the forlorn pyramids at Al-Jizah filled his mind once again. What had he said then? Ah yes, monuments in praise of oneself, as well as honors and fame, were in the end no more than vanity, quickly forgotten. To his surprise, he found he no longer cared for them. All he really wanted was Adela and a chance to live out his life with her in the place where they had been the happiest—in Fernshanz. He dropped his eyes to the floor and remained silent.

"Well, no matter," Charlemagne said, pulling at his mustaches as he did when he was baffled, "I'm sure you'll confide in me eventually. You will stay with me and go hunting, won't you?"

"I must see my sons first, my lord, and learn what they need. Then I long to go to Fernshanz and Adalgray and see my people again. I miss them." He paused for a moment, cleared his throat, and said softly. "Finally, I wish to visit Adela. I've not seen her for years now. And I long to be reconciled with her, even if we cannot live as man and wife."

"Ah, of course you must, then. Your sons will all be here soon, as well as your men Liudolf and Bernard. But after the reunion, go wherever you like. You've earned whatever reward you choose. And I promise not to call you up again for at least a year. All right?"

"Yes indeed, my lord emperor. I'm very grateful. And may I say, sire, I hope you like the caliph's 'large gift.' Sorry it took so long to get him to you."

"Nonsense, no one else could have done it, Sebastian. God bless you. Abul-Abbas is forthwith the most prized of all my possessions. Long may he live."

***

After the celebration in Aachen, he went back with the younger boys to Andernach on the Rhine, where he paid his respects to Duke Gonduin, now a very old man who could no longer sit a horse or take long trips. The emperor had made Gonduin an emeritus duke and given his responsibilities in the army to other generals. The old man could scarcely remember in the afternoon what he did in the morning, but he could talk endlessly about the army and the wars he had fought with Charlemagne. He was still first and foremost a campaigner, and now, at the end of his life, he cared to talk about little else. Unfortunately, conversation with him was hard going at best since the duke never heard responses or answered anyone's questions. So Sebastian was in for a long monologue each time he visited.

"Ah, Sebastian," Gonduin sang out lustily when he first saw his son-in-law. "You rascal!" he shouted, pounding him on the back. "Where have you been all this long time? Don't think I don't know. You've been up in the Saxon woods chasing that bloody hound Prince Widukind!"

"My lord," Sebastian shouted in the duke's ear, "that was nearly twenty years ago. Widukind's been long dead." But the duke didn't hear him.

Sebastian tried to learn news of Adela and was greatly saddened when the duke never mentioned her in his ramblings and responded to questions about her with a puzzled, "Who?"

The boys liked to come to Andernach. After all, much of their growing up had taken place there, and they still enjoyed the wide fields and extensive forests of Gonduin's sweeping estate. And they loved the chance to engage in mock combat with the many young men who still came there to be trained.

Sebastian joined them in the stables after a mock melee on horseback. They had been the best on the field, and he was bursting with pride. Still, he felt the need to push his parental responsibilities.

"Karl, don't you want to read a bit with me when we're through here? I just received some new scrolls. Very easy to read, wonderful stories."

"Not again, Father. I can read, but I don't like it. That was the worst part of grandfather's training program—it always included reading and writing in Latin. No one speaks Latin anymore. And none of our mates had to learn reading either. Only us. And we had to do it at the crack of sparrow fart in the morning. It was gruesome."

"Well, I can read, and it certainly has enhanced my life greatly. In fact, it's what first brought me to the attention of the emperor. If it weren't for that, I'd still be eking out a living at Fernshanz. What about you, Attalus, will you join me? You read well; I've heard you."

"Yes, Father, I can read and even write a little in Latin. And I have enjoyed some of it. But it takes too much time away from training. And I really don't quite see the use of it—at least for us. We're warriors."

"Ye gods! It's to enhance your life, you knuckleheads. It's to add to your knowledge of the world, of people, of your faith, of everything! What are you going to do when the emperor stops campaigning? You know he's fighting much less than he used to. He's actually trying to find other methods of maintaining peace and prosperity. You should be learning how to do that. And reading would help."

"Perhaps His Grace is slowing down a bit. He's certainly getting quite a paunch," Attalus retorted. "But that doesn't stop him from sending his sons or other generals off with the army to fight. Last year, I was with Prince Charles when he rode into Saxony to push the bloody Slavs out of our territory. I loved it; it's what we're trained to do."

"And I got to ride with Count Wido, father," Karl piped in. "He's commander of the Breton March now, you know. We went in to teach the sodding Bretons a lesson again. They still don't want to pay their taxes. We even got to see a bit of action. And I was only sixteen!"

"Well, Gonduin shouldn't have let you go. I wouldn't have."

"Oh, right! We know your history, Father. Heimdal has told us all the stories, ever since we were babes. You rode with Grandfather Attalus to fight Widukind, Prince of the

Saxons, when the war with them first began. And the blind man said you got your arse in a crack on that trip, pardon the expression. And you were only fifteen!"

"That'll be enough of that, Karl. Show your father some respect. Heimdal greatly exaggerates everything, you should know that."

"Well . . ."

"Enough! Tell me, when was the last time you saw your mother? Have you had word from her lately?" Sebastian tried to appear casual as he asked the question, busying himself with straightening a harness.

"She was here not too long ago; about a year maybe, wasn't it, Attalus?"

"Maybe not so long as that," Attalus replied. "She looked well, Father. Of course, all we could see was her face and hands. She's a nun all right. But I don't know why she can leave the convent if she is one."

"Your mother has never taken her final vows as a nun. Until she does, she still has some personal liberty. Besides, your grandfather gave the convent a good deal of gold when she entered. She can fairly well do as she pleases." He hesitated before asking, "Did she ask for me at all?"

"Of course she did, Father. But we couldn't tell her anything. We didn't know."

"Sorry, Father," Karl added, "but I think she thought you were dead."

"Did anyone think to tell her I'm not—I mean, when you found out?"

"Well, we thought Grandfather would. Anyway, Milo came home, and he said he stopped by the convent first and told her when they were coming up from Venice last year. So it's all right. She knows."

"Yes, she knows I was alive last year. Milo must have told her we were still in Africa. After that, what?"

"I dunno. We were away on campaign a lot of the time."

***

When Sebastian returned with the elephant, Milo was not in Aachen. Alcuin had left the academy in the palace to become abbot at Saint Martin's shrine in Tours, and Milo was visiting him when messengers came announcing Sebastian's return. He left immediately for Aachen.

By chance, on the way home Milo found Sebastian at Andernach and stayed with him several weeks, revisiting every detail of the amazing journey and trying to define what it meant in the long run. In their long conversations deep into the night, it dawned on Sebastian that his first son was indeed becoming an extraordinary young man. In his late twenties now, he was far more intelligent and better educated than most of the people Sebastian knew. He never spoke without thinking and had a knack for winning friends everywhere he went. People recognized his genuineness and sincerity and were flattered by his attentions to them. He was also clearly devout and did not hide his spirituality from anyone.

"What will you do now, son?" Sebastian asked at one point. "Will you go back to Aachen, or join Alcuin in Tours, perhaps?"

"No, Father, I have a notion to go to Rome. I wish to study more Latin, and I want to learn Greek well enough to read it fluently. There are many scholars there, and in several of the monasteries there are books about science in Greek— medical science."

"Really! Where in the world did that come from, pray tell? I'm surprised you even know what the term means. Do you?"

"Listen, Father, I'm thinking about Magdala. She made quite an impact on me, as well as on you, I might say. She could really heal people, not just bleed them to death like some of our so-called physicians. She was doing great good in Jerusalem. She gave me some ideas about how to set up hospitals for ill or injured people. We already have inns here and there for pilgrims, and in some monasteries there is care for the sick. But there's nothing for the sick and the dying in our towns and villages where the ordinary people live. There's so much suffering, Father. I feel I must do something about it, and I wish we'd made Magdala come with us."

"I invited her, son. You know what she said."

"Yes, but I think she might have come if I had asked her. I. . . I think she liked me."

"Milo, you can't have used that reason to bring her to Francia. It would be dishonorable if what you really want is to use her knowledge and skills."

"I know, but. . . I liked her, too. I just never mustered the courage to tell her." He got up and began pacing around the room. "In fact, I think I could have loved her. She's the first woman I ever even thought about in that way."

Sebastian waited, but all he was getting from Milo was anxious looks. Finally, he said, "If that's what you want to do, son, I might be able to arrange it. I can send a letter to Syncellus George in Jerusalem asking him to find Magdala and tell her there is great need for her in Francia—and that you, particularly, want her to come and work with you to build institutions, charitable places, financed by the great lords and bishops. I will write that you are willing to find the money and build a network of these small infirmaries if she would be willing to find and train healers for them.

"If she's willing, I'll instruct George to make sure she still has enough money and find her a safe passage to Italy. You could meet her in Rome. But if you're not there when she arrives, she already has the names of other contacts in Rome who would help her come to Francia. And we will tell her to bring along her silent young ward. What was his name?"

"Damien."

Within the week, Sebastian sent the letter.

***

This time he was admitted into the convent without having to beat the door down. The dwarf doorkeeper was still as surly as before, but at least Sebastian didn't have to wait for an hour. As soon as he was in the reception room, Adela burst through the door and fell into his arms. She even kissed his face over and over, and tears covered her cheeks. The sensation was so unexpected that Sebastian felt overwhelmed and light-headed. For the first time in years, he felt there might still be some hope for them.

"I thought you were gone forever," she said, crying and laughing at the same time. "And then I heard you were alive but still in danger. There was so little word for so long. Then finally Milo came. But wait, come and sit. Talk to me! Let me look at you." Sebastian was so stunned he could think of nothing to say. Finally, Adela composed herself and wiped her face with a kerchief. She seemed embarrassed to have lost her composure so completely.

"All right, it's your turn. I'll behave myself. It's just that I'm so relieved to see you—and so glad!"

"So am I, my love. You can't know how much I missed you. I have so much to tell you. Are you allowed to spend time with me? May I stay for a day or two?"

"You can. Mother Herlindis will allow it, I'm sure. She knows all about us and is my closest friend. You won't be able to stay here at night, of course, but there's an inn close by, and you can see me during the daytime."

Sebastian spent a week with her. It was an enchanted time, and they fell into the same intimate bond they had always enjoyed. The only thing missing was the physical connection. Apart from her initial abandoned greeting, Adela kept herself carefully at a distance. "I'm still a nun, Sebastian," she said ruefully. "But I've never taken my final vows. I don't know if I ever shall, but as long as I can't live with you, this is as good a life as I can have. I am content most of the time."

"I've learned to be at peace, too, Adela. The experience in Jerusalem with Magdala and in the desert changed my life. I've learned to be content with my life as it is and appreciate the many good things that are in it. But I know you still love me, and that fills me with joy. I tried in every way to forget you—to exchange you for somebody else or something else. But I've found I'm never really happy without you.

"Come home. If you still want to retain your status as a nun because of Konrad, I can bear that now—as long as I can be with you. We still have our sons to enjoy and be proud of. We've always been so happy at Fernshanz or Adalgray. I spend most of my time now on the land. The emperor has no need of me at present, and I hope he'll consent to let me retire from his service.

"And I no longer want to kill Konrad, thank God. I don't wish to pay for having you back with me by killing a human being, as bad as Konrad may be. In fact, I hope I never have to kill another living thing. I don't even want to go hunting with the emperor," he said with a laugh.

"Come back to me, love. You know we were meant to be together."

"Oh, my dear, my sweet love, you know I want to— with all my heart. But you also know we couldn't stay apart. It would be like the last time, when you were sick. It was adultery."

"Oh, for God's sake, Adela. No one believes that, not even the king."

"We have been all over this, my dear. You know how I feel. God does not allow me to make that decision."

He did not press her or make her miserable again with his disappointment. Instead, he contented himself with the knowledge that she still loved him and would come to him if she felt she could. One day. . . one day, he thought.

They parted very affectionately the next morning, both pretending it was not so sad this time and that Sebastian would visit more often, at least on Easter and Christmas and the anniversary of their wedding.

On the long journey home, he could not forget the image of a painting in the convent's reception room where they had met and talked so intimately every day. It was of a rude altar, placed on the dirt of the floor in a stable. On the altar was a simple cloth, and on the cloth were a loaf of bread and a chalice of wine. Running across the table and down the front of the altar was a small cutting of a vine of bittersweet, full of orange-red berries. Sebastian could not get the painting out of his mind. It stayed with him the whole way back to Fernshanz. By the time he arrived home, he knew what it was: the altar represented the faith their union was based on, the bread was Adela, and the wine himself. And the bittersweet was the story of their marriage.

Chapter 30

The Crucible

Summer 804

The emperor had not led a campaign for four years. There were always border problems in Spain, Brittany, Italy, and Saxony beyond the Elbe, but Charlemagne now preferred to send his sons or other generals to put out the fires. However, two years after Sebastian's return, the emperor called him up. The troubles in Saxony and in Denmark had become too big to ignore.

" Here's the thing, Sebastian," the king said as soon as they found time to be alone in his quarters. The news i'nt good with the East Saxons up beyond the Elbe just now. And it's worse, I'm thinking, in Denmark where that mule's arse Godofrid is making noises like he's really a king to be reckoned with. Pah! He's a coward and a loudmouthed boaster, is all. But I may have to go up there and teach him and the Saxons a lesson. They're unsettling some of our allies."

Indeed, as they soon found out, the news from Denmark was not good. King Godofrid of the Danes was mobilizing his whole nation and assembling a fleet of ships in the Baltic. There were border issues and increasing skirmishes with Viking ships who were poisoning the peace between Denmark and Francia. Charlemagne was particularly enraged by the fact that Godofrid was harboring traitors and fugitives from Francia. One in particular was named in his dispatches to Godofrid. It was Konrad, who had become notorious for his raids on Frankish ships and into Friesian ports. Charlemagne was sure that King Godofrid knew of Konrad's blatant pirating, and he wanted to go up to the border and see what the

Danes would do, even if it led to all-out war. But first he wanted to deal with Konrad's raiders.

"Listen, my old lad," the emperor said in a tone of assuagement, "I know I said I wouldn't bother you anymore unless it was a dire necessity. Well, I have one. You know that scoundrel Konrad is getting bolder than ever. King Godofrid says he doesn't even know him, the flaming liar! Konrad's got command of a whole fleet of Viking ships now, and he's bringing his bloody raiders right into our ports and sacking entire towns. When we send forces against him, he just picks up and sails away, and we're forever too late.

"You know that rascal better than anyone. You're probably even able to guess what he'll do next. And you were in at the beginning of our shipbuilding enterprise in Dorestad. They've been doing fine, and we've got the makings of a fleet of our own. But the problem is we still don't have enough sailors to man them. We need more men like the Viking raiders, fighters as well as sailors. I want you to go up there and see if you can stop Konrad somehow. And this time I'll send a good part of the army with you. Will you do it?"

A few years ago, Sebastian would have given anything to hear the king say that. Now he dreaded ever meeting his old enemy again. So far, he had been able to keep his resolve. He had killed no more men. But if they were able to bring Konrad to bay, he knew it would mean a fight to the death. No matter what else he might be, Konrad was never the kind to surrender.

***

Charlemagne gave Sebastian a contingent of five hundred men from the heavy cavalry, some of the best troops of the army. But having enough good men for the job was one thing, catching Konrad was entirely another. The Vikings were extremely elusive and mobile. They were never far from their ships and an easy outlet to the open sea. Once upon it, they could not be caught.

Before even talking to the commander of troops, Sebastian sought out his most trusted counselors, Liudolf, Bernard, and Heimdal. The blind man, old as he was, was still the source of the most useful ideas.

"Surprise is the only solution," Heimdal declared as soon as he was apprised of the task at hand. "You must draw him in and trap him. Think of how you might do that."

"That's precisely the problem, Heimdal," Sebastian emphasized. "We never know where Konrad will strike. And when he does strike, we can never respond in time."

"All right, then. Where is he most likely to strike? What does he want most?"

Surprisingly, Bernard, who rarely put two words together, spoke up. "He wants them ships we're building up in Dorestad, I'm thinkin'. He's already tried to get in there twice."

"He's right, Sebastian," Liudolf added. "Konrad knows we might beat him if we ever get a fleet into the Balticum or the northern sea. I'll wager he's spoiling to burn the harbor at Dorestad where we're building the fleet. Besides, that's a rich town, and he'd love to rape it. The only reason he hasn't succeeded yet is there's a pretty large Frankish garrison guarding the harbor. They fought him off twice."

"Do we know how strong Konrad is now, how many ships and men he has?" Heimdal asked.

"The word from the army is that he probably has at least two hundred men. That's about ten or twelve warships."

"Right, then. We know he would like to attack Dorestad. It's a tempting target, and he's got two hundred men to do it with. How many of our men are defending the port?"

"There's a big garrison," Sebastian replied. "Two or three hundred, I believe, and there are fortifications in the harbor area. I see where you're going, Heimdal. You want us to lure Konrad into the harbor and trap him there. The problem with that is the garrison is too strong. He'd lose too many men trying to beat them. And the other problem is he would know if we brought extra troops anywhere near the harbor. I'm certain he would have spies in the town."

"Very likely. But it's still the best solution. Lure him in, trap him, and destroy him. You just have to work out how to do it."

Liudolf offered a possible stratagem: "We could arrange to have several Frankish merchant ships sail into the port loaded with trade goods. Konrad's spies would be sure to report that."

"That's a good idea, Liudolf. We can do that. But it might not be enough if the harbor is still heavily defended." Sebastian paused for a long moment and then added another angle. "What if we removed most of the Frankish garrison troops in Dorestad, leaving just a skeleton force? We could march them out in broad daylight for everyone to see. The word would soon get back to Konrad."

"Good," Heimdal said. "Then you bring the fat merchant ships in. That's the bait, now how do you spring the trap?"

"We'll bring back some reinforcements at night, fifteen or twenty men every night over a period of a week or so. We'll disguise them as merchants or cart drivers and conceal their weapons. They'll look nothing like soldiers. That will raise our number by fifty of the best men we've got and keep them out of sight in the barracks area. The rest of our troops will have to be encamped at least a day's ride from Dorestad so as not to raise any notice. If Konrad takes the bait, we'll send riders out to bring them up. Those of us already in the town will just have to hold out until they get there. I think we can do it if we use the fortifications well. At least Konrad will be surprised when he meets more resistance than he bargained for. But I know him. Once he's committed, he won't back down."

***

Everything worked well initially. Sebastian was greatly pleased with the troops Charlemagne sent him. He worked with them for a month, training them specifically for the mission. Meanwhile, orders went out for merchant ships to begin plying toward Dorestad. However, when he was in the process of selecting the fifty men who would infiltrate the town, he discovered among them his own sons Attalus and Karl.

"You can't go. I won't allow it. You will distract me. I'll be too worried about you to concentrate on the fight."

"Father, you cannot deny us," Attalus said. "Even the emperor takes his sons along when he fights."

"Yes, but he has the whole army with him to protect them. And they are never in the front ranks during the heat of the action."

"That's just not so, Father," Karl broke in. "Prince Charles certainly got his sword bloodied when we invaded Brittany. I saw it."

"And may I remind you, Father," Attalus added, "you saw your first battle when you were barely fifteen. We're grown men now, and we have a right to fight by your side."

In the end, Sebastian relented, remembering how he had stubbornly inserted himself when his own father went off to war. But he insisted that both his sons stay close to his side.

In a quiet moment on the march to Dorestad, he gave them this advice: "You're too young yet, and you have seen too little of war. I've seen much of it—far too much. Let me tell you this, and I hope you'll remember it or learn it quickly: war can be exhilarating. When I was your age and I got into it, I felt I was at the top of my game at the time. We were winning. I was winning. It was a heady tonic.

"But I learned quickly that it is not noble. It's ugly and cruel. It ends life so casually and leaves good men crippled for the rest of their lives. It causes heartbreak. In the end, there's something obscene about it—an empty well. I'm sick of the memories of it."

"Then why do you continue to do it, Father?" Attalus asked.

"That's a good question. I've asked myself that same thing many times. The only answer I can give is that I believe in the emperor. I believe in what he's trying to do. If he succeeds, he'll bring unity and law and a lasting peace to the whole realm. And I do it because I don't see how we could survive if we don't fight when we must. Our enemies would destroy us. I've always tried to get the emperor to use other means to achieve the security we need. If I stay close to him, perhaps I can influence his decisions. But in the end, if we're threatened, I think we must defend ourselves."

***

There was no assurance that the plan would work. They ran the risk of whiling away their time indefinitely if Konrad did not take the bait. But, as planned, all but fifty of the garrison troops marched out in broad daylight, leaving the distinct impression that Dorestad's defenses had been seriously weakened. Sebastian slipped in during the darkest part of the night with his fifty men and kept their heads down. The cargo ships came in one by one, presenting themselves as fat and juicy targets. Konrad's spies would have to be blind not to see them.

Still, after two weeks, there was no sign of Konrad, and Sebastian worried that the troops he had left under Liudolf's command a full day's march away would eventually be discovered, and the plan would be thwarted. And then toward the end of the day on the first day of the third week, Sebastian's own scouts, placed carefully far enough upriver to give adequate warning, reported sighting the curved prows and checkered sails of Konrad's Viking fleet.

Sebastian sent three riders out on separate routes to make sure the word got to Liudolf to come as quickly as possible. Then he called all the men to their posts in the block fortifications around the harbor. He set ships, lashed together, to make a barrier in the inner harbor construction area where the merchant ships were moored, and then he brought out flaming pots for fire arrows if Konrad's ships came too close. As he expected, Konrad realized the danger and did not bring his ships within range. Instead, he beached the shallow draft warships downstream, and his men poured out of the vessels and came running toward the harbor fortifications, expecting to boil right over them. They were stopped cold by a shower of arrows from the defenders manning the low walls.

The defenders were stunned right from the beginning of the attack when they discovered that Konrad's band numbered at least twice as many warriors as Sebastian had expected—at least four hundred men—and they streamed into the harbor area, attacking the fortifications on both sides of the river without pause. But they had no scaling ladders, so they could do little but crouch behind their shields under the walls, screaming and milling about.

Sebastian spotted Konrad standing on an overturned fishing boat at the edge of the water, surveying the scene. At length, he raised a horn to his lips and called off his men. They retreated in a disorderly mob the way they had come. Sebastian's men cheered and bellowed insults at their retreating backsides.

Sebastian called his sons and the three subordinate commanders of his small troop. "Hear me now, comrades. Our enemy has two or three times the number we expected. We're not going to be able to hold this port area for long once they get ladders. But I don't think they'll come at us again today. It's getting too dark. I could be wrong, so we need to post sentries all around the town in case they leave the river and try to come around behind us during the night.

"But more likely they'll want the port first, and they'll build the ladders tonight and come at us again at dawn. We won't be able to hold this port area for long once they do, but we need to hold them off as long as possible before we pull back to the town."

There was a narrow wooden causeway through the marshes between the lower town and harbor area and the upper town where the trading center was located in the town square. The square also boasted a middling stone church. This would be Sebastian's citadel in case the harbor fortifications were breached. He now knew they most likely would have to use it.

He sent men to the town square and had them roll heavy wine barrels from the trading center into two curved lines on the wide steps in front of the church. Between these barrels and the church he planned to make a last stand, if it came to that.

He told his sons, "Look, boys, this is worse than I expected. Konrad has a great many more men than we thought. I'm not sure we can hold him off in time for Liudolf to get here with the main body. I want you to stay close to me, one on either side at all times. No heroics. No going it alone. Promise me." When they agreed, he embraced them both and whispered, "I'm so proud of you, and I'm sorry I led you into this muddle. But with God's help, we'll survive."

The defenders spent a frantic night trying to strengthen the fort complex. But it was never intended to be a real redoubt, only a temporary one, and they were woefully unprepared to withstand a determined assault by a superior force—there were no throwing rocks or oil to burn and pour on the foe, not enough arrows or javelins to throw, and not enough men. Sebastian knew they would have to give way at some point and retreat to the town. After that, their only hope was for Liudolf to get there in time.

As soon as the sun was up, the attack began again. The fort on the right bank of the river was quickly overcome, and its defenders fought their way over the bridge of boats to the left bank to join Sebastian's main force.

"They'll get around us now and burn the ships in the harbor," Attalus shouted as they stood on the defensive parapet firing arrows into the mass of Konrad's warriors preparing to scale the low walls.

"No, they'll want to keep the ships if they beat us. But they'll surely be able to flank us now. Pass the word to be ready to pull back over the causeway to the upper town when I sound the horn."

Sebastian could see Konrad in the midst of his warriors giving orders to begin an encirclement and scale the walls from several different directions. Sebastian had to thin the ranks to cover the additional threat.

The first wave hit the walls in a thunder of shouting and horn blowing. The Vikings just threw themselves at the walls, screaming insanely as they climbed, almost oblivious to their vulnerability on the ladders. The Franks took advantage of their unshielded bodies and made them pay dearly for the furious onslaught.

Four times Konrad's men hit the walls, each time succeeding in getting a few men onto the parapet. Sebastian and his sons and a few others acted as the reserve and raced to the points of penetration to throw the Vikings off the parapet. The Franks were holding on gamely, but there were too many losses. After the fourth attack, Sebastian blew the horn to pull them back across the causeway to the town. They did it quickly while Konrad's men were regrouping for another attack. But just as the last man was off the parapet and racing for the town, the Vikings came again. Sebastian and his sons were the last to leave the redoubt. Midway across the causeway, several Danes were coming too fast, and they turned to fight.

There were only a few feet of space on the causeway, and on either side of it was a swampy marsh, impossible to walk in. Sebastian, Attalus, and Karl stood shoulder to shoulder to delay the Vikings until all the men could get behind the wine barrel defense line at the church. They cut down the first few Vikings and withdrew steadily. The pressure was light because many of the pirate band were running through the port area to explore the ships in the harbor.

In the midst of the action on the causeway, Sebastian felt a pang of remorse that he had not been able to maintain his resolve never to kill again. But his sons were beside him and in mortal danger. He put it out of his mind and struck out with the same dauntless prowess that had made him famous. His sons matched him with deadly effect, and they cluttered the causeway with the wounded and the fallen.

Finally, they reached the end of the causeway and turned to run under the cover of Frankish archers on the church steps. Just as they reached the barrier line and turned to get behind the barrels Attalus cried out and pitched forward with an arrow in his back. Sebastian grabbed him up and burst through the line of barrels and up to the church.

The Vikings failed to press their attack across the causeway, and Sebastian got a chance to catch his breath and regroup his forces. He was relieved to see the arrow was only in Attalus's right shoulder and had not penetrated deeply through his chain mail. Nevertheless, the wound was bleeding and serious enough. Attalus was finished for the day.

The barrels stood in two lines, both curving up to the church to present an unbroken barrier. All of them were full of wine and heavy to move. One line of barrels was on a tier several feet from the first line and a foot or so above it. He placed spearmen with shields in the first line of defense. Above them, behind the second tier of barrels, he stationed the best archers. There was food and water and additional weapons in the church, and the men got a chance to rest a moment. It was mid-morning. Where was Liudolf?

Greed delayed the Vikings for another two hours as they stopped to assess the new situation and look over the full warehouses and heavily laden ships in the harbor. It was noon before Konrad made an appearance in the square.

Sebastian was sure Konrad had not yet recognized him, and he observed his burly, arrogant old foe with more than casual interest. He was still powerful by the look of him, and he still strutted around as if he were a king himself and invincible. Sebastian had hoped never to see his old nemesis again, but here he was, once more at a pivotal moment in their lives. They had fought each other twice now. Most likely this would be the third and decisive time. Strangely, Sebastian no longer hated the man. He no longer dwelt on the unlucky fate this man had handed him, the loss of his precious wife, the loneliness and nomadic life he was forced to live because of Konrad's hate. He had come to peace in the crucible of the long journey to the East. Now here was another and possibly final crucible—the final test for both men. He wished he could avoid it.

The advantage certainly leaned in Konrad's favor. Sebastian had lost more than fifty men on the walls and was now down to less than fifty unwounded men. Konrad had lost twice as many, but he still outnumbered the Franks three to one. As yet, there was no sign of Liudolf, and time was running out.

As Konrad was preparing a new phase of the attack, Sebastian decided to take a chance and possibly buy more time. He stepped out beyond the line of barrels and took off his helmet.

"Hallo, you old clot! Konrad, you great gob of spit, you scum-sucking prick! How'd you like a chance at me again, eh? The last time we fought, you had a little help from your friends. Perhaps you won't be so lucky this time, you coward!"

Konrad stopped cold, his jaw gaping in disbelief. He turned alternately pale as a ghost and then gradually red with fury. So far, he had been unable to speak.

"Come on, you stinking yellow dog," Sebastian taunted, brandishing his sword. "Let us finish what's between us—just you and me. Else it will be unsatisfactory, whichever side wins."

Sebastian knew that if he could make Konrad mad enough, he could get him to fight. He'd done it before—twice. This might be their only chance. He drew his sword, walked out boldly into the middle of the square, and pointed it straight at Konrad's head.

"Bastard!" came the scream Sebastian hoped for. Konrad came lurching out into the square, paying no mind to the shouts from his cohorts behind him. The two fighters confronted one another briefly. Sebastian smiled provocatively and drove Konrad to fury with an insulting wink. Everyone, on both sides, was shocked into silence by the drama unfolding before them.

As they moved around each other cautiously, looking for a weakness, Sebastian observed his old opponent with surprise. He was fat! And his face was as red as a beet, a telltale sign of too much whoring and dissipation. Well, Sebastian calculated, he just might have to pay the bill for all that now. It was a good bet the old brawler had lost a few steps.

Just then Konrad charged forward, bull-like, as always, trying to bowl his enemy over or close with him so he could get his powerful hands on him. Sebastian sidestepped, barely ahead of Konrad's outthrust shield.

Whoa, Sebastian cautioned himself, breathing deeply in relief. The old bully still has plenty of steam, even for a fat man. Konrad might not be as quick as he once was, but he was still a very dangerous fighter. He could still wield that long, heavy sword like a stick, and he was clever. He couldn't be given any leeway.

They began the familiar dance—continuous movement, lightning ripostes after every swing of Konrad's sword, relentless circling, back and forth, watching for an opening. Sebastian's best chance was to let Konrad wear himself down.

It was working. Konrad's reckless charges cost him drastically. He was sweating profusely and breathing hard, even after the first few minutes. And for the first time, Sebastian discerned a look of panic in his foe's eyes. Konrad's distress was obvious to the onlookers as well. The Danes could plainly see that their leader was losing the contest. They began to edge closer to him from behind. Sebastian saw the movement too and realized he needed to put an end to the fight quickly. He moved in closer to Konrad, presenting a tempting target. Konrad spun and lashed out. Sebastian caught his sword before it descended, deflected it to one side, and in a backhanded blow, smashed Konrad's helmet off, leaving him bleeding from a head wound.

Then he spun around behind his dazed opponent and dealt him a heavy blow precisely in back of the knee. It brought Konrad crashing to the ground on his stomach. When he rolled over, Sebastian's sword was at his throat.

In that moment, however, Sebastian remembered his vow. He had said he would not kill again if he could spare. He stared into Konrad's stunned eyes and then lifted the point of the blade off his throat.

Sebastian caught a threatening movement out of the corner of his eye; a Viking had burst from the pack of warriors and was racing toward Sebastian, blade held high above his head. Sebastian turned to parry. Konrad took advantage of the moment, regained his sword, and rolled to his knees, preparing to strike Sebastian from behind.

He was in the act of drawing his sword back for a swing with all his might when he stopped suddenly, dropped his sword, and stared down in shocked surprise at the point of a javelin protruding from his chest.

Following up his thrust, Karl stepped up quickly and jerked the lance out of Konrad's back, releasing a torrent of blood as Sebastian finished off the attacking Viking.

At that moment, there was a great shout from the Frankish defenders on the church steps. "Hurrah, hurrah!" they yelled. Sebastian looked up from the kill and saw Liudolf leading their reinforcements up the causeway and into the back of the Viking throng. The Franks needed no orders; they left their positions at once and surged toward the Danish warriors, who suddenly found themselves assaulted fore and aft. They broke in desperation and scattered in bunches, seeking a clear path of escape. The town square suddenly became a furious field of savagery, made more ghastly by the crimson color of the paving stones, where blood mingled with wine leaking from the punctured barrels to cover the surface of the square.

Sebastian had a single moment to look his son in the eyes before the battle swirled around them. But the fight moved quickly out of the square as the surviving Danes floundered through the marshes or fought their way down the causeway to their boats.

Sebastian let Liudolf and the garrison commander lead the pursuit. Then he turned to Karl, standing close by to defend his father. "Come," he said, "help me get this man into the church."

They picked Konrad up as carefully as possible and carried him into the church, all the way to the altar area to lay him down. Sebastian did what he could to stop the bleeding, but it was of no use. Konrad had already lost too much blood, and he lay gasping from a punctured lung and spitting up the blood in his throat.

Sebastian bent down and spoke into his ear. "Listen, Cousin, you're dying. We're in a church. Don't you want to ask forgiveness? It's not too late."

Konrad opened his eyes, struggling to focus. "Ah," he rasped weakly, "the bastard. Still alive? Ach. . ." He turned his head in disgust. "Go away, let me die."

"Konrad, I no longer wish you harm. I want to be reconciled to you. And I want you to be reconciled to your God. He will forgive you anything."

"Bollocks," was the reply. "I hate you, bastard. . . always have. As for God, he made me the way I am. If anything, he's responsible for my sins. No. . . I'll die as I lived. . . on my own terms."

Konrad's defiant reply cost him all the energy he had left in his body, and he quickly began to fade. He opened his eyes once more and saw Sebastian staring down at him. "Damn you!" he said, and turning his head, he exhaled his final breath.

Epilogue
Three Boats

September 804

The emperor was ecstatic. He had just come back with the army from a confrontation with King Godofrid, and he gleefully informed Sebastian that the Danish king had gotten cold feet, scattered his fleet, and taken his whole army back into the heartland of Denmark.

Charlemagne's delight was multiplied when Sebastian reported the success of the trap in Dorestad and the near annihilation of the Viking force. "Excellent!" the emperor pronounced emphatically when Sebastian told him of Konrad's death. "I hope you killed him yourself, did you? You deserved to."

"No, Your Grace, it was my son Karl who killed him. He saved my life."

"Well, outstanding, then! Perhaps we have another young paladin walking in his father's famous footsteps, eh?"

"He's as good a fighter as I've seen lately, sire. As is his brother Attalus, who, by the way, was wounded in the battle. Not seriously. He'll recover."

"Excellent, I can't wait to see them both and congratulate them. This is truly a superb victory. Perhaps we'll keep the bloody pirates away from our merchant ships for a while. Sit and tell me every detail."

Sebastian recounted at length the story of the trap, its near collapse and final lucky outcome. The emperor was captivated and swore he would have given half his empire to have been there. Sebastian seized the moment and came to the main reason he wanted to see the emperor. "Sire, I hope you will agree that Konrad's death makes my wife, Adela, free again."

"I certainly do," he said without hesitation. "I told you before, she could have been free long ago as far as I was concerned. I suppose you want to go to Bischoffsheim and get her."

"I do, sire, as soon as may be, and I was hoping you would excuse me from service for a while. I hope to bring her up to Fernshanz right away and start again there."

"Bravo! Of course you're free to go. You must." And then the emperor paused a moment with furrowed brow. "If she hasn't already taken permanent vows. . ."

"She told me the last time I saw her that she has not."

"Then go, by all means, and the best of luck to you!"

***

Adela greeted him with the same unreserved affection as the last time, and he was much encouraged by her delight in seeing him. Still, he had an uneasy feeling in the pit of his stomach about her reaction to the outcome of events in Frisia.

"Sit down, my love, I have something very important to tell you."

Without preamble, he simply announced, "Konrad is dead—for sure this time." He held her hands in his while he slowly recounted the battle. By the end of it, she was weeping.

"You didn't kill him, did you, Sebastian?"

"I did not, my dear wife. I could have, but I withdrew from it at the last moment. It almost cost me my life. While I was distracted, Konrad was poised to kill me, but Karl was by my side, and he saved my life. It was Karl who killed him."

"Why did you hesitate? You've always wanted to kill him ever since we learned he was still alive."

"I learned something from Magdala, that mystic girl we met in Jerusalem. She helped me realize fully that we're all part of the miracle of life, even Konrad. Since God is the author of it, we shouldn't seek to undo his work. It's a hard road for a soldier to follow, but I'm trying. That's why I wouldn't kill Konrad. In fact, I tried to help him to face his God as he was dying and ask for forgiveness."

"Did he?"

"He did not, love. He died as he had lived."

"I'm so sorry. I've never stopped praying for him. I will continue to do so. Perhaps God will have mercy on him after all."

Sebastian waited a long minute before he continued. "Adela, you're my heart. You know that. You've always known it. We're free now. Will you come back to me? We can be happy again."

For a long time, she looked into his eyes, and then she looked away and began to cry again. "Oh, Sebastian, I want to, with all my heart. But it's been years now that I have lived this nun's life. I managed to be content simply serving God. I've even written some things—spiritual reflections, things that have helped others. I feel useful here. I feel I've been doing what God called me to do."

"But what about me? Weren't you first called to love me? What about the boys? We lost the chance for you to be a mother to your sons. We had to sacrifice that, too. Now we have another chance. We've paid the price for our love. Please, dear Adela, let's start again. You don't have to abandon God. You can just continue to serve him in different circumstances—ones I'm sure he would approve."

In the end, Adela seemed to relent, but she begged him to allow her time to think. She told him tearfully, "Sebastian, my life has changed so much that I'm not even sure I can be a wife again. I don't want to disappoint you! I need to be sure. I beg you, try to understand."

Sebastian didn't understand. How could she love him and not want to be with him now that they were finally free? But he fought off the urge to be angry and full of blame. That would only make things worse, and the last thing he wanted to do was hurt her.

He said good-bye with a heavy heart, fearing she'd never return. But just before he rode away, she kissed him on the knee as he sat in the saddle, just as she used to do when he rode off on campaign. She seemed to brighten. "Don't despair, my love," she said, looking into his eyes. "I will pray about it

410

and talk to Herlindis. I promise you at least this: if you don't receive a letter from me within two months, I will come to you."

***

When Sebastian returned home to Fernshanz, Milo was waiting for him. Alcuin of York had died in May at Saint Martin's Abbey in Tours, and Milo had left Rome to go on pilgrimage to Tours to do homage. He had only recently returned to Fernshanz.

Sebastian had never seen his usually imperturbable oldest son so excited. "I have wonderful news, Father! When I left Tours, I went back to Aachen to see friends and pick up some books, and there were letters there, one for you and one for me—from Simon. He's bringing Magdala!"

"What? When? I wrote that letter nearly two years ago. We've heard nothing since."

"But she's coming. Our Jewish contacts in Rome sent for Simon as soon as she came to them. And he's written that he's bringing her straight here because that's where you would be. I can't wait to see her."

"I wonder why she would actually come, son." Sebastian said in a teasing way. "She's a desert creature. Never been out of it. And she can't even speak the Frankish tongue."

"Ach, that's nothing. She'll learn it in no time. She's very good at languages, as you know. She must speak five already. In the meantime, she'll make do with Latin till she learns."

Only five days later, a boat appeared on the river. Bardulf was at the docks fussing with his old boat and saw it first. He raced to the alarm bell and rang it long and loud. It put the whole town on alert, and many were already at the docks as the boat pulled in, including Sebastian. He watched until he could recognize the faces of the two people standing in the prow—Simon and Magdala. It was not what he hoped, but he was nevertheless delighted to see them. Behind them, mouth agog, was Magdala's speechless ward, Damien, looking as if he had seen ghosts.

"Bardulf, you old beggar, you didn't need to ring the alarm," Simon sang out gaily. "We're not the enemy. Good Lord, look at all the people. Quite a welcoming party."

Sebastian and Milo were the first to welcome Magdala, who maintained her equilibrium in spite of the hubbub. She came off the boat smiling broadly and embraced both of them warmly. Later, when they had settled her into the manor house, she explained her reasons for deciding to come.

"I told you I wouldn't come, Sebastian, but you were right," she said in her simplified Latin. "It became too dangerous in Jerusalem for Damien and me. The Arabs didn't like a woman healer of men, and the Greeks began to suspect that I was some kind of sorceress. They thought my medicines were devil's brew and my practices some kind of dark magic. We had to leave. Besides," she added with a grin, "I wanted to see my two pupils. I hope what we learned together has stuck with you," she said, looking pointedly at Sebastian.

"We will have many talks, my dear Magdala. I acknowledge gratefully, once again, that I have much to thank you for. And Milo has some very grandiose plans for what you might do together to revolutionize the care of the poor in this country. Meanwhile, let us have a feast with the whole town to welcome you to Francia. You and Milo and I shall do great things together."

***

A month passed and still no letter from Adela. A whisper of hope began to grow in Sebastian's belly. And then a second boat came up the river. This time Sebastian was inspecting the new beer brewery by the river, tasting its produce with pleasure. He ran out when someone gave a shout.

To Sebastian's profound astonishment, it was not Adela sitting in the middle of the boat wrapped in blankets.

"Of all people in the world," he muttered in amazement, it's Adelaide!"

She was sick. The beauty that once radiated from her face and body had faded so dramatically that Sebastian almost didn't recognize her. She had lost a great deal of weight, and the lustrous red hair she had been so proud of in Constantinople was now a lifeless brown with streaks of gray. When she saw Sebastian's astounded look, she began to sob and buried her face in her hands.

He went to her at once and hugged her head to his chest. "Don't cry, Adelaide. It will be all right. How in the world. . ." He signaled four husky men to come to him at once, but before they could reach her, Adelaide was taken up in the strong arms of her ever-faithful servant, the giant Ajax. He quickly bore her to the manor house as Sebastian stayed by her side, holding her hand and trying to calm her with assurances. "I'm so glad to see you, my dear, dear Adelaide. I was afraid of this. Afraid something would happen to you because of me. But we will make you well. You will be all right. We will take care of you."

Once inside, he shouted for Magdala, who came running at once. "Listen, my dear Adelaide, this is Magdala. She's a healer, the best in the world. You'll be fine now. Quickly, bring her to my room. She can have my room."

It was several days before Adelaide felt well enough to talk. She had arrived at Fernshanz in the nick of time, for she was completely worn out from the travel and almost at the end of her rope. She was attended by the huge, silent Arab who never seemed to leave her side and two Greek women, old friends and sisters-in-the-trade from her courtesan days. It was they who had gotten her out of the palace complex after Sebastian left and spirited her across the straits to the Asian part of Constantinople. They had laid low for weeks there in the roughest part of the city, never going out in the daytime and eating the food of their peasant hosts. At length, they found passage to Antioch and then to Alexandria and finally to Venice. Adelaide would not talk about what she had to do to

survive or how she eventually found—or earned—the money
to come to Fernshanz.

"I had no choice, Sebastian," she rasped in a voice
made hoarse with sickness. "My father would not take me
back. He said I deserved it. He wouldn't even let me stay the
night. We came on, hoping to God you would be here. Can we
stay? Will you forgive me? Please! You were always so good,
Sebastian, my love. I don't want to die."

"Nonsense, Adelaide. You're not going to die. And
there's nothing to forgive. We will make you well. Magdala is
here. She'll nurse you back to health. She's an amazing healer.
You'll see. You will be well in no time."

And Magdala was as good as he promised. From the
moment Adelaide arrived, Magdala tended to her, feeding her
personally, applying salves and making her drink potions and
warm herbal teas. In less than a week, Adelaide was sitting up,
eating a bit and breathing easily. Within two weeks, she could
even smile and walk out for a while into the open air. She
came to adore her nurse Magdala and she fawned over
Sebastian, following him with her eyes whenever he came into
the manor or when she spotted him outside. She begged him to
come and sit beside her. It was clear she saw him as her last
hope for any kind of a new life.

For his part, Sebastian was completely bewildered as
to what to do with her. He was greatly relieved to be able to
confide in Simon, who had decided to take a long sabbatical in
Sebastian's company.

"Well, it's your own fault, old son. I told you not to get
too attached to that lady. I knew from the first time I saw her
that she was like fire—if a man gets too close, he is very likely
to get burned. And now what are you going to do with her if
she does indeed survive?"

"I have no idea."

Simon couldn't help but laugh. "I'm sorry, my friend,
but it's the classic story—a man pursues a beautiful woman,
and when he catches her, he wishes he'd never met her."

"Oh, I don't wish that. I'm glad I've known her.
Whatever else she is, you have to say in her prime she was

possessed of the fullness of life, and nobody enjoyed it more than she. It was thrilling to be around her. I loved her very much once. She was a tonic for me when I thought I'd lost Adela forever—and everything else."

"Well, you will work it out. With any luck, Magdala will bring her back from the dead, and she'll be her old amazingly formidable self again."

"Don't you want to see her? She's much better now, and she'd be glad to see an old friend."

"Ha! I doubt that's what she'd call me. But I'll look in on her if you think she's up to it."

"Of course. She gets feistier every day. I'm sure she's already more than a match for you. I'll let you have her all to yourself. You both will have more fun that way." Sebastian walked off whistling.

***

When Simon walked into Adelaide's room, the Greek women were combing her hair. It was already beginning to recover its shine and thickness. Adelaide sat straight up and shrieked in surprise. "Simon! You rotten bastard," she said with a laugh. "I never thought I'd see you again. Come and kiss me."

He embraced her and then stood back to look. "Well, you're doing much better. I'm amazed. You were so sick when they brought you in that you didn't even recognize me. You were so focused on Sebastian it was like he was your last link to life."

"Well, he certainly was—and is. I knew if I could only get to my darling Sebastian, I might have a chance to live again. Not like you, you scoundrel—running off and leaving me like that in Spain."

"I seem to recall, madam, it was you who ran off from me. One moment you were all sweetness, the next you were gone. And then the next thing I knew about you is that you had arrived at the top of your trade. They told me you were the most sought-after courtesan in all Constantinople."

She pouted. "I would have gone on with you, Simon. You suited me. But you were more interested in your trade—and in money—than in me."

"Oh, that's unfair. I was indeed interested in you. Women could not be more perfectly represented than by you. But women, unfortunately, are only one of my compelling interests."

"You dog," she said, putting on a stern face, which instantly turned into a laugh. It was clear they still enjoyed each other's company. From then on Simon paid her a short visit every day. She thrived on it.

***

Later, out on a ride along the river, Sebastian groaned, "What in the world am I going to do with her, Simon? She can't stay here. What if Adela comes? How am I going to explain it? Won't you go off with her somewhere? I know you still like her."

"Wish I could help you, old son, but I tried that once. It didn't work out. We're too much alike, and it led to fighting. Besides, you know the kind of nomadic life I lead. Wouldn't do." He paused to consider.

"If Adela comes—and you have no assurance at all that she will—you're just going to have to tell her that Adelaide had no other place to go. Adela has a very soft heart. She won't be put off by it. In fact, she'll probably be in there with Magdala helping to save the woman."

"From your lips to God's ears. I couldn't bear it if Adela was coming back to me and then changed her mind thinking I already had another woman."

"Rubbish. She'll see at once the condition Adelaide is in. She doesn't need to know all the history behind you two."

"I'd hate having to lie to Adela. If it comes to that, I'll tell her everything and hope she understands."

"That's you all over, Sebastian. I admire you for it, but for what it's worth, it would be much easier to lie your way out. Well, time will tell. Listen, my friend," he continued with a grim face, "there's something else I've been meaning to talk to you about. It's serious. There's something going on amongst Emperor Karl's three sons."

"What do you mean?"

"They're quarreling. Pepin is the King of Italy, Louis is the King of Aquitaine, and Charles is supposed to be the King of all the other Franks. God knows how all that works. But the emperor's not getting any younger, and you know what happens when a Frankish monarch dies—all hell usually breaks out amongst his heirs. We'll be lucky if there's no civil war."

"Do you really think there could be?

"If history's any guide, they'll split the empire for sure, each one of them wanting to be his own man, not subordinate to a brother. I don't think any one of them is the equal of his father. Oh yes, there'll be war unless a way can be found to prevent it. I tell you this because I know you'll become involved. Each brother will want you on his side. And the emperor, in the meantime, is going to want your counsel, too—yours and Alcuin's. I'm surprised he hasn't already called up all his wise men to help him figure out what to do."

"Oh, I suppose you haven't heard: Alcuin died last May at Saint Martin's in Tours. He'd been abbot there for about the last eight years. God rest his soul. He was a good friend to me and a strong ally. We both wanted the same things for the realm. The emperor loved him, too."

"I'm sorry, Sebastian. There was no one like him."

"Right. Well, there's nothing for it now. We'll just have to remember his example and hope to save what he started. In fact, I've been thinking of going down that road myself in the future—giving up this bloody paladin thing. I've been thinking about it more and more lately. I don't think I'm fit for it anymore. It makes me sick to think of going out to do more fighting and more killing. I want to be free to live my own life, finally. And now, if Adela comes, everything could change for me again. I could have her back. I could have happiness again. She's all I've ever needed."

He paused, realizing with surprise that he had just revealed to his friend a whole new plan for his life. Until this moment, he hadn't even admitted it to himself. He said with some apprehension, "Do you think the emperor will understand?"

"Frankly, no. You know him. He has very little patience for personal things; everything and everyone must bend his back to the endless causes of the realm. You know he'll call you, especially if there's any threat at all of civil war. He depends on you too much."

"God, why now? I thought I was going to be through with all the emperor's business—for a while, at least. Damn it, he can't call me up now. I won't go—at least not until I've had time to see if Adela's coming back to me. For me, there's nothing more important. There's two more weeks until the two months are up. I still haven't gotten a letter from her. I'm beginning to hope. Until I know, the emperor can go to the devil."

"Er. . . right. We'll see about that. But what if she does come but still wants to be a nun? What if she just wants to be 'friends' here with you and be able to see her sons more often but still wants to live the celibate life she's been living and do the writing you say makes her feel so fulfilled? What happens then? Will you say, 'All right, then,' and marry Adelaide just to have a woman to sleep with?"

"Don't be ridiculous. I don't want Adelaide anymore. I would never have wanted her in the first place if I'd thought I had a chance to have Adela. I just want my wife back."

"Well, Adelaide will want *you*. And when she gets her health and her looks back, she's going to mount a campaign to win you over. I know her. She won't give up without a fight. And if Adela doesn't want to live with you as man and wife, I'd say Adelaide has a fighting chance."

"No, never. And the emperor can go to hell, too. I'm going to have a new life now—at least for the rest of the time I've got. It's going to work out. You'll see. I know it will!"

******

A week later, a third boat appeared on the river. At this point, Sebastian was spending most of his days down by the water. He was in the millhouse inspecting damage to the great wheel when he spied the small vessel tacking slowly against the current. As always, peasants working near the landing crowded down to witness the rare event. As the boat came closer, he could see two figures in the prow. A little closer and he could see one was a woman. She was dressed in white, the white of the convent. Adela!

His heart leapt. His first impulse was to run to meet her at the landing. But the singular way she was dressed made him step back into the shadow of the millhouse door. When he left her at Bishoffsheim, he had given up hope. She had all but told him outright she doubted she would be able to change her way of life again. She had come too far down the spiritual path, she said, and felt that God still called her to give herself completely to the contemplative life.

Her dress was white, but she wore no nun's headdress. The shawl around her head and shoulders was blue. What did that mean? When the boat docked, he watched as she stepped gracefully onto the pier, smiling and warmly greeting those she knew, all the while searching the faces of the crowd for his own.

A thousand memories, important and incidental, flooded into his brain—and as many questions. Why was she not dressed in the full white habit of the sisters? Had she come to stay or not? If so, would she live with him as wife or friend? What would she do when she discovered Adelaide's presence at Fernshanz? If she had indeed come home to be his wife, answering at last all his prayers, what would he do if the scent of war drew him away from her once again?

And there it was—war's harbinger—following close behind her. Sebastian suddenly noticed the second passenger. Wrapped in a fine long traveling cloak, a grossly fat man stepped with difficulty onto the pier, nose in the air, exuding an air of privilege and power. It was Arno, Charlemagne's former castellan at Worms and now his mayor of the palace at Aachen.

"Oh God, no!" Sebastian moaned aloud. There was no escaping the immediate conclusion that the emperor had send Count Arno to fetch him—now, just when Adela had come home! And the fact that he had sent someone as high up in the court as Arno meant that the matter was serious and that he would be expected to come at once.

He looked back in a panic at Adela and saw that she was searching the crowd for him, a look of concern on her face. That was enough. A single small voice emerged from his confusion, borne of the ruin and redemption of years of tumult and separation. She's your greatest gift, it said. She was taken from you, and now, God willing, she's returned. Run to her! Cherish her! Whatever it is, the emperor can wait. If you cannot keep her, there is nothing left but the bitter wine of violence. Go! Choose life. Make her stay!

He threw his doubts to the wind and ran to greet her, bursting through the crowd of Fernshanz folk to sweep her up in his arms and embrace her. The doubts and questions could wait for another day. At least they had now. And now was all that mattered.

Author's Note

The Paladin is a tale woven into early medieval times, but, as in Book I of the series, I have been at pains to portray those times as accurately and meaningfully as possible. Profound progress toward a new civilization occurred in the thousand years of medieval history, much of it in the early "Dark Ages," and Charlemagne remains one of the most memorable and effective rulers in European history. There is still an annual Charlemagne Prize for the institution or person who accomplishes the most to advance European civilization. Had it not been for the ninth-century devastations of the Vikings, the Magyars, and the Saracens, what Charlemagne started would have meant a much earlier flowering of European power, prosperity, and culture. Alas, in the two hundred years following his death, the light he lit almost went out. In Book III of this series, we will try to illustrate why it did not.

Most of the characters in the novel are fictitious, but history buffs will recognize that the story line of *The Paladin* follows real history as closely as possible—the Brittany and Avar expeditions, the plot of the Hunchback against his father, the king, the incredible journey of Isaac and Abul-Abbas. They were real, though more is known about the elephant than about Isaac. "Doggie" lived at least ten years after the journey and traveled with the king all over the empire. One thing seems certain, Isaac would never have made it without someone like Sebastian to protect him and help overcome the enormous logistical problems the journey must have faced.

Queen Fastrada was real, though the circumstances surrounding her controversial life and early death are shrouded in mystery. The Emperor Irene was also very real and even more ambitious, clever, and notorious than I have portrayed her. Harun al-Rashid was the great caliph of the golden years of the Abbasid Empire, made even more famous in the

Western world in the classic stories of *A Thousand and One Nights*, and Scheherazade was the lovely harem woman portrayed in chapter twenty-four.

I had a great time writing the story, but it wouldn't have come together without lots of help. I'm indebted to readers Peg Del Debbio and my old Cold War buddy Joe Kerr for their unswerving support and welcome ideas; to illustrators Denise Proctor and Karoline Banasik for the artful maps; to the encouragement and creative influence of long-time close friends and associates, Karen Fernengel, Don and Jo Ann Stovall, Frances Porteous Macdonnell, Janet and Terry Bartkoski, and my red-headed yoga teacher, Robin Krasnesky, all of whom inspired me or conspired with me to dream up the story and the characters. Special thanks to Father Ed Hays, who plotted gleefully with me until his untimely death; to Jennifer Quinlan, "the pro," my tough, uncompromising, and thoroughly constructive editor; and to the cherished memory of my lady, Mary Jo.